Patricia Scanlan lives in Dublin. Her books, all number one bestsellers, have sold worldwide and been translated into many languages. Find her online:

Facebook.com/PatriciaScanlanAuthor
Twitter @PatriciaScanl18
Instagram @PatriciaScanlan7224

The
Liberation
of
Brigid
Dunne

Patricia
Scanlan

SIMON &
SCHUSTER

London · New York · Sydney · Toronto · New Delhi

First published in Great Britain by Simon & Schuster UK Ltd, 2020
This paperback edition published 2021

3 5 7 9 10 8 6 4 2

Simon & Schuster UK Ltd
1st Floor
222 Gray's Inn Road
London WC1X 8HB

Simon & Schuster Australia, Sydney
Simon & Schuster India, New Delhi

www.simonandschuster.co.uk
www.simonandschuster.com.au
www.simonandschuster.co.in

A CIP catalogue record for this book
is available from the British Library

Paperback ISBN: 978-1-3985-0523-0
eBook ISBN: 978-1-4711-5119-4
Audio ISBN: 978-1-4711-9136-7

This book is a work of fiction. Names, characters, places
and incidents are either a product of the author's imagination or
are used fictitiously. Any resemblance to actual people living or
dead, events or locales is entirely coincidental.

Song lyrics to 'Finest Flower' –
a tribute to women who survived mother-and-baby homes.
Printed by permission of Ciara Sidine

Typeset in Bembo by M Rules
Printed and bound by CPI Group (UK) Ltd, Croydon, CR0 4YY

MIX
Paper from
responsible sources
FSC® C020471

This book is dedicated to *Mná na hÉireann*. The Women of Ireland, and in particular to the many dedicated activists who challenged a patriarchal society, where Church and State conspired to treat Irish women as second-class citizens.

We owe a debt to an illustrious list of women who challenged the status quo – and changed Irish society in the process. Too numerous to mention, they include Anna Haslam, Constance Markievicz, Hanna Sheehy-Skeffington, Hilda Tweedy, Nell McCafferty, Mairin Johnston, Margaret Gaj, June Levine, Mairin de Burca, Mary Maher, Moira Woods, Mary Anderson, Nuala Fennell and May McGee.

To Catherine Corless, for her unremitting efforts to bring justice for the Tuam Babies.

And to many courageous women today, inspired by the women above, who are still fighting the Church and State for justice, ethical behaviour, and equality for all Irish women. We owe you all a huge debt of gratitude.

If you want to keep a secret,
you must also hide it from yourself.

GEORGE ORWELL

PROLOGUE

CHRISTMAS EVE

1953

She pulls her shabby black woollen coat tighter around her and wraps her scarf snugly against her cheeks. It is bitterly cold, her breath forming an opaque mist in the frosty moonlight. The stony path that leads from her grandmother's cottage down to the farmhouse is slippery with ice, and she skitters and slides, grabbing a furze bush with her woollen-mitted hands to save herself from a fall. She pauses to catch her breath.

Venus, a radiant golden jewel, shines as brightly as the yellow slice of new moon against a black velvet sky speckled with glittering stars. Candlelit windows down in the valley and on the hillsides spill pools of light in the darkness. She'd lit the fat, red candle in her grandmother's parlour window

1

before she left, for the traditional welcome to the Christ child on Christmas Eve.

Normally she would feel delight and anticipation on this blessed night, though she is no longer a child and doesn't believe in Father Christmas, unlike her two excited youngest siblings at home, who have already hung their stockings at the end of their beds.

Tonight she is bereft, her heart shattered into a thousand sharp-edged pieces. She looks down to her left beyond the stony fields that quilt the mountain, where weather-bowed, bare-branched trees and hedgerows define the boundaries to the Larkins' farmland. Her heart feels as though a knife has stabbed and twisted it when she thinks of black-haired, brown-eyed Johnny Larkin, who had told her that he loved her more than he'd ever loved anyone. Who had pressed her up against the cold hard wall of his father's barn and kissed and caressed her in her most private places and done things to her that, even though she'd demurred and then protested, had shocked her, yet given her a fierce delight that Johnny loved and wanted *her* and not that skinny little rake, Peggy Fitzgerald, whose father owned the big farm next to the Larkins'.

Two days after Johnny told her he loved her, his engagement to Peggy had been announced. Tomorrow at Christmas Mass, Peggy will simper and giggle on Johnny's arm, flashing the diamond ring Pa Larkin has lent his son the money to buy.

She can't bear it. An anguished sob breaks the deep silence of the night. Her sorrow overwhelms her. A sudden, unexpected pain in her belly doubles her up, causing her to groan in agony. She feels dampness on her thighs and pulling up her clothes sees the trickle of blood down her legs. Another spasm convulses her and, frightened, she takes deep breaths until it eases.

In the distance, she hears the sound of the carol singers who go from house to house singing the glorious story of the birth of a child who would bring peace to all mankind.

As she loses her own child, in the shelter of the prickly furze bush, she hears the singing of 'Oh Holy Night' floating across the fields from her parents' house.

Christmas Eve

Mid-Eighties

Although the heat of the day has died down, she is hot and bothered. She thinks of Christmases at home when her fingers were numb with cold, and wishes for a moment that she could transport herself to Ireland, to Ardcloch, and feel the icy chill of a moonlit night in December. But she's half a world from home and she needs to focus on the task at hand.

The children are beside themselves, their excited chatter and awestruck expressions bringing smiles to the adults' faces. She casts a peek at the tall, lean man with the lopsided smile who is surrounded by them. How they love it when he is here. How *she* loves it when he is here. She has to be careful. Not by so much as a glance can she betray herself.

She is well aware that Mother has been watching her like a hawk since her arrival this morning.

Reverend Mother's presence brings a tension, an edge to the gathering. Everyone is on their best behaviour. Even laid-back Margaret is looking unnaturally spruce, her unruly red locks that usually escape in every direction imprisoned in hairpins.

Mother claps her hands for silence. 'We will sing "Silent Night",' she instructs as the room quietens down.

The old familiar carol brings a loneliness that catches her unawares. It is worse than loneliness. At home they have a name for it: *uaigneas*. That aching aloneness and loneliness that words cannot describe. She is apprehensive. What will become of her? With superhuman force of will she gathers herself and, by some grace, manages to join in the next verse.

Later, when all the guests are feasting on the eagerly awaited Christmas Eve supper, the children trying but failing to be polite as they cram food into their mouths, *he* comes to stand beside her at the buffet.

'*Bon nuit*,' he says casually, trying to ignore Mother's gimlet eye.

She keeps her head down, placing a slice of mango on her plate although her throat is so constricted she can hardly eat. '*Oíche maith*,' she says. She has been teaching him Irish. At that moment one of the children trips over and a plate smashes. There are squawks of dismay and flurries of activity as the broken pieces are swept off the floor, and while Mother's and everyone else's attention is elsewhere, she whispers urgently, 'I'm pregnant.'

'*Mon Dieu!*' he utters, his face turning ashen.

For one awful moment she thinks he is going to abandon her and leave her to endure the future alone, and then she hears him say, 'I am with you. We will face this together,' before someone comes to claim his attention.

Relief washes over her. Just as Joseph had stayed with Mary and helped her bring her child into the world on this Holy Night over two thousand years ago, *her* St Joseph will be with her on this new, unplanned journey that lies ahead. Joy fills her. There will be uproar when the news breaks. She knows a hard road lies ahead, but every fibre of her body rejoices at the new life she is carrying.

Christmas Eve

2017

She was a little girl again, back in the Four Winds. The easterly gale howling, keening like a banshee as it swirled around the chimney pots, almost drowning out the angry roar of the sea as it hurled itself against the rocks standing sentinel beside the half-moon bay at the foot of the bockety wooden steps at the end of the vegetable garden.

It was Christmas Eve. The old house creaked and groaned in the wind, and she wondered anxiously whether Santa's reindeers would be able to land on the roof. And then she heard it: the unmistakable sound of bells ringing, faint at first but getting louder. Her heart pounding with excitement and terror, she slid lower under her soft quilt, until only her peridot-green eyes were peeping above it, round and shining with anticipation. Santa was coming . . .

What was that noise? Marie-Claire woke reluctantly from her delightful dream, half expecting to see the glow of the fire in the darkness that surrounded her. Her mouth was dry, her arm stiff where she'd laid her head on it. A mobile phone was tinkling somewhere – not reindeers' sleigh bells – and it took a few moments to realize that she was on the small sofa in the recording studio, which was now in complete darkness. She'd come into the studio to listen, as twilight was falling, to a particular inflection that the actress who had been recording an advert earlier had got just right in one recording. Marie-Claire wanted to isolate that perfect tone and splice it into the voice-over, and the quiet of late afternoon was her favourite time to shut her eyes and *listen* to the recordings.

She could see it was snowing outside. Soft white flakes drifting and dancing down.

What time was it? How long had she been sleeping? She'd to go home and doll herself up. She and her partner, Marc, were having dinner in Edulis. He'd booked a table in November when he had taken her there to celebrate White Truffle season. Marc liked the good things in life. There'd be caviar and champagne on the table tonight, knowing him.

She was about to get up when the heavy, soundproofed door inched open, a slice of light from the hallway spilling in. A young woman was speaking excitedly in a low voice. The ON-AIR light was off and staff often stepped into empty studios to take private calls. She was about to sit up and announce herself when she heard a vaguely familiar voice say, 'Girl, you should see the gift he gave me: Tiffany love hearts on a silver chain! Not just the one – two! Which, obviously, is more expensive. What does that say? And when Marie-Claire goes to New York next week, we're spending a night in Niagara at the Embassy Suites. *The Embassy Suites!*' she repeated, her whispery voice rising in pitch. 'I swear Marc's falling in love with me. He keeps telling me I'm the best thing that's ever happened to him!' There was the muffled sound of a reply, rapid bursts of speech and then, 'No, I won't see him today. He has to take *her* to dinner. In *Edulis*, would you believe. That's want she wanted. She's so bossy. It's the Irish in her, he says. Listen, I have to go, catch ya later.'

Marie-Claire lay as still as a frozen mummy as the green light from the cell phone was extinguished and the hefty studio door opened once more and then closed silently.

So Marc was shagging butter-wouldn't-melt-in-her-mouth Amelia.

Struggling into a sitting position, she sat in the darkness, stunned. Marc, with his glinting amber eyes, six-pack abs and unruly black curls was a catch. But they'd been together for two years and were even planning on setting up a New York office to expand his recording business.

Aunt Brigid's oft-voiced refrain came into her head: 'Love many, trust few. *Always* paddle your own canoe.' *Well, paddle alone I will*, Marie-Claire resolved grimly, trying hard not to cry as a sickly tight knot settled in her stomach and the beginnings of a headache throbbed in her temple.

'Get up and get the hell out of here,' she muttered, trying to motivate herself. Because once she walked out of this building she knew with certainty that she'd never be back.

Tonight, in that posh restaurant, she would put on the performance of her life. Her *Irish* pride would see to that, she thought bitterly. This Christmas Eve would be one that Marc Bouchard would *never* forget.

PART ONE

The past cannot be changed.
The future is yet in your power.

MARY PICKFORD

CHAPTER ONE

MARIE-CLAIRE

The taxi cruised slowly along Niagara Street, the lights of Christmas trees in the red-bricked apartments twinkling into the snow-swirled night. Marie-Claire felt the tug of longing for Ireland, and home. Three hours ago she'd been a woman with plans and an idea where her future lay. Happy. Secure. Ambitious. One short, clandestine phone call had changed all that. Now she was in a maelstrom; shock, sadness, bitterness and rage tossing her on their churning seas. It was that roiling rage that would get her through dinner with Marc tonight.

She paid the taxi driver and wrapped her heavy green, faux-fur-trimmed cape around her. Marc had made a fool of her. Her anger was as much directed at herself as him, but he would *never* know what lay behind her decision to split, she decided with steely resolve. Let him think she was leaving him because she'd decided it was time to move on. Let *him* be the one questioning her decision. Let him be the one asking why. Whether Amelia was a mere distraction, fling, whatever, she didn't care. There would never be trust in their relationship if she stayed. And anyway, now she didn't want to.

Something unexpected solidified within Marie-Claire as she took a deep breath and walked towards the inviting lamp-lit entrance. What had happened today was life-changing. A kick in the ass! A wake-up call, her mother would say.

Was she to give up her life in Toronto and the career in sound engineering that she'd worked so hard to build? Running the Radio & TV Voice-overs department in a busy audio post facilities company that was going places. Marc's company, unfortunately. She'd have to go looking for another job. But where?

Right there, on that freezing night on a dark Toronto sidewalk, Marie-Claire knew exactly what she wanted and where she wanted to be. She wanted to go home. Back to the Four Winds and her snug little room in the eaves to take time to think and evaluate.

She'd even be able to go to Great-Aunt Brigid's surprise eightieth birthday party. An invite she'd reluctantly had to say no to because she'd originally been scheduled to be in New York.

Marie-Claire opened the restaurant door and walked in, preparing to put on the act of her life.

CHAPTER TWO

KEELIN

Keelin Durand stood at her bedroom window looking at snow-adorned Mount Canigou in the distance. The mountain seemed to shimmer in the early morning sun, a paler blue than the azure December sky that almost overwhelmed the vast plains of Roussillon and the lavender fields below. Canigou, the sacred mountain so beloved of the Catalans.

Keelin turned from the window. She and her husband, Armand, were closing up the house for two weeks to fly to Ireland to spend New Year with family. Her aunt, Reverend Mother Brigid, would be turning eighty and the family would be celebrating.

How nice it would be to stay in the Four Winds again. What a haven it had been, back when she needed it most, Keelin reflected. She loved the place so much that when she and Armand had inherited his grandfather's farm in the shadow of the Pyrenees, she'd named the house they had built Les Quatre Vents. It was very apt too, because the winds there came from every direction, each with its own distinctive energy. The Mistral. The Sirocco. The Tramontane. The eerie continuous howling of the Tramontane that blew in from the north-west set most people's teeth on edge, but it reminded Keelin of home.

She sighed as she expertly folded one of Armand's jumpers and placed it in the suitcase. She'd been dismayed when Marie-Claire had told her that she wouldn't make it home for the party. These days it seemed to be all work with her daughter. There had to be balance, Keelin counselled – as she did to her many clients who came to stay and renew themselves in the Healing, Spiritual and Relaxation Retreat Centre she and Armand ran in Les Quatre Vents.

But her advice fell on deaf ears with her daughter, to whom career was everything. Despite having been raised with a deep awareness of nature and the esoteric, both in Ireland and in France, Marie-Claire had turned her back on all that could nurture her spirit, preferring the bright city lights of Toronto, and soon, possibly, New York. Still, she had to get it out of her system, and far be it from Keelin to dissuade her from her chosen path.

She and her daughter were so alike, Keelin reflected, rolling a pair of PJs to make them fit better. She'd been a young woman once, with fire in her belly and a passion to make changes, to live life to the full – and look where it had got her. Far from where she'd imagined she'd ever be in this lifetime.

The catalysts for some of the great changes that had occurred in Keelin's life had been her mother, Imelda, and her aunt Brigid – two strong, determined and stubborn women. Who would be the catalyst for her daughter? When upheavals came – and they would – Keelin couldn't help but hope that Marie-Claire would be spared the torment and heartbreak that had once been visited on her, that she had kept so secret from her daughter. Keelin too had had to be strong, determined and stubborn when Marie-Claire was born; she hoped her daughter would be as resilient as the rest of the Dunne women, when she needed to be, although Brigid would be a more inspiring role model than Imelda, Keelin thought ruefully.

Yes, Brigid's eightieth would be interesting, that was for sure. She wouldn't miss it for the world.

CHAPTER THREE

REVEREND MOTHER BRIGID

Reverend Mother Brigid wrapped her cloak around her as she walked around the perimeter stone wall of the cloister. She was spending Christmas in the Order's Mother House on the outskirts of Paris. Dusk was falling, the sky turning deep indigo as the tangerine glow of sunset faded and was doused mercilessly by triumphant night. A Holy Night.

Brigid did not like Christmas Eve, never had since ... *Oh well, that was a long time ago*, she chided herself, dismissing the memory. She wasn't alone in disliking this particular eve. She remembered as a young nun, on her first posting out on the Missions in Africa, one of the older Sisters, crying, after imbibing some of the local brew – following midnight Mass – when the villagers had gone home.

'I wish I was at home, with a man's arms around me, and a baby to hold. And none of your Virgin birth nonsense. I want it all, the rub of the relic, everything, and now it's too late.

I'm nearly a dried up old crone,' Sister Pius had exclaimed, distraught, taking another swig of her drink before bursting into tears.

'Jesus, that's *blasphemy!*' one of the other nuns, Sister Francis, had blurted. Brigid had been so gobsmacked she'd been rendered speechless.

'Stop it, Pius,' the Almoner, Mother Veronica, ordered sternly.

'Well, it's true. Don't tell me you wouldn't wish for it. I'm sick of this place. Sick of pretending to be holy. I didn't *want* to be a nun. My father made me become one because I've a squinty eye and he said no man would marry me and he couldn't afford to keep me.' Pius was howling by this time, snorting and sniffling, and Francis had looked over at Brigid and thrown her eyes up to heaven and said, 'We'd better get her to bed.'

They had led their truculent, weeping colleague to her spartan room, with much hushing and 'don't wake the children' from Francis.

'Lord save us,' the other nun said later when Pius was tucked up in bed weeping inconsolably into her hard pillow. 'She's having a fierce hard menopause. I'm at my wits' end with her.' Francis was from the west of Ireland too, and still had her Connemara twang. 'I hate Christmas Eve here, too. It's too hot, and sad and lonely. Goodnight, Sister Brigid.'

Now, all these years later, when she'd gone through such longings and utter loneliness herself, she was glad she'd crossed the turbulent seas of life and was almost in safe harbour.

But next week she would return to Ireland, and retirement. Her sister nuns at home had suggested a small celebratory tea in the Four Winds, knowing how much she loved the sturdy old house by the sea, and she was touched by their thoughtfulness.

The opalescent lights shining in the windows of the large stone chateau were warm and inviting as the icy fingers of a northerly wind reddened her nose. Brigid shivered. Soon she would smell the salty, sea-tanged air of Ireland. Going home was always bittersweet.

So many memories. Now that she was almost eighty she might give herself some leeway. Brigid smiled wryly, knowing it was only her immense discipline and steely will that had kept her on the straight and narrow all these years as a nun. She should be proud of herself, but pride was a sin. Her younger sibling, Imelda, would tell her that quick enough.

Imelda, bitter and resentful still, after all these years. Holding a grudge that she couldn't let go of. So many grudges.

Did I say I was looking forward to going home? she thought, amused. *Perhaps I should make the most of the peace and calm silence of the Mother House while I still can*, she decided, turning to walk back along the rose-wrapped wall, the thorny branches harsh and unforgiving without the glory of their blossoms. A thorny branch. A bitter briar. Her sister, Imelda.

Reverend Mother Brigid sighed. She would pray for Imelda during Vespers and Compline tonight. It was all she could do.

CHAPTER FOUR

IMELDA

'Will I make the stuffing for you, Mrs O'Brien?'

'You will not, thank you. I'll make my own stuffing,' Imelda O'Brien rebuffed her daughter-in-law's kind offer sharply. What did they think, that she was incapable?

'No worries,' Felicity said drily, and Imelda knew that the younger woman was struggling to bite back a sharp answer.

'You can make a pot of tea,' she said, offering an olive branch. 'Everyone likes my stuffing. I've a secret ingredient,' she added in a more placatory tone. 'I want to make enough to freeze some.'

She couldn't afford to go alienating her daughter-in-law, Imelda reflected. Felicity and Cormac, Imelda's son, lived down the road, and were very good to her.

The best of all her children, Cormac, was. The most easy-going. He didn't get that from her. No one would ever call *her* easy-going, Imelda admitted with a rare spark of dry humour.

She wanted to make her own stuffing this Christmas Eve because she wanted to have plenty put by for when Keelin and Armand, her daughter and son-in-law, came home from France for their Christmas holiday. She supposed *Reverend* Mother would deign to visit as well.

Imelda's nostrils flared, and her eyes hardened like wizened olives. There was going to be a big do for her older sister's eightieth. A 'surprise' party. And they were all going to have to trek to that draughty, creaky old house by the sea in the first week of January to pay homage.

She could plead illness, she supposed, but she was rarely sick, and Keelin and Marie-Claire wouldn't be impressed with that behaviour. There was nothing for it but to go and pretend that she was enjoying the daft shenanigans that in her opinion were thoroughly unnecessary.

Imelda's lips tightened as she got her big mixing bowl and began to crumble breadcrumbs from the batch loaf she'd bought. She couldn't be doing with shop-bought breadcrumbs. They had no substance. She'd use proper bread and make her stuffing the way her mother and grandmother before her had made it, she thought crossly, feeling quite vexed at the prospect of the forthcoming party.

The way everyone went on about Brigid, as though she were a bloody saint! Well, the Reverend Mother was no saint, and she, Imelda, knew that better than anyone. Oh she could tell everyone a thing or two about *Sister*, who had abandoned Imelda to ... to ... *slavery* – that was the best word for it.

The way people had gone on when she'd left to join the convent had been sickening. 'You'll get to heaven quicker, having a nun in the family,' Aunt Lorna approved when she heard the news. *That* had pleased their father enormously.

'God always takes the good ones,' their grandmother declared, casting a sour eye over at Imelda, who had given her cheek earlier in the day. That was pointed and it had stung. Even now, all these decades later, this was what Imelda remembered of Brigid's decision to enter the religious life.

The tang of fresh herbs and onion wafting around the kitchen, mingling with the fruity aroma of Christmas pudding boiling on the cooker, soothed her agitation somewhat, so that when Felicity handed her the mug of tea, Imelda was able to accept it with a modicum of graciousness. Tea was the cure for everything, even the difficulties that came with having a saint for a sister and a party to attend in the depths of winter, when she'd rather be under the snug comfort of her own roof, minding her own business.

CHAPTER FIVE

MARIE-CLAIRE

Marie-Claire sat at the table Marc had reserved by the window. Outside, the snow frolicked in silent merriment. Inside, the hum of laughter and chat, the clinking of glassware, and cutlery on china, the delicious aromas from the kitchen, all seemed to mock her unhappiness. This was no place for the low of heart on such a night when the gods and goddesses of Gaiety and Seasonal Cheer insisted on participation. To her, it all seemed very surreal, as though she were living in a parallel universe.

None of the other diners knew, or cared, that she was in a state of utter wretchedness – and neither would Marc. Marie-Claire had to swallow hard to compose herself as a lump rose to her throat. She was in shock. Soon to be jobless, homeless, manless; and all because Marc Bouchard didn't think that a relationship with her was enough for him. Well, he could have Miss-Butter-Wouldn't-Melt and her fey, cloying obsequiousness, if that was what he wanted, but he damn well couldn't have them both.

Come on now! Chin up. Take control. Don't be a wimp, Marie-Claire told herself sternly, tensing when she saw Marc exiting his taxi. She took a sip of water, impressed that her hand was so steady. She would get through this meal knowing that the choice to play victim or victor was hers alone. And victorious she would be, she vowed, pasting a smile on as she saw her erstwhile partner's face light up when he joined her.

'*Chérie,* you look *stunning,*' he gushed, kissing her lightly on the lips, his mouth and nose cold from the biting air outside. He looked tired, but his gaze was admiring as it slid over her, taking in every aspect of her appearance.

She'd swept her auburn tresses up in a topknot, and taken extra care with her make-up, contouring her cheekbones, using smoky eyeliner to give her eyes extra depth. Her black off-the-shoulder dress clung to every curve. She'd nearly slipped a disc struggling into a pair of Spanx. Her feet were already aching in their skyscraper heels. It was as well she wasn't hungry because she was too trussed up to eat.

'Thank you, sweetie,' she said, lightly returning his kiss. 'Sit down and tell me all about your day. You must be exhausted.' How easily the faux sympathy dripped from her. She should be in Hollywood. She cupped her face in her hands and gazed at him expectantly across the table. The more talking he did, the easier it would be to get the meal over and done with and scarper.

'Oh, Marie-Claire, what a day,' he sighed. 'Families are such a nightmare. But let's order first – I'm starving.' He reached across the table and took her hand before catching a waiter's eye. Feeling her hand in his was a wrench. She'd always liked holding hands with Marc. He had big hands and long tanned fingers, and hers always seemed so dainty in his, though she was far from dainty, she thought wryly.

'Good idea,' she agreed, withdrawing her hand so she could peruse the menu. Her sight was blurred. She couldn't concentrate on the two set menus, with their seven courses of gourmet offerings.

As she'd predicted, Marc ordered the caviar and champagne. When they arrived, he took out his phone, placed the two glasses of sparkling golden alcohol side by side and the caviar in front, framing the photo just so, before uploading it to his social media accounts. He was an avid social media user, justifying it by saying it helped business.

> In Edulis, sharing caviar & champagne with my sexy, stunning girlfriend. Seven courses of Epicurean delights to follow. #HappyChristmasToAll.

'Let's take a selfie,' he suggested, raising his glass to her.

'Stop showing off,' she said lightly, clinking her glass to his.

'Why not? This is a go-to restaurant. One of the Diners Club "World's 50 Best". Why not show everyone how far we've come? And we're going much further, too. Next stop Noo Yark!' He grinned at her, and in spite of her misery

Marie-Claire laughed, because that was one of the things she'd loved about him. He could always make her laugh.

She leaned sideways across the small table, champagne flute in hand, and he did likewise, their heads touching. Marie-Claire smiled. *Suck this up, bioch*, she thought, beaming for the camera. She hoped Amelia would choke on her supper when she saw Marc's tweets and photos.

'So tell me about the funeral,' she said, nibbling on the caviar, once the waiter had taken their order.

'It was incredibly difficult,' Marc scowled. 'You know there's bad feeling between the families because my aunt was divorced and had a second family? Francine got cranky with me because I offered condolences to Raimondi, and . . .'

She listened to him describe what sounded like the funeral from hell and wondered what he would do if she suddenly said, 'I couldn't give a flying fuck about your crappy family and I know all about you shagging Amelia and giving her Tiffany love hearts and planning a trip to Niagara.'

Don't play the victim, she warned herself silently, taking care not to glug her champagne and loosen her inhibitions and resolve.

Marie-Claire ate the food that was set in front of her, the shucked, grilled scallops, the bass with porcini mushrooms and Brussels sprout leaves, and might as well have been eating sawdust. Marc wolfed his grilled prawns and milk-fed lamb, telling her that the offerings served after the funeral wouldn't have filled a gnat. He didn't even notice that she was toying with her food and not matching his drinking.

'I'm so glad we did this. What a fabulous meal!' he enthused as they sipped a postprandial brandy – which had also been photographed and sent off into social media ether.

'It was delicious, Marc. One of the best meals I've ever eaten,' she lied. 'What a great idea of yours to come and have this lovely Christmas Eve treat, *à deux*,' she added with a sarcasm that passed right over him, knowing he had shared every moment of their evening with Amelia and his other social media followers.

'That's not all we'll be doing *à deux*.' He rubbed his thumb along the side of her hand, his eyes glittering from wine and desire. 'Here, let me give you part of my Christmas present,' he said, taking a small duck-egg blue box out of his jacket pocket.

Her heart skipped a beat as she recognized the iconic Tiffany colour.

Was Marc going to give her love hearts too, she wondered, disgusted. But the box was small for a chain and pendants, she registered. Was he going to *propose*?

For one mad moment Marie-Claire thought she could pretend that she'd never overheard the phone conversation with Amelia. Pretend that she could live with Marc's fling – if she made it very clear that it was to end – and secure her future along the lines that it had been moving.

She had two choices, yay or nay. Depending on her answer, her life would be directed along one of two very different paths.

'Excuse me, Marc, I need to pee – all the champagne and wine,' she said. 'Back in a sec.'

'Don't be long, I've two surprises for you,' he said, taking out his phone to photograph the elegant box.

And I've a surprise for you, too, she thought grimly, wishing she could see Amelia's face, when *this* photo appeared on Instagram.

CHAPTER SIX

Her heart was thumping as she struggled with her unyielding underwear in the small toilet cubicle, listening to two women laughing heartily as they reapplied their make-up in the restroom. She banged her elbow off the side of the stall and the pain of it nearly brought tears to her eyes. What was it her Irish grandmother used to say? If you bang your elbow, bang the other one to even it out. She wanted to bang her elbow in Marc's solar plexus. *If* he was going to propose, how *dare* he think it was acceptable to ask her to marry him when he was shagging someone else? She sighed with relief escaping the confines of her detested Spanx. She was damned if she was pulling them back up, she decided, stepping out of them and rolling them up and shoving them in her handbag.

She washed up and retouched her bronzer and lippy. Time to make up her mind. Which path to take? The one with Marc? Or the one alone? She looked at herself in the mirror and saw a pair of troubled green eyes reflected back at her.

The eyes – mirror of the soul, or so they said. Her soul was spectacularly unhappy, just like she was. She was in a no-win situation. To leave Marc would make her as miserable as to stay with him. Whatever decision she made, her life would now be full of 'if onlys'.

'Woman up, Durand. Don't be a wuss,' she muttered, spraying 212 on her wrist and neck. The door to the restroom opened and a middle-aged woman with a lobster-red face came in, flapping her hand up and down to cool herself.

'Oh my gosh, it's so warm out there, when you're a woman of a certain age. Damn these flashes!' she grimaced, turning on a tap and dabbing her napkin in the water flow, before patting her face and neck with it.

'Not easy being a woman,' Marie-Claire remarked, tugging at her dress to stop it from clinging to her bare ass.

'You can say that again,' came the gloomy rejoinder to Marie-Claire's retreating back.

'Are you ready for your surprises?' Marc asked eagerly when she sat down at the table. His eyes were over-bright in the flickering candlelight. He was a tad inebriated. She was as sober as a judge. He waved a brochure at her and picked up the Tiffany box and handed it to her.

'Happy Christmas, *mon amour*, with all my love,' he said huskily.

It was as though time stood still for a moment. Marie-Claire gazed into his heavy-lidded amber eyes, speckled with flecks of gold, ringed by thick black lashes, now slightly glazed from all the alcohol he'd imbibed. His face was tanned from skiing. His nose slightly crooked from a break. His mouth, with a sensual lower lip, the top lip just the slightest bit too narrow, which could make him look mean sometimes if he was angry. The sharp cheekbones a woman would envy. Lean, tanned and taut. She knew the contours of that face so well. *So does Amelia*, a little voice taunted.

Marie-Claire cleared her throat.

'I have something for you first. And I need to say something,' she said, putting the box down and calmly opening her handbag to find his keys. Unfortunately, her handbag being its usual messy chaos, she had to rummage, and as her rolled-up Spanx fell into her lap she cursed herself for not being organized and having the keys in the small side pocket.

'You dirty girl, are you going commando!' Marc's eyes lit up and he laughed as she stuffed them back into the evening bag. 'I can't wait to get you in the taxi home!'

She was so annoyed with herself that when she found his keys, caught in the folds of her wallet, she grabbed them and handed them to him. 'Here. I'm giving you back your keys,' she said brusquely.

'What are you giving me these for? We're not moving yet.' He looked at them in surprise. 'Did you *know* I've put a deposit on a two-bed condo?'

'You did *what*?' Was she hearing right?

'This is part of the surprise.' He handed her a glossy brochure. 'I want you to move in with me. But we have to move fast. It's five floors up from mine. It's fantastic. Wait until you see—'

'Hold on a second and let me get this straight: you've put a deposit on a condo that you want me to move into with you, without me even seeing it?' How typical of Marc, she thought, to make a unilateral decision like that.

'I told you, Marie-Claire, I had to move fast. Half of Toronto wants one of those condos. And I know your rent is due for renewal the first of January, so you won't lose any money by not renewing. It's *perfect* timing,' he grinned impishly.

'Actually, it's not, Marc,' she said slowly. 'I'm leaving Canada. I'm going home to Ireland. Here are your keys. I've already moved my stuff out of your place. And I can't take your present. It wouldn't be fair.' She handed him back the Tiffany box.

'*What?* What do you mean, you've moved your stuff? And you're going back to Ireland? When? For how long? What about New York? What about us? What the hell is going on here, Marie-Claire?' He was flabbergasted, staring at her as though she'd lost her marbles.

Us? she wanted to shout, but she remembered her vow to herself not to play the victim. He would go to his end wondering why his 'Irish colleen' had dumped him.

'Hmmm, well, I've been thinking, especially with my rent coming up for renewal, that it was time to make a decision about what to do with my life. And while Canada's been great, and being with you has been really good, it's time for me to move on and try out something new, and—'

'Marie-Claire, are you for real?' His face darkened. His

voice had an angry edge. 'We've made plans to build up the company in New York. You've a meeting there next week. I'm asking you to move in with me. What are you talking about, leaving Canada?'

She noted sourly that his first priority was the meeting in New York.

'I'm sorry about the meeting in New York, but it's the same date as my great-aunt's eightieth birthday party, and I'd really like to be there—'

'~~Christ~~ Marie-Claire, you'd give up the chance of a lifetime to be at a damn birthday party? We're going places, you and me. Get a grip.'

'Yup, I'm going places – I'm going home,' she said mildly. 'Look, Marc, I'm . . .' She struggled to find a word that would wound without being offensive. 'I'm very, *very* fond' – that was so delightfully insipid, she thought proudly – 'very, very fond of you,' she repeated for good measure—

'Fond! You're *fond* of me?' He said it so loudly the diners at the next table stared over with undisguised curiosity. 'You're in love with me. We're really good together. What is *wrong* with you? Why are you behaving like this?' He couldn't grasp what she was saying. This had come as a bolt out of the blue.

'It's the *Irish* in me,' she said drily, remembering Amelia's derisive slur. 'Look, we had a blast, but I never made any promises to you. I kept my own apartment. I like my independence, you know that. I'm sorry you feel ready to take our relationship a step further and I don't. But that's life, *chérie*.'

'But *why*?' He was utterly bemused.

Marie-Claire smiled. *Mission accomplished*, she thought, proud of herself. He would *never* know the answer to that question. With exquisite timing, her phone tinkled. It was the driver of the cab she'd taken the precaution of ordering while she was in the loo.

'Marc, my taxi has arrived. Please give me the keys to my apartment. I'll be handing them in.' She held out her hand.

'You ordered a taxi! You're supposed to be coming home with me. We're going to visit my parents tomorrow. We're going skiing the day after!' He was totally flummoxed.

'Sorry about that, sweetie. Please give your parents my apologies, but I don't think it would be fair of me to take advantage of their kindness, or yours, now that we're breaking up—'

'Breaking up? Marie-Claire, are you on something? Did you—'

'Marc, the keys – they're on your key ring. I don't want to keep the taxi waiting. My resignation letter is on your desk; the holidays I'm owed can be in lieu of notice. I know it's all a bit sudden, and I apologize for that. But it's time for me to move on.'

'Please don't be hasty. Think about it. Come home with me tonight, Marie-Claire,' he urged. 'Let's—'

'Sorry, Marc, I don't want to take advantage of you. I *am* going home. A clean break is best,' she said firmly, taking a wad of dollars out of her wallet. 'Keys, please – and this is my share of the bill.'

He fumbled with his key ring and reluctantly handed her

back the silver keys. 'I don't know what's got into you,' he muttered. 'Is there someone else?'

'No! I don't two-time,' she said sharply, staring at him intently.

Flustered, he lowered his gaze and took a swig of brandy.

'Goodnight, Marc. Have a good Christmas. Best of luck with New York and the expansion plans. Thanks for the fun times.' Marie-Claire stood up, picked up her bag and walked away, leaving him speechless.

She collected her cape, wrapped it around herself and walked out of the restaurant into the glacial night, and out of Marc Bouchard's life, with her head held high.

CHAPTER SEVEN

'He's banging Amelia? You're *kidding* me!' Lizzie Ross almost spluttered her tea in surprise. When Marie-Claire had phoned to tell her closest friend and colleague that she wouldn't be returning to work at Bouchard and Clay's Sound and Post Facilities, Lizzie had told her to come over to her place immediately and spill.

'Yep – and buying her gifts in Tiffany's and bringing her to Niagara Falls when I was scheduled to be in New York,' Marie-Claire revealed half an hour later, sitting in Lizzie's kitchen.

'What a shit!' Lizzie scowled. 'And with that little weasel-faced pipe cleaner . . .'

Marie-Claire laughed at that, despite her heartache.

'Well she is, all bones and angles, and fried eggs for boobs,' Lizzie exclaimed loyally. 'What does he see in her when he has *you*?'

'I have asked myself that question,' Marie-Claire said drily.

'I've questioned everything about our relationship.' She took a glug of the chilled Chardonnay Lizzie had poured for her and nibbled unhappily on a cracker smeared with pâté.

'He's crazy! I don't get it.' Lizzie paced up and down the wooden floor of her light-filled kitchen. 'He respects you—'

'But he doesn't love me. Clearly, if he's shagging Minnie Mouse, I'm not enough for him.'

'Don't you dare blame yourself for *his* bad behaviour,' Lizzie retorted. 'It's not a lacking in you. It's a lacking in him. He's been a bit of a ladies' man as long as I've known him, but he really did change with you. He seemed so happy – I thought you'd tamed him. I was expecting an announcement, to be honest.'

'I thought we were heading in that direction myself. In fact, part of his Christmas present to me was a key to a two-bed condo in his building. He wanted me to move in with him.'

'Are you serious?' Lizzie stared at her.

'I am. Hasn't he got some nerve, expecting me to move in with him while he's cheating on me behind my back?'

'And what did he say when you confronted him?' Lizzie refilled their glasses, before checking on the chicken dish she'd put in the oven for supper.

'I didn't confront him. I told him I wasn't moving in, told him I was resigning from the job and going home. I told him it was time for me to move on. He couldn't believe his ears.'

'You dumped him! And he doesn't know why! I LOVE it!' Lizzie clapped her hands. 'Hoist by his own petard. Oh well done, woman, well done! I'd love to have seen his face!'

'He was gobsmacked for sure.' Marie-Claire managed a small smile. 'Don't you *ever* let on that I know about Amelia,' she warned her friend.

'As if!' scoffed Lizzie. 'But you do know he'll quiz me.'

'So tell him I felt like a change. And because my lease was up, it was the right time to do it.'

'OK,' Lizzie agreed glumly. 'I'm really going to miss you, though, Marie-Claire. Couldn't you leave the job but stay in Canada and look for another?'

'I'd like to go home for a while and sort out my head. I'm not sure what I want to do next in my life. I'll put my belongings in storage here. If I decide to come back, fine, if not I'll have them shipped home.'

'Please come back, Marie-Claire,' Lizzie begged. 'I can't believe you're leaving. Work won't be half as much fun without you,' she said mournfully, giving her a hug. Marie-Claire hugged her back.

'It will give you a reason to come to Ireland, if I decide to stay,' she comforted. Lizzie was a great pal. She'd made some lovely friends in Canada, but she'd great friends at home too, she reminded herself, and they would keep her going as she ended one chapter of her life and began another.

CHAPTER EIGHT

KEELIN

It was always bittersweet coming home, Keelin reflected when Armand took the slip road off the motorway and headed west. When they got to Ardcloch, ten minutes from where her mother lived, she would ring Imelda and tell her to put the kettle on.

This journey home never failed to bring mixed emotions. Delight because she loved Ardcloch and Glencarraig, the small town Imelda lived in and where Keelin had grown up. Sadness because she would be visiting the graveyard in Ardcloch where her beloved father lay buried with his parents. And painful memories too of a grim and fraught time when harsh words had been flung between them. That had been the worst phase of her life, and though the passage of time had healed some of the hurt, there was still an underlying residue of anger and resentment that Keelin didn't think would ever leave her, no matter how hard she tried to let go of it.

Her uneasy relationship with her mother was all the more prickly without the balm of her father's patient, even-tempered presence.

Please let her not be rude to Armand. Please let her not take the good out of Mère Brigid's party, Keelin prayed silently. Fervently.

Why did Imelda dislike men so much? No man was good enough in her opinion. Not even her loyal and tolerant husband.

'How can you put up with her meanness, Dad?' Keelin had asked her father once, furious with Imelda for not allowing her to go to a dance that all her school friends were going to. Larry had tried his best to get his wife to change her mind, but Imelda had snapped, 'You know as well as I do what goes on at those dances, and I'm not having her coming home thinking she's falling in love with some Romeo, and mooning over him, and having her school-work suffer.'

'That's a bit of an exaggeration now, Imelda,' Larry protested, winking at Keelin. 'Sure, it's the boys who'll be mooning over our lovely daughter!'

'She'd be better off keeping away from men,' Imelda scowled.

'Why? Weren't you very lucky to get a kind man like Daddy?' Keelin had exclaimed hotly, disgusted at her mother's derisory tone.

'Lucky! Is that what you call it?' Imelda retorted, stalking out into the garden to pick some peas and broad beans for dinner.

'She's so mean and nasty,' Keelin raged.

'Ah, she's having a hard time starting that old menopause thing. And with her own da being sick, she's worried and tired. Take no notice, pet, this too will pass,' Larry uttered one of his favourite sayings and gave her a hug. 'Put a pillow under your quilt. When it gets dark, I'll slip out and put the stepladder at your window and leave your bike down at the gate. But don't be too late home. And be as quiet as a mouse climbing in – although, knowing your mother, she'll be dead to the world by ten-thirty,' he added humorously.

'Oh, Dad, you're the best in the world. I love you so much.' Keelin had flung her arms around her father and hugged him with all her might.

Larry had been her champion, and she'd been his, so much so that Imelda had once accused them of ganging up on her.

'Don't be like that, Imelda,' Larry had said sternly. 'I don't like that talk and I *won't* have it. So we'll have no more of it.' It was almost unheard of for him to take that tone with her; shocked, Imelda had muttered an ungracious apology, but an apology nevertheless.

When her father had died, Keelin had wished bitterly that it had been her mother who had been taken first. But Larry was not the parent she'd to learn her life lessons from, she thought ruefully. It was Imelda who was teaching her tolerance, patience and forgiveness, much as she wished it might be otherwise.

'You OK?' Armand looked over at her, the expression in his brown eyes kind and loving as ever. 'Are you thinking of your father?'

'How did you know?' she smiled back at him.

'I know you.' He reached across and squeezed her hand.

'I'm so glad you got to meet him,' Keelin sighed.

'I'm glad too. I had and have a lot to thank him for.'

'Me too,' Keelin sighed. 'He was as good a father to me as you are to Marie-Claire.'

'High praise for me,' her husband said, expertly avoiding a pothole the size of a mini volcano crater as the winding road narrowed the further west they drove.

The pale wintery lemon sun flashed dazzling rays between the bare hedgerows and naked-branched trees. Keelin was glad she wasn't driving. The sun had been low in the sky, heading west, blinding in spots, but once they hit the Midlands, the fields shrouded in wisps of fine misty fog had an ethereal feel. The countryside was resting, deep in winter's grip. So Celtic, so druidic, she'd thought, relishing the energy of her homeland. Now, as they neared the west coast and home, the sun made an appearance again, dappling the bare grey hedgerows with sunlight.

Imelda had sounded tetchy on the phone when she had called her the previous day. Keelin knew it was because of Brigid's upcoming party. Her mother was annoyed because Keelin and Armand would be breaking their holiday with her to travel south to stay with Brigid for a few days.

The bond between Keelin and her aunt was strong, and

43

enduring because of what they had been through together. Imelda could not help but feel jealous, even though Keelin tried hard to be as loving and kind as possible to her mother and give her no cause to fret about their own relationship.

What could have happened to set off such resentment, Keelin wondered, as she always did when she thought about the relationship between Imelda and Brigid.

The familiar outline of Ardcloch's small church came into view, and below it, the houses and farms nestled in the valley. Memories surged back as she took in the patchwork of her grandparents' farm in the distance and the house where Brigid and Imelda had grown up, and where Keelin had spent much of her childhood and teenage years helping out. She remembered watching the rising sun exploding in glorious Technicolor over the top of the hills, her feet drenched with dew, foraging for mushrooms with her grandfather, to cook on the griddle with salt and butter for breakfast. Happy, sweet memories to counteract the sad ones, she acknowledged, looking eagerly along the main street of the village where Kennedy's shop and Post Office still stood, with its press-down brass door handle that rang a bell when you entered. Across the street stood the green cow-tail water pump, where in the old days the women of Ardcloch used to gather to chat and fill their water containers. The water from that pump made a great cup of tea, Keelin remembered nostalgically.

The primary school beside the church was closed now, while the bigger one in Glencarraig, where she'd been a pupil, had expanded. Always the rivalry between Ardcloch and Glencarraig, which dared to think of itself as a town. 'They have notions in that place. They think they're a cut above the rest of us,' her granny used to say scornfully when Imelda said how much she liked living there. Driving past the church and graveyard, Keelin felt the spirits of her long-dead relatives greet her in warm welcome. 'You're back. You're home,' she fancied she heard them say.

Keelin rooted in her bag, found her mobile phone and scrolled to Imelda's number. 'In Ardcloch now, Mam,' she said when her mother answered. 'Stick the kettle on.'

Imelda peered at herself in the mirror, inspecting the sides of her mouth and chin. She'd noticed, when she'd gone to clean the mirror in the guest room en suite, that she was sporting several curly white hairs that needed snipping. Thank goodness she'd been wearing her glasses. She wouldn't have seen the little buggers without them, and the last thing she wanted was to meet her French son-in-law looking like a walrus.

Armand Durand was not her favourite person. It was all his fault that she and Keelin had become estranged. His fault that Larry had died a troubled man.

It was only after Larry's funeral that Imelda, unable to bear Keelin's distress, had grudgingly held out the olive branch. For the sake of her daughter, and grandchild, she tolerated Keelin's French husband and tried to be civil to him. But it wasn't easy. Not easy at all!

It was a pity Marie-Claire wasn't coming home this year. There was something about her granddaughter that softened the atmosphere. She had a carefree way about her that was contagious, and she could make Imelda laugh like no one else could, with her impudence. Imelda smiled. She'd three other grandchildren and, while she loved them, Marie-Claire was her favourite.

She'd better get a move on; Keelin would be here in five minutes. She went into her own bedroom, patted her hair, powdered her cheeks with Mac bronzer and rolled her lipstick over her lips.

The Frenchman wouldn't find *her* lacking in her *toilette*.

The kettle had no sooner boiled than Imelda heard the rental car crunch over the stones in the drive. She whisked off her apron, placed it on the oven rail and went to open the front door.

'Welcome, home, Keelin. Happy Christmas,' she greeted her daughter. They hugged. Imelda was glad Keelin remembered not to kiss her in the French fashion, on each cheek. That nonsense irritated her greatly. Once was enough to kiss a person, there was no need for a pantomime, she'd said crossly to Armand after all the kissing eventually got too much for her.

'Armand, come in, happy Christmas to you, too,' she said in as friendly a tone as she could manage.

'Mrs O'Brien' – she'd told him sharply when she'd first met him not to call her *Madame*, she didn't run a house of ill repute – 'it's very good to see you looking so well. The felicitations of the seasons to you, also,' her son-in-law said, leaning down to kiss her cheek.

The felicitations of the season, indeed, Imelda thought irascibly. *Why couldn't he just say happy Christmas like everyone else?* 'Get in out of the cold' – *and don't be annoying me,* she would have liked to add, but she restrained herself. She'd given herself a stern talking to earlier and told herself to keep her sharp tongue under control. It got her into a lot of trouble, but keeping silent about things was not in her nature.

To take her mind off the antipathy triggered by her son-in-law's arrival, she busied herself making tea and cutting thick fingers of Christmas cake. Her cake had turned out particularly well this year; no sunken fruit or burned sultanas at the edges. She could serve it up to the Frenchman with pride.

'The house is lovely, Mam. The holly and ivy are so decorative along the mantelpiece with the fairy lights woven through,' Keelin lauded her mother's festive touches.

'I saw it done in a magazine when I was at the hairdresser's and there's plenty of holly out in the garden, so I cut a basket full and chopped the ivy off the wall. Even though I say so myself, I made a good fist of it,' Imelda declared.

'You certainly did, Mrs O'Brien, and your cake is delicious, if I may say so,' Armand added his praise to the conversation.

'Thank you,' Imelda said graciously, but didn't offer him another slice.

'Is there anything I can do for you, Mam?' Keelin asked, picking the crumbs of almond icing off the plate. Imelda noted what she was doing. 'I kept some almond icing aside for you – I know you have a weakness for it.' She smiled at her daughter.

'Ah thank you, Mam!' Keelin leaned over and gave her a hug and Imelda's cheeks went rosy pink with pleasure.

'Go on with you,' she said, but she was content with her daughter's response. She couldn't remember the last time she'd been hugged or kissed. It was a good feeling. 'Why don't the two of you go and unpack. I'll put a match to the fire in the front room. Even though the central heating's on, a fire is always that bit more festive at this time of the year,' she suggested briskly. 'We'll have a roast beef dinner today. I'll cook us a turkey dinner for New Year.'

'Do *not* go to trouble, Mam, we'll cook,' Keelin said immediately.

'Indeed you won't. It's no trouble. It will be nice to cook for someone other than myself. Off with you now to unpack,' Imelda ordered. She wasn't having that fella poking around her kitchen. Besides, she liked cooking for people. It wasn't the same cooking for herself now that Larry was gone. One thing about her husband, he'd always appreciated her cooking. A flicker of sadness crossed her face at the thought.

'OK,' Keelin said. 'If you don't mind, as soon as we've unpacked we might go and visit Dad's grave. I bought a lovely Christmas wreath in Dublin for him.'

'Right so.' Imelda stood up from the table. 'You go to the grave before it gets dark and then come back and sit in front of the fire and relax after your journey. I'll start dinner preparations now.'

'Let me put these dishes in the dishwasher.' Armand began to clear the table, and she was about to stop him but decided against it. Keelin was looking so sad at the prospect of visiting Larry's grave. There was no point in adding to her daughter's distress by being unnecessarily rude to Armand. If he didn't fill the dishwasher to her satisfaction, she would do it herself when they were gone.

CHAPTER NINE

MARIE-CLAIRE

When the plane had banked to make its final descent into Dublin, shortly before six-thirty a.m., and she saw the glittering lights of the city beneath her, tears brimmed in Marie-Claire's eyes. She had to struggle to compose herself before leaving the cocoon that had sheltered her from facing the world.

Marc had called constantly, as well as trying to Messenger her, before she left, but she'd ignored his calls and texted:

> Am up to my eyes packing, sweetie, I'll get in touch from Ireland.

She wouldn't give him the satisfaction of seeing her crying. That would ruin her plans for keeping him in the dark about her reasons for leaving.

Marie-Claire squared her shoulders and walked out onto the jetway feeling she was in some sort of a dream.

It was the first time she'd ever returned home with no one to greet her, and she felt a dart of loneliness when the opaque green doors parted and she walked out onto the Arrivals concourse. It was still pitch-black outside. She was glad she'd be getting into bed in the dark.

'Marie-Claire, Marie-Claire!' She heard her name being called and turned her head in the direction of the shout to find Ella waving frantically, heading in her direction. Her heart lifted. Loneliness fled. Ella, her best friend. Always in her life, steadfast and dependable as only best friends are.

'What are you doing here?' Marie-Claire held out her one free arm and was enveloped in a hug that made everything bearable.

'Did you think I'd let you come home at this hour of the morning after what you've been through and not be here to meet you?' Ella demanded, stepping back to look at her. 'Well, you might be going through a trauma, MC, but you look A-MAZ-ING!' she grinned. 'Love that cape. And your hair is so elegant, swept up. How come mine always looks like a bird's nest after I fly? And even when I don't fly,' Ella laughed, sweeping her fingers through her unruly chestnut curls.

'I can't believe you're here,' Marie-Claire exclaimed. She and Ella had met on their secondary school basketball court. Ella, a sixth year and captain of the school team, had been impressed with Marie-Claire's bank shots and blocking actions. Despite the five-year age gap, a friendship was born that had continued when they had both ended up sharing a flat in Dublin, where they had forged careers for themselves, Marie-Claire in sound production, Ella in the employment sector, where she'd eventually set up her own employment agency. As close as sisters, they shared each other's joys and sorrows. There was no one else in the world that Marie-Claire would have wanted to find waiting for her on her arrival back to Ireland.

'You know you can come home with me, but to be honest, I think you'd be far better off going to the hotel you booked,' Ella said as she took control of the trolley heading towards the exit. 'The girls held a sleepover last night and you wouldn't get a wink of sleep with them prancing around. I'm tempted to book in myself,' she grimaced.

'Ella, I'll take the courtesy bus, honestly. Don't go out of your way driving me there,' Marie-Claire protested.

'Are ya mad! I'm going to have a very peaceful break-fast and a natter with you, before you get into bed. Then I'm going into town to the sales. By myself! Oh bliss,' she grinned. 'I love my girls, but they do my head in. Our life was so uncomplicated when we were their ages. I swear to God, those Kardashians and social media have ruined a generation.'

'Is it that bad here too?' Marie-Claire followed her friend to the car park.

'You bet it is. I'll tell you about it another day. For now, it's all about you. Update me on EVERYTHING!' Ella demanded. Marie-Claire had told her friend all the gory details, starting with overhearing Amelia's furtive phone call and the evening with Marc, in several Skype sessions over the past few days.

'Well done, missus,' Ella had exclaimed approvingly when Marie-Claire outlined her strategy. 'Let him die wondering, the little shit.'

'Yep, that's the only thing that's positive about it for me: I'm in control and *I* dumped him and he'll never know why. He *hates* it. And I'll get over him. I'm not going to be defined by my relationship with him. I'm going to stop thinking of myself as a failure. It's time to move on.' But even as she said the words, they sounded hollow. Despite her best intentions, her heart ached as they walked out into the crisp cold air of Dublin, and the salty easterly breeze whispered across Marie-Claire's face and she caught the familiar scent of home.

CHAPTER TEN

'*Mon dieu!* What are you doing here?' Keelin's shout of joy was music to Marie-Claire's ears when she was hugged by her astonished mother in Imelda's front porch.

'Was that a good surprise?' she grinned, hugging back tightly, swallowing down the lump that rose to her throat at the sight of her much-loved mother.

'What's going on out here? Marie-Claire! *What* are you doing home? I thought you were working and couldn't come.' Imelda, hearing the commotion, bustled into the hall, her face lighting up at the sight of her granddaughter walking through the front door.

'That was a fib,' Marie-Claire lied, planting a kiss on her grandmother's soft cheek.

'Come in, have a cup of tea. Did you drive straight from the airport?' Imelda ushered them into the kitchen.

'No, I flew in yesterday and Ella collected me.' She omitted saying that she'd stayed the night in a hotel. 'It was great to

The Liberation of Brigid Dunne

catch up, and I did a bit of business in Dublin with the letting agency and the house and all that stuff, and here I am. Where's Papa?' She followed her grandmother into the kitchen and sat down at the round oak table, glad to be at her journey's end.

'He's gone over to Ardcloch to do a bit of work on the graves. We got new stones for them,' Keelin said lightly. 'He'll get such a surprise to see you.'

'I'll make up the bed in Keelin's old room, you can sleep there.' Imelda filled the kettle and took some mugs down from the press.

'I'll do the bed, Gran,' Marie-Claire offered. 'I don't want you going to any trouble.'

'*I'll* do the bed.' Keelin put milk and sugar on the table while her mother cut dainty fingers of Christmas cake to go with the tea.

'It's no trouble, I'm *delighted* to have you here, dear.' Imelda patted her arm.

'Thanks, Gran. Are you looking forward to the party? I can't wait to see Mère's face when I surprise her. Tell me all the plans for it.'

Imelda's lips tightened. 'Party! Party! Party! You'd think no one else had ever retired or got to eighty. Such a fuss!' she grumbled, spooning tea leaves into the pot. She didn't care for teabags and made tea the old-fashioned way.

Marie-Claire flashed a glance at her mother, who threw her eyes up to heaven. 'Ah sure, we'll have a big party for you, Gran, when you're eighty,' she said, deciding to ignore her grandmother's petulance.

55

'I don't want any of that nonsense, 'tis far from surprise parties I was reared,' Imelda sniffed.

'So Mère thinks it's a little party for the nuns and she doesn't know the family is coming, is that it?' Marie-Claire turned to Keelin.

'Exactly! We've all booked into Kirwin's Hotel—'

'Who's coming?'

'The four of us, now that you're home. Plus your Uncle John and Auntie Phil, Lucy and Laura—'

'Terrific!' exclaimed Marie-Claire, looking forward to seeing her cousins.

'And the Sheedys. Brigid is very fond of them. A few people from Butlersbridge, of course and the Mother General—'

'*She's* coming? All the way from Paris?' Imelda interjected sharply.

'Yes, and two other Sisters. They're only staying the night. Armand is collecting them from the station.' Keelin eyed her mother warily.

'For goodness' sake! Isn't it great for them all the same that they can spend a fortune on flights for a jaunt to Ireland? No doubt that money comes out of the charity boxes that people put their hard-earned money into,' Imelda griped.

'Mam, stop that,' Keelin said sharply. 'Brigid is highly thought of by her congregation. She's given a lifetime's service to her Order. She deserves a bit of recognition for it.'

'If we all got the recognition we deserved we'd be doing well,' her mother retorted as the sound of the doorbell chimes sent her hurrying out into the hall.

'I'm *so* glad you're here, Marie-Claire,' Keelin whispered. 'She's doing my head in. Brigid's party is going between her and her sleep, she's so annoyed about it. I swear to God, if it passes off without a hitch or a row, it will be a miracle.'

'Ah it's not that bad, surely,' Marie-Claire soothed, biting into the rich cake and taking a mouthful of 'proper' tea. Her heart sank at her mother's uncharacteristically stern words. She'd come home to Ireland looking for solace and landed in the middle of a family drama.

Imelda marched into the kitchen and plonked a beautifully arranged basket of flowers on the table. 'The O'Neills want me to give this to Brigid. Who do they think I am ... Interflora?' she snapped, glowering at the thoughtful gift. 'I got her fifty euros' worth of savings certificates and she can like them or lump them. I'm going to make up the bed.' She stomped out of the kitchen.

Marie-Claire giggled. '"Interflora!" She's a hoot when she's mad,' she whispered. 'Why is she so annoyed at Mère?'

'I have *no* idea, Marie-Claire. They've never got on, but it's more Mam's fault than Brigid's. I don't even think Brigid knows why. She doesn't want to come to the party. I told her to stay at home and she said she wouldn't have people talking about her. There's no winning with her. Uncle John opened his big mouth and told her he has a great surprise for Brigid, so Mam's curiosity is getting the better of her. That's another reason she's going. But if she upsets Brigid on her special day I won't hold back. I'm fed up of this carry-on, and Mam's walking on very thin ice with me.' Keelin sat poker-straight, rigid with disapproval.

Marie-Claire refrained from comment. She'd heard the wheels of a car on the drive and shot out of her seat and put a finger to her lips and hid behind the kitchen door. Keelin grinned, hearing Armand call her name.

'Am I blocking someone in the drive. Has Imelda got a visitor?' he asked, walking into the kitchen and bending down to kiss his wife's cheek.

'She has, but I don't think she'll be going anywhere for a while, so you're fine,' Keelin said non-committally. 'Would you like a cup of coffee?'

'I would. I'll stick the kettle on,' Armand said.

'Let me do it, Papa,' Marie-Claire offered, laughing.

Her father stopped and turned, doing a double-take. *'Marie-Claire!'*

'Oh Papa, it's *so* good to see you!' she exclaimed, launching herself at him, and he laughed with joy and hugged the daylights out of her, and for a while her sadness disappeared and she gave herself over to the immense pleasure of being with her parents.

CHAPTER ELEVEN

Una Farrelly was at her wits' end. She was doing her best to keep Reverend Mother Brigid's surprise party under wraps but the RM kept poking her nose into things that were really none of her business, commenting on the amount of bacon and eggs in the fridge, and the 'mountain' of sponge for the trifle she was going to make later. 'You're not going to be feeding the multitudes, Una. It's only a few Sisters from the convents and two from the Mother House,' Brigid remarked mildly, heading upstairs.

As soon as Brigid had left her in peace, Una picked up her mobile phone and dialled Keelin's number. She wanted to alert her to how difficult it was to keep on top of everything, with Brigid in situ. Keelin was like a sister to her, and Una felt the need for a bit of reassurance now that the pressure was on.

She heard her friend's cheery voice in her ear. 'Hi, Una, how are things? Can't wait to see you.'

'Keelin, I can't wait to see you, too,' she replied, keeping an eagle eye on Brigid, now out in the garden. 'I'm ringing to let you know that it's not easy trying to keep everything under wraps down here. Brigid's under my feet all day, wondering why I have so much food in the fridge. Thank God she doesn't know what's over at Maura's. I'm trying to keep her occupied, but I don't know how I'm going to set up the party and buffet without her copping on that it's going to be bigger than a little get-together with the Sisters.'

'Oh dear. We didn't think of that when we were planning it. Look, do your best. Get one of the nuns to take her out for a couple of hours. Or try telling her the parlour's out of bounds.'

'Ha! She might not take *too* many orders from me. I'm only the housekeeper,' joked Una.

'They're all afraid of you, Una. Look, don't worry about it. It will still be a surprise when we all arrive and that's the main thing.'

'OK!' Una sighed. 'I'll see you when I see you. How's Imelda behaving?' Una was privy to Keelin's difficulties with her mother.

'She's herself,' Keelin said caustically. 'Spoiling for a row.'

'Oh lordy!'

'Guess who's coming too?'

'Who?'

'Marie-Claire.'

'*What!* I thought she was tied up with work. Brigid will be thrilled, all the Sisters will be. Oh what a *treat*.' Una couldn't hide her delight.

'I thought that might cheer you up. It's going to be a great party.'

'If I don't have a heart attack first. I'll see you all tomorrow, pet.'

'What's up?' Marie-Claire asked when Keelin put the phone down. They were sitting at the table in Imelda's kitchen, Imelda was out getting groceries, and the Durand family were enjoying their time alone.

'Una was saying she's finding it hard to keep everything secret because Brigid's under her feet all the time and she's afraid she'll realize the party is more than a little celebration with the nuns. She's trying to think of a way to keep her occupied, away from the house, for a few hours so they can decorate the parlour and set up the buffet. Easier said than done.'

'I could go down and distract her,' Marie-Claire suggested, longing to get to her favourite place on earth.

'And how would you explain your presence? She'd know something was going on if you arrived unexpectedly,' Armand pointed out. 'Hercule Poirot had nothing on the Reverend Mother, as we well know,' he added wittily, and his wife laughed.

'Mère doesn't know anything about *all* of us coming to the party. I could always say that I took holidays owed to me. I'll tell her I flew in to Shannon.'

'You mean you're going to tell big whopping lies?' her father teased.

'Huge ones!' his daughter grinned.

'That's a good idea,' Keelin approved.

'Right! That's a plan. I'll go and pack.' Marie-Claire finished her slice of bread and carried her dishes to the dishwasher.

'Mam won't be too impressed that you're leaving already. And I was looking forward to spending the day with you.' Keelin followed her daughter to the sink with the rest of the plates and mugs.

'I know, Maman, but you'll be down tomorrow and we can spend time together then.' Marie-Claire hugged her mother when she straightened up from loading the dishwasher.

'Brigid will be over the moon—'

'Why will Brigid be over the moon?' Imelda came into the kitchen, at the tail end of Keelin's comment, and hefted her shopping bag onto the table before divesting herself of her hat, coat and gloves.

'I'm going to go down to the Four Winds to help Una out. She's a bit fraught, to say the least,' Marie-Claire said lightly, waiting for Imelda to erupt.

'For goodness' sake! You've only been here a night. Am I not going to get any time to spend with my granddaughter?' she exclaimed crossly, on cue, hanging her clothes up in the small closet off the kitchen.

There was a time you didn't want to know your granddaughter, Keelin thought sourly.

'Ah, Gran, don't be like that.' Marie-Claire put her arm around her grandmother's shoulders when she came back into the kitchen. 'Una's not as young as she used to be and it's a big undertaking, organizing a surprise party like that. Now come on, don't be cross. We're going to have a lovely family gathering with lots of fun and frolics – what could be better than that?' she cajoled, giving Imelda a squeeze before running upstairs.

It had started to rain lightly, a fine mist that swept in from the coast, as she threw her case into the boot of her hire car and blew a kiss at her parents and grandmother, who stood at the door to wave her off. Marie-Claire exhaled, driving through Ardcloch. She was glad to be on her own. Glad not to have to keep up a façade of cheeriness when all she wanted to do was to curl up in a ball and cry her eyes out. The long drive to the Four Winds was just what she needed.

She'd hardly left the main street when her phone rang on Bluetooth. 'Hi, Ella,' she said with pretend cheeriness. 'How are things?'

'I was ringing to ask you the same,' her friend laughed. 'Were they thrilled to see you?'

'Ah, they were, it was a huge surprise to them and it was great to see them and be with them.'

'And how's your little heart doing?' Ella asked kindly.

'Little heart's a bit battered,' Marie-Claire admitted, exceedingly glad that she didn't have to put on an act for her best friend. 'Actually, I was doing OK until I remembered that this morning, if I was in Canada, I'd be heading off to

New York to hold the interviews. But I'll get over it,' she said, swerving to avoid a large pothole.

'Ah, it's feckin hard though. One minute you're tootling along without a bother and then, whack! You don't know what's hit you. Anyhoo, remember I was telling you that Granddad Reilly, Mum's dad, stipulated in his will that he wanted Nana to go on a cruise with her friend after the house was sold and she'd settled in her apartment in Clontarf?'

'Yeah, I thought it was a lovely thing for him to do. I wish someone would leave me the money to go on a cruise,' Marie-Claire said humorously.

'Well, she's going in five weeks' time – for three and a half months, if you don't mind. Up to Alaska, then down the west coast of America, around the Caribbean Islands, across to the Azores, Portugal, Spain, France and Italy and then back to Southampton.'

'Wowza, I *love* it! Good woman, Nana Reilly,' Marie-Claire approved.

'The thing is, the apartment will be empty, and I was telling her you were home, and you'd have to give your tenant lots of notice if you planned on staying, and she said why don't you stay in hers, and she'll put you on the car insurance too. It's only a little Fiesta, but it would do for getting around until you figure out what you're going to do. Whaddya think?' Ella couldn't hide her delight. '*Please* say yes. Please stay in Dublin, I've missed you so much,' she added imploringly.

Marie-Claire was stunned. 'Jeepers, Ella, this is very

unexpected,' she said hesitantly. 'You can tell her if I'm staying I'll be paying rent. I'll get a job somewhere,' Marie-Claire said firmly. 'Even if it's only giving French grinds to students.'

'She'll say no!'

'Well then, I won't stay,' Marie-Claire retorted.

'You can sort it out between you,' Ella laughed. 'I'd better go, I'm back in the office and I have *thousands* of emails. 'Ring me after the party and let me know how it goes and what your plans are.'

The sun was shining by the time she drove through the open wrought-iron gates that led to the rambling, whitewashed, Victorian two-storey house that sat sturdily atop a cliff. The sight lifted Marie-Claire's heart.

She drove around the side of the house, got out of the car and walked into the back hall that led into the kitchen. The aroma of baking wafted around her, and her stomach grumbled at the smell. Marie-Claire inhaled the familiar scents of polish, and roses, that she associated with this house that had always been her refuge. She could hear murmured conversations and laughter and recognized Una and Mère's voices.

She opened the kitchen door and stood taking in the scene. The two women – her great-aunt in her black habit, Una in her floral apron, sitting together at the table, sipping tea out of china cups.

It was Brigid who saw her first. Her jaw dropped. Her face took on an expression of pure happiness. 'Marie-Claire!' she exclaimed joyfully, standing with the alacrity of a woman half her age. Arms outstretched, she crossed the tiled floor as Una clapped her hands and cried in delight:

'I declare to God, would you look who's here?'

'Dear, dear beloved girl,' Brigid murmured wrapping her arms around her great-niece, her cheek soft and unlined against Marie-Claire's. 'What blessing is this the Lord has sent us?'

They held each other tightly, and in the tender embrace of her great-aunt, in the place of her greatest solace, Marie-Claire knew that she was finally home.

Imelda sat in the armchair in her hotel bedroom and studied her surroundings. A Boutique Hotel was the way it was advertised. *Boutique, indeed!* she thought waspishly. A jumped-up B&B, more like it. Her bed was facing in the opposite direction to how she slept at home. She hoped it wouldn't affect her sleep. The room, though small, appeared clean and it did have tea-making facilities like a real hotel, Imelda conceded. The warm, buttery cream colour on the walls and soft yellow lamplight gave it a tranquil air. She was tired after the early start and journey to Butlersbridge. Keelin had advised her to take a nap. Everyone from Ardcloch was meeting up in the bar for a drink, later, before getting the hired minibus to take them to the Four Winds.

She had to admit, Keelin had done a good job planning the surprise bit of the party. All the guests were booked in. They wouldn't have to worry about walking in bad weather, or looking for parking. People would be able to have a drink. Every aspect covered. Would any of them bother to go to such trouble for *her*? Imelda wondered.

She doubted it. She knew she was an irritation to her children. Keelin had been her father's favourite, Imelda had always known that; truth be told, her daughter struggled not only to love her, but also to like her. She sighed deeply. Keelin had *no* idea of how things really were. None of the family knew any of it. Just as they knew nothing about Brigid, whom they all adored.

No, there'd be no surprise party for Imelda, when ... *if* she ever got to eighty. But if they knew the truth they'd feel sorry for her, Imelda thought forlornly as she got up to make herself a cup of tea. This party would have to be endured. She'd told Keelin she wouldn't be making a speech; their brother could do that.

Imelda eased her feet out of her suede court shoes and wriggled her toes. She was wearing a two-piece outfit, an indigo blue velvet dress and black sequined jacket she'd bought in Brown Thomas after Keelin had told her of the plans for a surprise party. Imelda was no Mary Hick. She'd hold her own anywhere, she thought proudly, hanging the ensemble in the wardrobe while she waited for the kettle to boil.

Not that anyone would be taking much notice of *her*. Tonight it would be all about her saintly sister – who really was no saint at all, if they only knew it.

CHAPTER TWELVE

THE PARTY

Brigid had had a most restful nap, sitting in the rocking chair in her bedroom, listening to the wind-tossed sea swirling and crashing against the rocks and shore. It had been twilight when she fell asleep after her tea and scone, now it was pitch-black outside, apart from the smattering of twinkling lights in Butlersbridge, across the fields, and the homes dotted along the headland speckling the darkness with pinpricks of light.

The sound of voices, and cases being trundled along the landing, had woken her. Brigid felt a fizz of excitement. She was looking forward to catching up with her fellow nuns, some of whom she hadn't seen in ages. She went to the door and poked her head out, to see Sister Marie-Hélène following Sister Veronique to the rooms at the end of the corridor.

'Marie-Hélène! Veronique!' she called, smiling broadly when they turned. They dropped their cases and hurried to her.

'RM, how are you?' Marie-Hélène encircled her in an embrace. From beneath her veil, bright green eyes full of love and mischief twinkled at back at Brigid.

'You look amazing. You never age, RM.' Veronique, who was on the portly side and nearer Brigid's age than Marie-Hélène's, puffed a little as she waited to hug her friend and colleague.

'What are you doing, wearing the veil? I thought you'd given it up.' Brigid eyed the younger nun, who wore a black skirt, white blouse, and a soft woollen short pink cardigan.

'I wore it to honour you. It's your party. You've never given it up, nor has Veronique and—' Marie-Hélène stopped. 'I can take it off if you like,' she teased, whipping the veil off her head to show her highlighted blonde tresses.

'You changed your colour,' Brigid noted. '*Très chic.*' The last time she'd seen Marie-Hélène she'd been sporting auburn locks.

'Blondes have more fun,' laughed her incorrigible colleague. 'Actually, I'm going to stop colouring it soon. I'm going grey. I might as well embrace it gracefully!'

'That will be the day you embrace anything gracefully,' Brigid said fondly. 'Who else is here? Let me freshen up and go down and greet them.'

'Freshen up by all means, RM, dear, but under no circumstances are you to go downstairs if you don't want Una to have a coronary,' Veronique said firmly, kissing Brigid. 'She's scurrying around making sure everything's perfect. She wants for you to make a *grand* entrance.'

'Good Lord, she's taking it all so seriously. She shouldn't be putting herself to such trouble,' Brigid tutted.

'She's in her element. She loves it! Bossing everyone around, baking her fabulous goodies, making a fuss of us, like she's always done. Don't be worrying, there isn't a bother on her,' Marie-Hélène soothed, her Kerry twang as pronounced as ever. She had taken the name Marie-Hélène, after one of the Order's founding nuns, because she thought it sounded more exotic than the more mundane Benedict they'd first suggested. It suited her greatly, Brigid thought, amused.

'Ah, Una's the best,' Brigid said fondly. 'I remember the day she started here as a young maid and she tipped a pitcher of buttermilk over Mother Patrick—'

'If she survived that, she'll survive your party. We'd better get ready. We've to be in the big parlour at six sharp. We'll see you down there,' Veronique interrupted briskly. If Brigid started going back to the early days they'd be there all evening. She loved to reminisce.

At that moment, Marie-Claire appeared on the return. 'I came to see if you were awake, Mère,' she said, from the top step.

'I am, dear. I'm just going to freshen up and change my habit,' Brigid assured her. Now that it was actually happening, Brigid was looking forward to her little party, although, at the back of her mind, the realisation that it was a swansong of sorts was unsettling. She was yesterday's woman now. A new order had taken over, Brigid thought, smiling at her little pun. Having Marie-Claire here was the icing on the cake for her.

Tonight would be a night of reminiscing, of happy memories, of love and sisterly affection. A fitting end to her career.

The Four Winds was a beacon of light at the edge of the cliff. Lamplight shone through every window. The Christmas tree lights sparkled in the bay windowpanes of the big parlour. Una's husband had strung fairy lights along the shrubbery that lined the drive. It looked like fairyland, Keelin thought, as memories came hurtling back with a fierce intensity that was almost painful, when she saw the old house lit up in all its glory.

'Isn't it *gorgeous*!' exclaimed Rita Sheedy in the seat behind Imelda's on the minibus. 'The nuns must have plenty of money to be able to afford a place like this.'

'Indeed!' sniffed Imelda, glancing out the window as the bus rattled along the drive. 'Wouldn't we all love a holiday home like it?'

'It was left to the Order, decades ago, by a wealthy landowner, who was very grateful for the nuns' care of his wife. She'd cancer. Their good deeds prompted his,' Keelin explained when the driver headed for the kitchen entrance, as per Una's instructions. The housekeeper didn't want Brigid seeing the guests arriving and entering through the front door, to spoil the surprise. The kitchen was at the side of the house, out of sight of Mère's bedroom window.

'They could have sold it and given the proceeds to charity. Or they could house homeless people in it,' Imelda retorted, unimpressed with talk of good deeds.

'Even nuns need a holiday,' Keelin said mildly, determined not to get into an argument with her mother, as the bus drew to a halt.

Imelda's lips tightened. '"Nuns need a holiday" indeed, and half the world starving and the Church owning assets worth billions. But then you can't criticize the nuns to Keelin. She always takes their side.'

Imelda could see that her dart had stung. She hauled herself out of the seat, listening to the excited chatter around her. Felicity, her daughter-in-law, was chatting on her mobile to Cormac, who had stayed at home to run the supermarket and mind the children, telling him they'd arrived at the party. Her brother John with his big booming voice, slagging Willie Sheedy about the fancy waistcoat that Rita had made him wear to the 'Nun's Party'.

''Twas more than my life was worth not to,' Willie said good-humouredly. 'And I see you're wearing a new pair of swanky braces yourself.'

'They'll see me to the grave,' John joked, and the two couples laughed at their good-natured banter.

Imelda had no one to banter with. She was a widowed outsider without the bulwark of a spouse, in social situations. A sharp arrow of self-pity pierced her heart. Why couldn't she be like all the others, looking forward to a night of fun and laughter? It was because of the secrets that she carried. And the sadness. It was hard keeping it all inside, especially when Keelin lauded Larry and his many great attributes. Imelda had attributes of her own that none of her family would ever give her credit for because they knew *nothing* of her stoicism and loyalty towards her deceased husband, despite the grief he had caused her.

Why was the past coming back to haunt her so much, these days? Hadn't she dealt with her demons? She'd got on with life, as she always did, but at moments like these – *especially* at moments like these, memories would surface and tsunamis of resentment would sweep over her and bring out the worst in her. She would make a *real* effort tonight. She might even enjoy herself. *Now wouldn't that be something,* Imelda thought in a rare moment of amusement, stepping off the bus to follow the Sheedys inside.

Una was standing at the back door, resplendent in tailored black trousers and a scarlet silk, boat-neck top.

'Well, don't you look posh, Una,' Imelda declared when the housekeeper greeted her.

'And pretty glam you're looking too, Imelda,' Una laughed. 'I love the outfit. That blue is a lovely colour on you.'

'I got it in Brown Thomas.' Imelda was immensely pleased with the compliment. She didn't let on that she'd got her dress in the sale, for half price. 'And I'm a great fan of the Radley handbags, so I treated myself to one.' She held out her clutch for inspection.

'How pretty,' Una said, but her attention was elsewhere, having spotted Keelin behind Imelda's daughter-in-law, Felicity. 'Go on into the big parlour, Imelda,' she said, ushering her in, leaving Imelda feeling she'd been dealt with and was now not even on Una's radar. She followed her neighbours into the large, high-ceilinged room, filling up with nuns and other guests.

At one end an enormous table, decorated with sprigs of red-berried holly and trails of ivy, awaited the feast from the kitchen. Beside it, a smaller table held shiny glassware, plates, and cutlery wrapped in linen napkins. Of course the nuns wouldn't use paper serviettes like the rest of them, Imelda thought, admiring the bushy, perfectly proportioned, decorated noble fir that dominated the bay window. The scent of fresh pine was lovely and she inhaled it appreciatively. A fire burned brightly in the grate, and the buzz of convivial conversation from guests seated on the old-fashioned chintz sofas, or standing in little knots chatting together, made Imelda feel unaccountably sad.

Oh why did I come? she thought wretchedly. She'd known all along that she'd hate it. This place brought back unhappy memories of the rows she'd had with Keelin, Brigid and Larry.

'It's Imelda, isn't it? You're Brigid's sister. I'm Marie-Hélène. I remember you coming to visit once, before Keelin moved to Dublin.' A bright-eyed, effervescent nun with a vaguely familiar face came and stood beside her.

'That was a long time ago,' Imelda remarked, glad of the opportunity to chat to someone.

'It's hard to believe so many years have passed, and Marie-Claire has turned thirty. Doesn't time fly? I was not long out of the novitiate, that summer she was born. In fact, I was there for her birth. I'd been in a car crash and was sent down here to recuperate after my surgery. RM was so good to me. So kind. I can't believe she's retiring – and eighty to boot,' Marie-Hélène said. 'I can't wait to see her face when she comes down and sees us all here.'

'And when will that be?' Imelda asked, glad of the change of subject.

'I'd say very shortly. There's our Mother General, and two of our nuns from the Mother House in France coming in now. Excuse me, Imelda, I'd better go and say *bonsoir.*'

Imelda watched the nun make her way through the room, casting a word here, a smile there, to the guests she knew. She remembered her now: young, vibrant, cuddling Marie-Claire and singing to her, charmed with the child in her arms. Imelda had felt at the time that Marie-Hélène would never stick religious orders, being too exuberant and full of life, and yet here she was, still a nun more than thirty years later, and as lively as ever. She must have had a *true* calling – unlike Brigid, in whose honour this party was being held, Imelda seethed, watching how all the nuns deferred to the Mother General as though she were the most important person in the room. The French nun carried herself with an air of great authority and hauteur. It was wasted on Imelda. She didn't take to people who had high opinions of themselves. She could be as haughty as any French Mother General, let there be no doubt about that.

A young waitress carrying a tray of glasses filled with red and white wine offered her a drink. Imelda took a glass of red. She might as well drown her sorrows and make the evening more bearable. She heard her brother's chortling guffaw and turned to see him enveloping Una in a hug. Well may he laugh, she thought resentfully. He'd never understood how she could be so angry with Brigid and Sean for leaving Ardcloch in their youth.

'Everyone has to tread their own path,' he'd pointed out once when she started on one of her rants.

'Convenient for them. You and I were left to carry the can.'

'Ah be easy, woman, and stop giving out. Didn't you do well out of it in the end?' was his tetchy response. She wondered what was the great present he'd bought for Brigid. *That* she was curious to know.

'Everything OK, Mam?' Keelin arrived at her side.

'I don't like this place. I never did. I'll be glad when this party is over, Keelin,' she said bluntly, taking a good slug of wine. Her daughter's face darkened.

'Keep your voice down, for goodness' sake, Mam. If you feel that strongly, you shouldn't have come,' she hissed.

'And have everyone talking? I think not. They had enough to talk about years ago,' Imelda snapped, annoyed at her daughter's rebuke.

'Mam, *stop* it!' Keelin turned on her heel and walked away, furious.

Imelda felt like going after her daughter and smacking her. Could no one on this earth understand *her* point of view?

A ripple of excitement at the door made her turn her head in time to see her older sibling, an expression of eye-widening astonishment, followed by delight and happiness chasing across her fine features. Brigid might be eighty, but she looked twenty years younger and her skin was soft and unlined beneath her veil.

'I don't believe it,' Brigid gasped. 'How? When? *Una!*' She turned to the housekeeper, who was beaming from ear to ear. 'You rogue!' Brigid declared before she was enveloped in a flurry of hugs as her sister nuns clustered around her.

Like a flock of chattering crows, Imelda thought unkindly as jealousy once again swept through her.

Brigid made her way into the room, guests hugging, kissing and congratulating her. She caught sight of Imelda and her face lit up. 'You came!' she exclaimed warmly, leaning forward to kiss her. 'Imelda, I'm delighted.'

'I'm your sister, why wouldn't I? Sure, don't we *have* to make a fuss of you?' Imelda pecked her on the cheek.

'Honestly, Imelda, I hadn't a clue. It's *such* a surprise,' Brigid confessed, the sly sarcasm sailing over her head. 'You look marvellous. That colour is lovely on you.'

Imelda softened at her sister's compliment. 'And black suits you,' she reposted humorously and they both laughed.

'And the Sheedys came, and the Mother General, and oh, Lord ... it's Keelin!' Brigid's face was alight with joy as she held out her arms to her niece.

'Mère, oh Mère, it's so good to see you. Happy, *happy* birthday,' Keelin put her arms around her beloved aunt and hugged her tightly. A pain, sharp as the thrust of a knife in her heart, stabbed Imelda, viewing the tableau of love and affection in front of her.

If she lived to be a hundred, Keelin would never kiss and

hug her with the love and warmth she had for Brigid. That look of joy would never cross her daughter's face for *her*! Afraid that she might cry, Imelda finished her wine and made her way out of the crowded room to find the downstairs restroom. She needed to be alone for a few moments to compose herself.

She heard Una announce that dinner was going to be served immediately so it wouldn't be overcooked, and that everyone was to tuck in, speeches could be made later and presents given to the guest of honour. Una was such a little dictator, Imelda thought crossly, wondering would she be able to eat anything when the lump in her throat was so big. She locked the door of the small bathroom behind her and leaned against it. Seeing how truly loved Brigid was, and how contented and serene she seemed, only emphasized her own sense of failure and disappointment with life.

Coming down here to the Four Winds had been a big mistake. It had stirred up memories and emotions she thought she'd buried deep. If only she had her car she could drive back to the hotel, her glass of wine notwithstanding. But she was trapped here until the party was over whether she liked it or not.

Imelda took several deep breaths and retouched her lipstick before opening the door. 'Howya, Imelda!' Maura, Una's younger sister, hurried past with a tray of condiments. 'Isn't it a splendid party? It all worked out perfectly,' she remarked gaily over her shoulder.

'Splendid,' Imelda echoed drily, promising herself one more glass of wine to get through the evening. She wasn't a big drinker, but sometimes, she acknowledged, a woman needed help to endure an ordeal.

Brigid, seated in an armchair by the fire, listened to the laudatory words of her brother, John and almost wept. She'd just finished Skyping with her brother Sean in Perth and his words of congratulation had touched her deeply. She'd never felt so loved in her entire life, never felt so cherished. To have her life's work affirmed so generously by everyone at the party was very touching. And, for the first time, she felt able to acknowledge that, *yes*, she had done good work during her time on the Missions and hopefully changed people's lives for the better. She could look her God in the eye on Judgement Day and say she'd at least done that.

' . . . and so my dear sister, Philly,' John smiled at his wife, 'and I want to gift you this, with all our love.' He handed her a small green book, and she saw that it was a Post Office book, with her name on it. 'We deliberately waited until you were retired, because we knew otherwise you would probably give it to the Order. It's our wish' – he glanced at the Mother General – 'that you use what's in this account to travel, spend time with us in Ardcloch or do with it whatso-ever you wish. Don't you agree, Mother General?' He turned to the nun who was standing beside him.

'*Mais oui!* Of course,' she agreed. 'Reverend Mother Brigid is now retired. The rules on personal wealth no longer apply.'

'Excellent,' John laughed. 'Because you're not getting it.'

'John,' murmured Brigid reprovingly, opening the book.

Her jaw dropped when she saw the amount. Thirty thousand euros! 'John, Philly, I can't take this—'

'You can and you will,' he decreed. 'Our parents left the farm to me because I was the eldest. Which I know was the tradition in those days, but which, as Imelda has pointed out on *numerous* occasions, is most unfair. Our Imelda always stands up for herself when she feels she is being hard done by,' he joked, winking at Brigid. 'I felt *you* were hard done by. Imelda and Sean got their whack when I sold some of the land to a developer a while back, and this is your entitlement. Enjoy it. You more than deserve it. You gave up your life for others, now it's our turn to give something back to you. And that's the end of my speech,' he added, 'because I hate making them.'

Everyone laughed as he stepped back to allow the Mother General to take his place, and, because he had his back to her, he didn't see the look of outrage on Imelda's face.

'I only served as any nun would serve God and her Order. I'm truly nothing special. It was an honour to work in Senegal. I can't thank you all enough for all your kindness to me, I don't deserve it,' Brigid said, eyes bright and shining with tears, showing how touched she was.

'You can say that again,' Imelda muttered from behind Keelin. She was incandescent and *mortified* at her brother's throwaway jibe. Everyone turned to look at her, standing with a fierce glint in her eyes that boded ill to all who knew her.

CHAPTER THIRTEEN

'Em . . . I see my sister is agreeing with me,' Brigid said with wry humour. 'Thank you, Imelda, for never letting me forget my place.'

'If you *really* knew your place you wouldn't be standing there, pontificating and pretending to be so humble!' Imelda's eyes were black beads of anger.

'Mam, stop it!' Keelin hissed. 'Don't ruin Aunt Brigid's party.'

'You needn't talk, madam,' Imelda said sharply as an awkward silence descended on the guests. 'You're as bad as she is.'

'Imelda, *please*. Control yourself,' Brigid said with years of authority in her tone.

'You're telling *me* to control myself? How dare you, Brigid Dunne. How *very* dare you!' Imelda marched up to her sister and turned to face the group. 'Look at her – the Reverend Mother. You'd think butter wouldn't melt in her holy mouth. Well she's not as holy and reverend as you all think she is. Sure you're not, Brigid? And you *never* had a vocation!' She glowered at her sister. 'Throwing yourself at Johnny Larkin. I saw the pair of you up against their barn. You weren't thinking of the Virgin Mary then, were you, when you were hooring around with him and letting him go all the way with you? I *saw* you. And then you legged it from Ardcloch when this lot' – she waved in the direction of the Mother General – 'gave you an escape route. I'm right, aren't I?' she demanded.

Brigid inhaled, shocked, blanching under her sister's vicious onslaught. '*Imelda!*' she whispered as the stunned guests gasped, not knowing where to look.

'*Mother!*' exclaimed Keelin, horrified. 'That's enough! Stop it right this minute. You should leave.' She went to take her mother's arm, but Imelda shook it off. 'You, miss! Don't *you* tell me what to do. You disgraced the family too, after she' – Imelda pointed a shaking finger at her sister – 'persuaded you to enter the convent, against *my* wishes, and then *you* forgot your vows of chastity—'

'*Imelda!*' Marie-Claire's stomach lurched and her heart began to race as she saw her normally placid father's eyes darken with fury.

'What's wrong with you, *Priest*?' Imelda sneered. 'Did you know, Father Donnelly,' she turned to Butlersbridge's parish priest, 'that my son-in-law here was once one of your lot, until he got his hands on my daughter and made her pregnant—'

'*Granny!*' Marie-Claire gasped, looking from Keelin to Armand in shock. Her dad had been a priest! Her parents had never told her *that*. 'Is this true?' Marie-Claire asked her mother, her voice little more than a whisper. The look of dismay and shock on her parent's faces was enough to confirm Imelda's revelation.

'Now, now, em ... Missus, eh ... Imelda, have you been drinking? There's no need for this,' Father Donnelly blustered, his florid face like a lumpy tomato atop his roman collar.

Keelin, weeping now, turned to her husband, 'I'm so sorry, Armand, that she would treat you like this. Marie-Claire, forgive me.'

'Imelda, that's *enough*!' Brigid raised her voice.

'Granny, you should be ashamed of yourself.' Marie-Claire couldn't hide her disgust at her grandmother's spite.

'You're one to talk, missy. Aren't you so lucky you live in an era when you can try out various men until you find the one that suits you? You don't have to worry about chastity like my generation did – not that your dear *Mère* was too bothered about it either,' Imelda snapped. 'At least I was chaste and pure until I got married. I didn't give myself airs and graces, and pretend to be something I wasn't. The hypocrisy in this room tonight is *sickening* – and my own brother there has the *cheek* to make smart comments about *me* in front of a crowd of strangers. I'm sorry if I've put a blight on the evening but I just couldn't take it anymore. I'm not condoning any of your lies—'

'Imelda, stop making a show of yourself. Get your coat!' John ordered, so sternly that Imelda stopped mid-sentence.

'Get your coat,' he barked. 'You're leaving. Brigid, I'm very sorry about this,' he said, taking his eldest sister's hand. 'Forget all she's said. She's only jealous of you. Always has been—'

'Jealous, you say!' Imelda's voice shook with anger. She didn't care anymore. All the resentment she'd swallowed down for years erupted out of her and she wasn't going to stop now. The wine had loosened her tongue. There was no going back.

'My sister took everyone I ever loved away from me. My first love was Johnny Larkin. Did you know that, Brigid?' She turned back to her sister. 'He stopped walking out with me when I wouldn't part my legs. Not like you. And then you had the nerve, the absolute hypocritical nerve to enter the convent and leave me to be a slave to that damned farm. Notions that were paid for by Daddy. There was nothing left for me after he paid your dowry to that French lot, so you wouldn't have to be cleaning their kitchens and toilets. Not for you to be on your hands and knees scrubbing floors and cooking and washing, like I had to for Mammy and Granny—'

'Imelda, please, *control* yourself. This is so unseemly,' Brigid commanded, amazed that her voice was so firm and authoritative, because her knees had started to knock, and she was shaking inside.

'That's rich, coming from you.' Imelda's eyes flashed fury. 'Do you know what it was like for me, to have to watch all the fuss that Daddy and Mammy made of you, knowing what

I knew and knowing that *I* would be the one left to look after them in their dotage? Oh, you took the easy way out, didn't you? And never looked back. But that wasn't enough for you, was it? You took my daughter, brainwashing her with your talk of life on the Missions! And then we had to live with the shame when she left the convent and came down here to have her illegitimate baby. Oh yes, the word got out eventually, after Larry died. The rumours flowed in Ardcloch and Glencarraig. But I kept my head high even though inside I was *utterly* ashamed.

'And now you,' she turned to Marie-Claire, 'you're my grandchild, and where do you come and spend your holidays? With your precious *Mère*, down here in the back of beyond,' she sneered. 'And I'm lucky to get a flying visit. And your parents, with their New Age nonsense, couldn't even be honest with you, while *I* have to stay silent? Not anymore. I've had enough. I might be out of line but *Reverend Mother* Brigid took you from me, too, and that's the way it is and—'

'Now you listen to me, Imelda,' Brigid said in a tone that brooked no argument. 'It was *never* my intention to take anything from you. I didn't *know* about you falling for Johnny Larkin. I didn't know you'd walked out with him, because you never spoke about anything like that to me. And yes, perhaps I *was* to blame for Keelin entering the Order, but I never took her or Marie-Claire from you – you drove them away all by yourself. I'm sorry that you feel this way and have held this bitterness inside you for so long. But now you've had your say, in front of all the ones I hold dear. And you should be very pleased, Imelda, because tonight *you* have taken everything from *me*.' Brigid was wraith white, but she held her head high and turned to her Superior.

'Mother General, I apologize on behalf of my sister, for the discomfort her behaviour has caused to you and all our guests. Una, I'm so sorry your beautiful party has been ruined. If you'll all please excuse me, I'm sure you'll understand that I need to be alone to pray about what has occurred here this evening. Continue to partake of the hospitality of the house. I will be at your disposal tomorrow and we can discuss what needs to be discussed.' She gave a small bow to everyone and left the room at her usual measured pace.

Maura's mouth was a round 'O' as she absorbed all she'd heard. Her Majesty Brigid had been royally shagged before entering the convent. She wouldn't die wondering. Strangely, Maura was glad for the elderly nun. At least she'd had one rub of the relic! A bit of ould sex couldn't be beat.

'Are ya happy now, ya mean-spirited briar?' Una couldn't contain herself, rounding on Imelda with fury.

'*Una!*' The Mother General's warning tone was enough to stop the housekeeper in her tracks. 'I'll deal with this.' She fixed Imelda with a basilisk stare. 'I think, perhaps, it's best if you leave, and that we retire.'

'I'm not one of your nuns. You can't tell me what to do,' Imelda retorted.

'Thank God, in His Divine Mercy, that you're not.'

The Frenchwoman's withering retort took the wind out of Imelda's sails and she flushed with anger, the red tide creeping up her neck to her hairline.

'*Aller!*' The nun pointed imperiously to the door. Imelda turned on her heel and followed her sister through the doorway.

It was as though everyone in the room exhaled when she disappeared out into the hall.

'*Bien.*' Mother General Aloysius gazed sternly at the dumbfounded partygoers. 'This is a sad state of affairs. *Oui?* I would ask from the bottom of my heart that not a word of this goes outside of this room. I beg your *discrétion* in the matter.' She glanced over at the cluster of nuns standing beneath the picture of the Sacred Heart. They lowered their eyes under her penetrating scrutiny. Aloysius did not want gossip about Brigid sidling from convent to convent and over to the Mother House and beyond. Brigid's fall from grace was catastrophic for her, and at this hour of her life. There but for the grace of God went any of them. The Mother General gave a little shiver. She too had her secrets.

Una went out into the hall. Imelda was at the hallstand, stony-faced, rooting for her coat. 'I'm getting the bus driver to bring you home on your own, right now,' she said coldly. 'Because I'd say the rest of your family would like to lynch you.'

With her head held high, Imelda marched out to the bus and never looked back.

*

Maura gave a discreet tap on the sturdy white door with the old-fashioned round brass knob.

'Please, leave me be.' Mother Brigid's voice had a hint of a tremor. Maura, ignoring the plea, opened the bedroom door. Brigid was in her dressing gown, sitting in her rocking chair looking out at the darkness of the windswept night. A flash of irritation crossed her face when she saw who it was. 'I asked to be left alone, Maura,' she said coldly.

'I hear you. And I will leave you alone. But drink this first.' She handed the nun a round brandy goblet half full of amber gold liquid.

Brigid sniffed it disapprovingly and made to hand the goblet back. 'I don't want alcohol, thank you. I rarely drink it.'

'Tonight, everything's changed,' Maura retorted. 'Drink it! It will save you tossing and turning all night.' The women stared at each other in the mellow glow of the lamplight. In that moment, they were no longer, employer and employee, religious and lay. A sisterhood, as old as time, bonded them together.

'Drink it, Brigid, and don't look back!' Maura bent down and gave the elderly woman a kiss on the cheek and a quick hug, and slipped quietly out of the room, closing the door behind her.

The last thing she wanted to do was to look back. The past was the past, what good was it to rake it up, like Imelda had just done? It only brought resentment and sadness, Brigid thought bitterly, trying to ignore the memories that crowded in around her.

PART TWO

The past is a foreign country;
they do things differently there.

L.P. HARTLEY

CHAPTER FOURTEEN

BRIGID AND IMELDA

1954

'Tidy up that bedroom of yours, you pair. And then, Brigid, you wash the eggs. Imelda, you can start black-leading the range—'

'That's not fair! How come she always gets to wash the eggs?' Imelda protested indignantly to her mother, who stood in the door of their bedroom with a vexed look on her face.

'Because you're too rough and you break them, miss,' Elizabeth Dunne snapped. 'We're not made of money that we can afford breakages. And then I want you to bring the tay over to your father on the bog, Brigid. You go to the well and get the water, Imelda, then the pair of you can help me finish wallpapering the parlour.' Elizabeth issued her instructions and hurried downstairs to pluck the chicken she'd left softening in a bucket of boiling water.

'I wish this bloody Station was over. There's so much work to do, on top of the usual,' Imelda groused, pulling her check pinafore over her head. She *loathed* the pinafores that her granny made for her. She wanted to be wearing tricot blouses with black velveteen ties, and taffeta skirts that swirled around, just like June Allyson and Debbie Reynolds wore.

'It's our turn to have the Station. It's an honour to have it, and we won't have to have it again for a few years,' Brigid said glumly, shoving her brogues into her half of the wardrobe she shared with her sister. They had half a rail each in the musty, mothball-scented, old-fashioned mahogany wardrobe. The left-hand side was Brigid's. Always a higgledy-piggledy mess. Shoes in a heap on the bottom shelf, her camogie stick sometimes straying into Imelda's territory, much to her younger sister's annoyance. Imelda's part was arranged neatly. Clothes hanging in order of length, shoes paired side by side. Magazines in a neat pile on the bottom.

They slept in a brass bed with a long bolster pillow and a patchwork quilt their aunt had made. Brigid liked the cheerful quilt with the blue, navy and white squares. It brightened up the room, darkened by small windows and elderly mahogany furniture. Imelda's side of the double bed was always made immaculately, sheets stretched, the woollen Foxford blanket straightened neatly under the coverlet. Brigid's side of the bed was always lumpy where she left the sheets as they were, pulling the quilt over the blanket not caring whether it was rumpled or not underneath.

'I don't know what the fuss about the bedroom's for,' Brigid observed crossly, cursing when a pile of books fell to the floor. 'The neighbours won't be coming up here.' Imelda didn't answer. She was studying her spots in the oval mirror on the windowsill. Brigid shoved the books under her side of the bed. Out of sight was out of mind.

She heard the sound of voices downstairs, then her mother laughing, and guessed it was their neighbour, Patsy, from across the field. The neighbours always mucked in when there was a Station being held, no matter who was hosting it.

The custom of the Station, an old tradition from Penal times – when it was forbidden for priests to say Mass in public, so they were forced to hold it in people's homes – was still practised in every townland and parish in the country. *Imagine not being able to go to Mass in a church. Imagine having to attend Mass at a Mass Rock, out in the open, no matter what the weather,* Brigid mused, glad she'd never had to stand outside in a howling gale and lashing rain to practise her faith. Irish Catholics had been persecuted in those terrible times. She shouldn't be so grumpy about it being their turn to offer up their home to the service of God.

It wasn't the idea of the Station that was really at the core of her annoyance; she *dreaded* that the Larkins, who owned the land next to theirs, would be coming. Her stomach coiled into knots when she saw any of that family. They would probably be next to be chosen for the Station and, knowing the Larkins and their propensity for showing off, it would be a big hooley.

For months now, her parents had been preparing for the great honour of hosting their family and neighbours for the religious celebration in their home. Brigid's father and her two younger brothers had whitewashed the house, painted the gate and pillars, tidied up the yard and garden, while their mother had organized a massive spring clean. Every nook and cranny in the house had been cleaned. The windows were sparkling. The smell of fresh paint permeated the air. Holding the Station meant best foot forward for everyone in the family, Elizabeth told her daughters when they grumbled about the extra work they had to do, as well as their usual chores of feeding hens, and calves, and bringing fresh water from the well, two fields away, come hail rain or shine.

Brigid picked her satchel off the floor and rooted for the tuppence-worth of sweets she'd bought for her younger brothers after getting paid on Friday. It was a little treat they looked forward to. She'd bring the sweets over to the bog for them, to cheer them up. She'd stopped buying a treat for Imelda since her sister had started being so spiteful to her before Christmas. Brigid couldn't understand why her general snippiness had reached a whole new level. 'She's *so* mean to me, Mam. She says really nasty things to me,' she complained to her mother.

'Ah take no notice of her. You were like that at her age. Turning into a teenager makes girls moody. The pair of you have my heart scalded with your humours and rows. You should be like me and Peg – best friends,' Elizabeth sighed.

'We'll never be best friends like you and Auntie Peg,' Brigid said morosely.

'Let me give you a piece of advice: count your joys instead of your woes, count your friends instead of your foes. You and Imelda will need each other sometime, and that's the truth,' Elizabeth advised her daughter briskly before hurrying off to churn her butter.

Would she ever need Imelda? She didn't think so, apart from needing her right now to make the bed, Brigid mused, dropping thruppence on the floor when she took the sweets out of her bag. She picked it up and put it back in her tartan purse. 'Come on and make the bed,' she ordered Imelda, who eyed the shiny silver coin enviously.

'You're lucky you have your own wages. *All* our money is going on this Station thing and I'm not even getting paid my egg money because Mammy needs it for provisions to feed all these people,' Imelda moaned, shaking the feather bolster and straightening the bottom sheet.

'Oh stop giving out, Imelda. I'm giving *all* my wages up next week. Mammy and Daddy are excited about the Station and they want to put on a good show. We don't want to disgrace ourselves in front of the neighbours and let them think we've nothing,' Brigid retorted.

'That's crooked!'

'I don't care!'

'Don't care was made to care.' Imelda glowered at her older sister.

'Oh shut up. I'm going to wash the eggs.'

'You got that job cos you're the favourite.'

'Ah yeah, washing hen shite off eggs, I'm the favourite all right,' scoffed Brigid, throwing her eyes up to the holy picture of a sad-eyed Jesus with a bleeding heart that hung on the wall, beside Imelda's poster of Paul Newman, and feeling quite the martyr herself. '*And* I've to traipse over to the bog,' she added for good measure.'

'I've to traipse over to the well,' countered Imelda, not to be outdone in martyrdom, flouncing out the door to do her chore.

It was a clear sunny morning, the salty sea breeze blowing in from the Atlantic and across the hills, rippling through the clumps of gay, yellow daffodils planted on either side of the freshly painted green gate. Normally Brigid would enjoy the walk through the fields to where her father and brothers were cutting turf. He wanted a supply in for the fire when they were having the Station. Today though, her heart was heavy. She wanted to be far away from Ardcloch, and the daily, repetitious grind that was never-ending. She wanted to be away from the past that intruded on her present, every day.

She hated her job over in Glencarraig, where she worked as a maid for the doctor and his wife. How Brigid longed to take the bus to Galway or Limerick, or – the dream of all young girls living in rural Ireland – to the bright lights of

Dublin. The sophisticated capital city had big department stores, cinemas, cafés and buses. What bliss it would be to live in a house with indoor plumbing and electric lights, and to have heating that wasn't dependent on a range or sputtering, smoky fire. Imagine being able to go to the pictures in proper cinemas instead of the galvanized tin-roofed shed in Ardcloch – that dump was no more a real cinema than the Dunnes' hen house – where, if it were a wet Saturday afternoon, the sound of the rain hammering down on the red roof would drown out the actor's voices, forcing the audience to lip-read.

Brigid had asked her parents if she could look for a job in Dublin or Galway, but her father had said she was needed on the farm to help her mother and grandmother, especially now that Granny was getting older and less able to run her own smallholding. 'Perhaps in a few years, pet,' he said, 'but not right now. The boys have to be educated as well. You did well that we could afford to get you to Inter Cert level. Plenty around here only got their Primary Cert. John will be going to ag college next year, if he gets a scholarship, so it wouldn't be the best time for you to leave us. Sure, I'd be lost without you,' he declared, his blue eyes crinkling, his tanned face creasing in a smile. Even though she loved her father, it wasn't what Brigid wanted to hear. What was the bloody point of having her Inter Cert if she couldn't put it to use? You didn't need a cert to do housework in Dr Murray's house!

Brigid climbed over the stile into Low Field, her wellies sinking into the mud on the other side. Was this to be her life? She was sixteen, and still stuck in the back of beyond. What, she wondered despairingly, could she do to escape from the binding ties of family and home?

Imelda pulled back the curtain under the press and rooted for the polish box to start black-leading the range. Her mother had finished plucking the chicken and was preparing mash for the calves. Sometimes Imelda reckoned the calves and the cattle were more important to her father than she and her siblings were. His whole life revolved around the 'stock' – buying, selling, rearing, milking them – and it was those large slobbery animals, chewing their interminable cud, that decided the financial circumstances of the Dunne family. Imelda loathed them.

She wanted to be a costume designer in Hollywood, like Edith Head, and design glorious gowns for Elizabeth Taylor and Grace Kelly and all the film stars who filled the pages of *Photoplay* magazine. *Photoplay* was her bible. Her Auntie Peg, Elizabeth's youngest sister, had emigrated to Boston, and the previous year she had sent them a package with a few of her old magazines, along with cuttings and magazines about Jack Kennedy's wedding to Jacqueline Bouvier. Auntie Peg adored JFK. Everyone in Boston did, she wrote to Elizabeth. Imelda wasn't interested in politicians, but she thought she was in heaven, immersed in the magazines her aunt had sent, reading about the film stars and studying their fashion.

She planned to emigrate to Boston too, after she'd finished her Inter Cert exam in the summer. She'd made the decision last autumn, when her first love had tossed her casually aside, betraying her in the most cruel way. It had left her heartbroken. Imelda hadn't told anyone of her plans, but she was sure her parents would agree. She'd be one less mouth to feed, and she could send money home from America. Perhaps when Brigid had to take on all the chores, she would appreciate all the work Imelda had put in. She would not miss her older sister one little bit.

'Imelda, would you run upstairs and bring me down my glasses, like a good girl. My eyes are tired,' her mother interrupted her reverie.

'OK, Mammy,' Imelda sighed, noting that her mother looked weary. All this work for the Station was wearing her out. When Imelda was a success in Hollywood she would pay a maid to do her mother's housework, she decided magnanimously, sashaying up the narrow stairs. Golden rays of sunlight slanting in through the landing window dazzled her, casting a warm opaque glow on the wall at the top of the landing. Pretending it was a spotlight and she was an acclaimed designer, ascending to the stage to collect the Oscar for Best Design – presented of course, by her idol, Paul Newman – she bowed and waved to an imaginary audience. For a few brief moments, Imelda's cares drifted away and she was happy.

The house was full to bursting, people crowding into the kitchen and hallway, chatting and laughing. The buzz of anticipation rippled through the throng as the Dunnes' family, neighbours and friends awaited the arrival of the parish priest and his curate. The priest, Father O'Connor, an affable Kerryman, and Father Foster, the curate, a bitter little man who had never had a parish of his own because of his fondness for the bottle (and a whispered past that had seen him moved from two former parishes), would shortly be arriving in Father O'Connor's battered old green Ford Anglia. Father O'Connor was a dreadful driver, and the curate always carried a hip flask filled with whiskey so he could take the odd nip to soothe his nerves.

Elizabeth took a last glance around the parlour. The table was set for the priest's breakfast. Her best linen tablecloth adorned the table. Two serviettes lay folded neatly on two side plates. The reverend gentlemen would be tucking into half a grapefruit each with a cherry in the centre, and sprinkled with caster sugar, then boiled eggs and toast. John was on call to toast at the fire with the long toasting fork. He was an expert at it, and never burned it. On a small side table beside the fire, covered with an embroidered Irish linen tray cloth, sat a silver salver with two cream candles in brass candlesticks, a crucifix, and holy water. The priest would bring his own Mass set to celebrate the sacrament.

Confessions would be heard in the parlour before Mass, and afterwards, when the sacraments were ended, the priests would be served their meal first, followed by a setting for the men, and finally the women would sit down to eat their food and chat and relax after all the excitement.

Elizabeth's two nearest neighbours had been helping her

out since early morning, making sandwiches of ham and cold roast beef, and egg and onion. They had used shop-bought, sliced bread for the sandwiches, a rare treat, and Elizabeth had rapped Sean on the knuckles when she caught him stealing one. There were loaves of currant bread and brown bread cooling on the kitchen window. She'd borrowed extra teapots for the gallons of tea that would be made. There was a rich fruitcake she'd baked a month ago, and apple tarts and scones brought by neighbours and friends. Herself and Tom and the children had worked hard to have everything right, and Elizabeth permitted herself a small frisson of pride, knowing that when people spoke about the Station held in the Dunnes' home, they would not be found lacking.

'Here they are,' she heard a shout. Hastily removing her apron, and patting her hair in place, Elizabeth went to the front door just in time to see the green car pull up in front of the gate. Nodding to her husband to follow her out, she went to greet the guests of honour.

'Thank God that's all over,' Brigid declared, stretching out in the bed, exhausted after spending the day making tea, offering food to their guests, washing up the dozens of dirty cups and plates and the final clearing up when everyone had gone. 'We won't have it again for another few years.'

'I won't be here for the next one, that's for sure.' Imelda yawned and got into bed beside her. She'd rolled her chestnut hair in three curlers that gave her a side wave like Rita Hayworth's.

'Why, where will you be?' Brigid sat up and blew out the candle so that only the pale lemon light of a waning moon illuminated the pitch-dark night.

'Far from here,' Imelda retorted tartly.

'Huh!' Brigid sniffed, turning onto her tummy and burying her face in the soft downy bolster. Where did her sister think she was going to end up? Imelda had such notions. Her parents had spent a small fortune on today's gathering. Things would be tight for a while now and they'd need more of her small wage. There was always something that stopped her from saving enough money to leave Ardcloch.

And then a thought – like a Divine revelation – struck her, lying in the bed under the eyes of her martyred Saviour. There *was* an escape route! Father O'Connor had mentioned that some Missionary nuns were coming to Ardcloch. French nuns! Soeurs du Secours Miséricordieux – the Sisters of Merciful Help, he had translated. They were seeking nuns to join their Order.

If she joined the Missionary nuns, she'd get to travel far from Ardcloch and escape a life filled with little opportunity. Brigid had recently overheard her parents discussing Granny Dunne's failing health. 'Brigid can go and live with her,' Elizabeth had said firmly. 'We don't have enough room for her to move in with us, and if Brigid's with her, we won't have to be worrying about her being on her own at night.'

Brigid had nearly had a heart attack. While she was very fond of her grandmother, her small cottage was dark and pokey. The toilet was down a winding path and not outside in the yard, like the one they had at home. Granny still boiled her kettle on the hook by the turf fire and baked her bread in the cooking pan hanging on the other hook. She was afraid of the 'electric', as she called it, and was adamant she wasn't going to have it connected up. Brigid would be stuck in the Dark Ages, reading by candlelight, if she was to end up living with her grandmother.

If she left to work in Dublin or Galway, Brigid knew she would be turning her back on her parents. She wouldn't be able to do that to them. She would be riddled with guilt. *Unless* she'd a vocation. She knew she didn't have one right this minute, but she could soon develop one, she was certain of it.

Sister Brigid. It rolled off the tongue. And she would be the best nun the Order ever had, so that perhaps, when she died, *all* her sins would be forgiven.

CHAPTER FIFTEEN

'I want to become a nun,' Brigid announced firmly as they walked home from early Mass two weeks later. It was a biting cold morning with the frost crackling underfoot, her breath a wispy film in front of her as velvet darkness began to give way to a soft light in the eastern sky and Venus sparkled over the dark hills.

'Arrah, everyone wants to become a nun when they hear the Missionaries speak,' her mother retorted. 'I'd like to become one myself, listening to them, instead of having to go and help your father milk the cows on this wicked cold morning.' She pulled the collar of her good Sunday coat up around her ears.

'No, I do, Mammy, I really *do*. I gave my name when you were in the shop getting the paper and the ice cream. They're going to write to me,' Brigid assured her earnestly. This was her chance. She must take it or a life of bitter regrets loomed ahead of her.

'Well for goodness' sake, Brigid. You can't make up your mind just like that – sure she can't, Tom?' her mother appealed to her husband, who was walking alongside them enjoying his Sunday-morning pipe.

'I think the best thing to do is see how you feel in six months' time. You're excited hearing the Sisters talk about helping the black babies in Africa,' her father advised sagely.

'But, Tom, this is nothing more than a figary – you know it and I know it. Don't be encouraging her,' Elizabeth said crossly. 'Honestly, Brigid, you're up and down like a yo-yo these past few months. Where are you getting your notions from?' her mother exclaimed in exasperation.

'It's not a notion, Mammy. It's what I want. God is *calling* me,' Brigid exclaimed in desperation.

'Well how come we haven't heard anything about Him calling you before now?' Elizabeth demanded. 'I've never heard one word of you wanting to become a nun. Ever.'

'I felt the Holy Spirit descending upon me at Mass,' Brigid fibbed, hoping that she would not be struck dead for her lies.

'Maybe it's because you're hungry. When you're fasting from midnight to go to Communion, the mind can play queer tricks on you. Mass was much longer than usual this morning because of the Missioners,' Elizabeth said firmly. Brigid knew what was behind her mother's opposition and could see her chance to escape from Ardcloch diminishing with every footstep they took.

'Mam, I read the *Lives of the Saints* every night. I pray to the Little Flower that she will make me selfless like her—'

'I'm sure the Little Flower didn't dance around the kitchen singing "Rose, Rose, I Love You", and "Tennessee Waltz",' Elizabeth said drily.

Brigid was stumped. She was so frustrated she began to cry.

'Stop that nonsense,' her mother ordered.

'I can't help it, I want to become a nun,' Brigid wept. She cried easily these days. She'd heard Patti Page singing, "I Went to Your Wedding" at the gramophone recital in the parish hall after Christmas and had been so overwhelmed with emotions she'd had to slip out the side door and sob silently behind the gorse bushes, trying hard not to make noise.

The memory of that made her cry even her harder now.

'There, there, lassie.' Her father patted her shoulder awkwardly. 'If that's what you *really* want to do, we'll think about it. Stop crying now, like a good girl. Pray about it. Talk to the priest. You don't have to rush into anything.'

'Tsk, Tom, don't be encouraging her.' His wife threw her eyes up to heaven.

'Wouldn't we be proud to have a nun in the family, or if one of the boys wanted to become a priest?' her husband said in his slow, measured way. 'And not a lay nun, like Margo O'Farrell. They don't get well treated, those lay nuns, I hear. Mind you, Tom O'Farrell was glad she entered, no matter what, because they have five girls to support, and he doesn't have to worry about her anymore, or feed and clothe her. Five of them would never make a good match here, there's so few men staying put on the land, and those two youngest are a dawny-looking pair. They'd be lucky to find a husband,' Tom remarked.

'Stop that! They're nice girls.' His wife scowled at him.

'But not good-looking like our girls.' Tom winked at Brigid. 'The O'Farrells have one down and four to go. Would you be wanting that, Elizabeth? We won't close the door on the idea of Brigid entering. She's got a good education – that will help too,' he added firmly.

'There's that, I suppose,' Elizabeth agreed reluctantly. It was rare for her husband to put his foot down. She usually ruled the roost. A nun in the family would be seen as a great blessing. But she had plans for Brigid.

'I wouldn't be letting you go in as a lay sister, now Brigid,' Tom assured his daughter. 'I'll pay your dowry and that will safeguard your future with the Order, if it comes to that.'

'Oh, Daddy, I hadn't thought about that.' Brigid was instantly contrite. 'I'll go in as a lay nun. I don't want to put you to expense.'

'You'll never get to the Missions so.' He puffed a stream of smoke into the frosty air, the scent of tobacco mingling with the whiff of sea breeze. 'You'll spend your life scrubbing floors, cooking and cleaning and minding the sick if you go in as a lay nun. Sure, you could do that at home – isn't that right, Elizabeth?' he said jovially.

Elizabeth pursed her lips, reminding Brigid of Imelda when she was annoyed. 'If she's going to enter, she'll enter the proper way. I won't have the neighbours talking and saying we hadn't the money for a dowry. I have that money I was saving for the new churn—'

'Oh no, Mam!' Brigid exclaimed, horrified, feeling utterly selfish. Her mother had been saving her egg money for a new metal butter churn to replace the old wooden one she'd had for years.

'Don't worry, I'll sell some stock,' her father replied easily, and Brigid had burst into a fresh bout of tears, overwhelmed by her parents' self-sacrifice.

'Stop your crying there now, like a good girl, and give me an extra sausage for my breakfast – and give yourself one because you won't be getting rashers and sausages in the convent,' her father joked when they reached the farmhouse, before he and Elizabeth had gone to change out of their Sunday best to go and feed the animals.

Her brothers were already home, chopping wood for the range. Imelda, as usual, was dawdling with her friends so she wouldn't have to help set the table. *Typical*. Brigid scowled, lacing slices of bacon in one pan and a pile of sausages in the other one for the weekly fry. While they were sizzling and spitting, she got knives and forks from the dresser drawer and set the table. It might be one of her last Sunday breakfasts with the family.

She was going to be a nun and dedicate herself to God, she thought, a little bemused by the suddenness of her decision, as the smell of the fry filled the warm kitchen. She was going to work in a country where people lived in mud huts with thatched roofs, and wild animals roamed the edges of the villages, and the rainy season turned scorched land into a lush green oasis, where dates and oranges and figs grew from the trees, ripe and sweet and plentiful.

How far more exotic a life would that be than cleaning the Murrays' house and going to live with Granny?

I'll be bringing the word of God to pagans. Could there be a better thing to do in life? Brigid thought, filled with a newly discovered missionary zeal. The early morning sun burst up from behind Hensley's Hill, and Brigid *knew* it was a sign that she was on the right path, and freedom beckoned.

'*You* are going to be a *nun*!' Imelda's pinched little face grew even tighter when she heard Brigid's news. They were doing the washing up after the breakfast, before peeling the spuds for the Sunday dinner.

'Yes, I am,' Brigid said, wiping the grease out of the big cast-iron pan before putting it in the soapy warm water she'd boiled up on the range.

'Don't you have to be *pure*, to be a nun? You've kissed boys, and probably more,' her sister accused slyly.

'I will make my full confession, Imelda,' Brigid said tightly. Sometimes she hated her sister. 'I didn't know I was going to be a nun when . . . when . . . Well, I thought I might get married. I didn't have the calling then.'

'You don't have a calling now, either! You're only pretending to have one,' Imelda observed astutely.

'Shut up, ya little cow,' snapped Brigid, stung that her sister wasn't fooled by her reason for taking the veil. 'I spoke to one of the Sisters and she told me I seemed like a bright girl who knew her own mind, and I was well educated. It's what I want and Daddy says I can.'

'I think you're very mean, putting that expense on Mammy and Daddy. They'll have to pay a dowry I bet. They won't let you go in as lay nun like Margo O'Farrell and I'll be left here to do *everything*!' Imelda said furiously, upon hearing this unwelcome information.

'Well that will be a first. You get away with blue murder,' Brigid retorted. 'And anyway, there's nothing to stop *you* entering.'

'Oh shut up,' her sister snarled.

'Ignorant bitch,' Brigid glared at her.

'And you're the one who's going to be a nun, with language like that! They'll throw you out when they find out what you're really like and you'll have to come back with your tail between your legs,' Imelda jeered, and it had taken all Brigid's self-control not to slap her sister's smug face.

One good thing about going on the Foreign Missions, if she was lucky enough to be chosen, was that she would have little to do with Imelda, who really was the most obnoxious creature on earth, Brigid comforted herself, wondering if the Little Flower had ever had to endure a sister like Imelda.

A month later a letter had come, addressed to *Miss Brigid Dunne*.

Written in elegant script, in a posh cream envelope, she knew straight away it must be from the French Missioners. Brigid slid out the single cream page and read it eagerly. It was an invite to visit the Reverend Mother and Mistress of Novices in the convent of the Soeurs du Secours Miséricordieux in Dublin, to be interviewed to see if she was suitable to become a postulant, and then a novice.

'I got called for an interview,' Brigid exclaimed breathlessly, her heart thumping. 'I've to go up to Dublin to meet the Reverend Mother. I'm going to become a nun!' She was beyond excited, and more than a little apprehensive. But utterly relieved. She would not be trapped in Ardcloch forever and a day. A new life was opening up for her. She would never look back.

CHAPTER SIXTEEN

Brigid's heart beat a fast tattoo against her chest when the grounds of the convent came into sight. She took in the high and forbidding grey stone wall, the black iron gates with their sharp pointed tips leading onto a gravelled drive and immaculately kept gardens. Once they drove inside them, the sound of the city traffic became muted and a silence, broken only by birdsong, enveloped them.

'Last chance to run, Brigid.' Her father smiled over at her and for one wild moment, Brigid was tempted. But where would she run to? Back to Ardcloch and a life too mediocre to endure? She'd been sent off to Dublin with the good wishes of the parish ringing in her ears. Her pride would not let her turn back.

'This is what I want, Daddy,' she said firmly.

'Grand,' he said. 'Let's go so.' He got out of the car, lifted her brand-new brown case out of the boot and they walked in silence up the steps to ring the bell beside the big wooden doors.

A nun in a black habit with a white veil let them in. 'Hello, and welcome to the house. I will bring you to the visitors' parlour, where you will wait until I come to collect you to bring you to the Mistress of Novices,' she said quietly, before leading them to a small parlour along the hall. The lay nuns wore white veils, Brigid learned. She would be wearing a black one when her novitiate was over.

Brigid and Tom sat side by side on two hard antique chairs, hardly able to speak. Brigid was her father's pet. She knew that, and it broke her heart that she would soon be saying goodbye to him, especially when there was no knowing how long it would be before she'd see him again.

'Write to us when you can,' he said eventually, to break the silence.

'I will, Daddy. I'll tell you everything that's happening, I promise,' Brigid assured him, hoping she wouldn't break down and upset him.

A light knock on the door made them start, and once again the lay nun came gliding in. *Did you learn to walk like that in the convent?* Brigid wondered distractedly, dreading the moment of farewell. 'It's time to say your goodbyes now,' the nun advised, and her grey eyes were sympathetic.

'Goodbye, Brigid, we're very proud of you,' Tom said, getting awkwardly to his feet. He put his arms around her and she was in absolute turmoil when she hugged her father one last time and smelled his familiar, reassuring scent of pipe smoke and tweed.

'Bye, Daddy, thank you for everything. I'll be the best

nun I can be,' she said, muffled against his shoulder. She would have liked to tell him that she loved him, but they didn't do that sort of thing in the family, and he might have been embarrassed. 'You're a great father,' she said instead, and his arms tightened around her and then he let her go, nodded to the nun and followed her out to the great wooden doors. When Brigid heard them clang shut, she knew she was on her own.

She waited until the nun came back, taking deep breaths to steady herself. Walking out of the visitors' parlour and passing beyond the white doors that led to the silent convent beyond, Brigid acknowledged that her past was now behind her, and her family no longer her concern. She was God's property now. The lay sister gave her a sympathetic glance from under her veil as Brigid wiped the tears from her eyes, but no words were spoken.

The Mistress of Novices, Mother Agnes, a tall, angular woman from Cork, informed her that she would be leaving all her worldly goods behind, except for the rosary beads and missal her parents had given her. 'You have a new life to learn now, Brigid. You must plant your feet firmly on your chosen path and devote every thought to self-improvement. You must give of yourself to the Merciful Works of God.' When Mother Agnes spoke the words 'the Merciful Works of God', her voice took on a most reverential tone.

Would she, Brigid wondered with a despairing heart, ever speak of, or think of the Merciful Works of God with such fervour? She'd entered the convent under false pretences;

she would have to work even harder than her fellow postulants, whoever they were, to convince the Soeurs du Secours Miséricordieux that she'd heard the call from God, just like they had.

Mother Agnes silently motioned her to a chair in the small, parquet-floored room where the new entrants divested themselves of their worldly attire and dressed in the habit of the postulant. Brigid sat down and saw the nun pick up a large pair of scissors. Her lower lip wobbled. She was proud of her luxuriantly rich, shiny hair and had always taken care to brush it a hundred times a day. Her crowning glory, her granny called it. The shock of hearing the harsh rasp of the scissors, and the feel of it tugging at her tresses, then seeing the long mane of auburn hair lying on the floor at her feet, and the unaccustomed lightness she felt, suddenly made her realize that her life truly was now changed forever. She was no longer Brigid Dunne, with dreams of love, marriage and children, no longer daughter, sister, friend. She was female, but no longer a woman. Her family were no longer her focal point. Her parents no longer her protectors. She'd a new family now and a new identity to show the world. Owned by God.

Mother Agnes handed her a white cotton cap, secured by a bandeau, to cover her head and neck with. Brigid's fingers trembled as she buttoned the bandeau, then she bowed her head as the nun placed the wimple that would hold the small grey veil on her head. Brigid knew that the yoke was now upon her.

She was given two cream calico chemises for nightwear, two slips and two cream calico shifts for daywear, over which she would wear a grey tunic. Two pairs of black woollen stockings and two corsets completed her ensemble. Mother Agnes instructed her to change into her new attire, in her brisk, no-nonsense tone. She would then be shown to her dormitory, which she would share with five other postulants, Mother Agnes informed her, before leaving the room with her hands tucked under her tunic, like a frozen statue on rollers.

Brigid sat back down on the hard chair for a moment to absorb the enormity of what was happening to her. At least she would hold on to something of her former identity: her name. Sister Laurence was the name the Order had chosen for her, but she'd pleaded her case successfully, saying that Saint Brigid was one of Ireland's patron saints, and she'd a great devotion to her. Not having to bear the name of a male saint was a small triumph, Brigid had thought with relief, gazing at her new uniform and realizing that she would never wear fashionable clothes again. *That* was something she hadn't considered in her haste to become a nun.

Just think of Africa, Brigid told herself firmly, as more tears threatened to fall when she stepped out of her good black and white polka-dot swing dress. It was her pride and joy. Her Aunt Maureen, a dressmaker, had made it on her trusty old Singer sewing machine, copying a dress Lauren Bacall had worn. Aunt Maureen's sewing room was an Aladdin's Cave of treasure. Boxes of buttons and beads, swags of material, and Brigid's absolute favourite, the big book of patterns that she would spend hours flicking through while her mother and aunt chatted over tea in the kitchen. The bridal dresses were what she liked best. She'd even picked out the one she would choose were she ever to marry.

An overwhelming tidal wave of grief washed over Brigid when she pulled on the scratchy black stockings. She would never walk up the aisle in a flowing lace bridal gown with a frothy white veil to marry the man of her dreams. Instead she would walk up the aisle as a Bride of Christ, in a nun's habit, living a lie, as punishment for her sins. All she could do was try to be as good a nun as she possibly could and hope that 'The Call' might yet come and she would be forgiven for her mendacity and the sins that had brought her to this place.

I'll make the best of it. I'll stick it out, Brigid vowed silently, slipping the grey tunic shift over her head and tying it with the corded black belt, before the lay sister came back to bring her to the dormitory. She led Brigid along another corridor that smelled of beeswax polish, and up wooden stairs to a narrow passage that had rooms on either side. They walked in silence to the end room and the young country girl, dressed in a habit similar to Brigid's own, but with a white tunic and white veil and white corded belt, opened the door and pointed to a cubicle whose curtains were open. 'This is yours,' she said. 'Put away your belongings and I'll bring you back down to Mother Agnes.'

'It's so small,' exclaimed Brigid in horror.

'Don't let them hear you say that. Ye'll get punished.

Never give criticism. Don't answer back. And do as you're told or they'll make your life a misery,' the young nun whispered. 'My name's Fausta, in here, and I'll help you as much as I can.' Fausta flashed her a shy smile.

'Thanks, Sister Fausta,' Brigid whispered back.

'Hush, I'm no Sister, I'm just a slave here,' the other girl said scornfully. 'That's the way they treat us girls that had no dowry and no education. We're here to do the dirty work. You'll do OK if you came in with a dowry. They'll send you teaching or nursing. The rich ones get away with murder, getting the easy jobs like sewing and working in the library. Come on, put your stuff away, and close your curtains to show your cubicle is taken. We'd better hurry or Agnes will come looking for us,' Fausta urged, whisking the curtain halfway around the metal rail.

Brigid entered her new habitat and gazed around her – not that there was much to take in. The cubicle was surrounded by cream curtains that screened off the narrow single bed and a bedside locker on which rested a lamp and a ceramic wash bowl and jug. A wooden crucifix hung on the wall behind the bed. The bed itself looked even harder and lumpier than the bed at her granny's, Brigid thought despondently. She placed her new apparel neatly in the bedside locker and followed Fausta back down the corridor to begin her new life.

CHAPTER SEVENTEEN

The shock of her incarceration, the shared sleeping space, and her tiny cubicle were the hardest things to bear during those early weeks of her postulancy, when all Brigid wanted to do was to run home and hide. The prospect of being kept awake by her fellow inmates snoring, sobbing and rustling behind the privacy of their curtains at night made her frantic with worry that she wouldn't sleep, because at five a.m. the harsh main lights were turned on by Mother Agnes, and Brigid would have to tumble out of bed, bleary-eyed, to kneel and pray at her bedside. Sometimes she fell asleep on her knees.

Brigid tried her best to read the Latin Office but she hadn't got a clue what it meant. After a half hour in silent meditation they would file down to the long, narrow, tiled refectory for breakfast.

Brigid was amazed on her first morning to be served tea in a bowl. It was the French way, she was told, and as the congregation was ruled from France, they followed the Mother House's rules and traditions.

In the days that followed, she and her fellow postulants, two Cork girls, a Dublin girl, and two Wexford girls, were introduced unceremoniously to the rigid daily regimes of the Soeurs du Secours Miséricordieux.

Porridge and brown bread and butter set them up for the day and prepared them for the duties ahead, which included clearing the tables, dusting the chapel, cleaning the dormitories, taking classes with Mother Agnes to study the Rule and the postulant's manual they had been issued with.

At midday they would have lunch but throughout the meal a nun would read passages of the Bible, and then there would be more prayers before it was time to work in the garden. Gardening was Brigid's favourite chore, no matter how cold the weather. She would breathe in deep lungfuls of fresh air and close her eyes and pretend that she was at home in Ardcloch and not confined behind high stone walls in a convent in Dublin.

The day was spent mostly in silence, and it was only after tea – usually an egg and bread and butter – that the community was allowed supervised talk time. The postulants and novitiates shared a small common room and Brigid and her five companions would gather together, under the watchful eye of a nun, and try to murmur little snippets of information to each other about where they were from, and what they thought about this new rollercoaster experience.

The strictness of the regime was difficult to tolerate,

especially for girls like Brigid who had minds of their own and were frustrated by the tyranny of it all. No wonder by nine p.m. at night when they lay in the dark, in their hard uncomfortable beds, many of them, including Brigid, cried themselves to sleep.

How will I ever stick it? Brigid wondered, knowing that when she got to the Mother House in Paris it would be even worse. The French nuns were sticklers for the rules – it was well known that life in Dublin was a doddle compared to life in the novitiate in France.

Three months later, Reverend Mother Celestine summoned Brigid to her office. A call to the Reverend Mother's large, book-lined office was a serious matter. Was she to be chastised for some misdemeanour such as chatting to Joan in the nun's garden when they were supposed to be meditating on the Word of God? Falling asleep at Vespers? Tearing a hole in her habit when she'd caught it on a nail in the potting shed while having a sneaky cigarette with the ancient gardener who looked after the grounds?

All her misdeeds came back to haunt her while she waited for her interview with *La Grand Fromage* as they irreverently called the Reverend Mother. What would the Big Cheese say to her? Had the nuns discovered that she hadn't a true vocation, Brigid wondered nervously, sitting on the hard chair outside the door of the inner sanctum.

'*Entrez!*' The door opened and the stern, austere nun crooked a finger at Brigid, who hastily stood up and bowed.

'Soeur Brigid, sit please.' The Reverend Mother indicated

a chair opposite her at the large, gleaming rosewood desk that dominated the room. Long sash windows looked out onto the manicured front lawns. Sunlight streamed into the pale, apple green and cream room, burnishing the desk and pastel green and gold rug with streamers of light. The décor of the room belied the nun's severe manner. Perhaps her austerity was all an act that she'd to put on because of her role, and the real Mother Celestine came to the fore through her use of colour and light in the décor of her office. Had she too once been a young woman with dreams and desires, Brigid wondered.

'We have made a decision about your future!' Reverend Mother interrupted her thoughts and Brigid's hands clasped each other in tension as she awaited her fate.

'We have decided,' continued the Reverend Mother in her slow, measured tones, 'that you are suited to become one of our nursing staff. You're practical, calm and hardworking, although lacking in concentration sometimes, but that will come when you are more focused. You start nursing training next month. After your year in a general hospital, you will transfer to a children's one. Paediatrics will be your speciality. Have you any questions?'

'No, Reverend Mother. I'm grateful for the opportunity,' Brigid said meekly. Her heart had lifted at the words of praise and the realization that she would definitely be going to the African Missions. She wouldn't have been given paediatric training if she weren't. For the first time since she walked through the doors of the convent, Brigid had a real sense of purpose. Once Mother Celestine had dismissed her with an unexpected smile, it took all Brigid's newly learned sense of decorum not to skip down the long parquet-floored hall yelling 'Yippee!'

It was an apprehensive but excited young novice who met her family in Dublin Airport two years later for a final goodbye, before flying to Paris to begin the next phase of her life. The respect and special treatment she and her travelling companions, Agnes and Orla, had received from the moment they had arrived at the airport had been enjoyable. Orla's family were waiting for her, and they were sitting at a table near the bar, enjoying their reunion.

Looking out at the propeller plane that would fly them to France – the St Coleman, it was called – Brigid felt somewhat reassured that a saint would be minding her on her first flight. How sophisticated she felt, admiring the white letters on the green fuselage. Aer Lingus Irish International Airlines. The sight of the shamrock on a green strip painted on the tail fin made her very proud to be Irish.

If she was going to flee the convent, this would probably be her last chance, Brigid mused. Joan, one of the girls from Cork, had left a week ago. Having played the game of subservient novice to the hilt until she completed her nursing training, Joan had pulled off a U-turn of epic proportions. The other novices could only admire her spirit and ingenuity.

Brigid wondered about following suit, but her circumstances were very different to Joan's. She'd insisted that she wanted to be a nun, and her wish had been fulfilled. Her parents had spent a lot of money on her dowry. She couldn't throw it back in their faces. How ungracious and ungrateful would that be – to say nothing of the scandal her behaviour would cause, if word ever got out that she'd done a runner. She simply couldn't do it to them. Nevertheless, she envied the Cork girl, who had become a good friend. She would miss Joan terribly.

A knot of people at the lounge door caught her attention and Brigid jumped up from her seat with delight, eager to get to her family, who were filing into the departure lounge to say goodbye and wave her off. It would be the first time they'd seen her wearing her habit, she thought proudly. There had been the occasional letters between them, but the letters were read by Mother Agnes, as were the ones Brigid wrote back, so they were pretty dull and samey. Her time apart from her loved ones had made her appreciate them more, and had brought home to Brigid that life in Ardcloch had had its good times as well as bad, and she was very lucky with her family compared to her friend Joan, who had been reared by a crabby aunt who had no love for her. In Brigid's case, absence had made the heart grow so much fonder, and she'd really missed her parents and younger brothers, and, strange to say, Imelda.

The Dunnes had all come dressed up in their Sunday best, Brigid noted, touched at the effort they had made for her. Her father was looking smart in his good brown suit and, because it was a special occasion, wearing his black fedora hat rather than his usual grey woollen flat cap. Her mother was dressed smartly in a new wool knit ensemble, a dress and jacket in heathery lilac colours, with a lilac headscarf. Imelda sported a pair of royal blue slacks and a blue and white cheesecloth blouse. She was wearing blue eyeshadow and mascara and had pink painted nails. Brigid thought she looked the height of fashion and couldn't hide the pangs of envy as she caught a glimpse of herself reflected in the big plate windows, in her woollen white novice's habit, hair hidden under a veil and wimple, and not a lick of make-up. Her brothers wore their white Sunday shirts and ties, their hair slicked back with Brylcreem.

'Brigid!' Her mother hugged the daylights out of her in a rare display of affection, her familiar scent of lily of the valley and Max Factor powder almost making Brigid cry with nostalgia as she buried her face in Elizabeth's neck and held her tight. Then it was her father's turn, and she saw with shock that he had tears in his eyes as he studied her with pride.

'You look wonderful, Brigid – a real nun,' he said proudly, enveloping her in a bear hug that made her feel like a little girl again.

'Daddy, Daddy, I've missed you so much,' she gulped, loving the feel of his lined, weather-beaten cheek against hers.

Joan's tearful goodbye kiss before she got into the taxi to go to Kingsbridge had been the first time Brigid had had any display of affection since her entry into the religious life, and now to be lavished with hugs and kissed from her parents made her realize how much she'd missed the comfort of touch.

Mortifying though it was for them to display affection in public, her brothers made the effort and kissed her on the cheek. However, Imelda, true to form, couldn't hide her jealousy. Given that they hadn't seen each other for so long, Brigid was unprepared for the frostiness of Imelda's lacklustre peck on the cheek and sullen, muttered, 'Hello.'

'I love your outfit.' Brigid offered the compliment with as good a grace as she could muster, hiding her indignation that Imelda wouldn't even try to make an effort.

'When you're stuck in the sticks, you have to do the best you can,' Imelda responded tartly.

'Well, it's very fashionable, Imelda. You look great in it.' Brigid tried to be the better person.

'Will we have a pot of tea and a few buns?' Tom suggested, glaring at his youngest daughter. 'And we can catch up with all the news. Sure, we've loads to tell you. Lads, go get a table for us. Come on, Elizabeth – you pick the cakes.'

'Are you enjoying working in O'Brien's?' Brigid asked Imelda while they waited for their parents to return with the tea and cakes.

'Eh ... no! It's a job in a hick country village when all I want is to be up here in Dublin living my own life and not sharing a bedroom with Granny and helping out on the farm because John's in ag college and you ran away to the convent,' her sister drawled derisively.

'Ah, don't be like that, Imelda. Don't ruin my last day in Ireland,' Brigid sighed.

'Am I to feel sorry for you? Is that it? Flying to Paris on

a plane? Heading for Africa? Being trained as a nurse? And what am I? A shop girl. A farm girl. A girl of no importance. Give over, Brigid,' Imelda retorted.

'Aren't you walking out with Larry O'Brien? Mam told me in one of her letters.'

'Brigid, it's bad enough being in the back of beyond without being left on the shelf. Thanks to you, I'm stuck helping out on the farm and living with Granny. So Larry's the best I can do. We can't *all* run away!' she added pointedly.

'I'm sure you could if you really wanted to,' Brigid muttered, wishing with all her heart that her sister had stayed at home instead of lashing out with her mean accusations.

'And leave Sean to do everything? Sure, all he cares about is his transistor radio, and making the few bob from Daddy to buy fags and a sneaky bottle of stout! He'll be gone soon as he's finished in the Tech. Where will that leave Mammy and Daddy? You knew what you were doing, entering the convent,' Imelda sniffed, lighting up a cigarette, much to her sister's envy.

'Shush, here's Mam and Daddy, we don't want them to hear us arguing,' Brigid snapped, spying her parents making their way towards them. She wanted to slap her sister's cross face and tell her where to go, in a most un-nun-like manner.

When the boarding time for their flight was called, Brigid's heart felt like lead. She'd no idea when she would see the family again. It could be years. She stood up and tried to keep her lip from wobbling. Her mother hugged her again, tightly, and whispered, 'Keep doing what the nuns tell you, Brigid. I'm very proud of you.'

Elizabeth's cheeks were damp with tears and that was nearly the undoing of her. 'Thanks for everything, Mammy. I'll write as often as I can,' Brigid promised, her voice breaking.

'Do, pet, do. I love getting your letters.' Elizabeth stepped away to let Tom take her place. He put his arms around her and told her she was the best daughter in the world, and she'd made the family very proud, and to remember them in her prayers. 'Travel safely,' he added, slipping a St Christopher medal into her hand. As her fingers closed around it, she knew it would be one of her dearest possessions.

John gave her an affectionate jab in the ribs and told her to write to tell him everything about the flight, before he handed her a pound note.

'We're not allowed, John,' she protested.

'It's your running-away money, in case you ever need it!' He winked and she laughed, and slid it under her bandeau.

Sean gave her the thumbs up and slipped a packet of cigarettes into her habit pocket. Her baby brother was taller than she was now, and his voice was breaking. He would be a man the next time she saw him, Brigid thought sadly, giving him a peck on the cheek, much to his embarrassment.

'Bye, Imelda,' she said quietly, turning to her sister.

'See ya, eh ... safe journey,' Imelda said offhandedly, clearly not interested in hugging or kissing her – until she caught her mother's gimlet eye. Grimacing, she leaned over and gave Brigid a quick peck on the cheek before wandering off to look out onto the tarmac.

A cold farewell, thought Brigid. Imelda had never been one for putting on a façade with people. She supposed there was integrity of sorts in being true to yourself. Imelda was more true to herself than she'd been, Brigid acknowledged ruefully. She'd grown quite accomplished at looking at herself in the mirror and not seeing the true reflection.

Imelda had been painfully perceptive in her accusations that Brigid had no vocation, and that she was using the lie to escape Ardcloch. There was no denying that.

'We have to go now, Sister Brigid,' Mother Agnes reminded her, turning to crook a finger at Orla who was bidding a tearful farewell to her family.

'Sister Brigid is a credit to you, Mr and Mrs Dunne. She's worked very hard at her nursing training and she will be a great asset to us on the Missions.' Mother Agnes shook hands with Tom and Elizabeth.

The memory of the look of pride on her parents' faces at the Novice Mistress's words would get Brigid through many difficult times in the Paris convent while she prepared to take her final vows. Even Imelda had looked surprised at the laudatory words of the older nun.

Brigid's last view of the family had been through the aircraft window. They were all standing on the rooftop viewing balcony, waving enthusiastically as her plane trundled slowly past, making its way towards the runway.

Tears slid silently down her cheek and Mother Agnes

handed her a fresh handkerchief and said kindly, 'The first time leaving the country is always the worst.' In the seat across the aisle from them, Orla was weeping into her cupped palms. The jet propellers began to whirr faster, the engines roaring into life, and then they were racing down the runway and, suddenly, with a heart-jolting lurch, the plane was hauling itself off the ground. Below them, Dublin shrank until it was lost amid a patchwork of green and brown fields. Brigid got such a fright she'd nearly pulled the curtains closed, but she slid her hand into her habit pocket and felt the St Christopher medal her father had given her and her fingers curled around it as they flew across the sea towards France.

CHAPTER EIGHTEEN

1960

Brigid lay prostrate on the cold tiles at the foot of the altar as the sound of her congregation singing the Magnificat soared through the convent chapel. *For he hath regarded the lowliness of his handmaiden ...* She was indeed a lowly handmaiden, but at least, she was no longer in a state of mortal sin.

Six months before taking her final vows, Brigid had taken a late lunch during her shift in *Hôpital des Enfants malades* and gone to confession in Chapelle Notre-Dame-de-la-Médaille-Miraculeuse. The Mistress of Novices would have frowned on her independent behaviour but Brigid had decided, the first day she'd joined the nuns, that she would not be confessing the sin of impurity to any of the priests who ministered at the convent; the thought of having to look her confessor in the eye when discussing her vocation and enduring the mortification of his knowing glances on a daily basis would be intolerable.

Thankfully, only a handful of penitents were waiting to confess that day. Brigid knelt with her head in her hands, praying earnestly to be given the grace to make a good confession. She was sick with nerves. Receiving the Body of Christ while in a state of mortal sin, as she had for the past few years might be grounds for excommunication. What would she do if that happened? Her mouth was dry and her voice trembled when she began her 'Bless me, Father . . .'

'Daughter, God is merciful, there is no need to be nervous,' a kind voice came from behind the grille.

Brigid burst into tears, thrown by this unexpected response. 'Father, I received Communion many times knowing that I was in a state of mortal sin. A boy once . . . he . . . I . . . Well, I said no, but he didn't listen . . . and there was sex, Father, even though I did try to push him away. I didn't deliberately lead him into temptation and be an occasion of sin for him,' she gabbled, the words coming out of her in a torrent of French and English.

When she was finished, Brigid knelt in silence, waiting for the words of condemnation to rain down upon her.

'My child,' said the priest. 'You are greatly loved by God and His Precious Mother. Your sins have been wiped clean. Today you start anew. For your penance, you will carry with you at all times the Miraculous Medal of Our Lady, to remind you of the great love and esteem in which you are held. Make your solemn act of contrition and go in the peace of God and His Holy Mother. Amen.'

'Oh my God, I'm heartily sorry . . .' she began her act of

contrition, stunned. This was it! No words of condemnation. No excommunication. The priests at home would have excoriated her. Brigid had floated back along Rue de Sèvres feeling that the burdens of the world had been lifted from her shoulders.

Now, lying on the cold marble floor she gave thanks for her second chance. The soaring notes of the nun's choir touched her so deeply that tears slid down her cheeks and she wished her parents had been with her to share the ceremony of her profession.

When her congregation raised her to her feet and removed the white robe and veil that covered her brand-new habit, before placing the black veil on her head, Brigid felt their pride and love for her. Her thumb caressed the slim gold band on her left finger that signified that she was now a Bride of Christ.

I've done it, Brigid thought happily that night, lying in the cell-like room that was would be hers until she left for Africa. She'd stuck it out and become a nun. A nun who was now free of mortal sin. She slept like a log that night.

The blast of heat, and the strange new smells, hit Brigid the minute she stepped out onto the silver metallic steps that had been wheeled out to the aircraft. *So this is Africa*, she thought excitedly, as a welcome breeze lifted her veil. It had rained earlier – this was what they called the rainy season – and the ground was still damp, almost steamy from the heat. Glancing over in the dark at the welcoming lights of the long low terminal building, she saw the high control tower.

It reminded her of a water tower near Butlersbridge, where the Order had a holiday home.

She collected her luggage and made her way into Arrivals, struggling to steer the ancient trolley with its wonky wheels. A smiling nun with a round, tanned, lined face under a white veil was there to greet her.

'Sister Brigid, welcome to Senegal,' she heard her say in an unmistakable Kerry accent. 'I'm Maria Goretti, but everyone calls me Goretti,' the nun introduced herself, holding out her hand. 'I hope you had a relaxed journey. This is Jakab, our driver; let him take your trolley.'

'Welcome, Sister.' Jakab bowed and smiled at her, his teeth the whitest she'd ever seen in another human, his brown eyes twinkling bright in the darkness of his skin. The airport was full of dark-skinned people and to Brigid, who had never seen a black person until she'd arrived in Paris, it all added to the magic of Africa.

She gazed around her, delighting in the glorious colours worn by the women, some with magnificent turbans on their heads, and the pristine white robes worn by men.

'It's so different, isn't it?' Goretti smiled. 'I've been here fifteen years and I never tire of it.' She led the way out of the airport to a red Citroën parked at the kerb, its two large round headlights looking like a pair of frog's eyes.

'Jakab will be teaching you to drive once you've settled in, and then you and I will be heading to St Louis, a large regional capital up north, to set up our childcare clinics. Malaria is the biggest killer of children here, especially in the rainy season. We use antimalarial drugs, quinine, insecticides and netting mostly – and of course, the local cures in the areas we go to. Hep A and Typhoid are our main problems, and yellow fever afflicts men who work in the heavily forested areas. So we've plenty to keep us going.' Goretti grinned and, as Jakab hoisted Brigid's case into the boot, she opened the passenger door for Brigid.

'So we won't be based at the convent in Dakar then?' Brigid asked, settling into the worn car seat.

'Oh no!' Goretti winked. 'We'll be far, far away from it, in our own little convent. There'll be five of us, living in a small house, which will be our base. We'll be on the road mostly,' the Kerry nun explained.

'Oh!' said Brigid, liking the sound of this.

'I'm dying to hear all the news. I hope you brought letters.' Goretti slid into the back seat alongside her. 'We love it when someone arrives from Europe.'

'I did, and some homemade scones that myself and another Irish nun made, and macarons, and some Gruyère, and boeuf bourguignon and some pâté and crackers. And two baguettes. They're in Tupperware containers in that big brown cardboard box. It went into the hold, so it's quite chilled.'

Goretti's eyes widened in pleasure. 'Yum yum! We'll be having a party tonight,' she said gaily. 'Get us home as fast as you can, Jakab,' she instructed their driver, who turned on the engine and took off like one of the rally drivers he so admired.

Driving through the narrow, dusty, dimly lit streets of Dakar felt almost surreal after being used to the wide, well-lit boulevards of Paris, and Brigid wondered, if she pinched herself, would she find she was dreaming? She was sweltering in her heavy habit, and envied Goretti her lightweight white dress and short veil. After many twists and turns through the dark, potholed streets, Goretti said, 'This is Yeumbeul, and about a mile ahead is the ocean. *We*,' she smiled, 'are just down this street on the left-hand side.' Jakab swung around a corner and drove a third of the way down a street lined with ramshackle cement buildings, before turning into a large compound, surrounded by high, whitewashed walls. The gravel drive led to a complex of one-storey buildings, one of which Brigid thought was a school, judging by children's paintings decorating some of the windows. To her left was a large whitewashed, two-storey, colonial-style building with blue shuttered windows and edged with long verandas, illuminated by lamplight from the rooms inside. It looked so comfortable and welcoming that Brigid yawned and realized how tired she was and how much she looked forward to getting into bed. That building had to be the convent, she guessed. The car drew to a halt beside some steps leading to a low porch on which a sleek black and white cat stretched languorously. Two large terracotta pots of orange and pink flowers were a splash of colour against the white.

Brigid could see mosquito nets draped from the ceiling and big fans whirring slowly. And then the big blue wooden front door opened and a group of nuns in white robes and short white veils like Goretti's came out onto the veranda. A portly, smiling nun extended her hand and said, '*Bienvenue, ma fille*, I am Mère Margaret Mary Alacoque, and we are delighted you have come to join us.'

Brigid unfurled the white mosquito netting from the top of the hut to enclose the mat on the floor where she would be sleeping. She was tired. It had been a long but satisfying day. She, Goretti and Khady, a young Serer nun, had left the small house they lived in, close to the banks of the Senegal River, some two hundred and fifty kilometres northeast of Dakar, to hold clinics in the small villages of the *Peuple Sérère*, the Serer people, indigenous to the area along the river. She'd been up since five a.m.

Tonight they were staying in one of the larger villages, and the villagers had held a party for them. They had feasted on *sombi*, a sweet milk-rice soup which Brigid, having a sweet tooth, loved, and *thiéboudienne*, a boldly flavoured combination of fish, rice, and vegetables simmered in tomato sauce. It had been cooked in one large pot, eaten outside, and Brigid had thoroughly enjoyed it.

Afterwards, she'd sat, surrounded by children, rocking a three-month-old baby, Mena, in her arms, listening to the *sabar* music of the Serer people, under the blackest, starriest sky she'd ever seen.

Brigid had never been so happy. Now at last she felt she had a vocation. This was where she was meant to be, and this was the work she was meant to be doing, she thought, cooing at the baby in her arms, thrilled when Mena's little face broke into a huge smile. How she loved working with babies. They satisfied every maternal bone in her body, and when she finally handed her back to her mother, Brigid kissed them both in gratitude.

Gratitude was her overwhelming emotion, every day. How her life had changed. Now she was driving the jeep, careering along the dusty trails from village to village. Driving made her feel as free as a bird, like a goddess in her chariot charging into the unknown.

The regimens of convent life were no longer imposed on her. Goretti was sister-in-charge, but the older nun wasn't the slightest bit interested in hierarchy. Her prime concern was to be out among the people, doing 'The Work', as she called it.

Brigid was in awe of her. It was only since she'd come to live in Africa that she truly realized what amazing work these women, these nuns she was sharing her life with, did with such generosity and ability. Their whole focus was on empowering the people, especially the women, to reach their potential. Getting an education was a goal for them, and she thought guiltily back to her own schooldays and the way she and her friends had moaned about studying, not realizing what a privilege it was to be educated.

She was the one being educated by these beautiful people, not the other way around, Brigid acknowledged; 'Thank you, thank you, thank you, God, for bringing me to this wonderful country.' For the first time since she'd entered, Brigid truly felt like she was a real nun. Slipping under the cover to lie on the mat on the floor, she fell asleep before she'd even time to say her prayers.

CHAPTER NINETEEN

IMELDA

Imelda Dunne was fit to be tied. From the moment Brigid had gone to Dublin to join the convent, with a fine fat dowry, Imelda had known that she was *doomed*. For that she would never forgive her sister. Her aspiration to carry on in secondary school and take her Leaving Certificate exams had come to nought. Her brother's education was deemed more important than hers, and because John was bright and hard-working there were high hopes he would get a scholarship to agricultural college after his Inter Cert.

She'd had to give up on the idea of emigrating to Boston. That had been a pipe dream, she acknowledged disconsolately, but her plan of getting a job in the Civil Service in Dublin and moving up to the capital had been more realistic and, she'd hoped, achievable.

To live in a flat or a bedsit, free from all parental control, able to do as she wished – that had been her goal. She'd so looked forward to the exciting social life that would have been hers to enjoy. Dances in the Ierne Ballroom. Nights out at the big-screen cinemas like the Savoy and the Carleton, so different from watching Laurel and Hardy or the Three Stooges in black and white at the parish hall, or the rackety crackling of the film reels in the 'cinema' in Ardcloch. She'd daydreamed of having afternoon tea in the Gresham or even the Shelbourne. Of getting her hair cut and dried in swanky hair salons. Shopping in the big department stores on Henry Street. Grafton Street, she'd decided, might have been too posh until she developed a more sophisticated persona. And she would have, Imelda knew. She would have been the most sophisticated girl in Dublin and she would have swanned back to Ardcloch like Nan Doyle used to, strutting around in her Capri pants and tight top, holding a long cigarette holder, for all the world like Lauren Bacall or Jane Russell, regaling everyone with tales of her glitzy and glamorous life in the capital. Nan was a bank clerk, a step up from a clerical officer in the civil service, but Imelda would have worked anywhere if it meant she could live a life of liberty in Dublin.

Instead, after Brigid's triumphant departure to enter the convent, Imelda had moved into Granny Dunne's dark cottage, trying to study for her Inter Cert by candlelight. A week after Imelda had finished her exams, Elizabeth had had discussions with a friend of hers who owned a small drapery and hardware shop in the next parish. 'It would be a grand job for you, and you'd still be able to help me out here,' Elizabeth informed her youngest daughter, who could think of nothing worse than standing behind a shop counter day in day out, being bossed around by Franny Moran, who wore a hat and 'best pinafore' in the shop, and loved the sound of her own voice. Imelda was put on a month's trial, handed a duster and Brasso and a white coat to cover her clothes, and told it was her responsibility to have the countertop, shelves and brasses *gleaming*!

Imelda was in despair. She was a slave to Franny, and a slave to her mother and grandmother, and there seemed to be no escape from the drudgery of her life. She scoured the Situations Vacant columns in the papers and *begged* her father to let her go to interviews in the big towns further afield.

'Will you just wait for another while, pet? Your mother and I can't lose two daughters in one year, not with John heading off to ag college, and me with a contract from the creamery. Maybe next year. Sure, you have your whole life ahead of you.'

When he put it like that, what could she say?

It was so unfair though. Brigid had not been made to feel guilty for leaving home, why should she? Imelda fumed resentfully to Teresa McHugh, her best friend.

'She got her chance to go, we'll get ours,' Teresa, who was a laid-back type, assured Imelda. 'At least we're getting a few bob, working. It could be worse.'

Later that autumn, Imelda remembered those words, 'It could be worse', and truly despaired. Elizabeth and Tom decided that Granny was too old to be living on her own, day or night, having suffered a couple of falls over the summer. They felt the best option was for her to come and live with them. Now that Brigid was gone, there was room for her.

The brass double bed that Brigid and Imelda had shared was sold, and two new divans installed. 'You'll have a bed all for yourself. No more sharing,' Elizabeth cheerfully pointed out the silver lining.

Imelda was beyond horrified. It hadn't been all bad, living with her granny. When the old lady went to bed, early, as she always did, Teresa would sneak in for a cigarette and a sip of the altar wine she robbed out of the parochial house where she worked as a maid.

'This is the only thing keeping me going, Teresa,' Imelda sighed the night before moving back home, exhaling a thin stream of smoke in her best Bacall impression before taking a sip of the wine, reassured by the thunderous snores coming from her grandmother's bedroom. She felt quite the sophisticate, drinking alcohol in the glow of the Tilly lamp, with the flames from the fire casting amber and gold flickering light. There'd be no way she'd be able to drink alcohol in front of her teetotal mother.

Imelda had hung gay coloured scarves over all the depressing holy pictures in the bedroom and brought her Paul Newman poster to hang on the back of the door. It had been bliss to have the whole double bed all to herself. Now she was going to lose the few perks she'd gained since Brigid's departure, and her life was going to be even worse than it had been.

'Let me stay on my own in the cottage and Granny can have the room to herself,' she pleaded.

'Indeed, I won't let you stay there on your own – and after me buying a lovely new bed for you. We'd only be wasting money trying to keep two houses going,' her mother retorted irately.

'But why do *I* have to share and mind her and do everything for her—'

'How very selfish of you, Imelda. I hope when you're that age you'll have children prepared to look after *you*, miss!' her mother snapped. 'When we were young, three of us shared a double bed and your Auntie Peg had a settle bed by the fire – and here's you turning up your nose at a lovely bed of your own.'

Imelda had had to listen to the old refrain 'Have you any idea how lucky you are?' and bury deep her bitter resentments because she knew she'd get nowhere arguing with her mother.

In the middle of September, when the nights became chilly and the trees were on the turn, Imelda and her grandmother moved back to the farmhouse. The welcome luxury of having electricity, rooms blazing into light at the touch of a switch, could not comfort her.

Granny snored like a hippopotamus, and farted great rasping gusts of wind, especially if she ate onions, which she loved. She wouldn't allow Imelda to read with the 'electric' on. What was the point in having this magical bright light if you couldn't use it? Imelda wept with indignation, to no avail.

So she'd had to read her precious Mills & Boon romance novels under the blankets by torchlight because Granny blew the candle out when it suited her. Worst of all though was that Granny Dunne insisted on Imelda accompanying her saying the Rosary, though the family Rosary had already been recited in the parlour at seven p.m. every evening. 'Two Rosaries a night! I'm saying more prayers than Brigid!' Imelda raged to Teresa one evening, when they met at the crossroads by the pub on their way home from work and stopped to have a chat and a smoke.

'That's cat altogether,' Teresa sympathized. 'You'd better come to the hop in Ballydoran at the weekend and see if you can shift a fella. It's a good dance for meeting farmers.'

'I don't want a farmer, I want someone to take me out of this kip,' Imelda moaned. 'I want to live in Dublin.'

'Don't we all,' Teresa said gloomily, dragging the smoke deep into her lungs. 'Did you see the new Mrs Larkin is driving around in a Beetle. Needless to say, it was her da that bought it, not Johnny. He did well for himself, marrying her,' Teresa added conversationally. Teresa always referred to Johnny Larkin's wife as the 'new' Mrs Larkin to differentiate between her and her mother-in-law.

'Lucky her,' retorted Imelda. 'My da won't ever be buying me a car because he gave all our money to those feckin' Missionary nuns so they'd take Brigid.'

'She thinks she's the bee's knees, that Larkin one. Why don't we let the air out of her tyres some night – that would bring her down to earth, literally!' Teresa guffawed.

'I have to go,' Imelda said, stubbing out her fag. 'I've to cycle over to O'Brien's with the eggs and there's a bloody howling gale. I'll be OK going but I may as well walk coming home, and I want to be home before dark.' One of her chores was to bring the freshly laid eggs over to O'Brien's grocery shop in Glencarraig, twice a week.

'Larry O'Brien fancies you,' Teresa teased.

'Well I don't fancy *him*,' Imelda said irritably. 'I'll see you at the dance on Saturday night.' She cycled off down the rocky lane to the farmhouse where her mother had the fresh eggs waiting in the pantry, ready to go.

As she set off for O'Brien's, her cycling punctuated by deep gusty sighs, Imelda was in a foul mood, thanks to Teresa bringing Johnny Larkin's wife into the conversation. Though she'd never admit it, she still harboured a deep and unrequited love for the handsome young farmer who had flirted with every girl in Ardcloch and broken more than a few hearts. Her face darkened, assailed by painful memories of her encounters with him the previous year.

Johnny Larkin had been her first kiss, even though she'd been only fourteen and he twenty. He'd been a bit pissed one day when he'd sauntered out of Nolan's pub and found her trying to mend a puncture on her bike.

'I'll do that for ya,' he'd said good-naturedly, hunkering down to find where the air was escaping and stick the patch on the hole. She'd looked down at his curly black hair and strong, tanned neck and felt an unaccustomed surge of quivery feelings that made her want to touch his hair and . . . *kiss* him. He was an older man, of course, but then the heroes in her romantic novels were always older than the heroines, older *and* more experienced. She'd watched as he'd pumped up the tyre, admiring the dark hair on his tanned, muscular arms, and his long, strong fingers that made her want him to touch her in her secret hidden places, places that gave her such pleasure.

'There ya go! All ready to take you to Timbuktu and back.'

'Thanks so much, Johnny,' she'd managed breathlessly. 'I'm very grateful.'

'Ah, you're a grand hoult of a girl. Give me a kiss now in return,' he said, grabbing her and planting his mouth firmly on hers, then sliding his tongue in between her parted lips. Imelda was so shocked she opened her mouth even wider, much to his approval. 'And a good kisser too,' he said, eventually drawing away from her when he heard the growling roar of a tractor heading in their direction. 'G'wan, before ya get me into trouble,' he laughed, and swung off in the direction of his farm, raising his hand in greeting to Milo Owens when the tractor crested the hill and the cab came into view.

Imelda's life had changed from that very moment. She was a woman in love – deep, passionate and all-encompassing love. Her thoughts were full of him. She went to sleep thinking about him, with her hands down between her legs, bringing herself to warm, wet pleasure-filled quivering throbs, though she knew it was a mortal sin and would need confessing. Imelda didn't care if she went to hell; the pleasure was worth it, although she'd blushed to her roots in the pitch-darkness of the confessional when Father Foster had asked her if 'actions' had accompanied her 'impure thoughts'.

There had been other interludes, whenever she encountered Johnny on her way between Ardcloch and Glencarraig with the twice-weekly delivery of eggs. Each time her beau, as Imelda thought of him, tried to go further with her. But when he touched her privates, she'd pulled away and said 'no'. Johnny's response was to call her a tease and tell her that he was finished with her.

Her romantic notions, fed by love stories and Hollywood fantasies, were dashed when real-life rejection showed her that dreams were not real and reality sometimes stung, hard.

Imelda had never forgiven him. Watching him parade around Ardcloch with that show-off wife of his was a constant reminder of the intolerable heartache unrequited first love brings in its wake.

'Don't think about him, the lousy skunk,' Imelda muttered, her words floating off in the air as she cycled.

Larry O'Brien was on his knees stacking shelves behind the counter when she walked into the shop with her basket of brown and white speckled eggs. 'Howya, Imelda,' he said politely, standing up. He was tall and broad-shouldered too, she noted idly, remembering her friend's teasing.

'Hi, Larry, here's the eggs.' She laid the basket on the counter.

'They're a grand size, thanks. Let me get you the money for them.'

'You've got a cash register!' Imelda exclaimed, admiring the new gleaming chrome machine on the counter.

'I did,' he said proudly. 'We have to move with the times. Besides, the mother was getting a bit confused with her tots on Sunday mornings when there was a crowd in after Mass, and I'd have to do hers as well as my own.'

'Franny Moran would love one of these, but she's too mean to buy one.' Imelda ran her fingers over the round keys.

'I heard you're working there. How are you getting on?' Larry pressed the key to release the till and counted out some coins.

'All I'm doing is cleaning and polishing, because she does all the serving. She's very particular. I even have to empty out the screw and nail containers and clean them once a week. She has me well screwed,' she added humorously.

Larry laughed. 'Well, I suppose technically my mam is the boss, but she's leaving much more of it to me now, and I have plans for this place. I'm going to expand and add a butcher's counter on because I hear so many complaints about Billy McKenna's down the road. It's filthy and he's spending any profits in the bookies and not putting it back in the business. He's mad. A good butcher's shop will always do well in a town or village.'

'That sounds like a great idea.' Imelda was impressed with Larry's business sense. He was only eighteen but he seemed like a man on a mission. She liked forward thinkers. 'I better be off, the weather's getting bad and I don't want to be drenched. It will be bad enough trying to cycle with the wind in my face.' She put the coins in her purse.

'Here's a bar of chocolate for the road, to keep you going,' Larry offered kindly, and she smiled delightedly.

'Thanks. I'll enjoy that,' she assured him, giving him a wave, and had two squares in her mouth before she hopped up on her bike.

When Larry O'Brien asked her to dance the following Saturday evening, in what was grandly called the 'ballroom' but which was in fact an old renovated barn with a corrugated tin roof, Imelda agreed. A shopkeeper's son who was presentable enough was as good, if not better, than a bought farmer any day, she decided, watching surreptitiously as Johnny Larkin whirled his young wife around the dance floor, oblivious to her. And it was that total lack of awareness of her very existence that was the sharpest cut.

'I was talking to the mother ...' Larry's words intruded on her thoughts as he guided her around the dance floor. He was a good dancer, Imelda noted. 'And she'd be happy just to come into the shop on Sunday mornings. She's been working in it all her life and she'd like to retire. I ... eh ... I was wondering, Imelda, would you be interested in leaving Franny's and coming to work in my shop?'

'And would you let me use the till?' she teased.

'I would,' he laughed.

'And would you pay me better than what I'm getting in Franny's?'

'I would do that too.'

'I'll hand in my notice so,' Imelda agreed. The shop in Glencarraig was busy all the time, unlike the hardware store, where the hours often dragged. Imelda liked being busy at work. Time went faster.

'Sure, we'll make a great team,' Larry smiled down at her, his brown eyes crinkling, and she thought if she hadn't lost her heart to Johnny Larkin, he might have been in with a chance. He wasn't particularly good looking. His smile was lopsided, his nose a tad crooked, and his brown hair floppy, but he had a quiet charm and he was a terrific dancer and Imelda *loved* to dance. And they had a lot in common, as Imelda was to discover in the weeks and months when they worked side by side in the small grocery store for which he had such plans.

He confided that he would like to have studied accountancy, because he loved working with figures. He'd like to have left Ardcloch and gone to live in Dublin, but that was impossible because he was an only child, and his father had built up the business from a small corner shop that had sold only the basics to a well-stocked extended store, only to die of cancer while still a relatively young man. It was expected, now, that Larry would take it over and run the business, and keep an eye on his mother, who was not in the best of health.

Imelda, who had been totally immersed in her own woes, without much interest in anyone else's, had realized that Larry was a comrade in arms.

He would listen to her ranting and raving about sharing

150

her room with Granny Dunne, or the utter drudgery of her farm chores, nodding his head in empathy. 'You're as trapped as I am, and I'm as trapped as you are. Duty bound, Imelda, that's us,' he observed one miserable rainy day as they stood behind the counter looking at the mist rolling in over the hills, obliterating the view, as the rain grew fierce and heavy, battering the plate-glass windows he'd had installed to brighten up the store.

Every Friday when he handed over her pay, he'd treat her to a box of Milk Tray, her absolute favourite chocolates, then he'd bring her dancing on Saturday and Sunday. And so it was they slipped into coupledom. Imelda had allowed Larry to court her in his shy, awkward way, even though he was second best and always would be, and his soft kisses in no way compared to the passion of Johnny Larkin's. And at the back of her mind she was always hoping that a dishy Sir Galahad would come and rescue her from the dreary drudge of life in the country and whisk her off to the bright lights of the capital.

But no knight in shining armour had come her way, so when, on her eighteenth birthday, Larry had asked her to marry him, Imelda agreed.

She liked her husband-to-be very much. He was kind and stalwart and he made her laugh. But she didn't love him, not even when she walked up the aisle of the small chapel in her white, swing tea-gown-style dress and short veil, and he put the ring on her finger and made her his wife.

She would have a house of her own, which thrilled her.

They were building it on a plot of land his mother had given them for a wedding present, and she was now, finally, her own mistress. It was, Imelda supposed, watching the roof being put on her new home, an escape of sorts – but a far cry from the life she'd planned.

CHAPTER TWENTY

December 1970

Imelda felt a wave of nausea wash over her. She was sitting in a hospital queue with her mother, waiting for Elizabeth to have a pulmonary function test. They were running late and she'd told her mother-in-law that she'd be back from the hospital by three-thirty, so she'd be able to feed Keelin and Cormac after school.

'Excuse me, Mam, I have to go to the loo,' she whispered to her mother.

'Don't be long in case I get called in,' her mother said nervously. She hated hospitals and doctors.

'Mmmm.' Imelda nodded, afraid if she opened her mouth she'd puke. She hurried down the grim, green-tiled corridor at a lick, praying there'd be a cubicle free in the Ladies. Moments later she was doubled over, retching miserably, breaking out in a sweat, the smell of bleach and stale urine making her feel

153

even sicker. When she was finished, she opened the cubicle door and stood at the hand basins staring at her reflection in the chipped, black-spotted mirror on the wall above them.

Her face was flushed, her brown eyes glazed and watery, and strands of her thick chestnut hair clung limply to her damp cheeks.

She looked like a woman in her fifties, not her thirties, Imelda thought glumly. She splashed her face with cold water, brushed her hair and reapplied her lipstick. This was her third day in a row to be sick. That and her missed period were enough to tell her that she was pregnant again, and not suffering from a tummy bug as she'd so fervently hoped.

Tears blurred Imelda's eyes and she struggled to compose herself. She wanted to lie down and cry out in despair at the thought of pregnancy and birthing and minding a new baby and all the stress and extra work it entailed. She had three children: Keelin, her eldest, and only daughter, and her two boys, Cormac and Peter. Three was more than enough. She didn't want any more. She could just about cope with her life as it was.

A care-worn woman carrying a squalling baby and a holding a lively toddler by the hand came in and Imelda felt a kinship as she swallowed hard and managed a small smile before leaving to rejoin her mother.

She knew Larry wouldn't mind that she was pregnant. He loved their children and had endless patience with them, far more than she had. She was lucky in that regard, she supposed. She had a good husband who provided well for the family, and who helped her out as much as he could with the children, and their elderly parents.

He had taught her to drive after Keelin was born, and bought her a car because he felt she needed to be independent. Being able to drive had balanced, somewhat, the overwhelming sense of being trapped when she'd held her baby daughter for the first time and realized, with a sinking heart, that here was another responsibility, another demand on her, pushing her dreams of living her own life, unchained by the needs of others, away for ever.

Imelda sighed. She'd felt so unlike most other women of her age, who seemed to adore their babies. She must be unnatural, she thought, because had she and Larry been childless, it wouldn't have upset her in the slightest.

Learning to drive had been a double-edged sword. Very few women in the townland had cars of their own and she was plagued to give lifts to all and sundry. She'd to bring her mother-in-law to a dental appointment tomorrow morning, and Peter to an eye clinic for a follow-up appointment after his surgery to correct his squint. She was practically living in hospitals these days. Imelda frowned, sitting back down beside her mother. And then she remembered she'd promised her mother she would help write her grandmother's memorial cards today, as well.

Granny Dunne had died in the autumn and Elizabeth wanted to have everything done properly so that people wouldn't be talking about how long it took to get the headstone for the grave, and to send the memorial cards.

Granny's passing had freed her up a little, Imelda admitted. But it had been a hard year, with her mother's bronchitis, Granny Dunne's last illness, and her father's fall from the tractor and subsequent back surgery, which left him limping and crotchety.

'We got a letter from Brigid. Your father read it to me. She's spent six months in Nigeria setting up a clinic like the one she's running out in the bush in Senegal. She wants us to hold a Bring and Buy Sale, for Christmas, to help her to raise funds. I've asked the new priest for the loan of the parish hall, and he kindly said yes. We can have it next Saturday. Will you ask Larry to give us a few contributions for the Wheel of Fortune? And will you sell some tickets in the shop, and bake a few fairy cakes? Yours are as light as a feather. And will you get a loan of the Burco boiler from the Tech and drop it down to the hall?' Elizabeth turned to her and issued her list of requirements, much to Imelda's chagrin.

Did her mother think that she'd nothing better to do than bake cakes and sell tickets and lug Burco boilers around Ardcloch? Didn't Brigid have the life of Reilly, flitting around Africa between convents! Not for her sister the washing of their grandmother's stinky, urine-sodden sheets, or ferrying ailing relatives around, morning, noon and night.

'I'll do what I can, Mam,' Imelda said dourly. Her parents lived for Brigid's airmail letters with all the news of their daughter's exotic lifestyle in the wilds of Africa. She was now practically a saint in their eyes.

'You're in bad form,' her mother noted. 'Is Aunt Flow in town?'

I wish, thought Imelda, unwilling to tell her mother that it was precisely the fact that she hadn't got her period that was causing her bad humour.

'No. I'm tired, that's all. Buying in the stock for Christmas is always a busy time in the shop and I didn't sleep great last night,' she fibbed.

'Are you going to Dublin for the eighth?' Elizabeth queried, taking out her knitting.

'I am. You didn't want to go did you?' Imelda's heart sank. The thought of the annual Christmas shopping trip to Dublin, on the eighth of December, the Feast of the Immaculate Conception – or Culchie Christmas, as the Dubs called it – had been keeping her going. She was meeting up with Teresa in Clerys, and spending the night with her best friend at her home in Glasnevin.

For years, she'd taken Elizabeth and her Aunt Dervla up on the train to Heuston station, where they'd caught the bus to the city centre. It had been a great day out. The atmosphere of gaiety and anticipation in the carriages as the train rattled along the tracks to Dublin was infectious, and half of Ardcloch and Glencarraig would be on the exodus of trains and buses leaving the West for the big day out. But Imelda had been looking forward to going on her own this year, and staying with Teresa, who had married a carpenter she'd met at a dance in Galway. He worked for Dublin Corporation and did plenty of nixers, and they'd bought a small bungalow in Glasnevin. Imelda envied her friend greatly, living in the city with buses and shops and interesting places to visit, all to hand.

'No, I'll stay put this year, Imelda. I don't want to leave your father on his own all day. God knows what he'd get up to. He's got no patience, that man,' her mother sighed.

'I'll bring you to Galway or Limerick some morning,' Imelda offered, relieved that she would be travelling solo and knowing how much her mother loved the lights and decorations in the cities at Christmas time.

'That would be lovely, Imelda. You're a good daughter. We'll have lunch. My treat,' her mother said gratefully, patting her arm. 'I don't know how I'd manage without you.'

It was rare for her mother to praise her, and Imelda felt a softening of her impatience. She loved her parents, but she resented the time she'd to spend looking after them and their affairs. It seemed to her that she'd never, not once in her life, had time to spend on herself, doing what *she* wanted.

'But sure, what woman ever gets time to spend on herself, Imelda?' Teresa laughed, a week later,, when they sat together sipping coffee in Bewley's Oriental Café on Grafton Street, and Imelda was regaling her friend with all that was going on in 'the sticks'.

'True,' Imelda agreed, sitting back to allow the waitress to place a steaming mug of coffee and a scone and jam in front of her. They had been lucky to get a table in the famous restaurant. It seemed half the country was up in Dublin for the Holy Day, and the streets were thronged with Christmas shoppers, and excited children gazing awestruck at the Christmas lights.

'Would you not have an éclair, Imelda? They're *delicious*! You always have one when we come here.' Teresa licked some cream from the side of her mouth and poured herself a cup of tea.

'I'd have liked to, but my tummy's a bit off these days.' Imelda eyed the choux pastry and chocolate treat with envy.

'A bug? I thought you were a bit down all right.' Teresa raised an eyebrow, before taking another mouthful of the sinful concoction.

'A baby!' Imelda replied glumly.

'Oh cripes, Imelda. So soon after Peter! How do you feel about it?' Teresa eyed her warily, not sure whether to congratulate or commiserate but, knowing her friend as she did, feeling commiserations would be more appropriate.

'Fed up, if you want the truth. I haven't told Larry yet. I'd say I'm about six weeks' gone.' Imelda sighed deeply and cut her scone in half and spread butter and jam on it.

'Were you not taking precautions?'

'Ah sure, my cycle's all over the place. Even bloody Mister Billings couldn't make head nor tail of it.' Imelda gave a wry grin.

Teresa snorted derisively. 'Don't you mean the recently elevated Knight Commander of the Order of St Gregory the Great? The Pope rewarded him with *that* title last year – that's when he's not writing encyclicals on birth control.

Humanae vitae, if you don't mind. *On the Regulation of Birth.* How bloody *dare* he stick his long beak and his pointy hat in women's matters—'

Imelda tittered at this piece of irreverence. Pope Paul VI had indeed a rather prominent nose.

'You may laugh. I bet you didn't know that Master Billings and his missus had *nine* children. His natural family planning method didn't work for them, and we're supposed to believe it will work for us. Huh!

'*Nine!* The randy little fecker. How do you know that?' Imelda was gobsmacked. When *Humanae Vitae* had been published, the parish priest had read parts of it from the altar and urged all his parishioners to follow the guidelines therein, and not be availing of unnatural contraceptives that were against the will of God and therefore a sin. The Billings Method was the only method of natural family planning approved by the Church, and it was universally loathed by most Irish women.

'A woman I met at a meeting told me: nine kids. And he and the Pope have the cheek to expect us to let them tell us what to do about controlling our own fertility—'

'That's very progressive talk, Teresa. What kind of meeting were you at?' Imelda eyed her friend curiously, taking a sip of her delicious coffee, the likes of which she would never get to drink back home.

'Wait until I tell you *my* news, Imelda,' Teresa said excitedly. 'I joined the women's lib movement.'

'Go way! Did you?' Imelda was stunned. 'The one they

were talking about on the *Late Late* a while back? That was a mighty programme that night! There was *ructions* when the women got going and put Garrett Fitzgerald in his place.'

'The very one. And it was started here – the organizers had their very first meeting in Bewley's. I must give you their manifesto: *Chains or Change.*' She took a gulp of tea and continued, 'You want to know what infuriated me so much I had to get off my arse and join them? I went to sign up for a library card and they told me they couldn't give me one without my husband's signature on the form as a guarantor. *Imagine!*' She shook her head indignantly. 'The number of women I've met who've had to give up their jobs because they got married. The differences in the salaries women are being paid, compared to men. Don't get me going, Imelda.'

'Sure, we've always been looked upon as second-class citizens,' Imelda shrugged.

'I don't know about you but I've had enough. I want equal rights, equal opportunities, the end of the marriage bar, the right to contraception. Guess what,' Teresa said gleefully, leaning conspiratorially across the table and lowering her voice. 'We're planning a trip up the North to buy contraceptives and import them back into the Republic. It will be breaking the law, and we could be arrested, and we'll be on the news, but you know what? The Church and State can go stuff themselves, because Irish women are finally putting their foot down. Why don't you come with us?' Teresa urged. 'We'll have a day out and a bit of craic.'

'Oh, I don't know,' Imelda demurred. This was radical

stuff. 'It's all right for you. You live in Dublin, it's far more liberal here. Could you imagine what they'd say in Ardcloch and Glencarraig if I was seen on the news buying French letters? The Church would organize a picket on the shop, Teresa. You know that. All them craw thumpers would be out. I'd probably be refused communion. I don't think I'm brave enough to bring all that down on the family.'

'I suppose you're right. It is much easier to do this kind of thing here in Dublin, without every nosey Norah knowing your business. Pity though,' Teresa agreed.

'Not that there aren't like-minded women of our age at home. Perhaps I could set up a little group and you could forward me the literature, and we could take the odd trip up to Dublin to go to the meetings,' Imelda said slowly.

'Now you're talking,' Teresa grinned. 'That's the Imelda I know.'

'Dublin's changed you. You were always so easy-going,' Imelda observed.

'I still am. Wait until you see the state of the house when we get home,' her friend laughed. 'But when I saw those two library forms, a green one for Kevin because he's the "house-holder" and pink for me, the second-class citizen, with a space for his signature approving my application, it opened my eyes. And I'm ashamed to say that I'd been sleepwalking through my own inequality until that moment.'

'Maybe you should have accepted Bernard Breen's proposal all those years ago,' Imelda teased. 'You'd be a landowner now that he's shuffled off his mortal coil, the poor craythur.'

'Oh don't remind me,' Teresa hooted. 'What was it he said when he proposed?' She half closed her eyes to think back. 'Oh yeah . . . "I have the place for ten cows and the waterin' of twenty, if we schtick together, like. And we'll live with de mudder." Poor oul' Bernard. I wouldn't have needed the Billings Method if I'd been married to him. He'd never have got near me.'

They erupted into gales of laughter and Imelda felt a rare moment of carefree light-heartedness that the gift of her friendship with Teresa always brought.

'Did you enjoy yourself, Imelda?' Larry asked her the following evening, as they prepared for bed.

'I had a great time, Larry. Teresa's such fun. And you know me – I *love* shopping.'

'I know you do.' Her husband smiled, buttoning his pyjama jacket.

'And I got a pair of white, wet-look boots for Keelin. She'll be *ecstatic*! I've got all the Santa stuff stashed over at Mam's.'

'I hope you bought something for yourself.' Larry got into bed and yawned, running his hand over his stubbly jaw. Imelda felt a twinge of guilt. He had made sure there was a stew cooked when she got home and the house had been tidy. *A*nd he'd been up to his eyes at work.

'I bought myself a quilted handbag, like the one Liz Taylor was wearing last year. They're all the rage now. I'll carry it to Mass on Christmas morning and be the envy of Glencarraig.' Imelda finished creaming her face, wiped her hands on a tissue and got into bed beside her husband. He'd been so good to her, and as always, so generous, she wanted to show her appreciation. At least having sex with him tonight wouldn't result in pregnancy, she thought ruefully, feeling a tad horny. She always felt horny in early pregnancy, so a ride would do them both good.

'You're the best husband in the world,' she said, switching out the light and snuggling down beside him, running her hand over his chest.

'And a man couldn't have a better wife,' Larry assured her, squeezing her hand. But, to her disappointment, he turned over on his side and was snoring within minutes.

Imelda lay wide-eyed in the dark, listening to his steady rhythmic breathing. Sometimes she wondered if Larry wasn't interested in her anymore. He hadn't come near her for a few months after Peter was born, eighteen months ago, telling her to 'let things settle'. She heard the baby whimpering in his cot and got out of bed and went over to tuck him in where he'd kicked off his blankets. She looked at his downy head of dark hair, illuminated in the moonlight. He was a sturdy wee chap, who got on with things. Keelin, her ten-year-old, was a stubborn little madam, like she'd been, Imelda acknowledged, smiling in the dark. Cormac, the eldest of her two sons, was placid and loving, like his father. She knew she shouldn't have favourites, but he was hers. By this time next year there'd be another baby in the cot, and that would be the end of it, Imelda vowed. She wasn't going to wait for the Women's Movement to liberate her from the rulings of the Church. She was going to bloody well liberate herself.

Imelda had crested the top of the big hill between Ardcloch and Glencarraig when nausea overtook her. She pulled in to the side of the road and got out of the car, afraid she might be sick. Twilight had fallen softly on the countryside; only the sound of a dog barking and the crackling of the hoarfrost underfoot broke the still silence.

Imelda took some deep breaths, the inhaled air burning her lungs with the cold, the exhaled forming a white mist in the dark night. Only the starlight, and the twinkling of window lights in the houses scattered across the fields, broke the velvet darkness in the valley to her left. To her right, the dim orange hue from the street lamps of Glencarraig, two miles away, called her home.

She'd no sooner climbed back into the car, when the first excruciating cramp struck, followed swiftly by another. She felt the blood flow through her, unstoppable, like another miscarriage she'd suffered.

'Oh Jesus,' she whispered. 'Help me get home.' She started the car, taking deep shallow breaths. This was her punishment for wanting to use contraception. For not welcoming the child she was bearing. She knew of two women in Glencarraig that were in the depths of despair because they could not conceive. Women who would have danced with joy to be expecting, unlike herself, who had seen her pregnancy as an act of oppression. Now she was paying for her sinful ingratitude.

She was being smote by the hand of God.

Later the following morning, lying in a hard, narrow hospital bed after having a D&C, drowsy from the anaesthetic, Imelda thought back to the guilt she'd felt when the child in her womb had ceased to be. Yes, she'd felt guilty, she acknowledged, but mostly, right now, she felt relief. And if that made her a bad person, so be it.

CHAPTER TWENTY-ONE

May 1971

The buzz of anticipation when the train from Belfast appeared on the horizon, chugging slowly into Connolly station – where supporters of the Irish Women's Liberation Movement were waiting to greet their sisters – grew to an excited clamour as the train clickety-clacked its way to the barrier before coming to a stop. A sea of placards waved in the air and the cheers grew higher, reaching a crescendo when the women poured out of the carriages, waving their contraceptives in the air, much to the bemusement of the customs officials. The TV cameras whirred, and Imelda waved her banner while making sure to keep her face partially hidden, unwilling to be seen on the news later, and envious of the women around her who had no such qualms.

'Let them through! Let them through!' The chant grew louder and louder as the women surged forward to encourage the lawbreakers on the other side of the platform. Imelda swallowed hard, overcome with emotion, and felt tears slide down her cheeks. The women beside her were crying too, tears of joy and relief, knowing that they were at long last beginning the journey to reclaim control of their own sexuality and fertility from the hands of men, and the Church.

Teresa had said that at one of her Women's Liberation meetings they'd been told that in many family units there were often as many as ten or twelve children, if not more. She'd already been pregnant five times, and she could still have fifteen years left of fertility. The sooner contraception was made legal the better, she'd decided, offering to be at the homecoming of the 'Contraceptive Train' to support her friend.

Imelda felt fiercely proud waving to Teresa, who was walking along the platform on the other side of the barrier, triumphantly holding up her haul of condoms and spermicidal jelly, and grinning from ear to ear. In one fluid movement, the crowd of women surged past the customs officials and out onto the concourse, singing 'We Shall Overcome', and Imelda knew she was seeing history in the making.

Teresa hugged her tightly. 'Imelda, it was *brilliant*,' she exclaimed. 'Look, there's Nell McCafferty,' she pointed to the renowned journalist who had come up with the idea of going up North to buy contraceptives. 'She told us *exactly* what to do and what to ask for. We had a list. All I'd ever heard of were French Letters and the jelly. There's something called the coil, and the diaphragm that you stick inside you, but you need a prescription for them. God, she's afraid of no one,' Teresa said admiringly.

'I know. I'd be a bit afraid of her myself,' Imelda grinned, watching the pint-sized Boadicea surrounded by her cheering comrades in arms.

'And that's Máirín Johnston—'

'She was great on the *Late Late*, she wouldn't let the men away with anything.' Imelda was excited to be amongst all these famous activists who were changing the lives of women in Ireland.

'The customs officer asked Máirín had she anything to declare and she waved the jelly at him and said, "Jelly! And you're not getting it. It's mine." And when he argued, she said, "No, you're not getting it." And he didn't know what to say to her. He was mortified.' Teresa grinned. 'Come on, let's walk up to the Capital and have something to eat, and we can get the number nineteen or the thirteen, whichever comes first, afterwards.'

Sitting opposite her friend in the dim interior of their favourite restaurant, Imelda felt far from her days of squelching across the fields to school in her wellies. Here she was, up in the capital, protesting with the Irish Women's Liberation Movement – unbeknownst to her mother-in-law, who was minding the children for the day – lunching in a fancy restaurant, and being highly entertained by her best friend's description of the groundbreaking journey that had taken place earlier.

'Imagine, though, that we could have been arrested, faced a large fine and social disgrace for breaking the law and bringing back contraceptives from the North. It's *outrageous*, Imelda. It truly is,' Teresa said indignantly, lighting up a cigarette, after offering one to her friend. 'The Church and State have worked hand in glove to keep women down.'

'I know. There's a real change happening, isn't there?' Imelda sat back in her red chair and exhaled a thin stream of smoke.

'It nearly all came unstuck though.' Teresa sat back, relaxed now. 'Nell asked for the pill and the coil and the chemist said, "Where's your prescription?" And Nell's looking at him like he's got two heads. Sure, getting a prescription for those things here would be like finding gold dust—'

'Oh no! After going to all that trouble of taking the train up to Belfast. What did you all do?' Imelda exclaimed.

'Well the pharmacist couldn't give us the pill so Nell told us to buy aspirin and take them out of the packets. None of the customs men had ever seen the pill. Neither had any of us, come to that. So they would be none the wiser. No contraceptive pill came into the Republic today, but a hell of a lot of aspirins did,' Teresa said drolly.

Imelda laughed heartily. 'No more sending off postal orders to England with stamped addressed envelopes for rubber goods to be back sent under plain cover then.'

'Ah, I'd say we're not finished with the days of "foreign correspondence" yet,' Teresa said sagely.

'Foreign correspondence?'

'Another name for French letters,' Teresa winked. 'The Church won't give up without a fight, and sadly what the Church says still dictates what goes on here.'

'It's changing though. It's changing. By the time Keelin grows up, it will be nothing like it is now.'

'You hope,' Teresa shrugged. 'One battle at a time.'

Imelda felt refreshed and revitalized driving into Glencarraig the following morning. Her trips to Teresa, and Dublin, were a godsend. She knew how lucky she was to have a husband as decent as Larry. He never moaned; in fact, he encouraged her to have her days out in the capital because, he always teased, she came back in good humour after spending all his money.

They hadn't had sex since she'd had the miscarriage at Christmas, nearly six months ago. And he was wary of the protection offered by condoms. He said he didn't want to risk her getting pregnant again. Well, tonight there'd be no risk because she'd a tube of spermicidal jelly to go with the French letters Teresa had bought her, on her 'Occasion of Sin' to the North.

On a whim, Imelda turned into the car park in front of the shop. Larry had had a new extension put on, and a chill room, and the plate-glass windows gleamed in the May sun. The cheery baskets of cascading pink, purple and white petunias looked almost continental against the whitewashed walls. She was proud of her husband. He was a hard worker. A man with a vision for his business and he treated her and the children very well. And she had standing in the community, as his wife. She might not have been in love with Larry when she married him, but she could say, at last, that she was reasonably contented.

Imelda was feeling uncharacteristically cheerful as she made her way through the busy store, greeting customers and neighbours. Larry wasn't on the floor so she poked her head into the office to see if he was there. 'I think he's out the back, Imelda,' Betty, the secretary said, lifting her head from her ledger.

'Grand. Thanks.' Imelda smiled at the middle-aged, grey-haired woman who always had a pencil stuck behind her ear. She pushed open the rear exit, immediately feeling the difference in temperature as she walked along the hallway, past the chill room, to the large storage area at the back of the building. Hoping to surprise her husband, she was glad she'd changed her high heels for flatties for the drive back from Dublin; her footsteps made no sound on the vinyl flooring. She took the jelly and a condom out of her bag and silently pushed the door open.

She heard the murmur of voices behind a stack of tinned foods and made a face. She couldn't very well prance up waving a condom in front of someone. She was about to call out, when she heard Larry's deep voice say with a passion that rocked her to her core, 'I love you, and I've always loved you, and I can't change that.'

Frozen, Imelda stopped in her tracks.

'I love you too. It's hell on earth, Larry. I wish we could be together,' she heard the soft response and, rounding the corner, she saw Larry and Fran Cassidy, the art teacher in the local secondary school, staring tenderly at each other, before their lips met in a passionate kiss.

CHAPTER TWENTY-TWO

Imelda gasped and turned away, and heard Larry call her name, in shock, but she kept on walking, desperate to get away and be on her own to absorb the impact of what she'd witnessed. She thought she was going to puke. Her legs were shaking. She hurried out the side door, into the back yard, and then ran to her car, heart thumping, mind swirling.

Larry and Fran Cassidy were lovers.

Fran with the soft, melting brown eyes, and the longest, blackest eyelashes Imelda had ever seen. Did Fran run those delicate, long painter's fingers over Larry's body and bring him to passionate delights that somehow she'd never been able to? Now it all made sense. She'd always been more sexual than her husband. He was much more passive. Larry had done his marital duty with Imelda, but he had made *love* to Fran, she thought bitterly, bursting into great gulping sobs in the safety of the car as she saw Larry rush out into the car park. She gunned the engine and sped out onto the main street. She couldn't go home and face her mother-in-law and her children after what she'd just seen.

Dazed with despair and shock, her eyes blurred with tears, she drove on autopilot, wondering if she was about to wake up and be overcome with relief that it was only a bad dream. But it was no nightmare. This was real, Imelda acknowledged, jamming on her brakes to avoid a black cat who was sauntering nonchalantly across the road. Her marriage was over, she thought frantically. Larry could go and live with his fey, artistic lover, because *she* was kicking him out of the house.

What a scandal it would cause if she did that though, she thought miserably. The townland would be riveted, the gossip spreading like wildfire. Her parents would be horrified. Marriage break-ups were unheard of. People got on with things in good Old Catholic Ireland.

Perhaps she should move to Dublin. Her thoughts skittered here and there, seeking a solution. She'd every reason to go now. What a relief it would be to live in an anonymous city where no one knew her business. She could get a house near Teresa. Larry would have to pay for the children's upkeep and she could get a job. She'd plenty of retail experience.

Could she uproot the children from their home, their friends, their schools? Could she wrench them from their father's loving care? They adored him. She couldn't do that to her children. Was she yet again going to have to sacrifice what she needed for others' happiness?

Imelda turned left down a side road that was more a

boreen than a road. There was a copse of trees halfway down and she pulled in and parked the car, got out and made her way to a round smooth boulder where she often liked to sit peacefully and look out across the valley. The breeze whispered through the leaves. Clusters of bluebells swayed gracefully at her feet but today Imelda, ensnared in turmoil, saw none of the beauty of Hedigan's Wood.

'Why?' she roared up at the clear blue sky. 'Why do you keep picking on me, God? What have I done to deserve this shite that you keep shovelling down on me?' Imelda sat on the rock and put her head in her hands and wept brokenly, her body shuddering with sobs until she'd no more tears to cry. She felt sick, tired and weak. Her stomach was tied up in knots, her head beginning to pound. After she'd composed herself, she went back to the car, rooted in her bag for her cigarettes and lit up.

She didn't know how long she sat on her stone, smoking cigarette after cigarette, but the sun had long reached its noon zenith when she took note of where she was and what time it was. Heavy-hearted, Imelda knew that she should go home. She'd children to take care of. Keelin and Cormac would be finished school and wanting their dinner and she'd to collect Peter from her mother-in-law's.

She was stubbing out her last cigarette when she heard the crunch of tyres along the boreen. Imelda's heart sank. She swore, wiping her tear-stained face with her hands, sure that her mascara had run after her bout of crying, and knowing that she looked a sight.

Her stomach lurched when she saw Larry's red van.

Imelda stood up and squared her shoulders as her husband parked behind her car and made his way towards her, his face ashen and drawn in torment.

'Imelda, I—'

'How did you know I was here?' she said dully.

'I went home. I went to Mam's. Saw no sign of the car and I thought I'd try here. I know you. This is where you come when—'

'You know me,' she derided. 'Am I that predictable? And I thought I knew you. Well, I was wrong about that, for sure. In a million years I would never have imagined you and Fran Cassidy together.'

'I want to talk to you about that—'

'Why did you marry me? It *certainly* wasn't for love,' she interrupted bitterly.

'I could ask you the same question,' Larry said quietly.

His unexpected answer left her without a response. Because it was true. She hadn't married him for love; she'd married him to escape.

'So it's all been a sham then,' she said. 'It must have been such an ordeal for you, having sex with me, when all that was in your head was Fran Cassidy. Oh, it explains so much, Larry. So much,' she raged.

'Don't say that,' he muttered, reddening.

'I *will* say it. I'll say what I bloody well like, you bastard. And I thought we had a good marriage, despite everything. What a fool I was!'

'We did well, until today.' He kicked a stone around, hands jammed in his jeans pockets, head lowered, unable to look at her.

'I want to leave.'

'I understand that – but, Imelda, I'm begging you not to take the children away from me completely. That I couldn't bear. I'll do *anything*. Give you anything you want. As much money as I can afford, but they are my world,' he pleaded, tears rolling down his cheeks.

'The *children* are your world. *Fran* is your world, and *I* might as well be a leper,' Imelda replied flatly. 'I hate you for what you've done to me, Larry. I will *never* forgive you, but I will do right by my children and I won't disrupt their lives. Our marriage is over. You know that, don't you?'

'Please let me try and make it up to you. I'll never see Fran again, I promise,' Larry begged. 'Imelda, I'm so sorry. I—'

'Larry, what I saw will live with me for the rest of my life. Nothing you say is going to change that. Maybe time will dull the pain of it, I don't know, but for now, let me feel the way I feel and don't make false promises to me—'

'They're not false, Imelda. I will never, ever see Fran again,' Larry assured her.

Imelda couldn't think straight. Everything in her life had changed in that instant. If she'd no children, she'd be gone. But she did have children and she had a responsibility towards them, whether she liked it or not.

'Do what you like from now on,' she said bitterly. 'I'm never going to speak to you about this again. Let the façade continue, because that's what it is and always has been. You're right. But you need to remember that once I became your wife, I was as good a wife and partner as I could be. I kept my marriage vows and I was never unfaithful to you. That counts for something, in my view. Here,' she scrabbled in her bag for the condoms and threw them at him. 'I won't be needing these. I'm the biggest fool this world has ever seen.'

The water lapped gently against the quay. The boats bobbed up and down on the silky blue-green water. Her children were enjoying their Saturday out in Galway, a summer holiday treat that had been long promised. Imelda was going to bring them to have their lunch in one of the cafés around the Spanish Steps and their excitement was mighty. The deep musical chimes of the church bell across the road signalled midday, and automatically she and the children blessed themselves and began the Angelus. 'The angel of the Lord, declared unto Mary,' she intoned, and Keelin's clear voice answered, 'And She conceived of the Holy Spirit.' A thought struck Imelda. She could bring Keelin to confession here; it would save her having to bring her tonight. One more chore of motherhood ticked off.

'Will we get confession here and then we won't have to go tonight?' she asked her daughter.

'OK, Mammy,' her daughter agreed easily.

'I don't want to go into a church.' Cormac made a face.

'We'll be in and out in no time. And you know what, we're going to get a big fat ninety-nine cone after we have our lunch,' she smiled at him.

'Yippppeeeeeee,' he yelled, dancing up and down.

'You're easily pleased,' Imelda laughed, in spite of herself. 'Come on, take Keelin's hand crossing the road.' She turned Peter's buggy around and checked for traffic before crossing over to the church.

'Can I light a penny candle?' Cormac begged as they walked up the long aisle, towards a confession box, which had a small queue waiting.

'Go on. Keelin, go with him and make sure he doesn't set fire to himself or the church. I'll sit in the queue.' She handed her son and daughter a bronze coin each, removed Peter from his buggy and carried him into the row of seats beside the confession box. She watched her children lighting their candles. They were well behaved, she acknowledged. A credit to her and Larry, her father had said recently.

The one good thing to come out of her marriage, she sighed, moving up a seat as the queue got shorter. 'Go on in,' she said to Keelin, when the door to the confession box opened and the penitent before them emerged, head down, blessing himself. Keelin scooted in obediently, the picture of piety, Imelda thought, amused.

She was out in less than five minutes. 'I'll mind Peter while you go in,' Keelin held out her hands for her baby brother.

'Oh!' Imelda was thrown. She hadn't planned to go to confession. But when she saw her daughter's innocent, trusting face looking up at her expectantly, she handed Peter over to her and slipped into the dark box that smelled vaguely musty, despite the polished wood.

She heard the click of the shutter as it was pulled across and saw the priest in dim shadow, head bowed, on the other side of the grille. He nodded his head. 'Make a good confession, my child.'

'Bless me, Father, for I have sinned; it's two months since my last confession, Father,' she murmured. 'I—'

'Two months! What sin has kept you from the sacrament that long?' The priest lifted his head and looked at her sternly.

'Anger, Father.' Imelda shrugged despondently.

'Anger at whom, my child?'

'My husband, and God!' She might as well be honest, she decided. She was, after all, in confession.

'And what has provoked this anger?'

'I caught my husband having an affair and—'

'What caused your husband to have a relationship outside of the confines of marriage? Have you been granting him his conjugal rights?'

'*What?*' Imelda snapped, not sure if she'd heard right.

'Have you been giving your husband his conjugal rights?' The priest looked askance at her disrespectful tone.

Wrath, primal in its origin, scorched through her. 'How *dare* you? You impudent article. What about *my* conjugal rights?' Imelda hissed. 'My husband is the one committing mortal sin, and you're blaming it on *me!*' She couldn't believe what she was hearing. She stuck her face close to the grille, and all the injustice that she and her kind had endured for centuries impelled the words that erupted out of her. 'This is my last confession, *Priest!* I'll never kneel before one of you lot again.'

Imelda stood up and marched out of the dark confessional, blinking in the daylight into which she emerged, wanting to open the door to where that so-called man of God sat and batter him with her fists. *The Church be damned*, she raged, ushering her children down the aisle ahead of her, and so what if she was cast into damnation? Hell couldn't be much worse than the life she was living now.

CHAPTER TWENTY-THREE

KEELIN

Summer 1972

'Put the good toilet roll in the bathroom, and fold the first sheet in a triangle. Give the sink a wipe, and for goodness' sake tidy up those magazines and straighten up your bedspread,' Imelda said exasperatedly, standing at the door of her daughter's bedroom with a cross look on her face. Keelin turned from where she was sprawled on her beanbag and lowered her *Jackie* magazine.

'Oh Mam!' she exclaimed, when she noticed her mother's new hairstyle. 'I *love* your hair. It's like Jane Fonda's in *Klute*.'

'Do you like it? I'm not sure about it.' Her mother stared doubtfully at her reflection in the oval mirror on Keelin's dressing table. 'It's shorter than what I'm used to.'

'It's fab, Mam! *Very* sophisticated. I like the feathery bits at the side. Wait until Dad sees it.'

'Huh, I might as well be wearing a pink wig for all the difference it will make to him,' snorted Imelda, and Keelin felt a surge of irritation. Sometimes her mam could be so mean to Dad and she hated it. But she knew better than to say anything in his defence, so she hauled herself out of the beanbag and went to her bed to straighten the offending bedspread. Why she needed to do this, she'd no idea. Surely the aunt, whom she'd never met, wouldn't be upstairs snooping in her bedroom.

'What time is Auntie Brigid coming?' Keelin changed the subject.

'Later this afternoon. She's going to the home place first to pick up Nana and Granddad, and to see Granny Dunne's grave. When you've tidied up here, come down and help me make the egg mayonnaise and cheese and pineapple skewers.' Imelda studied her daughter, frowning. 'Change out of those shorts and put a dress on,' she said briskly. 'I want you looking your best when you meet your aunt for the first time.'

'OK,' Keelin sighed, wishing this auntie who worked as a nun in Africa would hurry up and get her visit over with so that life could get back to normal. Since her mother had heard that her sister 'the nun' was coming home for her first visit in more than ten years, she'd nearly driven Keelin mad with all the extra housework that had to be done. The net curtains had been taken down and washed. Keelin had to clean all the windows until they gleamed. The tiles in the kitchen had had to be regrouted, and Imelda had ordered new lino for the floor. Larry was instructed to plant more summer bedding than usual, although Keelin had to admit the pots of cascading petunias, hollyhocks, busy lizzies and campanula that her father had planted made the garden look ever so pretty.

Keelin straightened up the flower-sprigged bedspread with the lemon frill. She had a pillowcase to match. Her friend Lisa thought Keelin had a very posh bedroom and envied her having a room to herself. Lisa had to share with her two sisters. Their room always looked like a pigsty.

She *was* lucky, Keelin admitted. She was one of only three girls in her class to have a bedroom to herself. But she was also one of the only girls who had to work on Saturdays, whether she wanted to or not. Keelin had to stock shelves in her parents' supermarket on Saturday mornings, and her brothers had to help their grandfather and uncle up on the bog in Ardcloch to earn their pocket money. Some of her friends were having the whole summer off, scot-free. She was babysitting for one of her mother's friends three mornings a week.

Lucky for Keelin that she liked the little boy she was minding. He was a real cutie. She smiled thinking of him. She was teaching him his ABCs on his toy blackboard, but one day she wanted to be standing in front of a real blackboard, teaching. It was what she planned when she left school. Study at Carysfort Teacher Training College in Dublin and become a primary school teacher. Her parents had told her if she studied hard and did well in her exams she could apply for a place in college. Imelda in particular was very keen that it should happen for her.

That was one of the things Keelin most liked about her mam. Imelda believed women should be educated, independent and have their own money. She believed in equality. She was even a member of the Women's Liberation Movement. She didn't make Keelin and her brothers go to Benediction and Devotions and Holy Hours, like a lot of her classmates had to. Once Keelin had overheard her mother saying to her dad that she didn't believe in all that 'religious shite' anymore and she only went to Mass on Sundays 'to keep up the façade, for the sake of the children'.

Keelin had been shocked. How could her mother *not* believe in the Church's teachings? Especially when she came from a religious family that had a nun on the Missions? Neither Imelda nor Larry went to confession, and Imelda had told Keelin that she could make up her own mind about continuing to go when she turned sixteen. In the meantime, Keelin went once a month or so, unlike most of her classmates who went weekly. Keelin wondered, did the nun who was coming to visit know of Imelda's controversial opinions?

When her mother was in good humour – which seemed to be a rare thing these days, Keelin thought glumly – she could be impulsive and good fun. Last week, on a gloriously sunny day, she'd called Keelin, Cormac and Peter to get up and give her a hand, because they were going to go to the beach for the day and she wanted to bring a picnic. She needed a day off, she declared. She'd had 'enough of everyone'. So Peter got a day off from school, much to his joy.

Her brothers had packed the boot of Imelda's Ford Cortina with windbreaks, tartan rugs, the yellow lilo, a football, a bucket, spade and towels and swimming togs, while Keelin had helped make the picnic. Imelda had sent Peter down to the shop to get Tayto crisps, lemonade and chocolate bars, then they'd set off, giddy with excitement to be spending the day on the beach, an hour's drive away.

The boys had set up the windbreaks, hammering the posts into the sand with flat stones while Keelin and Imelda had spread out the rugs and all their bits and pieces. Imelda had been first to dive into the surging Atlantic waves, squealing at the cold, urging Cormac to get down in the water and not be standing there shivering. Keelin dived in straight away, preferring to get the shock of the immersion in the freezing cold water over quickly. The sun had been warm on her face and shoulders and she'd felt she was in heaven, the blue-green sea glittering so brightly she had to squint to look at it.

It had been a perfect day, all the better for its unexpectedness, and Keelin was happy to see the lines of stress soften in her mother's face as she snoozed in the afternoon sun after their picnic. Imelda seldom took the time to relax. She was always on the go.

Perhaps after the nun's visit she might bring them on another beach day, Keelin thought hopefully, sloping down the stairs to help with the buffet.

*

'Well, hello there! Aren't you gorgeous! I can't believe I have a niece who's nearly as tall as I am.' Keelin stared at the woman with the smiling, startling blue eyes, a tanned face emphasized by the white band that held her nun's black veil in place, who was holding out a slim, tanned hand to her.

'Hello,' she said shyly, shaking her aunt's hand, which, she noted, had a very firm clasp. 'It's very nice to meet you. Erm ... I've heard a lot about you,' she added, not sure whether she should call her auntie, or Sister. The nun laughed and glanced over at Imelda.

'Have you?' she said. 'All good, I hope.'

Her mother looked a bit flustered. When Nana, Granddad and the nun had arrived, the two sisters had looked at each other, Brigid smiling, Imelda somewhat wary. But when Brigid had opened her arms, Imelda had reached in and hugged her sister briefly, and they had looked at each other and smiled. 'Good to see you, Imelda. You look amazing,' Brigid said. 'I love the trouser suit. Everyone's wearing them, I see.'

'And you look good, from what I can see of you, and *very* nun-like.' Imelda's face softened in a smile of rare affection and Keelin's grandparents beamed happily, delighted to have their daughter home from Africa.

'So what have you heard, Keelin? And what a lovely name that is.' Brigid gave her a light kiss on the cheek.

'Granny always reads your letters to me,' Keelin smiled. 'I love hearing about Africa.'

'And I love living there,' the nun said, turning to Keelin's brothers. 'And these are my nephews, Cormac and Peter. Isn't it wonderful to come home and have three lovely new relatives?' She shook hands with the boys, who bashfully shook hands back.

'Are you feeling better now?' Imelda asked her sister, ushering them all into the sitting room.

'I'm better than I was, but it will take a while. I was run down as well. But it's wonderful to be home in the gorgeous fresh air of the West. It will do my lungs the power of good.'

'Double pneumonia isn't to be sneezed at,' Imelda said, and the nun laughed, a hearty, infectious chuckle.

'I forgot how witty you always were, Imelda. Not to be sneezed at, indeed.'

'Sure, if you didn't laugh you'd cry,' Imelda said drily, but Keelin could see that her mother was pleased and had begun to relax.

The afternoon passed in a blur of anecdotes and reminiscences, and Keelin sat, fascinated, listening to her aunt talk about sleeping in wattle and bamboo huts, and eating with leaves as your plates, and using your fingers instead of knives and forks, and of plucking bananas and mangoes off trees to eat. Her brothers wanted to know if there were crocodiles, and their aunt told them that, yes, there were, and they lived in mangrove swamps and river basins, and she had seen them when she was in a boat going to the villages upriver. She'd shown some photos of the white house with the long veranda where she lived. And photos of people in exotic, colourful clothes. A picture of a man riding a scooter and carrying a baby goat on his shoulders, two children in front and a big bundle on his head.

She told them about the dust blowing in from the Sahara, when they would have to wear scarves, and Keelin longed to be there in that exciting world.

'I think I'd like to be a nun, and work in Africa,' she exclaimed, fired by her aunt's altruism and nobility of spirit.

Imelda did a double take and said firmly, 'You can forget that nonsense, Keelin. It's a whim. I never heard you show any inclination towards the religious life. You'll finish your Leaving Certificate and do your teacher training,' she told her daughter in a tone that brooked no argument.

Brigid, sensing the tension, said calmly, 'This is not a life you rush into, pet. It's very different now, since Vatican Two, than when I joined. Do as your mother suggests. Finish your exams. Train for something. Live life to the full. I'm not in favour of young girls entering before they've had a chance to experience things. It can lead to great unhappiness. And besides, there are no guarantees that you would be sent on the Missions. You could be placed in a convent in Ireland, or France. It's up to the Mother General where nuns are sent. Once you enter, you take a vow of obedience and give up free will.'

'It's good to hear you talk a bit of sense to this one,' Imelda said grudgingly.

'But, Mam, I think I'd like—'

'Enough.' Her mother raised a hand and Keelin seethed inwardly. How *dare* her mother make a show of her, and dismiss her feelings as a whim! If she wanted to become a nun, a nun she would become, Keelin decided there and then.

'You have plenty of time to make a decision,' soothed Brigid, noting her niece's crestfallen expression. Keelin saw the glare her mother flashed her sister and decided to say no more about becoming a nun. It would only lead to rows.

'We need to get going, Imelda. Thanks so much for a lovely spread and a very enjoyable afternoon.' Brigid rose to her feet and helped her father out of the armchair. Granddad Dunne was very stiff after a bout of lumbago, and Keelin, who knew she was his favourite, picked up his walking stick which had fallen down beside his chair. 'Here, Granddad, I'll cycle over and see you tomorrow,' she promised, giving him a kiss.

'You're a little treasure,' her grandfather smiled, hugging her.

Brigid turned to Imelda, 'I'm going to the Four Winds soon; why don't you bring the children down and stay over, if it's not too busy?'

'We'll see,' Imelda said noncommittally. 'I have to bring Larry's mother to a hospital appointment. Dad has one next week, and the shop's busy, what with the tourist season and everything.'

'Well, the offer is there,' Brigid said lightly, and Keelin knew somehow or another that she would get to see that house on top of the cliff before the summer was out, and that she and her Auntie Brigid were going to be the best of friends.

CHAPTER TWENTY-FOUR

Summer 1975

'*I agápi mou thélo*,' the young Greek soldier whispered in her ear, his finger tracing a light caress across her bare shoulder and down her arm.

Keelin knew, from a love song that everyone on the Island of Rhodes was singing, that *agápi mou* meant my love. She wasn't sure what the other words meant but she could guess, by the ardent desire that she could feel, as Christos Kostopoulos turned her head to look at him before he kissed her passionately, that he wanted more than kissing.

So did she. It was her first foreign holiday. She'd met Christos at a night club in the new town, down near Mandraki Harbour, a week previously, and he had taken her to see the Valley of the Butterflies on the back of his scooter and now they were strolling along a moonlit beach, the warm Aegean Sea lapping over their toes. The sound of bouzoukis drifted on the breeze from the beachside restaurant where they'd drunk retsina and eaten olives and kleftiko, a lamb dish that melted in the mouth, and baklava, the heavenly filo pastry, chopped nuts and honey dessert that Keelin and her two housemates had fallen in love with.

This truly was the holiday of a lifetime, she thought happily, kissing her companion back, enjoying the delightful sensations coursing through her body. When Christos slid his hands over her hips and pressed her tight against him, and she felt how hard he was, she wanted him as much as he wanted her.

Keelin knew it was considered sinful to have sex before marriage. She'd been brought up with the notion that sex was dirty. It had permeated her school days, her college days and would, if she let it, colour every relationship she had with a fella until she got married ... *if* she ever got married. Here on this beautiful island where nothing felt sinful, and the slow, melodious flow of life made her feel vibrant and free, the straightjacket of dogma, so invasive at home, seemed a world away.

He was very gentle with her, lightly caressing her, and then his touch becoming firmer, insistent, and she was longing for him, her body delighting in the sensations he was arousing in her. When he came into her she gasped with pleasure and, briefly, pain, but pleasure took over and Keelin cast away her inhibitions and gave herself up to the moment, and felt utterly liberated as her young, healthy body made her forget, momentarily, all that she'd been taught in her Catholic upbringing.

*

'You did it with Christos,' Eva grinned, pointing an accusatory finger at her.

'How do you know?' Keelin said, laughing and blushing at the same time.

'You're *glowing*! You lucky wagon. He's gorgeous.'

'I know,' Keelin agreed, flinging herself down on the bed. 'If someone told me I'd come to Greece and lose my virginity to a man I only met a week ago, who hardly speaks a word of English and who I'll never meet again after the holiday is over, I'd have told them they were raving.' Keelin stretched sensuously. 'Girls, I tingle all over!'

'Oh, stop boasting,' Norah scowled. She was still an unwilling virgin. 'I'd be riven with guilt. I know I would. I was in the Children of Mary when I was younger. I know I'd feel impure. I can't help it. I'm indoctrinated with it.'

'We all were, Norah. Get a few of these in you tomorrow night and feck the indoctrination. But make sure you use a condom.' Eva handed her a glass full of ouzo.

'So we're not going to Mass tomorrow, I take it?' Norah took a swig of ouzo and raised an eyebrow at her friends.

'Nope!'

'I can't. I'm in a state of mortal sin,' Keelin giggled, a tad tipsy.

'My mother was right. You're a bad influence on me, the pair of you,' tittered Norah, draining the shot glass and holding it out for a refill as the first rays of dawn whispered through the curtains of their hotel room.

*

'I can't believe it's over,' Eva sighed, fastening her seat belt. 'It was a brilliant holiday.'

'I'm so glad you persuaded me to come,' Keelin smiled at her friend. She was sitting in the window seat of the Aer Lingus jet that would fly them home. Norah was in the aisle seat, rooting for her Jackie Collins novel.

'I bet Christos was too,' she said *sotto voce*, and the other two laughed. Norah, sadly, was returning home *virgo intacta*, having not been able to summon up the courage to go the whole way with Stavros.

Keelin sighed deeply. She wasn't looking forward to returning to Ireland. She'd enjoyed so much about the holiday: her delightful interludes with her soldier, the laid-back culture, the heat, the food, the friendly islanders. The very foreignness of the place had been intoxicating. This was probably how Brigid felt about Africa.

What would her aunt think of her loose morals, sleeping with a stranger on holiday? She might not be too impressed, Keelin reflected. And would she think Keelin immodest for dressing in shorts and wearing no bra under her halter-neck top? What was so awful about the female body that it needed to be kept hidden, as if it were something tainted? Her legs had a sexy, even tan after her holiday. *They look great and I'm proud of them*, Keelin thought as the plane roared into the sky, wishing she'd the nerve to prance around the college grounds in her shorts and halter neck.

Her holiday had been a turning point. She'd left Ireland a girl; she was returning home a woman. It was time to change her attitudes about how women should be in the world, she reflected as the passengers settled down for the long flight home.

'Teacher, Teacher, she pulled my hair!'

'Did not!'

'Did so!'

Keelin held up a warning finger to the two warring five-year-olds who were glowering at each other in the straggly line that was forming at the classroom door, waiting for the bell to ring.

'What did I say about fighting, Sheila Kelly and Cathy O'Flanagan? Down to the end of the line with you.'

'But, Teacher, I did *nuttin*,' came the outraged howl from Cathy O'Flanagan.

It was Friday afternoon. Keelin had a thumping headache from being in a stuffy classroom all day, on top of a hangover from the previous night's carousing, in Zhivago. She couldn't wait to see the back of her infants' class and go home to bed for a couple of hours, before hitting Leeson Street with the girls. The bell rang, saving her from having to hold an inquiry about the hair-pulling incident as a crescendo of excited chatter swept through the line and her charges waited for her to lead them out the classroom door to the school entrance, where their parents were waiting.

We opened a new clinic a hundred miles downriver. We had two hundred and fifty women and children on our first day, we got so many gifts of chickens, fruit and eggs, we made a big feast and shared it with the villagers. Jakab made a pot of chicken and couscous stew, and cooked yams in banana skins over the fire. It was all delicious.

I feel I'm making a difference, especially in the lives of women, here, in Senegal, and that is deeply satisfying. It wasn't until I got to working on the Missions that I felt my true vocation. I'm so glad that you love teaching so much, dearest Keelin, and that life is very good for you.

Love and Blessings,

Brigid XXX

PS Keep up your French language studies.

Keelin read the last lines of her aunt's letter, sitting in the staff room having a cup of tea. *I feel I'm making a difference.* Why had that jumped out at her? Why was it unsettling her, Keelin wondered irritably, stuffing the letter back into the envelope and shoving it into her bag. The old niggling longing that she'd kept at bay rose up again. Her life was so good right now, how could she possibly want to become a nun? She knew how little respect the Church gave to women.

But I could help change that, she thought, *and that's how I would make a difference.* Maybe this was what her vocation, if she had one, was about. One thing was certain, she needed to see once and for all if the religious life was for her and get it out of her system. That nagging voice that she had shushed for so long was making itself heard again.

Cycling along the Ballymun Road after school, she kept

pedalling straight on instead of turning for home, freewheeling down the hill to The Rise. She scooted left onto Griffith Avenue, wondering was she mad? Autumn had come early. Great drifts of red–gold leaves banked up against the trees that lined the long elegant avenue. She sailed through the lights at Whitehall, cycling on until the high convent wall loomed up ahead. She'd passed it many times on her bike, or on a bus, the convent of the Soeurs du Secours Miséricordieux, where Brigid had been a postulant and then a novice.

Keelin slowed down to turn left into the entrance to the large, graceful redbrick building. Her heart was thumping. She was surprised when a nun in a smart knee-length pleated navy skirt and white blouse opened the heavy wooden door. She wore no veil and her hair was cut in a neat bob. She looked quite modern, unlike Brigid in her traditional habit.

'Come in, I'm Sister Frances. Mother Veronica asked me to keep an eye out for you. She's talking to a builder about a renovation we're doing and she'll be down in ten minutes or so. Can I bring you some tea while you're waiting?' the nun said pleasantly, leading her into a small parlour off the hall.

'Thanks, that would be lovely,' Keelin murmured, fighting the urge to run. She'd a good job, money of her own, freedom of sorts. Wasn't that enough?

The tea and Mother Veronica arrived simultaneously, and Sister Frances asked her Superior if she'd like a cup.

'A good strong one, please, Frances,' the older nun, who wore the traditional habit, said agreeably, shaking Keelin's hand.

'So you think you might have a vocation, Keelin. Tell me

about it,' she invited kindly, sitting in a chair opposite Keelin. She was a tall, angular woman with a thin face dominated by bright, hazel eyes that had a humorous glint in them, despite her austere appearance.

'Well, I suppose it was meeting my Aunt Brigid the first time and hearing her stories of the Missions that ignited my interest. My aunt is one of your nuns, she works in Senegal.'

'Your aunt is Brigid Dunne?' exclaimed the nun delightedly. 'I worked with her in St Louis, before I was recalled home and promoted. Well goodness, you couldn't have a better role model.'

'I know,' Keelin agreed. 'I just don't know if I have a vocation or not.'

'Being a postulant and then a novice gives a person time to decide if the religious life is for them or not. Final vows aren't taken for several years, so you will have plenty of time to make your decision,' Mother Veronica explained. 'Tell me why you think you might have the call to enter.'

'It's a feeling I've had for years, something that won't go away—'

'The Lord keeps knocking until we listen,' Mother Veronica smiled.

'You're not serious, Keelin! In the name of God, *why* would you want to give up the great life you have to become a nun! Are you *mad*!' Imelda was aghast at the news Keelin had imparted. 'It's all bloody Brigid's fault, writing you those letters. Brainwashing you—'

'Mam, stop. That's not fair – Auntie Brigid didn't brain-wash me. Remember when I met her that first time, she urged me to live life and travel, and have fun,' Keelin protested.

'I supposed she's delighted,' Imelda snapped.

'I haven't told her yet. I wanted to tell you and Dad first,' Keelin said gently.

'I can't believe you're even *considering* entering. I reared you to be free of religion. To have a life of your own and to be independent. Don't forget that.'

'I know,' Keelin agreed. 'And I'm grateful to you and Teresa, and all the other women who are fighting for our equality. But, Mam, some of the work those women do out on the Missions is life-changing for the people they're work-ing for. And they don't all wear the habit anymore. They're very emancipated now, and Auntie Brigid does her own thing in Senegal. So it's not *all* of them,' Keelin pointed out.

'Keelin, I once told you that if you ever entered a convent it would be the end of us,' Imelda warned grimly. 'I've no time for nuns, priests, religion or any of the claptrap associ-ated with it.'

'And I'll make up my own mind. So much for me being independent and liberated,' Keelin snapped.

'Well, they're two things you won't be in a convent,' Imelda retorted furiously. 'For God's sake, Larry, talk some sense into her.'

'It's a hard life,' Larry said slowly. Keelin could see that her father was as shocked by her announcement as her mother was.

'But it's a lot different now. Being out in the community rather than being stuck behind convent walls – unless you're a contemplative nun, of course – is now seen as the way forward. It's exciting actually,' Keelin explained.

Imelda gave a derisive snort. 'Sure, aren't you working in the community, teaching? Can't you continue your education and go for a degree?'

'Mam, I won't be taking final vows for years. I can always leave if I've made a mistake. But something's pushing me and I will always regret it if I don't listen to that inner voice.'

'Pshaw, inner voice,' scoffed Imelda.

'Imelda, don't be disrespectful,' Larry said sternly, and his wife glowered at him but said no more.

'When do you go in?' her father sighed.

'Next January.'

'Not too far away. At least we'll have you with us for Christmas.' Her father held out his arms to her and Keelin hugged him tightly, grateful for his quiet understanding.

'I know you, Keelin. You're too strong-willed and argumentative to subjugate your personality. It will all end in tears,' Imelda said grimly, marching out of the kitchen.

'Don't mind your mother. You know what she's like: bark worse than her bite. Do what you have to do. If it works out, it works out, and if it doesn't you always have a home to come back to,' her father said reassuringly.

His words were a balm to her agitated spirit. It was good to know she had a safety net.

CHAPTER TWENTY-FIVE

It was in the Mother House in Paris, a week before she was to fly to Africa, that Keelin began to wonder whether she had made a huge mistake entering the religious life. She was in the large common room with other novices, sitting in front of the big colour TV that had recently been installed and watching a televised event in St Peter's Square. The commentator spoke with hushed reverence as the cardinals appeared in their scarlet robes and red birettas, followed by the bishops with their mitres, monsignors and priests in their black cassocks, but to Keelin they seemed a self-important flock of peacocks on parade. A thought struck her with stomach-lurching clarity: *There is no place for Jesus here. And where are the women?* Women as well as men were supposed to be created in God's likeness. There was no equality in what she was seeing. Or in the life she was living. It was as if a bucket of ice-cold water had been poured over her.

Surrounded by her fellow Sisters, Keelin felt a surge of

silent, primal rage as she watched the smug, self-satisfied princes of the Church and their cohorts cheering their leader. Pope Paul VI, austere and cold, had none of the kindly, warm-hearted humility of his predecessor, Pope John XXIII.

Humanae Vitae, On the Regulation of Birth, an encyclical written by the Pope, had reaffirmed the orthodox teaching of the Catholic Church regarding married love, responsible parenthood and the rejection of most forms of artificial contraception. It had caused a lot of controversy on its publication. Imelda had been scathing about it and Keelin, once again, had been impressed with her mother's progressive stance, particularly at a time when so many women in Ireland accepted what they were told from the pulpit without question.

Keelin's rage grew as the programme continued and she wondered, were these doubts and observations merely part of the process of assimilation into the life of an obedient nun? Doubts were normal, she and the other novitiates were often told by their Superiors.

But what Keelin was experiencing went beyond the usual doubts voiced by her peers. This felt like an awakening in the very depths of her being, a realization that the suppression of women perpetrated by the Church through the ages, and still to this very moment, was the antithesis of all that Jesus had preached. Now she could understand the attitudes of those American nuns who were demanding equality, despite being frowned upon by their French counterparts for being, as Mother General had put it, 'too lacking in humility'.

If humility meant putting up with this continued

repression, supporting an organization that perpetuated such abuse, she wanted no part of it. Why had it taken her until now to see what was under her very nose? How ironic, that it was in a convent, in the process of offering her life to God and the Church, that the scales were falling from her eyes, she thought ruefully.

The following day she went to confession. 'Bless me, Father, for I have sinned. It's a week since my last confession, Father. I have grave doubts about the Church, and becoming a nun. I have fears about taking my final vows,' she declared.

'That's normal, my child, I would have fears for you if you didn't,' Monsignor LeFrey, the chaplain to the convent, said humorously. 'Tell me about your doubts about the Church, firstly, so I can allay them for you.'

It poured out of her, her sudden awakening. Why could women not be priests? It was a man-made law, not the law of Jesus.

In the dark of the confessional, kneeling to a man who sat with a barrier between them, looking down upon her, Keelin was too upset to see the irony of her position.

'So you are one of these new feminist types that I'm seeing so many of, lately,' the monsignor said slowly.

Keelin felt a wave of relief at his words. She wasn't alone. There were others with doubts, here in France as well as America.

'Wanting equality is important,' she said quietly. 'I don't like to label people.'

'And you imagine that *you*, a young, untried girl, know

better than the finest theological minds in the Church? You think *you* know more than the Pope, who is infallible when he makes decisions concerning the Church. Jesus had twelve apostles. They were men. His women followers played their role also, just as you will, dear Sister, but first you must overcome this uprising of the ego. The ego is the greatest enemy to those of us in Holy Orders. Your greatest battles will be with your ego and not Mother Church, as you imagine. Suppress the ego so that humility will triumph and you have won the battle. Be humble in your thoughts. Be meek and self-effacing in your daily duties and you will come through. Leave these thoughts about women's place in the Church, and the Pope's encyclicals, to wise and experienced theologians whose job it is to rule on such things. Go teach the little children in Africa of the love of Jesus and the glory of the Church. Pray to our Holy Mother to make you unpresumptuous in thought. Say five rosaries and fast for two days as your penance. Now say your act of contrition and ask for forgiveness, my child, that I may grant it to you. Oh my God . . .' he began patronizingly, as though she were a six-year-old.

'Oh my God, I am heartily sorry for having offended Thee, who art infinitely good, and I firmly resolve with the help of Thy Grace never to offend Thee again,' she murmured, heavy-hearted.

Was it her ego that was causing her such doubts, radical thought and angst? Keelin agonized, returning to her pew to begin her penance.

True, subduing the ego was the greatest struggle in Holy

Orders. If Brigid could do it, surely she could, Keelin assured herself, beginning the first of her five rosaries.

'Sister Michael, I'm afraid we expect you to wear a veil and white habit here in Nigeria,' the Mistress of Novices, Mère Benedict, said firmly after Keelin followed her fellow novices from the convent church after Lauds.

It was her first morning in the convent in Ikorodu, a city in Lagos, where the Order had a primary and secondary school on a large, enclosed compound. Keelin had come to church wearing a patterned green and gold cotton shirtdress. She'd never worn a veil, not as a postulant, and not in the six months she'd spent in the novitiate in Dublin.

She'd been sent to Ikorodu to teach in the primary school while continuing her novitiate. And when the Boeing 707 had taken off from Heathrow to Lagos she couldn't have been more excited. *This* was what she'd entered for.

Keelin had spoken to nuns who had worked in Nigeria and read up on the country she was going to. As in Ireland before colonization, when the Brehon Laws gave a woman the right to retain all land, flocks and household goods she brought to the marriage, in what was quite a matriarchal society, women in Nigeria had traditionally played a major role in social and economic activities, wielding considerable power and even becoming tribal chiefs. Colonization had altered gender relationships and eroded that power. Keelin was determined to empower her young female charges and be a champion of women's rights.

Now she was being told to wear the veil by her Superior. That was a bit disheartening, she thought, dismayed. 'I haven't worn a veil or a habit since I entered, Mère,' she said politely.

'My dear, you're in Africa now, we do things differently here. It's a requirement of this convent that you wear the habit. We expect it of every nun, indigenous or not.' Mère Benedict smiled sweetly but her voice was firm, and her brown eyes steely.

'Very well, Mère,' Keelin acquiesced politely.

'A word of advice, Sister. I and many of my colleagues do not agree with the liberal regime that is running rampant through religious orders. We still abide by the rules and regulations set by Rome and endorsed by our last Chapter, a year ago. If you remember this, you will settle in quicker. Go to the Almoner to get a habit,' Mère Benedict instructed.

'Thank you, Mère,' Keelin said calmly, but her heart sank. She'd heard that the African religious were still very traditional. This was surely the proof. Mother Veronica's parting words when Keelin left Dublin came to mind: 'You and your vocation will be tested in Africa. Prepare for that.'

The days slipped into a pattern that Keelin found hard to adjust to. The teaching was a joy to her. She'd a natural affinity with children and loved their honesty and view of life, but once school was over and she'd corrected homework and prepared the following day's lessons, she was expected to behave in a 'nunny-like' way, as she privately called it, and pray and study the Bible, and say her Office. She'd done all this in Dublin and Paris, but she'd also been encouraged to take courses in social justice, and she'd volunteered with the St Vincent de Paul charity to visit vulnerable families and the elderly. When she'd expressed a wish to Mère Benedict to undertake similar community work in Ikorodu, her Superior had told her, 'In time, Sister. For now you must concentrate on your spiritual studies, for they are equally important.'

Keelin felt utterly restricted. Despite tales of bag snatching and robberies, she longed to explore the city, but because she was in the novitiate she was denied the freedoms enjoyed by professed nuns. Every Saturday she had to confess her sins and Father Eze probed more than she liked. 'Your resentment towards the rules of the community comes from ego, Sister. It is something you must battle,' he'd informed her the previous Saturday, and she'd longed to tell him to feck off. She'd much more to offer than to be kneeling in churches, trying to pray, when she could be teaching young women in the city ways to help themselves out of poverty.

It's not what I imagined, she'd written to Brigid. *I feel very underused, despite my confessor's accusations that it's my ego that's causing me to feel like this. I thought I'd be like you, out in the community, not trapped in a convent.*

A month later the sage reply had come back:

Dear precious niece,

You are being taught humility and patience, something we all have to learn. But I truly understand your frustration. Were I in your shoes, I'm not sure that I'd cope either. I've got used to my 'freedom' from the rules and regulations which convent life binds us to. If it gets too much, my advice is to leave. No point in being miserable, and thankfully, you have a profession to go back to.

I think Veronica sent you to Lagos to test your vocation. And that's fine too, Keelin. It's much easier to leave now than it was when I joined, and if that's what you decide to do, at least you will have peace of mind knowing the life of a nun was not for you.

Try and be happy,
Your loving aunt,
Brigid

Her aunt's letter came as a shock. She hadn't expected Brigid to urge her to leave so easily. She couldn't leave. She *wouldn't* leave this early in her novitiate. Keelin shook her head angrily, remembering her mother's prediction: 'It will all end in tears.' She'd stick it out for at least six more months, which would bring her up to a year as a novice, and then she'd consider her options.

Four months in, Mère Benedict told her the Reverend Mother wished to see her. Keelin's heart sank. She'd very little to do with Mère Gertrude, a wry, spry seventy-year-old

Frenchwoman who had spent most of her life in Africa. Was the Reverend Mother going to tell her she wasn't good enough for the Order? Keelin wondered anxiously, thinking how ironic it would be if she got the boot rather than resigning. Perhaps Mère Benedict had complained about her attitude. Keelin found it hard to restrain herself sometimes when the nuns bossed her around. Taking a deep breath, she knocked on the Reverend Mother's office door.

'*Entrez,*' came the command. 'Ah, Soeur Michael. Please sit down.' The Reverend Mother gestured to the empty chair at the other side of her burnished teak desk. 'You speak French, reasonably well, is this true?' The question, in rapid French, caught Keelin off guard.

'*Oui*, Mère Gertrude.'

'Excellent. One of our teaching nuns on the Ivory Coast has been stricken with TB and must return to the Mother House in Paris to recover. The nun we had selected to replace her has suffered a nervous breakdown, so we are temporarily stuck. It has been decided to send you there until we sort out a permanent replacement from our professed nuns. The position is in one of our smaller compounds along the coast. Are you agreeable to this?' The nun, sitting straight-backed with steepled fingers, eyed her keenly.

'*Certainement,* Mère Gertrude.' Keelin tried to keep the excitement out of her voice, for fear the offer would be withdrawn. 'I am God's willing servant,' she added in a humble voice, hoping this would make her seem less eager and more pliable.

She wouldn't be in a convent compound in the city. She'd be out where she'd always imagined, in the countryside, the real Africa, and it was going to be a smaller community, hopefully something like Brigid's where she'd have much more freedom from the 'nunny' stuff.

'*Bien*, we will book a flight for you the day after tomorrow. This will allow you to prepare your pupils for your departure, and give you time to say goodbye to your community. Until you are back with us, I wish you Godspeed and His blessings, my child.'

'*Merci*, Mère Gertrude,' Keelin murmured, bowing and backing out of the door as quickly as she could in case the Reverend Mother changed her mind.

CHAPTER TWENTY-SIX

'*Petite chérie.* Little puddin', aren't you?' Brigid crooned, caressing the cheeks of the plump six-month-old baby boy in her arms. When Joseph had first been brought to the clinic, three months previously, he had been suffering from malnutrition and diarrhoea. Now, after their care, observation, and nutritional advice and aid to the young mother, her first child was thriving, alert and smiling at Brigid. 'Here you are, Yacine, he's doing great,' Brigid said, reluctantly handing him back to this mother. 'See you next month.'

'*Merci*, Soeur, *merci*.' The young woman handed Brigid a bottle of bissap juice, made from the hibiscus flower native to West Africa. The ruby-coloured drink was most refreshing and Yacine always added orange peel and ginger to her homemade blend.

'*Merci*, Yacine, I will drink this with pleasure.' Brigid took the gift gratefully. She'd already been presented with a chicken, yams, a bead bracelet and a hand-woven basket in the clinic this morning.

'Yacine's the last,' Sister Dominique said cheerfully, closing the door to the examination room. 'We should be home before dark.'

They had a fifty-mile journey ahead of them, and Brigid was relieved that they would be navigating the dirt trails in daylight.

'Do you want to drive?' she asked the young Senegalese nun.

'Oh Brigid, you're the best,' Dominique whooped. She loved driving.

'We're not in the Dakar Rally now,' Brigid reminded her colleague, laughing. Dominique was fast, and Brigid, who liked to drive fast herself, often had to tell the younger woman that she'd like to get to their destination alive!

They ate some chicken and rice stew, drank a glass each of Yacine's bissap, and had a mango, before locking up the clinic and packing up the jeep. It had been a busy day and Brigid was tired but satisfied with how it had gone.

Darkness had fallen by the time they arrived at their small compound, and the welcoming light in the sitting room window shone out onto the veranda, where Sister Philomene was reading under the mosquito net, moving backwards and forwards in the rocking chair.

'Hi, Brigid, there was a call for you from Dakar. Mère Perpetua is flying in from Paris tonight. You have to go to St Louis tomorrow.'

'But I've a clinic in Diama,' protested Brigid.

'Dominique and I will take it. She wants to see all the regional heads,' Philomene said sympathetically. 'Go and have a quick shower. The water and the electricity went off earlier. I wouldn't be surprised if it goes again,' her friend advised. 'I have lamb casserole for dinner, so go wash up, the two of you, and we'll have it when you're ready.'

An hour later, sitting in the light of a paraffin lamp – the electricity had indeed gone off – they watched lightning zig-zag on the horizon. The lamb was melt-in-the-mouth delicious, and Brigid sopped up the gravy with a piece of bread, wishing the feeling of apprehension that had enveloped her would evaporate. Why was Perpetua flying in from Paris? Visits from the hierarchy in the Mother House didn't happen that often, but they always spelled change.

Was it time for her to be moved to another convent in another part of Africa, she wondered distractedly. She loved Senegal and the warm, friendly people she worked with. But a new challenge might be a good thing. She had so much experience setting up and operating the mother-and-child clinics. Brigid prayed silently that her wings would not be clipped, nor her 'freedom' curtailed.

'You want me to go back to *Ireland*?' Brigid couldn't hide her shock as she sat in front of her Superior in the airy, white-painted office in the convent in St Louis.

'As Reverend Mother,' Mère Perpetua reminded her in her soft, whispery voice. 'You will spend some time in Paris with us, preparing for your promotion—'

'But, Mère, I'm needed here. I've set up a dozen clinics, I love working here.'

Mère Perpetua held up a hand and Brigid fell silent.

'That is part of the reason you have been recalled. Strong attachment to place and job is strongly discouraged in the Order. You know that. You know also that pride in our accomplishments nullifies them in the sight of God.'

'But my nursing training, Mère. I've been able to help so many mothers and babies,' Brigid protested heatedly, raging that she'd been accused of the sin of pride.

'Indeed, but you have also been able to train the Sisters in Senegal to take over the work, and you've trained them well. It is wonderful, is it not, to have been able to do that?' the Reverend Mother said sweetly.

'Yes, Mère,' Brigid said heavily. It was true; part of her remit had been to work with indigenous nuns so that they could take over and, as she'd thought erroneously, free her to set up new mother-and-child clinics elsewhere on the Missions. *That*, Brigid had truly believed, had been her path in life, and she'd loved the work.

'Sometimes God needs us to do different work than what we feel we should be doing,' Mère Perpetua said briskly. 'You have *tremendous* organizational skills, and we have a convent in Limerick that badly needs reorganization. The last Reverend Mother had an affliction that unfortunately affected every aspect of the community. It's in complete dis-array and needs a younger, more energetic person in charge. We also want it to be a hub for our American postulants and novices. We're getting a lot of enquiries from young American women about joining our Order. We propose to build a new wing in Limerick where these youngsters can stay and be assessed for their suitability to enter. We feel you are the ideal candidate for the position.'

Brigid's heart sank as low as it could go. She, who had entered in a state of mortal sin, was not the ideal person to veto anyone who wanted to enter the religious life.

'What was the Reverend Mother's affliction that has affected the community so badly?' she enquired, wondering how she could get out of this nightmare situation.

'Alcoholism, sadly, and engaging the caretaker to buy drink for her with money from community funds. It's been going on for a long time, it seems. She's drying out now in rehab, and retiring to Scotland from whence she came.'

'Truly, Mother, I don't feel I'm the right person to take over the convent in Limerick. I have *never* sought a position of authority. I am more suited to a less exalted position,' Brigid argued desperately.

'False humility is a sin, Soeur Brigid. *We* feel you're the right person to do God's work in Limerick. So be it! Now go and pray and give thanks for the new opportunities the good Lord has given you to do His work. You will fly to Paris in two weeks' time. You will be warmly welcomed in the Mother House.' Perpetua stood up and walked around to Brigid's side of the desk. 'Congratulations, my child. We expect great things of you.' She kissed Brigid lightly on each cheek and ushered her out the door.

Brigid made her way to the chapel in a state of utter shock. If her niece's vocation was being tested in Africa, *hers* was going to be severely tested in the country of her birth. Brigid feared what the outcome of that testing might be.

Her fellow Sisters held a party for Brigid in the garden of the small white house where she'd lived so happily for so long. When word had got around that she was leaving, she'd been inundated with gifts, including a goat from one of the tribal chiefs. Although she tried to put on a happy façade, her heart was raw and full of sadness as she said goodbye to the people she'd loved and made a difference to through her dedicated work.

The following afternoon, all her worldly possessions packed in a large brown case, which Jakab had stowed in the boot, Brigid said a subdued farewell to her housemates, hugging them all tightly, trying hard not to cry. But it was hopeless, and she sobbed bitter tears as Jakab drove her away from the life she loved to face the unknown.

'Thank you for what you have done for my people and my country, and for the kindness and respect you have always shown me.' Jakab had tears in his eyes as he placed her case on a trolley at Set Down in St Louis Airport, where she was taking an internal flight to the capital, Dakar.

'Jakab, you have been my friend and guide since I arrived in your beautiful country. I could never have done the work I did without you. I was *blessed* by your friendship,' Brigid said with heartfelt earnestness as they hugged each other tightly.

The Senegalese man had been a true friend and had gently instructed her in the ways of his country as he had driven her in the course of her work. Brigid had depended on him greatly and had found comfort in his stalwart presence at her side.

Eyes blurred with tears, she'd got through check-in and sat awaiting her flight with a heart like lead.

Four hours later, she settled herself into a window seat in an Air France flight to Paris. Eager to catch her last glimpses of the country she loved, she was dimly aware of someone sitting in the seat beside her.

'Sorry, Sister,' Brigid heard an unexpected Irish voice say as she was poked in the leg with a handbag. She turned to find an elderly nun trying to locate her seat belt.

'Sister, I think you're sitting on it,' Brigid said kindly. 'Stand up and I'll pull it out from underneath you.'

'Oh, that's very kind,' said the other nun. 'You're Irish too.'

'I am, for my sins,' Brigid sighed. 'I'm going home from my beloved Africa. I'll miss it,' she said, assisting the older woman to fasten her seat belt.

'I'm going home too, I'm retiring.'

'Should I congratulate you?' Brigid smiled.

The old nun shook her head. 'I'm only still in the Order because I hadn't the guts to leave years ago when I should have, but I've no time for the Church or religion after what happened to my community during the Suez Crisis,' she confided morosely.

'The Suez Crisis, that was a long time ago,' Brigid replied. 'You must have been very young when you joined.'

'I was. Fourteen. It's all so different now, isn't it? I'm Martha, by the way.'

'Brigid! Delighted to meet you,' Brigid said, thinking how glad she was to have someone who spoke English, and a fellow countrywoman at that, sitting beside her for the journey home. 'So what happened that made you want to leave? Or can you talk about it?' Brigid enquired delicately.

'I can talk about it all right. It helps me, actually.' Martha's bright blue eyes darkened with anger. 'We were in a small convent in Suez, about ten of us, and late one night there was a banging on the gates of the compound. I was the one with the best Arabic, so I went out and asked what they wanted. It was the military. They wanted to come in and interrogate us. I told them it was a house of women and they could not enter, hoping that would put them off, but no, they broke down the gates and herded us all at gunpoint into the refectory.'

'How frightening,' Brigid exclaimed. 'But you survived, thank God.'

Sister Martha looked utterly sad. 'I was told to hand over our passports. There were ten of us. Two Irish nuns, five French, and three Egyptian novices. I knew what was going on and I refused. One of the soldiers pointed a gun at the Reverend Mother and said if I did not do as I was told, they would shoot her.'

'God above! Were you terrified?' Brigid gazed at her in horror.

'Oh, I was. I most certainly *was* terrified,' Sister Martha said grimly. 'They were so aggressive and full of hate. But then they'd been invaded by the Israelis, the British and French. Nasser was a very good president, I had a lot of respect for him,' she sighed. 'But I knew once those soldiers got our passports they would become death warrants.

'They took our French Sisters away. I heard later that they were raped and murdered. The Egyptian novices were told to leave. Our Irish passports saved my fellow nun and me. We managed to flee the country with the help of some kind locals. When we eventually got home to the Mother House in Ireland, the Church reprimanded us for deserting our posts. Imagine! That was Rome's response. Nothing about our trauma or our grief, knowing our fellow nuns had been raped and murdered.' Sister Martha shook her head. 'That finished me with the Vatican. If we had been priests, there would have been no rebuke. Priests would have been welcomed home with open arms. We were different. We were only women. I was sickened, and to this day, I have no time for the Vatican and its unchristian hypocrisy.'

She took Brigid's hand. 'You're a young, intelligent woman – get out before it's too late,' she said earnestly. 'We've all been duped, lied to, used to fill the coffers of the Vatican. Read, read, read. *Never* was there a truer saying than the one attributed to Pope Leo the tenth: "The myth of Christ has served us well." Because the Church's version of Christianity *is* a myth,' she added bitterly. 'And I try my best to subvert the Church in my own little way, from the inside.'

'Oh!' murmured Brigid, unsure how to respond. Sister Martha, though frail, was in full command of her faculties.

Brigid had been lucky. Apart from being robbed, several times – and that had been frightening enough – she'd never suffered violence.

'If I could, though, I would liberate a young woman like yourself from unwittingly spreading this false religion, and from wasting your life, a life that should be lived in freedom. Were I to accomplish that, I'd feel I'd done the work of Our Lord.' Sister Martha's vivid blue eyes shone with sincerity as she stared at Brigid.

'How interesting. Sister Martha,' Brigid said quietly, 'I will reflect on your advice and thank you for it.'

'One thing I'm glad about is that I lived long enough to find my own truth. I hope you do the same,' Sister Martha confided as the engines came to life and the aircraft began to race down the runway.

Over the weeks that followed, Brigid felt extremely unsettled. She'd the strangest feeling that Sister Martha had been sent to her, to make her think about the life she was living.

CHAPTER TWENTY-SEVEN

The small convent along the coast from the busy port of San-Pédro was nestled in a well-kept compound between the main road and the beach. Keelin loved it. The Reverend Mother was the only French nun in the convent, in charge of a small community of twenty nuns.

The single-storey house was built around a courtyard. All the bedrooms led onto the verandas that surrounded the convent. The sound of the sea was music to her ears. The beach was a two-minute walk away. There was a much more easy-going air, which soothed her frazzled spirit and gave her some respite from her doubts about her future in the Order. She was the only novice and Mère Germaine, who was unimpressed with reforms and expected her nuns to dress appropriately in their habits, set aside two hours on Tuesdays and Thursdays, after school was over, for Keelin to spend time on her spiritual studies.

How ironic it was *she* who was now feeling the sense of

freedom to do the work she wanted to do, as Brigid once had, and her aunt had been sent home. She'd been shocked to hear of Brigid's return to Ireland and wondered if she would ever adapt to life there after her time in Africa.

Keelin was kept busy and that suited her and the months passed and still there was no sign of her being recalled to Nigeria. But Keelin guessed, reading between the lines of her aunt's occasional letters, that she, too, was struggling with her vocation.

It was one Friday afternoon months later, and Keelin was sitting in the shade of the veranda, surrounded by her young charges. This was their favourite day of the week because after lunch there was no more schoolwork. It was a time she'd set aside for a chat about the events of the previous week, followed by Keelin reading aloud to her pupils.

They were discussing their aspirations for adulthood with great vigour and enthusiasm, and Keelin was about to end the chat and begin her story-reading when she saw the new priest, Father Durand, striding across the compound, his surplice flapping in the breeze that blew in from the sea.

He waved at the children and they waved back. They loved this new young priest who had come to assist the convent's chaplain, Monsignor Kelly, who had developed heart trouble. Father Durand often played football with the children and drew cartoon characters on the board when he was teaching a religion class. There was something about the earnest, kind man in his thirties that she was drawn to. He'd suggested they set up a folk group for the teenagers who came to Mass and she'd eagerly agreed.

It was a joyful collaboration. The young people loved singing and Father Durand played the guitar while she conducted their lively group. They had rehearsals on Saturday evenings, and a few of the indigenous nuns came and played some of their traditional music, and there was a lot of laughter and banter that Keelin found very enjoyable.

'Soeur, Soeur!' One of her young pupils was grabbing her arm to gain her attention. 'Yes, Sisal.' She smiled at him. The boy was one of her brightest pupils.

'I'm going to be an astronaut!'

'That's marvellous, Sisal,' she congratulated him. He beamed proudly.

Miriam, a feisty little Serer girl, turned to her and declared enthusiastically, 'I'm going to be a priest like Father Durand.' Her classmates broke into howls of laughter.

'Don be so *silly*, Miriam. You can't be a priest, you're a *girl!*' Sisal jeered.

Outraged at being sneered at, and taken aback by his response, Miriam turned to Keelin, fixing her huge brown eyes on her confidently, 'I *can* be a priest, can't I, Soeur Michael?'

Keelin's heart sank as she gazed into the little girl's eyes and saw the hope and belief shining through.

'I'm sorry, *chérie*,' she murmured. 'It's not possible for a girl to become a priest.'

'Only *men* are priests,' interrupted Sisal triumphantly.

'But why, Soeur Michael? Why?' demanded Miriam, shocked.

Why indeed? thought Keelin despairingly as all the doubts and questions she'd suppressed roared back with the force of a tsunami.

At her weekly confession she was dismayed when Father Durand and not Monsignor Kelly pulled back the curtain in the confessional. Monsignor Kelly would always say, no matter what she confessed, 'You're doing your best my child, that's all any of us can do,' before giving her a light penance and sending her away. Would this new priest be full of righteous dogma, unable to understand what she was about to say? Would he accuse her of lacking humility and allowing her ego to dictate?

'Bless me, Father, for I have sinned. I am troubled, Father. I have grave doubts about my vocation.'

'Can you tell me your doubts, Sister?' came the calm response from the other side of the confessional.

'It's like this,' she said, and in a torrent of words, sometimes in English if she couldn't remember the word in French, Keelin unburdened herself to a stranger, a young man not much older than her, who too was in the service of God.

When she finished, a long silence pervaded the confessional and she almost held her breath waiting for words of derision to come her way. Eventually, she heard the priest say with a deep sigh, and in a sad, grave tone: 'Sister, I cannot help you. I am not the right person to hear your confession. I too have doubts. I agree with all you say. You have come here and mirrored my beliefs and brought up *my* reservations. Reservations I have struggled with since before my ordination. I too have been told it was ego. But, in truth, I don't agree. Suppression by the Church is, as I see it, a form of control. If it is any comfort to you, you are not alone,' Armand Durand said quietly, and she raised her eyes to his and in that moment felt a connection so deep and true, it took her breath away.

'Thank you, Father,' she whispered. 'I should leave now. I've been in here too long. My Sisters waiting outside will think I've committed many mortallers.'

'Mortaller? I do not know this word,' he spoke in English.

'Mortal sins,' Keelin explained. 'It's what we Irish call them.'

Father Durand smiled, making his lean, austere face look years younger.

'Indeed,' he agreed. 'But we will talk of this again, soon. Try to be unperturbed.' He raised his hand and murmured a blessing and she was sorry to leave the place where, for a few brief moments, peace had embraced her.

'You are not alone,' Father Durand had told her. He too had doubts. It couldn't *all* be ego.

Unable to sleep that night because of the turmoil she felt, Keelin put on her swimsuit and wrapped a towel around her and slipped down to the beach below them. It was dark but a million stars sparkled in the sky and a small sliver of moon threw rays of silver onto the shimmering sea. In the cove where the nuns bathed privately, Keelin padded barefoot over the sand to the sea and felt the waters embrace her – warm, soothing, ethereally welcoming. She floated on her back, looking at the stars, and felt at one with God and nature. If only she could always feel this peaceful, she reflected, but she knew that she could no longer carry on her life as a nun.

Her mother would be horrified now. Imelda hadn't wanted her to enter a convent, but she was now quite happy to boast about 'my daughter the nun'. Her father only wanted Keelin's happiness; he would support her whatever she decided. The least surprised person, Keelin felt, would be Brigid. Her aunt had tried to stop her from entering, knowing her niece and knowing the pitfalls ahead.

She would stay until after Christmas, and tell her Mother Superior on the first of January that she was leaving the Order, Keelin decided.

Relieved that she'd finally made her decision, Keelin swam in the star-lit sea for a while longer, knowing that she should make the most of such delightful pleasures for her final months on the Ivory Coast.

A month later, Father Durand was again hearing confessions. Keelin's heart thumped. They had become very friendly, making the most of their snatched conversations at the folk group rehearsals, discussing their doubts and reservations about the religious life and the inconsistencies of the religion they both practised.

Armand drew back the curtain in the little window between him and Keelin. She immediately dispensed with the formalities and blurted, 'I've made my decision, Armand. I'm leaving after Christmas.'

'Keelin, you're so brave,' he whispered back. 'I wish I had your courage.'

'I can't do it anymore. I can't live a lie. It all makes me so unhappy,' she confided.

'I wish I could talk to you properly, unafraid that Germaine will chastise you. It's so frustrating.'

A brainwave struck Keelin. 'I often go swimming in the cove at night. It's beautiful. Why don't we meet there tonight soon after lights out at ten? We can talk about everything.'

'It would be a great cause for scandal if we were caught,' he said doubtfully.

'Well, I'd better get out of here or we'll be the subject of scandal in the confessional too,' she said crossly. 'I'm going swimming tonight, if you're there you're there, if you're not, you're not. *Adieu*, Armand,' she said, not even bothering to make a confession.

'It's you and your good name I was thinking of,' he said quietly.

She apologized, wishing she hadn't snapped at him. 'I'd better go.'

She was on tenterhooks all day. Would Armand join her in the cove? Or was she fooling herself that feelings had developed between them?

That night, wrapped in her towel, she slipped like a wraith down to the cove. Her heart sank when she saw Armand wasn't there and Keelin cursed herself for behaving like a love-struck teenager. She dived into the glistening sea and swam parallel to the shore, feeling alive and unrestricted, her hair stuck damply to her face, unhindered by the veil. As she turned on her back to float under the stars, she caught sight of Armand's shadowy figure striding along the beach. She waved and he waved back and her heart lifted with happiness. How lovely to be able to speak in peace at last. They had so much to talk about.

She heard the splash as he dived in and swam towards her. 'I came,' he murmured, his white teeth glinting as he smiled in the semi moonlight.

'Isn't it beautiful?' Keelin threw her arms wide, encompassing the magnificence around them.

'I brought some wine and bread and cheese,' he said, floating beside her. She had never felt so happy in her life.

'Have a swim and then we'll have our picnic,' she said. 'Race you.'

He beat her easily, his long powerful strokes slicing through the water. She was breathless and laughing when she caught up with him. 'This is such fun,' she grinned. 'I feel like a child on the mitch.'

'The mitch? What is that?' he asked, smiling back at her.

'Skipping class.'

'It's so sad. We're adults and something as natural as this make us feel like naughty children.' He looked stern in the moonlight.

'I know, I can't stand not being treated like an adult any-more. I can't go on with this. Germaine chastised me today for having a stain on my habit. One of the kids knocked over my juice by accident. I'm a teacher, for God's sake, not a mannequin,' Keelin exclaimed irately. 'It's a load of nonsense.'

Armand laughed. '"Nonsense"! I love it. Could you imagine the RM and the bishop if we said that to them?'

'He'd have us excommunicated immediately and Germaine would have me packing so fast I wouldn't have time to bless myself!' Keelin remarked, laughing.

'I love you,' Armand said, staring at her intently.

'I love you too,' she said simply, smiling at him, utterly carefree and joyful.

He reached for her and drew her to him and under the African moon they kissed so tenderly and lovingly that Keelin knew with every atom of her being that she and Armand were meant for each other.

'Now it won't be hard for me to leave the Church,' he murmured as they held each other tightly. 'This feels so right. I thought I would be consumed with anxiety, guilt and doubts, even shame. I feel none of these emotions. I simply feel happy.'

'Me too,' Keelin agreed with heartfelt empathy. 'I think our theological discussions have made it much easier for us. Or it could be that I'm just not a very good nun.'

'You're a great nun,' he assured her, kissing her neck and shoulder. 'But I'm not the ideal priest.'

'You're *my* ideal priest, Armand,' Keelin murmured. 'So kind and compassionate and unjudgemental. You know the kids love you and so do your parishioners. You never scare them with talk of a wrathful God, you only talk about the love of God.'

Armand sighed. 'The bishop told me off about that. He's advised me that my sermons should focus more on the commandments and the severe consequences of breaking them.' He took her hand and they walked out of the sea to where their towels were laid. He wrapped her towel tenderly around her and set out their picnic. They devoured the cheese and bread, hungry after their swim and then she laid her head against his damp chest, loving the sound of his heart beating so steadily beneath her cheek.

'This is paradise,' she murmured.

'Some would think that you and I will go to hell for committing this mortal sin of being happy in each other's company.' Armand gave a wry smile, his arms tightening around her.

'I don't think we're committing sin. This feels so loving, so peaceful. In your arms, I feel I've come home,' Keelin said, stroking his jaw, which had a hint of bristly stubble.

'That's *exactly* how I feel, Keelin, You have put it into the most perfect words,' Armand exclaimed and they stared at each other in the darkness before they kissed with a passion that left them both breathless.

'I should go,' Armand drew away from her. 'If I don't, you know what will happen.'

'I want it to happen,' Keelin sighed, bereft, as they stood not touching.

'It will, when the time is right,' Armand promised her. 'I

am on my parish visits for three days; I'll see you when I get back. *Bonne nuit, chérie.*' He kissed her chastely on the cheek and then he was gone, loping up the beach, disappearing into the darkness.

The loneliness Keelin felt watching him go was indescribable. Three days seemed such a long time when they had so much to talk about, and so much to plan. She tightened her towel around her and hurried back to the convent, alternating between moments of great joy and loss.

How her heart lifted when she saw him striding across the grounds to say Mass the following Sunday. The Monsignor was feeling poorly and Armand was taking his place. But once in the small chapel, with the Reverend Mother, her fellow Sisters, and the lay congregation, she felt a strange disquiet. Armand was about to say Mass and she would have to take communion from him. It seemed so hypocritical to pretend she was devout and demure when she was neither. Keelin knew she couldn't do it.

'I feel a little dizzy. I have to leave,' she murmured to the nun beside her, who stood up to let her pass. As discreetly as possible she walked quietly down the side aisle as everyone stood to welcome Armand to the altar.

For form's sake she should go to the infirmary, she supposed, and wait for Sister Frances. Reverend Mother would want to know why Keelin wasn't at Mass.

'I think I have a migraine coming on, may I go to my room and lie down for an hour?' she said dolefully. The nun took Keelin's pulse.

'Racing a bit. Show me your tongue,' Francis ordered. She was a wiry little Scottish woman who had worked in Africa all her life.

'It's only a dizzy headache, Sister. A cool cloth and a dark room will help.'

'If it doesn't clear, come back to me. And drink plenty of water,' her colleague instructed, and Keelin hurried along the arched corridor and crossed the courtyard to where her room was. She could hear the singing in the chapel and tears came to her eyes.

By Friday of the next week, Keelin still hadn't seen Armand. The Monsignor had recovered enough to say their daily Mass and Keelin went about her duties heavy-hearted, wondering had she dreamed the encounter in the cove. She was angry with Armand that he wouldn't make an effort to see her. Perhaps he was rethinking what had happened. Maybe he was overpowered by guilt.

She was sitting on the steps, reading aloud to her pupils as usual, when she saw him walk across the lawn with the Reverend Mother. He glanced in her direction and he seemed to be shaking his arms as if they were caught in his surplice and then she realized he was giving her a subtle sign. Swimming, that was it; Armand wanted to meet her at the cove. She nodded her head but barely glanced at him. Reverend Mother Germaine was as sharp as a tack.

The day seemed to go on forever but she put on her best façade while inwardly sizzling with impatience. She made herself lie on her bed after lights out, so thankful that in this convent she didn't have to share or sleep in a dormitory.

At ten-fifteen she was on the beach, wrapped in her towel, and Armand was waiting for her. He took her hand and led her to a small sheltered stretch of beach behind some rocks and wordlessly they kissed and caressed, holding each other tightly, whispering words of love.

'I want us to make love,' Keelin whispered.

'So do I,' Armand murmured against her ear. 'But this will be the road of no return for us. Are you sure?'

'Very, she said emphatically. 'Are you?'

'Very,' he echoed smiling at her in the moonlight. 'I found some condoms in my predecessor's bedside locker. Perhaps he left them for me,' Armand said awkwardly. 'You know some priests don't keep their vows of celibacy.'

'Well, here's one nun who won't be keeping hers,' Keelin teased, touched by his embarrassment, drawing his head down to hers before sliding the top of her bathing suit down to her waist.

'I will have no shame with you, Armand. I give you my love and my body freely,' she whispered placing one of his hands on the round curve of her breast and gasping with pleasure when his thumb caressed her hard nipple. He pressed her body close against him and she felt a wild and wanton surge of delight at his arousal. This was what her body was made for, Keelin thought, exhilarated, as they lay down together on his towel and brought each other to heights of pleasure neither of them could have imagined.

It was after their second time that Armand realized the condom had burst. '*Mon Dieu*,' he muttered, horrified. 'Oh Keelin, I pray I have not made you pregnant.'

Satiated, euphoric, Keelin nestled against his broad chest, loving the roughness of the dark patch of hair against her cheek. 'If I was to have your baby I would think it the greatest gift I was ever given,' Keelin said tenderly, knowing that there was no going back for her now. Once the first of January came, she was renouncing the veil and taking her place in the world again.

CHAPTER TWENTY-EIGHT

Keelin realized that she was pregnant days before Christmas. Her period was late, she felt constantly nauseous and her boobs were sore. She *knew* she was pregnant. So much for her grandiose notions of a baby being her greatest gift, she thought in utter dismay. Yes, it would be wonderful to be expecting a child if she and Armand were lay people and married, but they were nun and priest, without a penny between them. She raged at the unfairness of it all. She and Armand had only made love twice. Now what was she going to do? Where was she going to go? An unmarried mother and ex-nun hadn't many prospects.

The next morning at Lauds, she felt overcome with nausea and had to leave the chapel. Later, after breakfast, Mère Germaine accosted her on her way to class. 'Soeur Michael, I'm concerned. This is the second time you've had to leave the chapel during prayers. You're looking pale. I think we should have the doctor take a look at you.'

'The second time?' Keelin said, confused, and horrified that the Reverend Mother was taking a keen interest in her health.

'One Sunday at Mass,' came the stern response. Reverend Mother Germaine was an excellent administrator but she'd no warmth, nor empathy.

'Oh yes, I forgot that,' Keelin said flustered, remembering her alleged 'dizzy' spell. 'I'm fine, Reverend Mother,' she said brightly. 'I ... eh ... think I ate too much fruit yesterday and it had an effect on me this morning. I suffered a migraine episode that Sunday,' she fibbed weakly wilting under her Superior's laser-like stare.

'Moderation in all things is advisable, even eating fruit, Soeur Michael. Remember that!' came the cold response before the Reverend Mother swept down the corridor, robes fluttering in the breeze.

Keelin felt herself break out in a cold sweat and nearly puked on the spot. No one ever wanted an eagle-eyed Reverend Mother's keen attention. She least of all in her present predicament.

Armand had been visiting the outlying parishes some hundreds of miles away, so she couldn't tell him the news. Her constant queasiness made her more forlorn but she tried her best for the sake of her pupils to pretend to be excited and happy about their forthcoming Nativity play.

Oh the irony of it, she thought that Christmas Eve when young Lelia, who was playing the part of the Virgin Mary, discreetly pulled the baby doll from under the manger and placed it on the straw, signifying the birth of Jesus. If only it were that simple and that painless. Ibraham, who was playing St Joseph, stood proudly beside Lelia, beaming at the audience, the epitome of a proud father.

Keelin saw Armand enter quietly and stand at the back of the chapel and her heart twisted with anxiety. She would have to try and tell him her news tonight at the Christmas Eve party, but there would be no opportunity to talk for long. He would have to mingle with the parents and children and the other nuns, as she would.

'*Bon nuit*,' Armand murmured, coming to stand beside her at the buffet a while later. Keelin kept her head down and placed a slice of mango on her plate; although her throat was so constricted she felt she could hardly eat.

'*Oíche mhaith*,' she said, trying to ignore her Reverend Mother's sharp-eyed stare. Keelin had been teaching Armand Irish so she added '*Nollaig shona dhuit*,' to wish him a happy Christmas.

One of the children tripped over another and a plate smashed in pieces. There were squawks of dismay and flurries to get the broken pieces off the floor and while Mère's and everyone else's attention was elsewhere, she whispered urgently. 'I'm pregnant.'

'*Mon Dieu!*' he uttered, his face turning ashen.

For one awful moment she thought he was going to abandon her and leave her to endure the future alone and then she heard him say, 'I am with you. We will face this together,' before someone came to claim his attention.

*

Later, at midnight Mass, she tried not to look at Armand as he concelebrated with the Monsignor. His lean jaw was tight and tense, and she knew he was in turmoil. If only he had been hearing confessions earlier there would have been some time to talk privately, but it had been the Monsignor who had been in the confessional and she'd said nothing about no longer being celibate.

Keelin tried to sing the old familiar hymns but the memories of home that they evoked tugged at her heart and she wondered how her parents would react to the news that she was carrying a child and would be leaving the religious life. Her father would hear the news with stoic acceptance, her mother would be furious. Imelda would take a long time to forgive this transgression, Keelin knew.

The morning after Christmas Day she excused herself from breakfast and narrowly made it to the toilet in time to be sick. Afterwards she leaned her head against the cool marble tiles and waited for her stomach to settle. She splashed water on her face, dried it and opened the bathroom door to find Reverend Mother Germaine outside. 'Please follow me to my office,' she instructed coldly and swept ahead of Keelin, who followed with an enormous sense of dread.

'Sit please.' The Reverend Mother pointed imperiously to a wicker chair in front of her desk. Keelin did as she was bid. The other nun remained standing, staring at her with cold, hooded grey eyes.

'Are you pregnant, Soeur? Is this the reason for your morning sickness, pallor and lack of appetite?'

Keelin's heart thumped. She could deny it, but what was the point?

'Yes,' she said calmly. 'I wish to leave the Order and renounce the veil.'

'Who is the father?' the Reverend Mother asked grimly.

'It doesn't matter.'

'I *demand* to know!' Germaine's eyes were flashing with anger at being spoken to with such a lack of respect.

Keelin stood up. 'Reverend Mother, with respect, that is my business, not yours.'

'Go to your room and pray and return to this office at eleven a.m. I need to contact the Mother House. I should have sent you back to Nigeria when they wanted to recall you for your novitiate, but I argued to keep you here for another six months because you're a good teacher. What a *fool* I was. Get out of my sight,' Germaine dismissed her, puce with temper.

It's done now, thought Keelin, feeling strangely liberated, lying on her bed, overcome by weariness. She yawned and closed her eyes, her hands slipping down to her belly, hardly able to believe that she was pregnant. Her eyes drooped. She slept.

A loud rapping on the door woke her and she sat up hastily, not knowing where she was. Flashes of memory filtered into her consciousness. She glanced at her watch and saw that it was eleven-fifteen. She was late for her meeting.

She opened the door to find Mother Germaine standing

there. 'I do *not* appreciate being kept waiting, Soeur. Pack your case, please. You're leaving immediately.' She handed Keelin her suitcase.

'Leaving! *Now*? Where am I going?' Keelin was shocked.

'Ismael will drive you to the convent in Abidjan. From there, you will be put on a flight to France. Please hurry. Your sinful presence dishonours our convent,' Germaine added viciously.

'Wait a minute, Reverend Mother,' she protested. 'I've people I wish to say goodbye to, my friends, my colleagues, the—'

'You are allowed to speak to no one. Pack!' Mother Germaine hissed, the nostrils on her sharp aquiline nose flaring. 'Be ready in ten minutes.' She turned on her heel and stalked wrathfully along the corridor.

Keelin was stunned. 'Horrible bitch,' she muttered, closing the door. Although she didn't have a lot to pack, her hands shook as she folded her habits and nightwear and few small personal items and books that she owned. She hadn't expected instant dismissal and so swift a return to France. Would the Mother General in Paris be as unforgiving as her subordinate in San-Pédro? What was to become of her? Keelin's stomach knotted in anxiety. Was there any way she could contact Armand to let him know what was going on?

She wasn't a prisoner! But she'd no money, not even enough to phone her father to get him to wire some to her.

Ten minutes later, to the second, Germaine knocked peremptorily on the door. Keelin picked up her suitcase and with her head held high marched past her Reverend Mother. Because it was the Christmas holidays, the usual hustle and bustle was absent. No children in classrooms. No patients in the small clinic on the compound. The convent was silent; none of her colleagues walking hither and yon as they normally would on a busy weekday. She heard laughter from the common room where some of the Sisters were relaxing. She would miss the friends she'd made, and she'd miss her beloved pupils. A lump rose in her throat but she swallowed it down. She wouldn't let Germaine see her distress. She had some pride.

The young Ivoirian driver was waiting on the wide front step and he took her case and put it in the boot of the car. 'Drive *directly* to the convent with Soeur Michael, please, Ismael,' Germaine instructed. 'I've left instructions that you be fed and rested before you make your return journey. I will see you anon.' She glanced at Keelin, 'You have let your God, your Order, me, our community, your pupils and yourself down.'

'And *you* don't have one ounce of Christian charity, and that is *your* shame!' Keelin retorted and felt some satisfaction when she saw the nun flush crimson with anger.

Ismael's jaw dropped, his brown eyes darting from one to the other. He couldn't *believe* a nun had just cheeked Mère Germaine. Keelin walked around to the passenger side of the car, got in and stared straight ahead. When they drove through the wrought-iron gates, she never looked back.

CHAPTER TWENTY-NINE

'You cannot stay here in Paris for the remainder of your pregnancy. You understand that we have a duty to our postulants and novices. You would be a bad example to them, Soeur Michael,' Mother General Perpetua said in her soft voice that was, nevertheless, steely firm.

'Where can I go?' Keelin asked wearily. She was exhausted after the long, bumpy flight from Abidjan.

'I'm arranging for you to be sent to a mother-and-baby home in Cork. They will also arrange for the adoption of your baby. As you have not taken final vows, you will be leaving our Order. Your family will have to assume responsibility for you.' The Mother General looked at her appraisingly. 'I'm sure you would like to rest after your journey. You will be taken to guest quarters; please remain there. Your meals will be brought to you and you will be collected for your flight home tomorrow, when the arrangements are made.'

'I'm not to contaminate the community with direct contact, is that it?' Keelin said bitterly.

'Something like that, yes, if you wish me to be blunt.' The nun did not dodge the question.

'I'd like to make a phone call to my parents and my Aunt Brigid, please,' Keelin said firmly.

'Very well. You may use my phone. I will provide Mère Brigid's number for you, or do you have it?'

'No, Mère,' Keelin said.

'Dial zero for the receptionist and ask her to put you through.' She flicked through a Rolodex on her desk and wrote the number on a notelet.

'I'd like to speak to my relatives privately,' Keelin said politely.

'Ten minutes,' Perpetua instructed, sweeping out of the room.

Keelin swallowed hard when she finally heard her aunt's voice on the crackly line. 'Auntie Brigid, Mère, it's me, Keelin. I've something to tell you: I'm pregnant.'

'Oh Lord, Keelin.' Brigid couldn't hide her shock. 'You weren't raped, dear, were you?' The dismay and anxiety in her aunt's voice almost brought Keelin to tears.

'No, Mère. Nothing like that. It was consensual. With a man I love and who loves me,' she assured her aunt.

'Well, that is something to be thankful for, I suppose. Who is this man, may I ask?

'His name is Armand. He's—' now that she had to tell her aunt she found it awkward – 'he's a priest,' she murmured.

'A *priest*!' Keelin cringed at the shock and dismay in her

aunt's voice. 'He'll never leave for you. I know that. I've seen it too often out there,' Brigid exclaimed.

'He was going to leave anyway, before he met me,' Keelin said, almost in tears.

'Ah, they all say that,' Brigid sighed. 'Have you told Germaine?'

'Oh yes, she knows. I'm actually in Paris – she got rid of me the moment she heard,' Keelin said bitterly. 'And the Mother General has said I can't stay here or in *any* convent. She's sending me to a mother-and-baby home in Cork, and she told me the family have to take responsibility for me. I can imagine Mam's reaction to *that*!' she said despondently.

'You are *not* going to any mother-and-child home, Keelin, I can tell you that right now,' Brigid said grimly. 'Leave it with me. I'll ring Perpetua myself. I'll phone you back, dear,' she assured her niece.

'Can you give it ten minutes? I'm in her office. I've to ring Mam and tell her. I wanted to ring you first. I'll ring you back when I've spoken to her.'

'Keelin, I hate to say this, but be prepared for your mother's wrath. I don't think Imelda will take your news well,' Brigid said matter-of-factly. 'And perhaps don't tell her yet that the baby's father is a priest. She has a dislike of them.'

'I know that. It will be bad enough telling her I'm pregnant – then again, she *might* surprise us . . .' Keelin said hesitantly.

'She might indeed,' Brigid replied with false optimism. 'I'll talk to you after you've spoken to Imelda.'

'Thanks so much, Mère.' Keelin hung up the phone. Her aunt's concerns about Armand leaving the priesthood for her had shaken her to her core. Brigid had been on the Missions for years. She knew what went on. She was far more of a realist than Keelin had ever been. With trembling fingers she dialled the international code for home and followed it with the telephone number she knew so well.

Keelin felt a knot of apprehension. She hoped her father might be home from work to take the call. She longed to hear his comforting, reassuring voice and feel his arms around her. Then she needed to find a way to contact Armand.

She had to know what his intentions were towards her and their child. Everything had happened so quickly since her confrontation with Germaine.

Keelin's heart sank when she heard her mother's 'Hello'.

'Hi, Mam, it's me.' She didn't even bother to put on a cheery façade.

'Keelin! My goodness, I wasn't expecting a phone call from Africa. How are you? Is something up? You wouldn't be ringing home otherwise,' Imelda asked immediately.

No flies on her mother, Keelin thought ruefully. 'Actually, I'm not phoning from the Ivory Coast, I'm in Paris.'

'Paris! What on earth are you doing there? You're not sick or anything, are you?' Her mother, picking up on the despondency in Keelin's tone, was instantly alert.

'I'm pregnant and I'm coming home tomorrow. I was wondering if you'd collect me from the airport?' Keelin said, figuring it might be good for her mother to have twenty-four hours' notice so that she could be over the shock before they met face to face.

'*What!*'

'I'm pregnant,' Keelin repeated dully.

'Was it your own doing?'

'Yes!' Keelin sighed, imagining Imelda with pursed lips and narrowed eyes standing in the hall at home.

'I *knew* nothing good would come from you entering the convent. I said it. I said it would end in tears and no one would listen to me,' Imelda ranted. 'You won't be coming home here in that state. I'm telling you that straight away. Pregnant! And you a nun! How could you, Keelin? Have I not got enough to put up with, without this? I won't have disgrace brought on the good name of the family. I'm not going to be standing in the shop having the gossips in the town talking about you. Absolutely not. You go to your aunt and let her look after you. It's all her fault that you went traipsing off to Africa. Let *her* deal with it, Keelin, because I'm not having anything to do with it.' Imelda slammed down the phone, leaving Keelin staring at the handset, tears sliding down her cheeks.

'Mère Brigid, I was expecting to hear from you.' The soft birdlike tones of Mother General Perpetua came down the line. Perpetua might be tiny and birdlike but she'd a will of iron and ruled the Order with a steely determination that bordered on tyranny.

Summoning all the courage she had, although inwardly

she was quaking, Brigid said coolly, 'I've just spoken to my niece.'

'Ah yes, Soeur Michael. Very unfortunate indeed. Luckily, she hasn't taken her final vows. That would be an even greater disgrace.'

'And it would be *our* disgrace, Mère Perpetua, if she was put on the street. Her mother won't let her come home. She has nowhere to go.'

'She's not a *professed* nun. She can leave at any time,' Perpetua said icily.

'Nevertheless, she's a nun of our Order and in our Order she will stay until she decides what to do after her baby is born.'

'Are *you* telling *me* what to do, Mère Brigid?' Perpetua couldn't believe her ears.

'If you will let me continue, I will propose a solution,' Brigid heard herself say, equally coldly. Fortunately, her Superior couldn't see the pen trembling in her hand. 'I propose that Soeur Michael stay here in Limerick with me for the duration of her pregnancy and then we will see what is to become of her and the child. It is a solution I believe Our Lord and His Holy Mother would bless. We are, after all, an Order that gives *succour*,' Brigid added slyly.

'I couldn't sanction that! She would be a bad example to the novices and postulants. Under *no* circumstances will I agree,' Perpetua rallied.

As though a voice whispered to her, Brigid heard 'the Four Winds'.

'Very well, then. She can stay in the Four Winds, away from the postulants and novices.' Brigid strove to keep the desperation out of her voice.

There was a long silence on the phone. 'I'm very concerned that this would set a precedent. All those young nuns with their feminist views. Vatican Two was a catastrophe.'

'Times are changing and we must change with them,' Brigid said calmly.

'I wonder, did I make a mistake in promoting you?' Perpetua said snippily.

'I'm trying to find a Christ-like, merciful solution, Mother General. I feel at fault in a way. It was because of me that my niece entered the convent.'

'Very well, but under no circumstances is she *ever* to set foot in your convent in Limerick.'

'Thank you, Mother General; I will make sure she doesn't. *Bonne journée.*' Brigid hung up immediately in case Perpetua changed her mind. She was taut with tension. She rested her head in her hands, taking deep, calming breaths before redialling the number. The nun on the switchboard in Paris must be wondering what on earth was going on, she thought as she asked to speak to Keelin.

'Hello, dear. It's sorted. You're going to live in the Four Winds until you have your baby, and for as long as you need afterwards. I'll check your arrival time with the airport tomorrow and I'll collect you,' Brigid said crisply. 'Don't be worrying about anything else. Just get yourself home.'

'Oh, Auntie Brigid, I'm so grateful. I can never thank you enough.' Keelin burst into tears of relief.

'Don't get upset. All will be well,' Brigid said reassuringly. 'Now try to stay out of Perpetua's way, and if she says anything to you be as humble as you can. She can be mercurial.'

'Yes, Mère. I'm very sorry I've brought shame on you,' Keelin answered shakily.

'You haven't brought shame on me.' Brigid's heart ached for her niece. If only she knew, she thought in despair, wondering what Keelin would think if she knew Brigid's truth, and that she was living the greatest lie of all pretending to be pure and undefiled. 'It could happen to any of us. Come home, dear, and we will get through it together. Stop crying now, it's not good for the baby,' her aunt instructed. 'Go and rest and I'll see you tomorrow. Good night, dear.'

'Goodnight, Mère,' Keelin gulped, hanging up the phone. The doors of the convent were firmly closed against her. Her mother had disowned her, but Brigid would stand beside her come what may, and knowing that gave Keelin the courage to face the future and whatever lay ahead.

CHAPTER THIRTY

She didn't know who she was angrier with, Imelda or the Mother General! Or that bloody priest. How could they all turn their backs on a young pregnant girl, in this day and age? It was the eighties, not the fifties; gone were the days when young girls who 'got into trouble' were spirited away to a life of misery. Imelda was Keelin's birth mother, and the Mother General her spiritual one, yet neither of them had shown one ounce of motherly compassion to her.

No one knew better than she did the utter trepidation and loneliness Keelin was feeling right now. How well Brigid remembered, even after all these years, the terror and dawning realisation that *she* was pregnant, when her period was a month late, and she was feeling sick when she woke up every morning, after her final encounter with Johnny Larkin. What would become of her final she'd thought in despair. She'd have to leave Ardcloch and take the boat to England, so as not to shame her family. Or else go to one of those grim places that girls whispered about when someone 'got into trouble'. The Magdalene laundries, the 'holy' workhouses or the mother-and-baby homes struck fear in every young girl's heart.

The parish priest of Ardcloch had taken Lorna Murphy to a Magdalene laundry in Limerick and she'd escaped after having her baby, and drowned herself in the Shannon, because the nuns had taken the child from her and sold it to an American couple. Mrs Murphy had let out a blood-curdling scream that half the village had heard when the priest had come to tell them the news. 'Murderer!' she'd shouted. The poor woman never got over her daughter's suicide.

And Imelda knew this! Wasn't she fearful for Keelin's future? Her own daughter?

And what of Larry? Brigid would have expected more of him. Keelin was the apple of his eye. But then he was so hen-pecked he did everything he was told, Brigid mused, closing the door to her book-lined office in the convent in Limerick.

Brigid couldn't help the pangs of guilt that assailed her. If she hadn't written to Keelin about her life on the Missions, her niece might never have joined the Order. Imelda had been furious with her. But Imelda was always furious with someone, Brigid thought crossly, picking up the phone to ring the housekeeper in the Four Winds to tell her to prepare a room for Keelin, and to say she'd be staying a few days herself. The Four Winds was never too busy in December and January, so Brigid was quite sure there'd be beds for them.

It would be nice to spend a few days by the sea in that homely old house, she thought, flicking through the Rolodex on her desk to find the number. Keelin had said that she loved the priest who got her pregnant. But did *he* love her and would he stand by her? With all her heart she hoped so, but she had her doubts. Being a single mother in a judgemental society was a hard path to tread, as Keelin was already discovering, and there but for the Grace of God was a path Brigid had once thought she would walk herself.

Thinking about the baby she'd lost all those years ago brought a lump to Brigid's throat. Taking care of the babies in Senegal had helped heal the gaping wound that her miscarriage had caused. But here in the convent in Limerick there were no children, no babies to hold and cuddle and she missed that part of her life more than words could say. She was going to be a great-aunt in more ways than one, she reminded herself. Keelin's baby couldn't come at a better time in Brigid's life.

'But she's our daughter, Imelda. Of course she can come home! I'm going to phone that convent right now and tell her so! How could you be so heartless?' Larry raged at his wife. She'd just told him that Keelin had phoned to say she was pregnant and was coming back to Ireland, but under no circumstances would she be taking her in.

'I told her it would all end in tears. I knew the life of a nun wouldn't suit her. I said it and you all pooh-poohed me. But I was right, Larry. No one ever *listens* to me.' Imelda glowered at her husband. 'Brigid got her into this, Brigid can take responsibility for her.'

'But she's not Brigid's daughter, she's ours. And she's having a baby. Our grandchild! For God's sake, Imelda, have you no feelings?' Larry was aghast at his wife's intransigence.

'Don't you dare talk to me about feelings, Larry O'Brien, after what you put me through,' Imelda shouted. 'Everyone will be talking about her. It's bad enough leaving the convent, but coming home *pregnant* – the gossips will have a field day. She won't be able to walk down the street without someone pointing a finger at her. Is that what you want for her? For me?'

'People are kind, Imelda; it will be a sensation for a few days and then they'll forget about it,' Larry tried to appease his wife.

'Would you listen to yourself? "People are kind"!' she snorted. 'You know as well as I do, there'll be people in this town that will be delighted to see us get our comeuppance. People who think we've got notions because we hauled ourselves up by our bootstraps to become the elite of the town.'

'The "elite"? What are you talking about, Imelda?'

'Yes, the elite. We're up there with the priests, the doctor, the teachers, the creamery owner. You're one of the biggest businessmen in Glencarraig. Sure, don't I get it every day – "You wouldn't know what it's like to have to do your own shopping and carry your own bags anymore."' Imelda put on a sneery, sing-song voice. '"Sure aren't you *loaded*?"'

'Ah, you'll always get people like that in any town.' He shrugged.

'Yes, you will. Begrudgery is part and parcel of who we are, and that's why when shame befalls us, people enjoy it and rub our noses in it. I won't have it, Larry. I've had enough to put up with over the years. Why is it *I* have to endure the consequences of other people's bad behaviour and no one gives a shite about me? I'm sick of it, Larry. Sick! Sick! Sick of it! Do you hear me?' Her face was blotchy red, her eyes sparking with fury.

'The whole *town* can hear you, Imelda,' Larry snapped. 'I'm going up to Dublin to collect Keelin from the airport tomorrow whether you like it or not.'

'Do what you like. Do what you bloody well like, Larry,' Imelda shouted as she left the room, slamming the door behind her.

'God Almighty,' muttered her husband, at his wits' end. There were times when he longed to walk away from his life in Glencarraig and never look back. He and Imelda had come to an uneasy truce years ago, and in fairness to his wife, she'd put the children first. But whenever she found life difficult, she would fling the past in his face. It would never end, Larry thought wearily, thumbing through the address book on the hallstand to find Brigid's number.

'I need to talk to you, Monsignor,' Armand said agitatedly.

'Is that so? "I need to talk" nearly always indicates something serious is up. Pour us both a drop of the hard stuff, if that's the case.' The Monsignor pulled himself up in his chair while Armand got two glasses and poured a measure of whiskey into each of them, a larger measure for the Monsignor than for himself.

'I've made a girl pregnant.'

'Ah, *Armand*!' Did you not use a johnnie when you were dippin' your wick? Have you young lads no sense?' The Monsignor shook his head in exasperation. 'I hope she's over age?' he added sharply.

'She is, and I *did* use a condom. The damn thing burst.' Armand sat down on the chair opposite his parish priest.

'Well, we have to get the girl properly looked after. That's the important thing. We can put her living with a family away from here. We'll pay them to take care—'

'It's one of the nuns, Monsignor.' Armand explained wretchedly.

'Ah Chrisht above.' Monsignor Kelly's Irish accent got more pronounced. 'Do ye meant to tell me I'm going to have that she-devil Germaine breathing down me neck? Oh Almighty God, what did I do to deserve this torment?' the Monsignor groused. 'Does she know yet?'

'I don't think so,' Armand muttered. 'Keelin, I mean Sister Michael, only told me on Christmas Eve and I never got a chance to speak to her because of going up country.'

'Ah, the little Irish lass. God love her.' The Monsignor shook his head. 'What were the pair of you thinking?'

'We love each other. We both want to leave Holy Orders. It's not the life for us. I was troubled before I met her. She knew she wasn't going to take her final vows; I suppose this will make up both of our minds for us.'

255

'I knew this life wasn't for you,' the old priest said heavily. 'You can't cope with the injustice of it all. You younger ones want to change the Church and its injustices more than you want to spread the word of God. Have a bite to eat and go to bed, we'll meander over to the convent together tomorrow and see how the land lies,' he said gruffly.

Armand felt a great worry slide from his shoulders, knowing that the kind old man did not judge him, or Keelin, and he would do his best for them. The greatest relief of all was knowing that the internal struggle about his vocation, or lack of it, was finally over.

Armand felt a new sense of purpose as he assisted the Monsignor in Mass the following morning. He tried to locate Keelin but couldn't see her with her fellow Sisters. Reverend Mother Germaine was stern-faced as always, but today she seemed particularly thin-lipped. The niggle of anxiety increased to a full-scale blast and after Mass, disrobing in the small sacristy, Armand whispered to the Monsignor, 'I didn't see Keelin out there.'

'Stay calm, lad, they'll be offering us tay and breakfast. Let's see what the RM has to say. You say *nothing*. Maybe the girl is sick.'

'I suppose if I ask about her it might seem odd?'

'Whatever you do, don't mention her name in front of that Germaine one. I'll try and suss out what, if anything, is going on. Say nothing now!' the old priest warned.

*

Pascal, the houseboy, had barely finished clearing away the dishes when Reverend Mother Germaine swept into the small dining room.

'I trust your breakfast was satisfactory, Fathers,' she said in her cool, clipped tone.

'Very tasty, Reverend Mother,' Monsignor Kelly answered genially. 'Are you and the Sisters enjoying the holidays?'

'We were, until I had to send one of our nuns back to France.' She gave Armand an unyielding stare. Dread swept through him but he held her gaze.

'Oh dear,' interjected Monsignor Kelly swiftly. 'Nothing serious, I hope.'

'*Extremely* serious!' The RM continued to stare at Armand. 'She was guilty of dishonouring her God, her Sisters here and her Order. *What* could be more serious than that?'

'I see,' the Monsignor said calmly, pouring himself another cup of tea. 'Father Durand?' He raised an eyebrow and held up the elegant silver teapot.

'Thank you, I will.' Armand managed to keep the shake out of his voice, taking his cue from the Monsignor.

'And apart from that unfortunate event, and we must remember that Jesus in His mercy and charity never condemns and always forgives,' Monsignor Kelly added pointedly, in the same matter-of-fact tone, topping up Armand's tea. 'Have the holidays been restful?'

'Quite,' snapped the Reverend Mother, who did not appreciate being chastised about her lack of mercy and charity in front of that young upstart of a priest, whom she suspected knew more about Soeur Michael's condition than he was letting on. Was he the father? They were always chatting and laughing together and singing with the folk group they had set up. Who else could it be? She'd racked her brains, even wondering if it were Ismael, who had a great teasing way with the younger nuns.

'I was gifted with half a dozen Nile perches up country, if you would like some, Reverend Mother . . . ?' Armand busied himself pouring milk into his tea.

'I'll send the cook up to you; you can discuss it with him. I have to go and see what arrangements I can make to replace Soeur Michael. I now have a class with *no* teacher and *you'll* need to find someone else to play the guitar for your folk group. She's left them in the lurch too,' Reverend Mother said frostily, glaring at Armand. He knew she was hoping for a reaction but resisted the urge to speak in Keelin's defence.

'God will provide,' Monsignor Kelly said mildly. 'Drink up, Father Durand, we have work to do ourselves.'

'Yes, a she-devil of the highest order, that Germaine,' Monsignor Kelly said irritably as he climbed into the jeep beside Armand. 'She's very old school. Sister Celsus, who plays the piano so beautifully, would be the ideal replacement for Germaine. She's from the Ivory Coast, did you know that?'

'I did not,' Armand said miserably, gunning the engine and scorching down the drive to swing out onto the Boulevard Houphouët-Boigny.

'Easy there, I'd like to get to Quartier de la Corniche alive!'

'*Pardon*,' Armand apologised glumly, slowing down.

'So my boy, your Irish lass has been sent back to France in disgrace. But at least she will be looked after. I want you to *seriously* think about whether you want to be laicized. It's a big step to turn your back on Holy Orders, and I don't want you to be regretting it in ten years' time.' Monsignor Kelly fished a packet of mints out of his cassock pocket and offered his companion one.

'*Merci, non.* I won't regret it. There's no peace of mind for me as it is, and that was the case even before I met Keelin. It shouldn't be such a struggle.' Armand overtook a ramshackle lorry, carrying a load of timber. 'It's time to go.'

The old priest sighed. 'All right so. I'll ring the bishop and tell him to start your laicization. Keep your powder dry, Armand. Germaine's in the dark.' Monsignor Kelly advised sagely. 'And let's keep her that way. The less she knows, the better for *all* of us,' he added, with a wry smile.

'I won't leave you in the lurch, Monsignor Kelly,' Armand promised. 'As you say, Keelin will be looked after by her Order. I'll contact her in Paris and tell her I'll go to her as soon as I can be replaced.'

'Dad, oh Daddy!' Keelin ran into her father's outstretched arms. She'd been expecting to see her aunt standing at the Arrivals barrier, and her heart had lifted in joy when she saw her father, a broad smile on his face, holding out his arms to her. She rested her head against the tweed of his coat, and knew she was home, safe and sound.

'You're home and that's the main thing. I spoke to Brigid and we'll work something out for you and your little baba, so don't be worrying,' Larry said comfortingly, taking her trolley as they headed for the car park.

'Mam will never forgive me,' Keelin sighed, tucking her arm into his.

'You and I know she is the way she is. But she's a good woman at heart, Keelin, don't forget that,' Larry said loyally. 'Part of the reason she doesn't want you to come home is that she's afraid you'll be the subject of gossip, and she doesn't want that for you. To be honest, neither do I.' Her father dropped some coins into the ticket machine. 'Now let's go and have a cuppa somewhere. I'm gasping for the tay.'

'I'd love a cup myself. A real good strong cup of tea and a rasher sandwich,' Keelin confided, relieved that he had not asked who the baby's father was. Larry was kind like that. He'd let her tell him in her own time.

'Dad, it's great to be home, I only wish it was under different circumstances,' Keelin said sadly.

'Everything happens for a reason, love, and your precious baby will bring joy to many. So chin up. Chest out. Best foot forward,' he smiled, quoting one of his favourite lines from her childhood.

Keelin laughed and felt a frisson of happiness for the first time since she'd found out she was pregnant.

When he'd finally got through to the convent in Paris, with the assistance of a helpful international operator, Armand had been politely told that Keelin was no longer there and that she'd flown to Ireland.

'Stay calm,' the Monsignor ordered. 'I remember she once told me her aunt was a nun in Senegal. Leave it with me and I'll try to find the number for the convent in Dakar and see if they can tell me how to find her. It's a bit late now to ring. I'll do it first thing in the morning.'

The following morning, Armand hurried to the small office, his heart thumping in his chest to hear what news there might be. 'Armand, I've located a number in Ireland. Seemingly the aunt is now a Reverend Mother and no longer in Senegal. She's in charge of a convent in Limerick. We're getting places, son. We're one hour behind them, do you want me to ring her now?'

'Oh please, Monsignor; let us not lose a moment. I will of course pay for the call.' Armand could hardly contain himself.

'Arrah, you will not,' the Monsignor said irascibly. 'The Vatican has plenty of money, they don't need yours – the little you have of it.'

Armand's mouth was dry as the operator connected them to the number in Ireland. *Please let me be able to contact Keelin*, he prayed fervently as he heard the Monsignor say politely: 'My name is Monsignor Patrick Kelly; I'm ringing form the Ivory Coast. Would it be possible to speak to Reverend Mother Brigid please?'

Armand heard a female voice on the other end but couldn't hear what she was saying. 'Thank you very much.

I appreciate your help,' Monsignor Kelly said, scribbling a number down on a pad.

'The Reverend Mother is in a place called the Four Winds, down the coast from Limerick,' he said, dialling the long international number.

Another conversation and then the Monsignor gave him the thumbs up and Armand heard him say, 'Good morning, Reverend Mother, I'm ringing from the Ivory Coast. I wonder could you help me? I'm trying to locate your niece, Sister Michael—'

He stopped speaking and Armand could hear the nun at the other end saying something.

'Excellent, excellent, he's here beside me.' He handed the phone to Armand and said reassuringly, 'She has her safe and sound.'

Armand took the phone, his heart skipping a beat when he heard Keelin's beloved voice. 'Hello, Armand, I'm here with my aunt in Ireland.' Her voice quivered and his heart went out to her.

'*Cherie*, I'm so sorry to be the cause of this for you. I've asked Monsignor to ask the bishop to start my laicization process. I'll be with you as soon as I can,' he said earnestly.

'Oh Armand, thank goodness.' He smiled, hearing the note of relief in her voice. 'I'll be fine here, don't worry about me,' she added reassuringly.

'I will worry about you and our child until the day I die, *mon amour*,' he assured her, wishing with all his heart that he was with her right now. 'I will be by your side soon.'

*

'I suppose the pair of them are calling me a right bitch,' Imelda said forlornly, watching Larry unpack his travelling bag. He'd stayed in a B&B in Butlersbridge for a few days while Keelin was settling in to the Four Winds.

'I did explain that the main reason you didn't want Keelin home was the finger-pointing and gossip she'd have to endure,' Larry said coolly. He knew of old that when Imelda was feeling guilty she either went on the defensive or put on the 'doleful me' act.

'Well, that's the truth,' she retorted.

'*Part* of the truth, Imelda. Be honest. You're ashamed of our daughter. But let me tell you, she's a great girl and I'll be helping her out financially.'

'That's fine with me,' Imelda muttered. It wasn't only shame she felt about Keelin, it was *disappointment*. Huge disappointment *for* her. Her daughter had been living a life *she* would have given anything to experience. A life of freedom in Dublin. Sharing a flat and having a great social life and, the icing on the cake, foreign holidays with her friends. And most importantly of all, being financially independent.

It was the throwing away of all of that, so carelessly and unthinkingly, that wounded Imelda. She'd been so proud of Keelin. Her daughter was a liberated woman. It was unfathomable to Imelda that she'd given it all up to join an organization that was stuck in the Middle Ages, keeping women firmly in their place.

And now Keelin was even more trapped. Penniless, pregnant and soon to be an unmarried mother in a society that had little sympathy for women in that situation. Could she not have used protection, if she was going to have sex? It was easy now for women to prevent pregnancy. How *could* she have been so stupid and foolish to turn her back on such privileges? She'd had it *all* – and she'd taken it for granted.

Let her stay in the Four Winds with Saint Brigid, Imelda thought bitterly. It was what she deserved.

CHAPTER THIRTY-ONE

'Oh God! My waters have broken, Una, and I'm getting terrible cramps,' Keelin gasped, puffing and panting her way into the kitchen, where Una was peeling spuds for the dinner. 'Am I in labour? The baby's not due for another three weeks.'

'Oh Jesus, Mary and Holy Sweet Saint Joseph,' Una exclaimed in dismay, assisting Keelin to a chair. 'I'll call Maura and tell her to ring Doctor McCormack. Or should we drive you to the hospital? It's a long enough journey in case anything happens on the way.' Una went to the kitchen door and yelled for her sister, who was upstairs changing beds. There had been a lot of nuns staying the previous week, but thankfully there was a lull in the big house.

'What's going on? Why are you yelling at poor Maura?' Sister Marie-Hélène limped into the kitchen on her crutches. She was recovering from a car accident, spending the summer in the Four Winds to recuperate and write her thesis.

'Marie-Hélène, Keelin's waters broke and we think she's in—'

Keelin groaned and doubled over as another spasm of pain engulfed her.

'Oh Lordy! What do we need? They always say hot water and towels—' Marie-Hélène looked panicked. She was the same age as Keelin, they had become good friends. 'Lie down and we'll time the contractions,' she said, helping Keelin up from the chair. 'Can you make it up to the bedroom?'

'I'm scared, Marie-Hélène,' Keelin confessed.

'Nothing to be scared of, Keelin. Giving birth's the most natural thing in the world,' the young nun said confidently. 'Maura, ring Doctor McCormack and tell him Keelin's in labour and he needs to get over here,' she instructed. Keelin felt a modicum of comfort at her friend's authoritative instructions and the way she was taking charge.

Another contraction hit and she felt a wave of sweat break out across her forehead. If Brigid were here, she'd know what to do, and how far gone she was – she'd helped to deliver babies in Africa – but it would be two hours before she got to Butlersbridge from Limerick, Keelin thought, trying not to panic.

'Doctor McCormack is out on a call. Mrs McCormack said she'll give him the message as soon as he gets back.' Maura hurried up the stairs after them. 'Why don't I go and get Katie Wickham? Everyone calls on Katie to come when there's a birth or death in the village,' she suggested.

'Great idea,' approved Marie-Hélène. 'Get her *now*, Maura.'

'Sure,' Maura agreed, clattering down the stairs at speed.

'You'll be grand, Keelin. We'd better get your drawers off ya, in case the baby surprises us,' Marie-Hélène grinned. And in spite of her labour pains, Keelin laughed at the irrepressible nun.

Two hours later, after a fast and intense labour, Marie-Claire Durand shot into the world in an almighty hurry. Katie Wickham and Doctor McCormack, Una and Marie-Hélène were there, urging Keelin on, while Maura supplied the hot water and, when required, hot sweet tea.

'Now child, here's your daughter, and she has a fine pair of lungs on her, and she's a grand size even if she's early,' Katie smiled at Keelin, placing the baby in her arms, having wiped her off after the doctor had cut the umbilical cord.

'Oh, look at her! Look at the head of hair on her! Oh, she's *beautiful*!' Keelin gazed in awe at her daughter.

'Just like her mama,' Marie-Hélène smiled, kissing the top of Keelin's head. 'You did great.'

'Thank you so much for helping me, Marie-Hélène, thank you, everyone,' Keelin said with heartfelt gratitude, stroking her baby's soft cheek.

'Thank Katie and Doctor McCormack, and thank God they were here. Because now that it's all over I have to tell you, like Prissy in *Gone with the Wind* once famously confessed to Scarlett O'Hara ... "I don't know nothin' 'bout birthin' babies",' Marie-Hélène admitted drolly.

'You should get a best actress award, then,' Keelin laughed, and then her baby opened her eyes and stared up at her, and

Keelin knew as she stared into those big blue orbs fringed by long black silky lashes that she was the luckiest, most blessed woman in the universe.

'Awww, Keelin.' A voice at the door made them all turn. It was Brigid, newly arrived from Limerick, and she hurried over to kiss her niece.

'Do you want to hold her, Mère?' Keelin gazed up at her aunt who had been such a stalwart support to her and Armand.

'Oh yes, more than you'll ever know,' Brigid exclaimed, taking the tiny bundle into her arms and tenderly kissing her grand-niece's downy head. 'So here you are!' she murmured. 'I couldn't be happier.'

'Well now, isn't she the most beautiful baby you ever saw,' Larry said proudly, cradling his first grandchild. 'Was it hard, Keelin? I got a shock when Brigid rang me to say you were in labour.'

'I was fairly yelping all right,' Keelin grimaced. 'How do women do that twelve and more times? They're hardy women, our mothers' generation.'

'They are,' her father agreed.

'And speaking of hardy women, did Mam make any comment when she heard I'd had the baby?' Keelin asked.

'She's in Dublin. Up with Teresa. She doesn't know yet. I told the lads to tell her if she phones. They send their love and are looking forward to seeing their niece,' Larry explained gently.

'She probably wouldn't have come anyway.' Keelin's resigned tone told him his daughter knew her mother as well as he did.

'She'll come around eventually,' he said with fake optimism. 'Don't give up.'

'So it all went well, then and it was a girl,' Imelda said unenthusiastically when Larry got home that evening.

'Yes, a little beauty. She's a couple of weeks premature but she's a feisty little thing, like her mother,' Larry said proudly. 'Wait until you see her,' he added tentatively. 'You'll come to the christening, won't you?'

'No, Larry, I won't. And please don't ask me again,' Imelda said in a tone of voice that left him in no doubt that his wife meant every word she said.

'Is she as beautiful as her mother?' Armand asked Keelin, his voice such a welcome sound to hear down the phone from his grandparents' home in France.

'The most beautiful baby in the world, Armand,' Keelin said happily.

'I wish I'd been with you, *chérie*,' he said regretfully. My flight is booked for next Saturday.

'I know. I wish you'd been here too, but she came early. And everyone says I'm very lucky the labour was so short. She was certainly in a hurry to come. You'll be here in another week, and then you'll see what a beauty our daughter is,' Keelin consoled him.

'It can't come soon enough,' Armand said fervently. 'Have your parents seen her yet?'

'Dad has. I don't think Mam will be visiting us in the foreseeable future, if ever.'

'I'm so sorry to hear that, Keelin,' Armand said sadly.

'It's her loss, beloved. I'm not going to let it spoil this wonderful day.' Keelin was adamant about that.

'Good, that's very good, *chérie*. It *is* a wonderful day for us. We've been blessed by the arrival of our child. Soon we'll all be together. A family at last. As soon as I have my qualification to teach French as a foreign language I will be able to support us,' Armand assured her.

'I could go back teaching. I might have to pretend to be married though, because ... well you know the Catholic ethos in schools ...' She trailed off.

'You won't have to *pretend*. We will be married, never you fear,' Armand said resolutely.

'No! I don't want you to feel forced into a marriage,' Keelin replied firmly. 'An unplanned pregnancy should never be a reason to marry.'

'Keelin, pregnant or not, I always wanted to marry you, once I'm laicized. *Chérie*, we are meant to be together. It's been divinely ordained.'

'Oh, I feel that too, Armand. So strongly. *Now* I know why I was meant to join the nuns and go on the Missions. It was to meet *you*.'

CHAPTER THIRTY-TWO

'Look at the size of her. And look at the smiles out of her for her granddad.' Larry was delighted with himself as Marie-Claire cooed up at him, beaming a toothy grin that seemed to stretch from one ear to another. 'Can I lift her out?'

'Of course you can, Dad,' Keelin laughed. 'Though Una will probably give out. She says we're giving Marie-Claire bad habits, holding her all the time.'

'But sure, I'm her granddad, and I don't get to see her half as much as I'd like to,' Larry retorted, lifting the baby out of her pram. 'Make me a mug of tea and tell me all the news,' he smiled at Keelin.

'Armand will be here at the weekend. He has a job interview next week, in a school in Whitehall. We're going to look for a place to rent in Dublin in the New Year.'

'Now that's something I want to talk to you about,' Larry interjected, stroking his granddaughter's cheek. 'I lodged a couple of bob into your account. It should go some way to getting a deposit on a house for ye. Rent is money down the drain. Buy your own place as quick as ye can,' he advised.

'Aw, Dad, you're so good to us.' Keelin was overwhelmed by her father's kindness to her. 'Does Mam know? Does she mind?' she asked, placing his mug of tea on the table in front of him.

'Yes, she knows. I told her. She never put up any protest. I think she's glad, in her own funny way, to be helping you out.'

'And she knows you were coming to see me today?' Keelin queried.

'She does.'

'And she'd never say she'd come with you?' she asked wistfully.

'It will happen in time,' Larry predicted. 'She'll get used to the idea eventually.'

'She's had nearly a year,' Keelin said glumly, thinking how hard it was to believe that this time last year, she had been pregnant but hadn't realized it.

'How's the job going?' Larry changed the subject, dunking a chocolate biscuit into his tea.

'Great. I love it. I'm finished this week. The hotel closes for Christmas until mid-January. The few extra bob are great and the hours suit me.' Keelin sat down at the table beside him. She'd started working part-time in reception at the local hotel, filling in for the regular receptionist who was on maternity leave, and she enjoyed it very much. Una and Marie-Hélène had insisted she take the position, offering to mind Marie-Claire for her.

'That's good to hear. We're up to our eyes, of course. This time of the year is always busy for us, but I'm not complaining. It would be worse if it wasn't.' Larry made a funny face at the baby and she chuckled.

Her father looked tired and Keelin felt guilty that he had taken time out of his busy schedule to drive all the way to the Four Winds to see her and Marie-Claire. He'd been so good to her since the baby was born. She knew she would never have managed without him.

Larry had lunch with her and Una, and at Keelin's urging he left around two-thirty so that he would be on the main road well before night-time. She didn't want him driving home in the dark.

'I'll be down over the Christmas, Keelin,' he assured her, hugging her tightly before placing a tender kiss on his sleeping granddaughter's head.

'I'll be looking forward to it, Daddy. I love you,' she said, walking to the car with him.

'And I love you, Keelin. Very much,' her father smiled, giving her another hug before he got in the car. She waved him off until he disappeared from view, wishing with all her heart that Imelda would change her mind, so that Keelin and her baby could go and visit them in Glencarraig and save her father the long round trip.

'Imelda, you should get down here. Larry's taken a turn.' The secretary sounded panicked and her tone frightened Imelda.

'What sort of a turn, Betty?' Imelda felt suddenly shaky.

Larry had been looking weary lately, a grey-hued pallor shading his face. She'd put it down to winter and driving backwards and forwards to see Keelin and the baby.

'I think he's having a heart attack. We've phoned for an ambulance—'

'I'm on my way.' Imelda slammed down the phone, turned off the hob where she'd been cooking bacon and cabbage, grabbed her coat and keys from the hall stand and ran out the front door.

'Oh God, let Larry be all right,' she prayed fervently. 'Don't let anything happen to him. He's a good man. I'll be a better wife,' she promised in a lather of impatient anxiety when she got stuck behind an elderly lady who was tootling along at snail's pace.

'Jesus, Mary and Joseph! Get out of my way,' she groaned, sick with apprehension. Larry's secretary was not one to panic easily.

Larry was sitting in his worn leather office chair, his face the colour of chalk, grimacing in pain. 'What are you doing here, Imelda? It's only indigestion.' He tried to smile at her when she knelt beside him and took his hand.

'You're going on a diet, mister! No more biscuits and cakes,' she said in a calm voice that surprised her.

'Ah now, Imelda, no need for that.' He squeezed her hand and gasped when another spasm of pain hit.

'Don't talk, Larry. Save your energy,' Imelda urged, frightened at his colour. His hand grew limp in hers and tentacles of terror squeezed her insides. In the distance she could hear the howling wail of a siren. Thank God: the ambulance.

'They'll sort you in hospital soon, Larry. The ambulance is nearly here.'

'Imelda,' he murmured, his eyes dimming, 'I'm so sorry about Fran. I should have told—'

'Shush, forget about that now,' she urged. 'That's all in the past.'

'Imelda,' he whispered his voice low so that she had to lean in to hear him.

'I'm here, Larry,' she said tenderly. 'You'll be fine. The ambulance is here.' The blue flashing lights outside lit up the office in the gloom of the late afternoon.

'Imelda, promise me you'll let Keelin come home?' His voice was firm but very weak, as though he was speaking from somewhere far away.

'I promise, Larry. I'll invite her home for Christmas,' she assured him as the ambulance men hurried in to the office. 'I'm so sorry I behaved so badly. I'll make it up to her and you. I promise.'

'I know you will.' Even in his hour of affliction he was kind to her, she thought, riven with guilt. 'We did good in spite of everything.'

'We did, Larry!'

Imelda felt tears prick her eyes in this most tender moment when it seemed as though time was standing still and everyone else in the room had faded away and there was only the two of them.

'Excuse me now, ma'am! We need to examine your husband.' The ambulance man gently but firmly assisted her to her feet and edged her out of the way.

'Imelda!' Larry breathed.

'I'm here,' she gulped in terror, watching the light fade from his eyes as they become glassy and dim. Imelda didn't need the sharp intake of breath from the ambulance man at his side to know that her husband was dead.

'Larry!' she wailed. 'Don't leave me. Don't go! Larry! Larry! Larry!'

'This *is* a surprise. We don't usually get to see our favourite Mère, mid-week,' Keelin exclaimed when Brigid walked through the door into the kitchen.

'Keelin, I ... sit down, dear. I have bad news for you,' Brigid said sombrely and Keelin felt a jolt of apprehension.

'What's wrong?'

'It's your dad, love. He had a heart attack in the shop, earlier. He didn't make it to the hospital. Imelda rang me and asked me would I tell you. She didn't want you hearing the news that he died on your own. She asked me to be here with you.'

'Daddy's *dead*?' Keelin whispered. 'Dead!' How can that be? He was with us a few days ago. He's coming to visit us at Christmas. He *can't* be dead.' This had to be a nightmare, she thought frantically, as her body started to shake with shock.

'I'm so sorry, Keelin.' Brigid put her arms around her.

'It's my fault,' she cried. 'He shouldn't have been driving

up and down in the one day, in bad weather. If he'd have stayed at home he wouldn't have had a heart attack.'

'Shush, you and I both know that when it's your time, a time agreed between you and your Creator, external circumstances make no difference. Don't do that to yourself, Keelin. Larry would hate it.' Brigid held her tight.

'Oh my God. This is a punishment for what I've done!' Keelin wept, devastated.

'Don't think like that, Keelin. God doesn't punish. That's attributing human thinking to a Creator who is all loving. You *know* that,' Brigid rocked her niece in her arms, heartbroken for her.

'I'm going to his funeral, Auntie Brigid. I don't care what Mam thinks, or how mortified she is by my presence. I'm going and she can't stop me,' Keelin said heatedly, cursing God for taking the parent she loved and who loved her, and leaving her with a mother she hated.

'Keelin, I *beg* you. Don't make a scene with Imelda. Don't fight with her and say things that can't be unsaid. Your father would hate for that to happen. You know that,' Brigid said quietly, taking her niece's hand. They were sitting in Brigid's car outside the family home in Glencarraig, watching people entering the house to pay their respects.

'Perhaps it would be better to say that you're staying at the convent house in Butlersbridge, and not mention anything about leaving, or having a baby. This isn't the time for it,' Brigid advised, diplomatically but firmly. 'Imelda has enough to be dealing with, without noisy ould wans poking their noses in your business.'

'OK,' Keelin agreed dully. She was sick to her stomach with nerves and shock. A row was the last thing she wanted.

'Come on then. Let's go inside and pray for your dad,' Brigid said gently.

The front door was ajar when they reached it, and Brigid could see a throng of people in the kitchen, the low buzz of chat and the odd laugh reaching her ears. It seemed almost surreal. Wakes were such convivial occasions, she thought wildly, remembering the many she'd attended growing up.

'Keelin!' her brother's cry of surprise caused her to start and she saw him walk down the hall with his arms held out to her.

'Oh, Cormac,' she said brokenly when he hugged her. 'Where is he? Where's Daddy?'

'Come on, he's in the front lounge – I'll bring you in. Hello, Auntie Brigid.' He kissed his aunt, then led them into the front room.

The blinds were half shut, and the room was dim in the winter gloom. Candles flickered at the top and bottom of the gleaming mahogany coffin. Two neighbours, sitting on the sofa quietly, murmured a rosary. Imelda sat, head bowed in misery, in the chair opposite the one her husband always sat in.

'Mam,' Keelin said hesitantly, edging further into the room. She could see her father, dressed in his best suit, nestled in the white satin frill that lined his coffin, looking peaceful and serene, almost as though he was asleep. Rosary beads were entwined in his fingers.

'*Keelin!*' Imelda exclaimed, taken aback at the sight of her daughter and sister. She looked pale and very drawn, with big dark circles under her dull eyes. 'I thought you wouldn't be here until this afternoon.'

'I *had* to see Daddy,' Keelin said, starting to cry as she moved over to stand at the side of the coffin. 'Oh Daddy, Daddy, Daddy,' she wept. 'I love you. I'm so, *so* sorry for dragging you all the way to Butlersbridge.' Keelin's heart felt as though it was going to break into a thousand pieces, as grief, the like of which she'd never experienced, overwhelmed her. The physical pain of it shocked her, and she sobbed aloud in her anguish.

Imelda came and stood beside her, and Keelin heard her mother begin to weep. In a gesture that was utterly instinctive, Keelin reached out and put her arm around her, while on the other side of Keelin, Brigid came and stood next to her, also slipping a comforting arm around her.

Joined together in sorrow, the three women wept over Larry's remains, and the strife that had kept them apart for so long was temporarily forgotten.

PART THREE

Other things may change us,
but we start and end with the family.

Anthony Brandt

CHAPTER THIRTY-THREE

*Felicity, I've gone home. I had to get out of here. You can
take a lift with Keelin, John, or the Sheedys.*
  Imelda

She folded the note and popped it into an envelope. She'd
slip it under Felicity's door when she was leaving. She made
coffee, adding two sachets to the cup to sober her up, and
drank it quickly.

Time was of the essence. She wanted to be gone before
the minibus arrived with the others. Keelin would argue
with her about driving after drinking, let alone making the
two-hour journey in the dark on a wild night. And there'd
be another row. Well, her daughter wasn't 'the boss of her',
to use a phrase she often heard her grandchildren use on each
other. Still, it would be best to be gone, all the same.

Imelda glanced around the pretty lamp-lit room. She
would have enjoyed staying the night and having a room

service breakfast and watching TV in bed. Tears welled in her eyes and she blinked them away irritably. She hadn't time for tears. Was Brigid crying in her room in the Four Winds, she wondered guiltily. Were Keelin and Armand devastated because she'd revealed their secret to Marie-Claire? The memory of her granddaughter's stricken face caused a wave of guilt to wash over her. She should not have done that, Imelda admitted, ashamed.

'Don't think about it all now. What's done is done!' she muttered. She'd need all her wits about her to drive those windy roads in the dark, until she reached the motorway. Time enough to reflect on the events of this evening when she was safely home behind her own front door.

'Dear Lord,' Imelda prayed, five minutes later, swinging the car out of the small car park, 'please get me home safe, without harming myself or others, and please don't let me be stopped at a Garda checkpoint. Amen.' Torrential rain, so heavy the wipers could barely clear it away from the window, and gusting winds, blowing in from the sea, shook her hatchback, causing her to momentarily ponder the wisdom of her decision to leave Butlersbridge on such a stormy night, especially having partaken of two glasses of wine earlier.

It was too late now. She'd checked out, and she just wanted to go home to her own bed and try to forget all that had happened. Nor could she bear the thought of dealing with any of the family the following day. No, onwards she would go, Imelda decided, slowing down at a bend in the road, feeling the wheels almost aquaplane before she regained control.

In the distance, to her left, she saw the lights of the upstairs bedrooms in the Four Winds. She would never set foot in that place again, she vowed, turning at the end of the village's main street to begin her journey inland. As she drew further from the coast, the hedgerows along the narrow, winding roads offered a little more shelter from the harsh night, although after a particularly violent gust, she prayed, again, that there would be no fallen trees to cause her to crash.

The Flight into Egypt had nothing on this, Imelda thought ruefully, popping a mint in her mouth to help her concentrate. She could imagine what would be said about her, when the family discovered that she was gone. Let them say what they liked, she thought defiantly, squinting against the full-beam headlights of an oncoming car. They hadn't lived her life. She knew she should feel bad about the way she'd behaved, but right now she didn't care. Imelda felt strangely liberated, as if letting out all the poison trapped inside her had freed her from a past that had imprisoned her for years.

CHAPTER THIRTY-FOUR

'Why didn't you tell me? Why did you both lie to me?' Marie-Claire demanded bitterly of her parents. The three of them were alone in the small parlour; the nuns had all gone to their rooms, and the minibus driver was rounding up his charges to bring them back to Butlersbridge.

'I *wanted* to tell you. Your mother dissuaded me. She didn't want you to know,' Armand said angrily. He was furious with Keelin and Imelda. And he was mortified. He should have listened to his gut all those years ago and insisted on nothing being hidden.

'Is that true, Maman?' Marie-Claire rounded on her mother.

'Yes,' Keelin said miserably. 'But I wanted to protect you. I was worried you'd feel you were different to other children. Was that so awful—'

'You were ashamed, and I had to live with that shame,' Armand accused, his lean face tight with anger. 'I wanted the truth to be told so that we could begin our lives with a clean slate. No more secrets, no more lies. But you wouldn't listen to me. And this is the result. I hope you're satisfied, Keelin and I promise you one thing: I will not set foot in *la maison . . . de . . . de cette femme horrible! Jamais.* I've spoken to your mother for the last time. I will never darken her door again.' Armand was so upset he strode out of the room, banging the door behind him.

Keelin burst into tears. She and Armand rarely quarrelled, and he'd never shown such naked anger towards her. Who would ever have thought their past would come back to haunt them like this? And in such a horrible, public manner.

She'd hidden the truth of Armand's past very well, and hidden it from herself too, over the years. Her husband had never wanted to deny his past, once they left their religious orders. Denial would cast a shadow on their marriage, he'd argued, set it apart from others. He'd always felt it was their daughter's right to know their history, but nevertheless he'd gone along with it when she'd asked him not to tell people that he was an ex-priest. All Marie-Claire knew was that her mother had entered a convent, then left before taking her final vows – which was not a lie. She thought it was only *then* that her parents had met and fallen in love – which wasn't quite a lie, surely, more a sin of omission. Keelin wanted Marie-Claire to grow up carrying no religious baggage of guilt or shame. Back then, Ireland had still been very much under the dictatorial rule of Rome and the bishops, forcing Keelin to hide her pregnancy in the Four Winds while she waited to give birth.

'You could have told me when I was older, Maman! I wasn't brought up to adhere to the rules of Catholicism. You never wanted that for me. So why would I consider it to be a big deal that my dad was once a Catholic priest? I would have considered it a badge of honour that he left the Church. He's right. You're *still* ashamed of your past and his. How can you run courses on healing, and clearing the past, when you can't even heal your *own*? You need to do some work on *yourself*, Maman,' Marie-Claire fumed.

'That's *typical* of you. You always take up for your father,' Keelin snapped, stung by her daughter's accusations.

'Do you know who you sound like now?' Marie-Claire demanded. 'You sound just like Granny,' she retorted, walking out of the room in disgust.

Keelin watched her go and wanted to go after her and slap her. How *dare* she accuse her of being like Imelda! Sick to her stomach with anger and shock, Keelin slumped into a chair. What a night this had turned out to be. And now the whole family was in upheaval. All their secrets had been laid bare for the world to see. There was no hiding place for any of them anymore. She couldn't wait to get back to the shelter of Canigou and her lovely home. She might never visit this benighted country again – and that would cause her no regret, she thought bitterly.

And then she remembered what Marie-Claire had said about owning her past and healing it, and Keelin's heart sank. That was far easier said than done. Her daughter was right, much as she hated to admit it. It was utterly hypocritical of her to be giving courses about healing the past when she was unwilling to face her own.

'Physician heal thyself,' Keelin muttered irritably, knowing that until she dealt with her issues with her mother, there would be no peace for her.

'Don't look back,' Maura had said. But what was left to look forward to? Brigid lay rigid under the duvet, her fingers curled into tight fists, her nails biting into her palms, inflicting pain she wanted. *Deserved*. She would have to prostrate herself before the altar of God and beg His humble pardon. Her past had come back to haunt her, when she least expected it, Brigid acknowledged dolefully. She'd lost everything! Her good name. Her dignity. *And* her authority, which she'd always rather enjoyed. There would be talk. In the convents. In the Mother House. Here, in the Four Winds, her haven, her little bit of heaven on earth.

Brigid had seen the shocked expressions on her fellow Sisters' faces when Imelda had revealed the secret that Brigid had buried so deep. Something she thought, as the years passed by, would *never* come to light. She'd seen pity too, and not only from her congregation. Maura pitied her. Una pitied her. They *all* pitied her. Tears slid down Brigid's cheeks. All of those women who had always looked up to her – she was their 'Superior' and, if she was truly honest, she'd sometimes felt superior – had witnessed her downfall.

Her heart contracted as a thousand blades of mortification stabbed mercilessly, unrelentingly, as she lay in her bed, in her room under the eaves, and listened to the roar of the sea crashing against the shore and the rain hammering against the window.

'Pride comes before a fall,' her grandmother had often said. Even the Proverbs counselled that 'Pride goes before destruction, And a haughty spirit before stumbling'.

Well, her haughty spirit had taken a fine stumble tonight. One she might never recover from. Heartsore, Brigid sat up against her pillows, the small red lamp under the picture of the Sacred Heart illuminating the darkness.

She thought she'd reached calm seas in her vocation, until tonight. Was this her punishment for becoming a nun under false pretences, and staying a nun by burying truths, or lack of truths, about her faith that she did not wish to acknowledge, she wondered miserably, staring at the shadowy lamp-lit image of her Saviour.

She reached across and took the brandy goblet in her hand, raised it to the mournful visage of Jesus, and took a drink of the amber liquid. Tonight was one of the worst nights of her life; she might as well keep sinking until she hit rock bottom.

She choked and spluttered as the alcohol hit the back of her throat, her cheeks flushing with heat. Why did people like the stuff, she wondered. It didn't taste nice. It made her insides feel warm though, took the chill off them, she realized as the liquor coursed through her.

She tried to banish the memory of Imelda's bitter and twisted face, full of spite and anger, spewing her appalling tirade of vile rancour. Tonight her sister had burned every last one of the women in her family, right down to Marie-Claire. How could Imelda do that to her own child and grandchild? The knowledge that her sister carried such levels of animosity and resentment towards the family shook Brigid.

That Imelda had carried a torch for Johnny Larkin had come as news to her. But then, Imelda had always kept things to herself, in a sly, sullen way, even as a little girl. She wouldn't share her toys, or books, and was mean spirited and spiteful when Brigid was brought to the fore, on her birthday, or Holy Communion, or Confirmation days.

She was so *jealous*, always! Had she never once looked back and seen what a shallow, sleazy ladies' man, Larkin was? Pawing every girl in the parish. Feeling nothing for *any* of them. And then marrying a girl purely to get his greedy paws on her father's land. Did Imelda not realize that he had used both of them? What a waste to have held on to that childish hurt. And it seemed Imelda's obsession had blinded her to the gifts she had been given: a good husband, children, grand-children, a home of her own ... How could Imelda possibly have remained so envious, when she'd such graces in her life? All the things Brigid would have loved to have.

Brigid had never begrudged her sister the life she'd had. But she'd never understood why she wasn't happier and more content with her lot.

A ripple of guilt spread through her. She'd never under-stood because she'd dismissed too easily Imelda's moans about being abandoned to slavery – as she termed it – looking after their parents. The accusation that their father had given her

291

a good dowry to the detriment of Imelda's chances of bettering herself stung! And it stung because it was true, Brigid admitted guiltily.

Only one of them had been given the chance to escape the life of drudgery on the farm – and she had not only seized that chance, she'd taken it under false pretences. She'd had no vocation when she entered the convent, and Imelda knew it, just as she'd known all along that Brigid's only thought was to get away from Ardcloch and her broken dreams. And Imelda was right, she'd been thoroughly selfish, uncaring and insensitive, giving no thought to the dreams her sister had harboured but would never realize. Brigid felt shame at the realization of how high and mighty she had been. For years she'd had a wonderful life, driving around the African bush in her jeep, feeling mighty important, telling herself what a difference she was making to the lives of mothers and babies. She'd never spared a thought for the life of unrelenting hard work Imelda had endured, rearing her own babies and looking after her parents and mother-in-law.

Everything Imelda had accused her of earlier was true, Brigid thought, looking at the metaphorical mirror that had been held up to her by her sister. It was time for her to face her own past and be honest with herself. 'To thine own self be true,' she murmured sadly.

She took another mouthful of brandy, draining the glass. Maura had been generous in her pouring, Brigid recognized, replacing the empty goblet on the bedside locker and easing herself back onto her pillows. Unaccustomed to drinking alcohol, she was feeling a tad woozy. Her eyelids began to droop. She felt disconnected, as if she were floating off somewhere. Not an unpleasant feeling, to be sure. She was warm now, the earlier chilliness of delayed shock having thawed under the effects of the brandy.

A thought struck her. This was *not* the worst night of her life, despite the humiliation inflicted on her by Imelda. The worst night of her life had been on that lonely hillside on Christmas Eve, when her precious baby had flowed out of her and her heart had broken into a million pieces for all that she'd lost.

Imelda might have thought she'd revealed the most shocking details of Brigid's shameful past, and perhaps she had, but Brigid still had one precious secret: her pregnancy. Her brief, never to be forgotten experience of motherhood, when she'd cherished the knowledge that her child was growing in her womb. That would always be hers and hers alone.

It was rare that she permitted herself to even think about it. The memory of her pregnancy was her most precious jewel, locked away until the occasion it was needed. Tonight was such an occasion. Tonight she would allow herself to remember that fleeting primal joy, once the immense shock of realizing she was pregnant had waned, that had infused every cell and atom of her being, before worry and apprehension had quenched it.

Brigid's eyes closed and her thoughts drifted back to all those years before when she'd loved, and thought she'd been loved in return, and her body and spirit had felt vibrant and alive in a way it had never been before or since.

'Maura brought Brigid up a glass of brandy, Keelin. If I were you, I'd leave her alone until the morning,' Una murmured, putting her arm around her friend's shoulder. They were sitting in the kitchen having a cup of tea, the detritus of the party all around them. The guests who were staying in the hotel had departed, and the nuns had all gone to their rooms, distressed and dismayed at what had unfolded. The minibus driver had told Keelin and Armand that he'd come back for them after dropping the others off.

Armand was in the big parlour removing all the party accoutrements and stacking dirty plates and glasses. Marie-Claire was helping Maura divide leftover bourguignon and chicken tagine into containers.

'She won't drink that brandy,' Keelin sighed. 'I could do with one myself.'

'Me too!' Una grimaced. 'She will drink it, Maura insisted and she didn't argue. What in the name of God possessed Imelda? I mean, it was one thing to have a go at Brigid about what she sees as the unfairness of her entering the convent and leaving her to take care of the parents. But the other stuff! Lord above, there was no need for that – and in front of Mother General too.' She shook her head, still in shock at the viciousness of Imelda's attack.

'Marie-Claire and Armand are so angry with me now. Armand blames me because I made him keep it secret. Well, the secret's well and truly out now. Rita Sheedy won't be able to keep it to herself – it will be all over Ardcloch and Glencarraig in no time. I'll never be able to go back there. Not that I'd want to.' Keelin's hand shook, raising her cup to her mouth. 'There'll be no going back from this. She's caused a rift that will never be healed.'

'Time heals. This too will pass,' Una counselled sagely, patting her friend's shoulder.

Keelin shook her head. 'Imagine hating your mother,' she said sombrely. 'Because tonight I certainly hate mine! If I ever see her again it will be too soon.'

CHAPTER THIRTY-FIVE

Keelin lay beside her husband, listening to his steady breathing, wondering how he could sleep after the harsh words he'd spoken to her after the disastrous party. It wasn't *his* family that had been torn apart. Armand wouldn't have to live with the consequences like she would. Marie-Claire would take his side, and blame her for not allowing him to reveal his past. And now he could wash his hands of Imelda, and forget about her, Keelin thought resentfully, lying wide awake in the darkness, waiting for a text from her brother to say that her mother was home safe.

Felicity had knocked on her door earlier and shown her Imelda's note. 'The bloody old cow,' Keelin had cursed, 'If I could get my hands on her, I'd murder her, driving home on those country roads on a night like this, and after drinking as well. How feckin irresponsible is that! None of us can go after her because we've all had a drink.'

'Your mother is nothing if not determined. She'll be fine,' Felicity tried to pacify her.

'I don't know how you put up with her,' Keelin said through gritted teeth. 'She's impossible.'

'I asked Cormac to text me when he sees a light on in her bedroom – he'll be able to see it from our bedroom – and I'll text you. I did try to ring her but she has her phone turned off,' her sister-in-law said.

'Thanks, Felicity. At least you won't have to put up with her, driving back to Glencarraig.' Keelin managed a weak smile.

'Go to bed, Keelin. Things won't seem as bad in the morning.' Felicity urged. She was used to her mother-in-law's behaviour, and had decided in the early days of her marriage that she was not going to let it impinge on her life, knowing that if she did, her marriage to Cormac wouldn't last. She was an easy-going woman, the antithesis of her mother-in-law, and she suspected that was one of the reasons Imelda's eldest son had fallen in love with her.

'You're a great sister-in-law,' Keelin said gratefully, hugging the other woman.

'And you're not too bad yourself,' Felicity laughed, returning the hug.

How did Felicity cope with living in such close proximity to Imelda? Keelin wondered, turning onto her front and burying her face under her pillow. Keelin only saw her three or four times a year and that was more than enough for her.

More than three decades had passed, yet her mother still hadn't forgiven her for getting pregnant and having a baby out of wedlock, *or* for marrying a former priest even though he was the father of her child. The fact they'd opted for a civil wedding, in France, rather than a Catholic wedding hadn't gone down well with Imelda either; she'd professed 'grave doubts' that they were properly married at all.

Keelin rubbed her wedding band with her thumb. Marrying Armand had been the second happiest day of her life. Giving birth to Marie-Claire had been the happiest. Whatever she did or said, her mother would never take those joys away from her.

The ping of a text brought Keelin out of her reverie, and she picked up the phone, blinking in the dark when the screen illuminated and she saw it was from Cormac to say he had seen the light come on in Imelda's bedroom.

Keelin keyed in her thanks and turned off the phone. So Imelda was home safe after driving through that awful weather; that at least was a relief, she thought wearily as the wind howled in off the sea and the rain battered the bedroom window.

Beside her, Armand slept on, breathing deeply, rhythmically. She wished she could sleep with such serenity. But after the events of this evening she wondered would she ever be serene again.

CHAPTER THIRTY-SIX

Marie-Claire studied the post she'd typed in on her Facebook page:

> A lovely reunion with the Sisters, and family and friends in the Four Winds, at the surprise party to celebrate my great-aunt's eightieth birthday and retirement. When all is said and done, family is more important than anything.

Was the family bit over the top, especially when it was 'family' that had wrought havoc at the party? Should she post at all? It wasn't really appropriate because the party had ended in disaster, but who, apart from those present, would know it?

She'd taken photos in the early stages of the party, when everyone was happy and having fun. She'd a few lovely selfies of herself and her mother, and a great one with

Marie-Hélène laughing uproariously as they clinked glasses of Prosecco.

All taken before the party had turned to disaster and she discovered her parents had lied to her for her whole life. Didn't they trust her? Marie-Claire felt her understanding of her parents shifting, like puzzle pieces she suddenly realized didn't fit together as she'd thought. Was she posting to avoid thinking about what really happened?

This is all so shallow and immature, Marie-Claire upbraided herself. *What age am I? Thirteen?* Posting photos on social media to pretend to an ex-boyfriend that she was having fun in her life and getting on fine without him. How truly pathetic was that?

The *real* truth, Marie-Claire admitted to herself, was that she wanted to post about the party because today was the day she was supposed to be in New York, with Marc, holding talks to expand his company. She wanted her ex to see that she was enjoying life without him, although in reality quite the opposite was true.

She was about to delete it all when a small green light caught her eye and she saw, with a jolt, that Marc was also online. Her finger hovered over 'Post'. She erased the last line about family – that was going too far after tonight's shenanigans – and sent the post winging its way into the ether, watching as the photos began to upload on her Facebook and Insta pages.

Marie-Claire studied them critically. She looked bright-eyed and happy, she thought with satisfaction, and pretty glam too. She'd wound her hair up, little tendrils escaping to frame her face, which had got thinner because she'd lost a couple of pounds having been too busy to eat while she was making preparations to leave Canada, and then with all the travelling she'd done since.

The image on her iPad changed to an image of Marc and a little tinkling ringtone made her swallow and sit up straight. Accept or reject the FaceTime call? The choice was hers.

She saw her own image reflected in a small square at the top of the screen. She looked fine, Marie-Claire assured herself. Taking a deep breath, she accepted the call and felt a deep pang of heartache when Marc's handsome face settled into view. 'Hi' she said lightly, admiring the studied nonchalance of her tone.

'*Chérie*, I saw you online and I so longed to speak to you,' Marc said huskily. Hearing his voice almost undid her.

'How are you?' she asked, determined that she would not show by one flicker of her face the turmoil she was feeling. But a piece of her longed to be in his arms, in his big bed, his body warm and firm against hers.

'I'm missing you, that's how I am. I'm in New York and you should be with me. Please get on a flight and come back to me,' he urged. 'Look, it's snowing.' He panned around to show her the view of Central Park. 'We could be having such fun – please come back to me, Marie-Claire,' he entreated again.

How *tempted* she was to fly back to him and leave the family drama behind her. She longed to feel her lover's mouth on hers, and pretend that nothing had happened to ruin their relationship.

But it *had* happened, she reminded herself, and she

suddenly wanted to ask him if he had taken Amelia to Niagara Falls, and hear him stammer and stutter. But then he'd know the reason why she'd left him, and she wouldn't give him that satisfaction . . . *ever!*

'Oh Marc, it would be nice to have dinner with you in NY,' she said lightly 'but it won't be in the near future, I'm afraid. I'm making plans! I'm moving into a lovely seafront apartment in Clontarf next month and I've some job opportunities coming up,' she fibbed. 'And it *really* is lovely to be at home with friends and family. I'm having such a good time.' The lies flowed from her lips one after another.

'But what about *us*, Marie-Claire? We were a great item. Why did you suddenly decide to leave? I don't understand. I wanted to take it to the next level. I felt you did too,' he asked, still utterly bewildered by what he saw as her thoroughly unreasonable behaviour.

'Look, sweetie, I need this time to reassess, and take a step back, *precisely* because you want us to go to the next level. Have patience with me,' she heard herself say. 'It's never too late to change plans. Who knows, in six months' time, I could be missing you so much I'll be on that plane so quick you won't have time to think,' she said earnestly.

'*Do* you miss me?' he asked.

'Desperately,' she sighed and leaned in to the iPad and kissed his image.

'Aw, Marie-Claire, I miss you like hell. I miss talking to you and sharing all our work stuff. I want to tell you about New York, it's going to be a real—'

'I'm dying to hear all about it, Marc,' she interrupted, 'but, sweetie, it's the early hours of the morning here and I simply have to go to bed. I can't keep my eyes open. I'll catch you again soon. Night, darling.' She blew him a kiss and ended the call.

'You bitch,' she muttered, leaning back against the chair. The plan to keep him dangling had formed, right there and then. She could play as dirty as he could, with his little two-faced sweet-as-syrup floozy, Amelia.

Thank God she hadn't weakened. She wouldn't get in the habit of FaceTiming him too often, Marie-Claire decided, wishing that she was above playing mind games. Not mature, not adult, but satisfying nevertheless, she admitted gloomily, noticing that Lizzie had now come online. Can I FaceTime you? she messaged.

She'd barely sent off the message before her iPad vibrated again and Lizzie's face appeared on screen. Marie-Claire pressed accept eagerly.

'Hiya,' she said warmly. 'It's great to see you, I've *loads* to tell you!'

'Hi, MC, shoot,' Lizzie grinned. 'How did the party go?'

Marie-Claire shook her head. 'Don't ask,' she sighed. 'It was an *absolute* disaster!'

'Oh no,' her friend exclaimed, taking a swig of coffee. She was lounging on her sofa, and Marie-Claire wished she was there with her so they could have a drink and a girly natter and that life could be the way it had been, before her discovery of Marc's betrayal. 'What happened?'

Marie-Claire gave Lizzie the gist of it, keeping her voice low so as not to disturb any of the guests on her landing.

'OMG! Is she for real?' Lizzie exclaimed when she got to the part where Imelda made the revelation about Brigid. 'That was downright nasty.'

'Tell me about it,' Marie-Claire said gloomily. 'Guess who FaceTimed just before I messaged you?'

'Don't say Mister Bouchard!' Lizzie made a face.

'Yep! From New York, begging me to come back—'

'I hope you said no to the two-faced lizard,' her friend retorted.

'I won't deny it – I was tempted.'

'Marie-Claire,' said Lizzie sternly. 'You do know who he took to New York with him?'

Marie-Claire's heart sank. 'Amelia?' she said dully.

'The very one! She's been prancing around the office like the cat who got the cream since we came back after the break. Soon as she heard you were gone, she was trying to find out why. She even had the nerve to ask *me*, knowing that you and I are besties.' Lizzie scowled.

'What did she say?'

'She said ever so sweetly in that breathy little voice of hers, "Lizzie, is everything OK with Marie-Claire? I hear she's gone back to Ireland without giving notice, leaving Marc completely stuck." So I stared at her and I said, "*Excuse me?*" and gave her one of my looks—'

'Lizzie!' Marie-Claire laughed. One of Lizzie's looks was enough to intimidate anybody. 'What did she say to that?'

'Oh, she started to stutter, and I said, "Amelia, if you need to talk to me about anything work-related, fine, otherwise I'm very busy. I don't have time for idle chitchat and office gossip." She was twittering something about being concerned about you as she backed out the door. I was SO tempted to say, Girl, if you were *that* concerned, you wouldn't be sleeping with her partner – and I would have, if you weren't keeping shtum about it,' Lizzie said grimly.

'So he took her to New York with him?' Marie-Claire said dejectedly.

'He did. No point in me sugar coating it, honey.'

'And then he has the nerve to beg me to come back! I don't get it.'

'He's an opportunist. If you married him, you'd never have a minute's peace of mind. Guys like Marc are genetically incapable of being monogamous. You know something, Marie-Claire, you had a lucky escape.'

'I know. But it still hurts,' Marie-Claire admitted as an aching pain tasered her heart. 'I told him to give me a while—'

Oh, *do* keep him dangling.' Lizzie clapped and gave her the thumbs up. 'Honestly, he's like a bear with a sore head these days. He asked me why had you left. I said his guess was as good as mine. "Didn't she confide in you?" he asked. "Didn't she confide in *you*?" I asked back. You should have seen his face! He didn't know whether he was coming or going.'

'Oh, Lizzie, you're such a great pal,' Marie-Claire laughed. 'I miss you.'

'I miss you too, honey, but I'm glad you finished with him before you got in too deep. Go to bed and put everything out of your head, it won't look so bad in the morning,' Lizzie advised kindly and blew her a kiss before hanging up.

Marie-Claire turned off the iPad and took some cotton pads out of her toilet bag and began to wipe off the expensive products that had gone into making up her elegant façade. Would things look better in the morning as Lizzie suggested? She hardly thought so.

CHAPTER THIRTY-SEVEN

Brigid woke to the shrill beep of the alarm clock on her phone. It was six-fifty a.m. She had ten minutes' snooze time, a luxury she allowed herself when she was in the Four Winds. She was so snug and warm and she lay drowsily enjoying the comfort of her bed until a memory slithered into her consciousness and her stomach lurched.

Best face the music and get it over and done with, Brigid decided. She got out of bed reluctantly and brushed her short grey hair in front of the mirror, noting her pale visage. Thanks to the brandy, she'd slept the night through, much to her surprise.

Her pallor was the only outward sign of her inner turmoil. The stomach-knotting, heartsick, roiling emotional havoc that last night's incident had wrought would be kept suppressed. It was her way.

She gazed at the veil and habit she'd worn for practically all of her adult life, hanging on the hook on her bedroom door. It was a garment she had no right to wear. *I'm a fraud*, Brigid thought sadly.

She hurried into the bathroom across the landing and performed her morning ablutions, listening to the rattling of the elderly radiator pipes that already had the house warm from the frosty chill outside. Slipping silently back into her room, she donned her habit. Though she felt undressed, unfinished without her veil, she had decided she would never wear it again. Next week, after she'd things sorted out, she would ask Marie-Claire to bring her shopping for lay clothes. Taking a deep breath, she opened her door and stepped onto the landing.

She could see lights under doors. The occupants, like her, were getting ready to attend Lauds in the small oratory downstairs. Her lip trembled and she bit it in an effort not to cry. *Be composed*, she told herself sternly. *This too will pass.*

A door to her right flew open, and she knew without looking that it was Marie-Hélène. There was nothing calm and serene about the younger nun. She'd always been a whirlwind of action.

'Ah, mornin', RM. I hope you slept well in spite of everything. Are you doing OK?' Marie-Hélène dropped a comforting arm around her shoulder.

Brigid's face crumpled at her colleague's kindness.

'Come in here.' Marie-Hélène led the way into her bedroom, which looked like a bomb had hit it. Fortunately, Veronique, who had slept in the other bed, which was made perfectly and untroubled by cases, clothes and other personal belongings, had already gone downstairs.

'Oh dear, this is dreadful. I need to be composed,' Brigid said in a voice that shook, as tears slid silently down her cheeks.

'No you *don't*, Brigid,' Marie-Hélène said firmly, handing her a tissue. 'Now you listen to me. You have been an outstanding nun. You have given of yourself *selflessly*. The past – and it's the far distant past, I hasten to remind you – should not be allowed to diminish one iota of all the stupendous good you've done with your life. And it certainly should not be allowed to ruin your future.'

Brigid smiled through her tears. 'Marie-Hélène, you're such a beacon of positivity. It's something I hugely admire about you, but all I feel now is shame, emptiness and utter mortification.'

'The shame isn't yours, it's Imelda's. Her behaviour was totally unacceptable. Remember the time I was hauled up before the Mother General and the congregation for getting pissed the night we celebrated getting the Papal award? Dr Onondaga produced a bottle of gin, and boy did we give it socks!' She grinned at the memory. 'And when Mother Perpetua *berated* me – and let me tell you I had the mother and father of a hangover – and said I wasn't fit to be a nun, I told her, "Let he or she who is without sin cast the first stone."'

Brigid laughed. 'Marie-Hélène, you always were incorrigible. I well remember the stunned silence and then the titters.'

Marie-Hélène chuckled. 'First time *ever*, Perpetua was

309

stuck for words. She was incandescent. But that's my motto. If it was good enough for Jesus, it's certainly good enough for you and me. Now, come downstairs with me and hold your head high, RM. Let's go.'

'Thank you, dearest Marie-Hélène,' Brigid said humbly, greatly moved by her friend's support.

They were at the return on the stairs when Brigid heard the Mother General say behind her, 'Good morning, I trust you both slept well. Isn't it a beautiful morning?'

'Good morning, Mother General.' Brigid glanced behind her to look at her Superior.

'Last night's storm has passed.' The Mother General looked at Brigid kindly as they continued into the Oratory. 'We will walk together,' she said as Marie-Hélène opened the door and stood back to allow the two Reverend Mothers to precede her.

The candles on the altar reflected their flickering light in the beautiful stained-glass window of the Holy Family, and Sister Anthony's organ music rippled around the lamp-lit, peaceful room where several of the nuns were already kneeling in prayer. It had been Brigid's intention to take a seat at the back, but with the Mother General's firm pressure under her elbow, she was ushered to the front row and knelt beside her to pray. Her knees were shaking but a wave of relief and gratitude enveloped her at the support of stalwart friends.

When Lauds was over, they all trooped into the refectory where Una was ready to serve breakfast. Brigid found herself surrounded by her fellow Sisters, everyone asking if she was all right, telling her not to worry about the previous night, and urging her to enjoy her retirement. There was not one word of judgement, not one snide remark. As she sat nibbling on a piece of toast – all she could manage to eat – Brigid realized her harshest critic was, and always would be, herself . . . and of course Imelda.

Later, when it was time for the French nuns to depart, Brigid stood in the small parlour thanking Mother Aloysius. 'Brigid, if everyone in our Order was even half as conscientious and dedicated as you have been, we would be doing *very* well indeed. My last instruction to you as your Mother General is to enjoy every second of your well-deserved and hard-earned retirement. This is your time now. Use it well. And spend every penny your brother gifted you on *yourself*,' she added, laughing.

'Thank you, I'm so grateful for your understanding and kindness, and so sorry for—'

The Mother General laid a gentle finger on her lips. 'We *all* have secrets, Brigid,' she murmured.

Standing on the front step, waving at her fellow nuns as the pale wintery sun made a dazzling appearance from behind the hills on the horizon, Brigid heard the words pop into her head: *A new dawning.* It was almost as though a voice had said it to her.

It *was* a new dawning in her life, and today was the beginning of it. She had the strangest sense of liberation.

'I think,' she said to Una, who was waving vigorously

beside her, 'that I'll get the number of the hairdresser in the village and see if she can fit me in for a haircut. My veil-wearing days are over.'

'Morning, Maman,' Marie-Claire said warily, standing at her parents' hotel room door. She'd walked along the beach from the Four Winds.

'Morning,' Keelin said.

'Are you in a snit?'

'Why wouldn't I be? You and your father ganged up on me last night,' Keelin retorted, stepping back to let her in.

'Yeah, well, I got a shock. It's not nice, finding out that your parents have lied to you.' Marie-Claire walked over to the window and looked out at the glistening sea.

'We never *lied*,' Keelin protested. 'We just never told you.'

'You lied by omission,' Marie-Claire pointed out snootily.

'What are you, a *priest*?' Keelin raised an eyebrow and stared at her daughter.

Marie-Claire, taken aback at the riposte, stood with her mouth open for a second before catching her mother's eye and dissolving into giggles.

'That's good! That's very good,' she chortled.

'I have my moments.' Keelin smiled and held out her arms. 'I'm sorry, dearest. I *did* feel shame, on my behalf and your father's. How could we not feel shame here in Ireland? It's in our blinkin' DNA!' she sighed into Marie-Claire's hair, hugging her daughter tightly. 'And as you've so rightly pointed out, I need to deal with my feelings about the past and let them go, if I'm to live any sort of an authentic life.'

Marie-Claire leaned into her mother's embrace. The shock had not fully worn off that they had hidden something about her origins from her, but she was glad to be reconciled with her mother.

'Keelin, I'm heading off with John and Philly now, I'll go round to Imelda's and sort out your luggage, pack whatever needs packing, then you can collect it from our house. That will save you having to go back there until you feel you want to,' Felicity said kindly, leaning down to kiss her sister-in-law, who was sitting in the conservatory, enjoying a second cup of coffee.

'You're so good, Felicity. Thanks a million.' Keelin stood up and embraced the other woman warmly. 'I need time to calm down and ... what is it the Americans say? *Process* all that's gone on with Mam. If I went near her in the next few days she'd be a very sorry woman.'

'That's understandable. And don't worry, we'll keep an eye on her,' Felicity reassured her.

'I won't be worrying,' said Keelin. 'And I know that's a horrible thing to say. Do you wish you'd married an orphan?' she grinned. 'Have you ever met a family like us?'

'Well, look at it this way: you're never boring,' Felicity chuckled.

'I don't know how you've managed not to throttle my mother, living so close,' Keelin remarked.

'Ah, she's a sad old soul really, and who'd want to be like her? I ignore her carry-on for the most part. It's the only way to deal with her,' Felicity said matter-of-factly.

'She's gone to the hairdresser's, to get her hair cut,' Una informed them, when Marie-Claire and Keelin walked into the kitchen, red-cheeked, after walking from the hotel. 'She's not wearing the veil anymore and she wants you to bring her shopping for clothes, MC,' she added for good measure, enjoying the look of astonishment on their faces.

'Isn't that marvellous? Every cloud has a silver lining,' Keelin rejoiced. 'I never thought she'd give up wearing the veil.'

'It's very significant, if you ask me. Retirement from veil and job bodes very well for the future,' Marie-Claire enthused. 'Una, we're going to ask her to come to France with us. What do you think?'

Una turned to look at them where she was filling the kettle at the sink. 'I think that's a great idea, ladies. And you know it couldn't come at a better time. That cranky old boot Emmanuelle has booked in for a few days next week. I didn't tell RM. I didn't want to ruin her stay.'

Keelin's face darkened, but Marie-Claire didn't notice, she was too entertained by the housekeeper's description. 'A cranky old boot? Is she a nun?' she asked, cutting a couple of slices of brown soda bread.

'Allegedly,' sniffed Una derisively.

'I take it you don't like her.' Marie-Claire grinned, spreading butter on the bread.

'I do not, nor does RM – or your mother for that matter,' Una said chattily, heating the teapot. 'She's a mean-spirited, nasty little witch and I'll never forget the day she called you a—'

'*Una!*' remonstrated Keelin warningly.

'Oh Keelin, I'm *so* sorry. I wasn't thinking. Forgive me.' Una's hand shot to her mouth.

'What did she call me?' Marie-Claire asked, staring at her mother.

'Don't ask me that. It was a long time ago and best left in the past,' Keelin snapped, glaring at Una.

'Was it because you were a nun and dad was a priest?'

'Yes, something like that, although she didn't know your father was a priest.'

'Did she call me a bastard?' Marie-Claire probed.

'Oh, what does it matter, Marie-Claire?' Keelin sighed. 'Let it go!'

'You know this was my first home. The nuns are my family. Una is my family. I'm fed up with secrets. *Tell* me,' Marie-Claire demanded.

'Please, Marie-Claire, leave Keelin alone. I shouldn't have opened my big mouth,' Una pleaded.

'She called you a child of sin. She didn't want you and me living here. She was the only one of the congregation to raise an objection when I came back to Ireland, pregnant, and Brigid asked if I could stay in the Four Winds until you were born. She was here the day Brigid asked the staff if it would be OK by them. When she was overruled up in

Dublin, Emmanuelle took her complaint to the bishop. He told her she should be more Christian like her Sisters. She never came back to the Four Winds until you and I had moved to Dublin,' Keelin said flatly.

'Oh!' Marie-Claire murmured. What a horrible woman this nun seemed to be. 'A cranky old boot indeed, Una.' She tried to lighten the mood, although she was gutted for her mother.

'Oh she was something else, that wan. But RM let her have it that day. I never saw anyone skedaddle out of here as quick as she did. Of course, she was always jealous of RM, especially when she got promoted. Emmanuelle never made it to the top like Brigid – and why would she? She hadn't a Christian bone in her body and she was as thick as a plank. A plank with notions, I might add,' Una scowled, pouring out the tea for them.

'Stop it, Una,' Keelin murmured. 'Don't say things like that.'

'Indeed and I will, and I'll be giving her the lumpiest bed in the house, too. I have me ways and means,' the house-keeper said crossly.

CHAPTER THIRTY-EIGHT

Why did she have aching shoulders, Imelda wondered drowsily, stretching luxuriously in the warmth of her double bed. She yawned and turned sideways to glance at her alarm clock and got a start when she saw it was almost midday, and sunlight was peeping through the top of the curtains. What on earth was she doing sleeping in until this hour on a Saturday morning?

And then she remembered. She should have been waking up in that nice little hotel in Butlersbridge, having celebrated Brigid's eightieth and retirement party. Her heart sank.

No wonder her shoulders ached, she thought wearily. Driving through the torrential rain and gusting winds on those winding country roads until she got to the motorway had been nerve-racking. At times the rain had been so heavy the wipers couldn't cope and she felt she'd been driving through a waterfall, unable to see where she was going.

Imelda got out of bed and threw open the curtains. It was

a sparkling, clear-skied, sunny day, all traces of yesterday's stormy weather erased. The blackbirds were feasting on the apples she'd left out for them; the robin was perched on the birdbath surveying his territory.

All seemed normal, but Imelda knew she'd gone too far this time. It was possible neither Keelin nor Brigid, nor even Marie-Claire, would speak to her for a long time, if ever, she thought as she slid her feet into her slippers and wrapped her snug pink dressing gown around her. Well feck them, she told herself grumpily as she marched into the bathroom. So what if she'd offended them – none of them had had to put up with what she'd had to put up with.

Ten minutes later, Imelda stood at the back door feeding the neighbour's black cat, Sooty. It was bitterly cold but there was a hint of warmth in the sun's rays when she lifted her face to the sky. Sooty weaved around her ankles, head-butting her in gratitude before scoffing the dried food nuggets Imelda had poured in his dish, as if he were starving. The neighbours thought nothing of going off on holidays and leaving the young cat to fend for himself, Imelda observed crossly. They counted on someone taking pity on him and throwing him a bit of food.

'Taken us for granted, Sooty,' Imelda complained. 'But sure, everyone takes me for granted,' she informed him, patting his furry head as he ate, ecstatically happy to be fed. 'I'm in the dog house now because I had a row with them all and told them in no uncertain terms what was what. But does anyone see my side of it? No!' Sooty glanced up at her companionably before resuming his eating.

She left the door ajar, in case he wanted to come in when he was finished feeding. Imelda liked it when Sooty came and sat beside her on the sofa. It was comforting to have another heartbeat in the house, someone to talk to, even if he couldn't talk back. She filled the kettle and dropped two slices of toast into the toaster.

With a frisson of apprehension, she flipped open her phone. Would there be accusatory texts berating her for her bad behaviour? She glanced at the notifications and saw nothing. Not one message. She didn't know whether to be relieved or indignant. For all they knew she could be lying in a ditch in an overturned car, stone dead!

'They couldn't care less about me, Sooty,' she grumbled to the cat, who was now sitting looking up at her.

And why should they? The thought came unbidden. What was it about her that wouldn't let things go?

'Well, he *was* a priest, and he defiled my daughter and brought shame to her,' she muttered angrily, taking a sip of tea. Sooty rubbed his velvety nose against her leg.

When Keelin had phoned and told her she was pregnant, she'd been horrified. Nuns didn't get pregnant. They took vows of chastity. She knew of a couple of young girls who'd got in the family way and taken the boat to England and never been seen in Glencarraig again. How could her daughter even expect that she could come home under such circumstances and not have people talking about her? In those days, getting pregnant outside of marriage was a shameful thing. A stain on the family. So different from today, Imelda mused. Now they had the children and *then* got married!

She'd had enough on her plate, what with looking after her parents and Larry's mother, and all while starting the menopause. 'She's *our* daughter, not Brigid's,' Larry words came back to her. Keelin could do no wrong in her father's eyes.

Last night when she'd seen Keelin and Brigid's loving reunion, she'd been hit with the undeniable knowledge that when Keelin needed a mother most, Brigid had been more of a mother to her than Imelda had. She'd been torn apart with unexpected guilt at the knowledge.

And then when John had presented Brigid with the money – money that she'd not lifted a finger to earn – Imelda had been overcome by the unfairness of it. His final disparaging remarks had ignited the fire of her wrath and she'd said what she'd said. Now, Imelda thought ruefully, she was going to have to live with the consequences.

CHAPTER THIRTY-NINE

'I'm sorry, Armand, please don't be mad at me. You were right. I should never have hidden the truth about your past from Marie-Claire. It was my issue, not yours, and I did you an injustice.' Keelin's voice came down the line and Armand smiled at his wife's earnest tone.

He was walking along the narrow road that led to the Four Winds and his brisk walk, the long way round from Butlersbridge, had cleared his head and dissipated his anger after last night's row.

'I'm not mad, at you, Keelin. Perhaps I'm mad at myself for having agreed to hide my past in the first place. On some level, I think the reason I never brought it up again when Marie-Claire was old enough to understand was that I still hold some underlying shame.'

'Yeah. It brought up guilt in me too. Maybe all this happened so we can *finally* put the past behind us. Or maybe it happened because my mother is an absolute briar!' she added sardonically.

Armand laughed. 'I walked the long way round over to the Four Winds to see if Marie-Claire's OK—'

'Oh! We're here at the wooden steps,' Keelin exclaimed. 'We walked back across the beach. Marie-Claire came to the hotel this morning. She's not long gone up to put the kettle on. I wanted to give you a call to sort things out,' Keelin explained.

'Is she OK?'

'She's fine. We had a bit of a standoff and then we got over it and started to laugh. You know her, she never holds a grudge,' Keelin said lightly.

'Good! I hate when we're fighting. Look I'll be with you in a couple of minutes,' he said. 'Put my name in the pot.'

Walking briskly to get to the Four Winds, Armand saw a sprightly figure marching along ahead of him. It must be one of the nuns. He'd been introduced to quite a few of Brigid's Order the previous evening – thank God he didn't have to remember all their names; a 'Good morning, Sister,' would do, he told himself as he came abreast of the nun who was walking at a fast clip.

'Morning, Sister … Good heavens! Mère! It's you!' he exclaimed. Brigid stopped walking and gave him a self-deprecating smile.

'It is me, Armand. The *new* me.' Her silvery grey hair was styled in a soft feathery cut that emphasized her creamy skin and luminous blue eyes.

'You look beautiful, and if I may say, years younger.'

Armand hugged the woman who had been one of his greatest benefactresses.

'I like it,' Brigid declared stoutly. 'Although my ears are cold – I should have brought a woolly hat. Are you all right, Armand? Are Keelin and Marie-Claire all right? Imelda certainly knows how to end a party in double-quick time.' She threw her eyes up to heaven.

'I know,' Armand sighed, falling into step beside her. 'Keelin's upset, we're all very upset for you too.'

'What a strange night it was. There must be a Divine purpose to it, though what it is I have no idea,' Brigid sighed.

'Perhaps it was so you could get a stylish hairdo,' Armand teased, opening the red swing gate for her.

'Well now, I never thought of that,' Brigid laughed, and they were still laughing when they walked into the kitchen.

'Mère! It's *gorgeous!*' cried Keelin.

'Well, she did a great job on you!' Una added.

'Helen Mirren, eat your heart out!' Marie-Claire grinned with a flourish.

'Helen Mirren – I'll take that,' Brigid said, a tad abashed by their compliments. 'I was just saying to Armand, it's the new me.'

'Mère, Maman and I have come up with a brilliant idea: you must come to Le Quatre Vents with me when I fly over to join her and Papa for a holiday. You're retired now. You can do as you please. What do you think?' Marie-Claire gazed at her expectantly.

Brigid looked at her great-niece, astonished. 'Well, now!'

she said slowly. 'I *am* retired. I *can* do as I please. And now I'm a woman of independent means ... when do we go?'

Laughter erupted around the table as the Angelus bell chimed noon, and Marie-Claire took her iPad out of her bag to book Brigid's flight to France.

At last, thought Armand, delighted. Now he could *finally* show Keelin's much-loved aunt how grateful they were to her for taking them all under her wing when they had needed it most.

CHAPTER FORTY

Brigid sat staring at her reflection in the mirror, admiring her styled hair. She loved the way the silvery ash fringe feathered her forehead and swept sideways. It was very sophisticated indeed. *Well, now I can add vanity to my ever-growing list of sins*, she told herself. As for the new dress: that was indeed an occasion of sin, Brigid thought giddily. And she *loved* it!

When Armand had first suggested bringing her, Keelin, Marie-Claire, Marie-Hélène, Una and Maura, to dinner in the hotel, she'd demurred. She knew the gossip about the party was spreading like wildfire around the village. She'd got a few sideways glances and averted eyes when she'd walked into the hairdresser's this morning, but Vera, the hairdresser, had handed her a book of hairstyles and she'd sat down to flick through them, fighting the urge to get up and run.

'That would be a nice one on you,' said the girl who came

to bring her to the basin to wash her hair, pointing to a picture of the feather-cut style Brigid now sported.

When Vera had finished and she went to pay, Brigid's spirits had been lifted when Peggy Flynn, the butcher's wife, had complimented her: 'Very nice, Reverend Mother,' she approved. 'And enjoy your retirement.'

'Thank you, Peggy. I'll do my best.' Brigid smiled at the other woman and left the hairdresser's, glad that she'd not delayed in making her first foray into the village. The next time wouldn't be so hard.

Going to the hotel for dinner though had been a step too far for her nerves, and when Armand issued the invitation, she'd said no.

'Ah come on,' urged Marie-Hélène. 'That hair needs celebrating!'

'It would do you good,' Una interjected. 'What's the point in moping around here?'

'Do you know what we could do?' Marie-Claire's eyes lit up. 'We could nip over to Kilrush now and get something nice for you to wear—'

'Yay ... a girls' jaunt! I'm in,' exclaimed Marie-Hélène.

'No, no, no!' protested Brigid, laughing.

'Mère, think of the fun we'd have,' Keelin urged, cheering up at the prospect. 'It will only take half an hour or so to get there, an hour and a half to buy an outfit and have a cup of coffee, and we'll be back here before dark. We can all have a rest and then an early dinner in the hotel. A little celebration of your new life, with us,' her niece wheedled.

'Oh, all right then!' Brigid succumbed. Imelda's accusations had been as upsetting for her niece and great-niece as they had been for her. Perhaps the 'girl's jaunt' as Marie-Hélène called it was exactly what they all needed. The day was fine. The driving would be easy. What harm could it do?

A lot of harm to her purse, it turned out. Brigid smiled at the memory. It was the first spending spree she'd ever gone on in her life.

While Armand had gone fishing, the women had piled into Una's station wagon, made a pit stop at the hotel for Keelin and Marie-Claire to change their shoes, then headed for the town of Kilrush, twenty-five kilometres away.

She'd felt a frisson of nervous excitement when she'd walked into the clothes shop. She wouldn't buy anything too flashy. Plain cardigans, blouses and skirts, like most of her fellow nuns wore.

Marie-Claire and Marie-Hélène had other ideas. She ended up with two pairs of beautifully cut trousers, a tailored ruby-red jacket, three tops, two skirts – not pleated, at Marie-Hélène's insistence – and two jumpers. And then the dress she'd worn to dinner. She ran her fingers over the soft russet velvet jacquard material that flared out slightly from her narrow waist to drape in elegant folds to mid-calf. The small gold cross on its fine chain that her parents had given her when she took her final vows was the only jewellery she wore. Keelin had seen the dress and held it up against her.

'Mère, it's beautiful. So simple, so elegant, so perfect. Try it on.'

When she'd looked at herself in the mirror, Brigid could not believe it. Who was this elegant, slender woman? A pang of regret for that woman who had been so firmly repressed – by her own choice, Brigid admitted – brought tears to her eyes, knowing that her life could have been so different. She swallowed hard. She'd made her choice, even if it might have been a mistake, and she'd to live with it. Strange though how she'd never seen 'herself' when wearing the habit.

Vanity had been ground down to dust in the early years of her vocation. She only looked in a mirror to make sure her wimple was straight, and her only concession to her facial appearance was to rub in Nivea Creme moisturizer in the morning and to make sure her eyebrows didn't grow wild, or that the odd facial hair around her mouth and chin was plucked.

The woman who was looking back at her now in the full-length mirror was feminine, stylish and unknown to her. How dainty and neat her wrists were, and how long her fingers. How gracefully her calves tapered into neatly turned ankles, and her petite bosom was still firm, the dress material outlining her womanly shape in a way her habit never had.

Life as a nun had taken so much from her. It had all been about the denial of self. Innate human inclinations, needs and desires were suppressed, unless you were a rebel like Marie-Hélène. Brigid had always admired the younger nun's courage in being herself. It was different now, of course. Convents had been transformed since her day, and individuality and self-expression were now encouraged.

Here she was, at eighty years of age, reclaiming her femininity. A moment of liberation. The liberation of Brigid Dunne, she acknowledged as she stood silently rediscovering herself for a few moments before she wiped away her tears, straightened her shoulders and emerged to await the verdict of her 'girls'.

Their gasps of admiration brought a faint pink blush to her cheeks. 'Part of me wants to get straight back into my habit,' she confessed in embarrassment.

'No!' said Keelin firmly. 'You will *not* hide yourself. Never again.'

'You *shall* go to the ball, Cinderella, and this is the dress you'll wear. Buy it,' Marie-Hélène commanded.

'You can't order your Reverend Mother around like that,' Brigid retorted.

'My *retired* RM,' the younger nun had winked, and Brigid and the others laughed.

They had laughed a lot at the candlelit dinner that evening, as if by unspoken, mutual consent, the events of the previous evening had been put aside. Embracing a hedonistic lifestyle with gusto now that she was eighty, she'd allowed herself a small sherry beforehand. 'It's never too late to go to the dogs,' she joked to the others.

Brigid slipped out of the first beautiful dress she'd ever possessed and hung it neatly in the wardrobe. There were very few people she could be as relaxed with as she was with Keelin, Marie-Claire, Marie-Hélène, Una and Maura, she reflected. Perhaps it was because they'd all stood shoulder to shoulder when the Order had sent her niece home in disgrace from Africa, and Imelda had turned her back on her.

When Marie-Claire had been born and Brigid had held her for the first time, she'd wept, overcome with emotion at the memory of the child she'd once carried. A child who would have been Keelin's first cousin. She would have been a bit older than her niece – if it were a girl, and somehow Brigid had always felt her lost child had been a girl.

Holding Keelin's new baby, her tiny fists waving in the air, her beautiful big blue eyes drooping in sleep, Brigid had had the strangest feeling that God was giving *her* a baby to replace the void left by the loss of her own, all those years ago. How precious were those moments whenever she got to cuddle her great-niece, and, after a few months, when she was weaned, give her her bottle.

On Friday evenings she would drive down to the Four Winds and stay the night, and Brigid could not describe the joy and balm to her spirit when she would take the baby to her room and sit in her rocking chair and feed her and change her and sometimes bathe her, cooing lovingly to her, pretending that she was her own child. On Saturday night she would return to the convent renewed by her joyful interaction with Keelin and Marie-Claire.

It had been a time of love and joy in the Four Winds, when Marie-Claire had been born. Una and Maura were young housemaids back then. Marie-Hélène, convalescing after a car accident, had been such a support to Keelin when she'd been most vulnerable. They had *all* rallied around mother and baby in the most loving and practical way and, in the process, had become a tight-knit little family.

She'd watched her fellow Sisters interact with the baby, some of them nervous at first, others hardly able to wait their turn to 'get a go of her', and seen their maternal instincts, which had been dampened by the way of life imposed on them, awaken. Marie-Claire had truly seemed a gift from God.

'False humility is a sin, Sister Brigid. *We* feel you're the right person to do God's work in Limerick. So be it! Now go and pray and give thanks for the new opportunities He has given you to do that work.' Brigid smiled, remembering the haughty tone of her spiritual director all those years ago. What would she say to her *now*, after Imelda's revelations?

Something about humility, certainly. Last night had brought her as low as it was possible to be in her position as Reverend Mother. But it had also brought freedom. Her secret was out, no longer to be carried like a yoke on her shoulders. She was freer than she'd been the last sixty-four years. And that in itself was another gift from God. A gift she was going to enjoy every second of, Brigid resolved, switching out the light and climbing into bed and snuggling down under the duvet, drawing it up under her chin.

The red lamp under the picture of the Sacred Heart glowed comfortingly and Jesus's kind smile seemed to assure her that all would be well.

CHAPTER FORTY-ONE

For the umpteenth time, Imelda glanced at her mobile phone. She was a tad vexed, to say the least. Not *one* message from anyone to see if she was alive or dead.

She glanced at her phone again, wondering should she text Felicity to see if she was home. It wasn't her Sunday to have lunch with them; perhaps her daughter-in-law might think she was looking for an invite. No, better not to text.

She had Sunday lunch with her son and daughter-in-law on the first Sunday of every month and would always text Cormac if she was dropping in for an unplanned visit. Instead of hastening to assure her that she didn't need to go to the trouble of texting, the first time she'd done so, he'd told her it was a great way of seeing what suited everyone. 'Setting boundaries' was the term now used, seemingly. Imelda had read it in a magazine article at the hairdresser's and it had stuck in her head.

They might not be so smart about their boundaries if she told then she was leaving all her money to charity – particularly those charities who cared for elderly people living alone – Imelda had sniffed, spending a thoroughly enjoyable half-hour under the hairdryer imagining the reaction when her will was read out to the family.

The whole lot of them were now giving her the cold shoulder, Imelda thought bitterly, wondering could she send a text to them all to say FYI – she liked that very much, sharp and businesslike – I will be updating my will next week, and, as previously, the updated document will be with Fitzpatrick's Solicitors, in the event of anything untoward happening to me.

That might give them all a hop and let them see she wasn't to be trifled with. Larry had left her very comfortable. They'd all be getting a fine lump sum when she was gone, *if* she didn't change her will.

Even next door's kitty had abandoned her, it seemed. Sooty was another one who suited himself, Imelda thought crossly, divesting herself of her coat and hat and filling the kettle. He could feck off if he came to the door later, looking for food.

She leaned her elbows on the kitchen counter, waiting for the kettle to boil, imagining the look on her children's faces if she sent the text. They'd probably call her childish, Imelda acknowledged, sighing so deeply her breath fluttered the petals of her indoor cyclamen. Or, worse, that other term she'd read in an agony aunt's letter recently ... What was it again? She racked her brains, annoyed that she couldn't think of it immediately. She hated not being as sharp as she once was. Passive-aggressive, that was it, she thought trium-phantly. They'd say she was being passive-aggressive, which apparently was much worse than coming right out and saying things straight, which was her preferred method of dealing with something.

Keelin and her lot and Brigid were probably all down in the Four Winds, giving out about her right now. Or perhaps Brigid was sulking in her room while Keelin, Armand and Marie-Claire were holed up in the hotel, bad-mouthing Imelda over their cappuccinos or lattes or whatever fancy nonsense they called coffee these days. Well, bad scran to them, let them say and do what they liked. They could all go to hell in a handcart for all she was concerned.

Sundays were the days she missed Larry most, she thought sadly, admiring the daphne in all its pink and white glory, a winter jewel amongst the bare-branched trees and shrubs. Her husband would close the shop after the congregation from the ten-thirty Mass had bought their papers and ice cream and cream, the biggest sellers on Sunday mornings. He would come home, change out of his three-piece suit, and join her in the kitchen to prepare the Sunday lunch.

He would peel the potatoes and chop the vegetables while she made an apple tart or crumble, the smell of the roast-ing joint pervading the kitchen. He'd tell her who'd been in to the shop and if there was any news doing the rounds and, once she started making the gravy, he would drive off to collect their parents to bring them back for their much-looked-forward-to home-cooked meal.

After tea and a finger of home-made ginger cake had been served, later in the afternoon, Larry would drive their parents home, with a foil-wrapped dinner each for the next day. Keelin and the boys would have done the washing up and gone to meet friends, and Imelda would lie on the sofa, exhausted, and take a rare nap.

In wintertime, Larry would build up the fire and they would sit together companionably and read the papers and watch TV, or in spring, summer and autumn, they'd take a drive to the coast and walk along the beach enjoying the fresh salty air.

Larry was the only one who had accepted her the way she was, even with her sharp tongue and sense of injustice. He'd been a very understanding husband, but then, by the same token, she'd been very tolerant of him when she'd had to be. And that hadn't been easy. After all the emotional upheaval brought on by his relationship with Fran Cassidy, there had been mostly affectionate companionship in the latter years of their marriage, until Keelin got pregnant, that she greatly missed.

Feeling in need of comfort, Imelda went into the small pantry off the kitchen and cut herself a thick slice of tea brack and slathered it with butter. Not great for her cholesterol, but she didn't care anymore. If she died this minute, no one would give a damn, she thought bitterly, adding milk to her tea.

No one would weep for her like they'd wept for Larry. Such a strange disease, haemochromatosis, and so common to Ireland. He had succumbed to it when all it needed was for him to be monitored regularly by their GP. But no one knew that back then. At least nowadays there was a Haemochromatosis Society with up-to-date information.

She hadn't known until she read it in the autopsy results that Larry had suffered from the illness. She'd blamed his heart attack on the stress of all that had gone on with their daughter. How bitterly they had fought over Keelin. But she'd argued back with every weapon in her armoury and, looking back on it now, she could see that his creeping illness had weakened him so much, he hadn't been able to rally sufficiently, especially when she'd shot her parting arrow of bitterness, about Fran, that he had no answer for.

Even now, remembering the cruelty of her words brought tears of shame and regret to Imelda's eyes and she sat at her kitchen table weeping.

'Leave her up there to stew for a while, Felicity. She's a bitter old pill and what she did to Brigid and Keelin at that party was unforgivable. If I'd have been there, I'd have lambasted her,' Cormac growled, draining the steaming mushy peas.

'Well then, I'm glad you weren't.' Felicity cut thick succulent slices of beef from the roast and set them on a plate for her mother-in-law. 'There's enough bad feeling in the family without *you* getting involved.'

'She's *too* smart with her sharp tongue.' Cormac snaffled a crispy bit off the top of the beef and got his knuckles rapped with the carving fork. 'She's mean-spirited and always has been. She didn't tell Keelin for months after Dad died that he had haemochromatosis and that was what weakened his heart. She let Keelin believe his heart attack was all her fault, and I won't ever forgive her for that.'

'I know,' Felicity sighed, spooning creamy mash onto Imelda's plate. 'But that was all water under the bridge and they'd made up, years ago. Why could she not have kept her mouth shut at the party? She's her own worst enemy.'

'And you're too good to her, and too soft.' Her husband put his arm around his wife's shoulder and gave her a hug.

'Ah, she didn't have it easy in those years after your da died, and before it. It was no joke looking after her parents and his, and then running the shop when Larry passed.'

'I took that over,' Cormac said indignantly. 'Despite the fact I wanted to study architecture.'

'It wasn't meant to be. You'd probably have met some posh totty in uni and married her and been miserable. And here you are, with a thriving business and *me* for a wife. How lucky are *you*?' she teased, flicking him with the tea towel and he laughed, picking up the colander of mushy peas to pour them into a dish.

After they'd eaten the lunch and the dishwasher had been loaded, Felicity placed the Clingfilm wrapped plate of dinner into a shopping bag and added a dessert dish full of trifle.

She was dreading the visit to her mother-in-law's. She didn't like being involved in family rows. She was half sorry now that she'd offered to collect Keelin and Armand's luggage.

Imelda would be shocked to know that they weren't intending upon coming back to Glencarraig. It was a real slap in the face, even if a deserved one, and Felicity would much prefer not to have to break that news to her. Now she was stuck in the middle of them all when it was really nothing to do with her. One way or another she was in a no-win situation, Felicity thought gloomily, reversing out of the drive to make the short trip down the road to Imelda's house. She should have kept her mouth shut and let them sort it themselves but she'd felt so sorry for her sister and brother-in-law the night of the party.

'Were you too lazy to walk?' her mother-in-law asked smartly, when Felicity knocked on the back door and let herself in.

'No, Mrs O'Brien, I wasn't. I'll tell you why I drove in a minute,' Felicity said calmly, placing the shopping bag on the table. 'I've brought you a dinner and some trifle for dessert. Would you like to have it now? I'll heat it up in the microwave if you want.'

'That's very kind of you.' Imelda's eyes brightened. Felicity was a great cook and she always enjoyed the meals her daughter-in-law served. 'I wasn't expecting that. I'll have it now, then. I'm a bit peckish. I wasn't in the humour for cooking a full dinner. Eh ... were you talking to anyone ... ?' she enquired delicately while Felicity put the plate in the microwave.

'Not a sinner,' Felicity said lightly. 'Cormac and myself had a lazy morning.'

'I went past the house and saw the cars there as I was going to Mass,' Imelda remarked, fetching cutlery from the dresser to set her place at the table. The aroma emanating from the microwave was mouth-watering and she suddenly realized that she was famished.

'A glass of milk?' Felicity enquired.

'Huh, the way I feel I'd be as well turning to the vino. I've upset everyone, I suppose,' Imelda came straight out with it.

'Sit down there and enjoy your dinner.' Felicity ignored the comment, placing the steaming plate in front of her mother-in-law.

'I'll never eat all that,' Imelda declared, dipping a spoon into a small dish of horseradish sauce and spreading it over the roast beef.

'Eat as much as you can,' Felicity said. Imelda always said the same thing every time a meal was put in front of her, before clearing her plate. 'Will I light the fire for you while you're eating?' she asked, anxious to get the visit over as soon as possible.

'That would be lovely. I'll sit looking at the Christmas tree. It's nearly the sixth. Time to take it down. The season flew in,' Imelda observed, filling her fork with mushy peas and creamy potatoes.

Felicity set the fire and put a match to it, and placed Imelda's Sunday paper on the small side table beside her chair. Her mother-in-law was tucking into the trifle when she went back into the kitchen ten minutes later.

'That was delicious,' Imelda declared. 'I didn't realize how hungry I was.' She indicated the empty plate. 'You can put that in the dishwasher.'

'Will I make you a cup of tea to bring into the lounge?' Felicity was used to her mother-in-law's imperious ways and she did as she was bid.

'Yes, that would be grand,' Imelda nodded, scraping the trifle dish.

'Em ... Mrs O'Brien, I'm going to collect Keelin and Armand's luggage. They're not coming back to this neck of the woods before they fly home to France,' Felicity said in as matter-of-fact a tone as she could muster. 'I'll meet them with it along the motorway one of these days.'

Imelda's jaw dropped. She blanched, reddened and swallowed, reminding Felicity of a guppy she'd seen on one of David Attenborough's documentaries.

'You'd better go up and get it so,' she said tightly, her eyes glittering, when she'd recovered some composure. 'I'll make the tea myself while you're doing it.'

Felicity avoided catching Imelda's eye. Her mother-in-law was clearly mortified and stunned; she didn't want to add to her discomfiture.

There wasn't much to pack away and Felicity lugged the large case downstairs and hefted it into the car boot before returning to say goodbye. Imelda was ensconced in her armchair, back straight, head high. 'Thank you for my dinner, Felicity. It was tasty as always. Enjoy the rest of your evening.' She nodded dismissively.

'Can I get anything else for you?' Even though she

could have strangled her, Felicity's heart went out to the elderly woman.

'Not a thing, thank you. If you could close the gate, I'd be obliged.'

'I will indeed. Ring me if you need anything,' Felicity assured her, hurrying to get into her car and make her escape.

Imelda's heart felt as though a thousand thistles had stung it. Keelin and Armand weren't coming back to spend the last week of their holiday with her. All that lovely stuffing and gravy she'd made, now languishing in her freezer, would do her until Easter, she thought distractedly. When Felicity had told her they weren't coming back to Glencarraig, it had taken all Imelda's self-control not to burst into tears and make a show of herself.

This time there would be no forgiveness. And she only had herself to blame. She'd given in to herself and let her tongue, and bitterness, run amok.

With the fire crackling merrily and the lights of the Christmas tree illuminating the gloom of the evening, Imelda sat alone in her armchair, tears rolling down her cheeks.

CHAPTER FORTY-TWO

Brigid pulled her woollen hat down over her ears. In the past she'd relied on her veil to keep her head snug in wild and windy weather; without it, she felt strangely different. As if the 'wholeness' of her was now emerging. She recalled someone describing a workaholic as a flower with only one petal unfurled. In a way, she too had only unfurled one petal on her beautiful flower. Now, with her symbolic discarding of the veil, and her forthcoming trip to France, other petals were opening out as a whole new life beckoned.

She sat on the small wooden bench on top of the bank overlooking the ocean, one of her favourite places in the world. White clouds scudded across the sky and far on the horizon a dark grey line hinted at the rain to come as a weather front made its inexorable progress toward the coast. Much as she'd love to take a walk along the strand, it was time to say goodbye, for a while, to her beloved Four Winds, standing robust and resolute atop the cliff, no matter what the weather. '*Slán agus beannacht,*' she said in her native language. 'Until I see you again, God willing.'

'I'll miss you. It's been great having you all to stay, even if the party didn't quite go to plan,' Una remarked as she and Keelin finished changing the last bed and were folding sheets to add to the pile on the landing.

'I didn't think Armand and I would be staying as long as we did,' Keelin said ruefully. 'Thanks for taking us in when we had to leave the hotel.'

'Not a bother,' Una straightened the duvet on the single bed, now ready for whatever nun might arrive for a few days' respite in the holiday home.

'The Four Winds has always been a haven for me. I love it and you dearly.'

'And everyone here loves you, Keelin,' her old friend assured her. 'Any word from Imelda?'

'No!' said Keelin grimly, walking out to the landing to gather the dirty linen to bring to the small laundry room downstairs. 'Felicity has been popping in and out. She says she's subdued.'

'A rare description of Imelda,' Una observed, following her down the stairs with her arms full.

'Yeah well, apparently she's not subdued enough to apologize. I swear to God, Una, this time I'm *not* giving in. She can get lost. She's got away with offensive behaviour before, but this was beyond the beyond.'

'So you won't be taking a detour to Glencarraig?'

'Absolutely *not*! My mother needs to learn that there are consequences when she behaves the way she does. And I'm not enabling her bad behaviour anymore. I'm fed up with her treating me like shite.' Keelin glowered, shoving sheets into the washing machine and adding a washing tablet.

'It will all settle down eventually,' Una soothed, pouring in the conditioner and switching on the machine.

'You know something, Una, right now I don't care whether it does or not. I know it's a horrible thing to say, but I don't like my mother – and I never have.'

'Ah don't say that, Keelin,' Una murmured in dismay.

'It's true,' Keelin said miserably. 'But you know, that's OK. To paraphrase Florence-Scovel-Shinn: "No man is my friend. No man is my enemy. Every man is my teacher." So I suppose we're teaching each other lessons of *some* sort or another.'

'So what's going on with you and your chap? Something's up, isn't it?' Brigid cast a knowing look at Marie-Claire. She was sitting propped against the pillows of her hotel bed, in the room that they were sharing, watching Marie-Claire cleanse, tone and moisturize.

Marie-Claire met her great-aunt's keen gaze in the mirror opposite the bed, where she was seated surrounded by beauty products.

'Why do you think that?' Marie-Claire paused her cleansing ritual, wondering why she was surprised at the question. Mère knew her so well, and it was almost impossible to pull the wool over her eyes.

'Your eyes are sad. Your *joie de vivre* is gone. You're making a big effort to appear normal – and doing a good job, if I may say so – but you haven't spoken about him like you always do. And the length of your stay is surprisingly long, and you've not mentioned the trip to New York that you'd been telling me about,' Brigid said, looking out at her over the top of her glasses.

Marie-Claire turned to face her great-aunt. 'You always were good at sussing me out. Hercule Poirot would be proud of you, Mère.' She managed a smile.

'What happened, *alannah*?' Brigid's tone was full of love and sympathy.

The old, familiar Irish endearment caught Marie-Claire off guard and tears brimmed in her eyes.

'He cheated on me.' Her voice shook.

'Well then perhaps he's not worthy of you. Better to find that out now than later,' Brigid pointed out.

'But it hurts so badly. I feel I've wasted those years with him. Now I have to start all over in a relationship, if I ever find someone, and I've to get another job, too.' Marie-Claire burst into tears.

Brigid threw back the duvet and got out of bed with a sprightliness that belied her eighty years. She put her arms around her beloved great-niece's shoulders and Marie-Claire cuddled into her embrace.

'I could tell you there are other fish in the sea. I could tell you there's a whole fresh start awaiting you, a new chapter in your life. But you don't want to hear these clichés now.

The wound is too raw and you think it will never heal. It will. I promise you. All I can say that might bring you some comfort is that this too shall pass, and it's all right to grieve what you perceive as your loss, but time will change your perception of it. And you know it's always possible to forgive, when the hurt has lessened. If you feel you could forgive this young man in time, do it. Forgiveness can be a very power-ful gift for both of you. It could even strengthen your bond immeasurably,' Brigid counselled. She gave Marie-Claire a comforting squeeze. 'I'm eighty, remember? I'm supposed to be wise,' she added lightly.

'Oh, Mère, thank you for your advice. It's been hard pre-tending everything's OK.'

'I think your parents know something's up.' Brigid kissed the top of her head before getting back into bed. 'Mothers and fathers know their children and know when something's wrong, so my advice is to tell them and let them comfort you as only they can,' she advised sagely.

'You're right, Mère.' Marie-Claire wiped her eyes with a tissue. 'There is a bright side, though. If it hadn't happened, I wouldn't be going to France with you.'

'I can't wait. Now get into bed, we have a very early start in the morning.'

'Yes, RM,' grinned Marie-Claire. 'But when we get to Le Quatre Vents. *I'll* be bossing *you* around.'

Later, in the dark, listening to Brigid's soft breathing, Marie-Claire felt certain that she would never be able to forgive Marc. It was natural that Brigid would tell her to forgive, she being a nun and all, but being realistic, she didn't think it was going to be an option she would take. And on the subject of forgiveness, she wondered how her grandmother was faring. Imelda would never have been able to utter endearments like '*alannah*', or 'dear' the way Brigid had upon hearing Marie-Claire's tale of woe. Imelda would have been brisk and no-nonsense, telling her not to cry over spilt milk and to get on with it.

They were so different in their ways, the two sisters. But for all her sharpness, Imelda's prickliness came from wounds that had never healed. As furious as she was with her grandmother for the upset she'd caused, she felt a tiny bit of sympathy for her. Perhaps when she came back to Ireland, Marie-Claire would drive down to her grandmother and see if she could get her to make that first move towards reconciliation. Because, right now, Keelin was uncharacteristically adamant that she wasn't going to be the one to make the first move in healing the rift. Surely, with time having passed, Imelda might be open to the idea. Marie-Claire hoped so. Life was hard enough without the family being at loggerheads.

Imelda picked up her mobile and scrolled down the numbers until she came to the Four Winds. It was three weeks since the row, and she hadn't heard a peep from any of the family, apart from Felicity, and Cormac, who was being cool with her.

She hadn't believed that Keelin and Armand would actually go back to France without saying goodbye, despite

Felicity coming to collect their luggage. Her pride had prevented her from asking her daughter-in-law what day were they meeting her en route to Dublin, and Felicity hadn't mentioned it. But as the days dragged by and it became clear that they weren't going to phone, let alone visit, Imelda felt bereft. Keelin was clearly very angry. Brigid might be a little more forgiving. There was nothing to do but make some sort of apology to her sister and hope that Brigid might persuade Keelin to let bygones be bygones.

The thing was, Brigid's phone seemed to be constantly off. Or perhaps it was a dodgy signal down at the Four Winds. Imelda's best bet was to ring the landline and ask to speak to her, though she wasn't particularly enamoured of the idea of speaking to Una. She clicked on the name and pressed dial, her heart thumping a little faster, wondering what sort of a reception she'd get from her sister.

'The Four Winds.' Una's familiar west of Ireland burr came clearly over the airwaves.

'Una, it's Imelda here. I'd like to speak to Brigid, please, I can't seem to get her on her mobile,' Imelda said briskly, not even bothering to say hello.

'Well I'm afraid you won't reach Reverend Mother here, Imelda. She's gone to France. You'll have to ring her at Les Quatre Vents.'

'Gone to France! For how long?' Imelda was astonished.

'Indefinitely, Imelda. As I say, try ringing Les Quatre Vents. Bye bye,' came Una's crisp response, and then the phone went dead.

Imelda stared at the receiver, stunned. Brigid had gone to France too, without even a text to say she was leaving. How long had this jaunt been planned for? It had to be since before the party, she'd imagine. No one had said anything to her about it. Typical! The whole lot of them couldn't care less about her. All going on holidays behind her back. Did they not think that a holiday in France might have done her good? If she'd been invited to go with them, she might have kept her powder dry at the party and not been driven to vent her resentment at their treatment of her. But this slap in the face was one more example of the way she was treated by her so-called family.

Well, she'd had enough of them. If they could hurt her, she could hurt them.

Imelda slammed down the landline handset, picked up her mobile phone and scrolled down her contacts until she came to her solicitor's number and pressed dial. It was answered almost immediately. 'Annie, it's Imelda O'Brien. Can you give me an appointment to see Garrett, please? I want to revise my will,' she said, her lips a thin line of disapproval, her eyes narrow slits of fury as she drummed her fingers impatiently on the kitchen counter, waiting to be given the date that would see Keelin, Marie-Claire and Brigid summarily disinherited. No ifs, ands, or buts about it!

CHAPTER FORTY-THREE

Brigid flung open the duck-egg blue shutters and opened the window to breathe in the fresh Pyrenean air. Below her, the fields of the Durand family's vineyard stretched to meadows and hillsides beyond, shaded by the majesty of Mount Canigou. It was a view she never tired of.

It was hard to believe she'd been in France for nearly three months, but the heat of the morning sun, shining on the red roof tiles of the houses in the village below, was growing stronger daily, and the long shadows of winter were shortening as spring blessed the Pyrenees.

How she loved this sturdy, stone-walled *maison de maître* with the shuttered windows and big wooden front door. Her bedroom was on the third floor. A large square room, with a double bed and an old-fashioned, gleaming, cherrywood wardrobe and dressing table. A winged armchair placed beside the biggest window was her favourite place to read, or simply watch the changing light of the sun and sky over Canigou, and the vineyards, fields and village below. Today the sky was clear and bright, right across to the coast, the peaks of the mountains sharply etched against the azure palette.

Two days previously, Canigou's majestic snow-capped peak had been shrouded from view by the mist weaving its way across the vineyards towards Les Quatre Vents. Brigid had spent a gloomy afternoon reading in her armchair; engrossed in a book Keelin had given her. The memoir of a woman, Fiona McLaren, who came to the conclusion that the painting that had hung in her farmhouse for many years was a lost Da Vinci. The subject of the painting was Mary Magdalene – hidden in plain sight, as were many of the artist's depictions of the woman believed by some to have been married to Jesus. The journey to authentication was full of revelations, and Brigid had flipped from reading the book to googling names and facts on the new iPad she'd treated herself to. The Gnostic gospels, the gospel of Mary Magdalene and the gospel of Saint Thomas, made intriguing reading.

Since she'd been in the Languedoc, where the Magdalene was revered, Brigid, who would once have dismissed the notion of her marriage to Jesus out of hand, was beginning to realize that the Church she'd served for so long, and with such blind faith, had suppressed much knowledge that would have diminished their authority.

Keelin, who was an expert on such esoteric knowledge, had driven her places where the Magdalene was venerated, and even up to Rennes-le-Château, which had become famous after the publication of *The Da Vinci Code*. Keelin explained knowledgeably that Rennes-le-Château had been known about long before the American author had spotted its potential as a money-spinner. Keelin had given her a copy of *The Holy Blood and the Holy Grail*, one of the first books to draw attention to the esoteric secrets of the small French village, but it was the books of a superb writer called Patrice Chaplin that had most resonated with Brigid, especially when the author wrote about the mysterious, mystical Mount Canigou, a mountain of initiation, where many, including the author, claimed to have experienced a portal that led beyond earthly realms.

Brigid had visited the famous monastery on the Mount, with Keelin and Marie-Claire, and they had climbed the winding path upwards for an hour, immersed in the mystical powerful energy that the mountain seemed to radiate. As they climbed, the summit disappeared, veiled in ethereal cloud, and the wind rose, pushing against them; it was kinder in their descent, blowing against their backs and speeding their way. A path of initiation, Patrice Chaplin had called the route in her book *The Portal*.

She too was on a path of initiation, Brigid reflected, as a dove cooed in the eaves. Having wasted years in dull acceptance, controlled obedience, and institutionalized rigidity, she was now hungry for knowledge. Unlike Marie-Hélène, who reasoned and questioned and was true to her own sense of self, and whose religious life was vibrantly alive as a result, Brigid had been intellectually lazy, suppressing every trace of individuality to become part of the hive mind. Now, at eighty years of age, she chastised herself for her passivity and cowardice. She'd thought she was leading a spiritual life, when all she'd done was toe the party line and accept the rulings of a patriarchal, misogynistic controlling clique of men who would never know what true Christianity meant, despite their so-called theological knowledge.

She'd had such interesting, thought-provoking conversations with Keelin and Armand on all the scandals, lies, and abuses of power that were so prevalent in the news. She read accounts of nuns throwing ice-cold water over children who had wet the bed, leaving them shivering and terrified; and mothers who had babies torn from their arms to be sold to American families. Brigid had wept reading the stories of the women trapped in the Magdalene laundries. And of their children, ill-treated and fostered to families as slave labour. It beggared belief that anyone could treat young women and children with such *cruelty* – let alone do it in the name of God. And then there were the accounts of those who didn't survive: the bodies of nearly eight hundred babies found in an old septic tank in a mother-and-baby home in Tuam. How could her fellow nuns in that religious Order condone and be a part of such horror? Where was their humanity?

What would have been her own fate if her pregnancy had run to term, she wondered. Would her parents have sent her to a mother-and-child home? The shame of being pregnant outside of marriage and carrying an illegitimate child was so enormous in those days, Tom and Elizabeth Dunne might have thought they were doing their best for their daughter, hiding her shame by sending her to such an institution. After all, the nuns ran them, and no one questioned the holiness of nuns back then. There but for the Grace of God went she, Brigid thought to herself whenever some new revelation broke about the cruelty perpetuated by the Church on young, unmarried pregnant women and their babies.

She'd trained with nuns who were cruel and sarcastic in a mentally abusive way, but she'd known far more Sisters who were kind, patient and giving, and who had inspired her own behaviour when she'd become a Reverend Mother herself.

These last months in France had changed her radically. Brigid had never felt so free physically or intellectually, and as she cycled into the nearby village of Bois d'Abbés to get the daily bread and pastries from the boulangerie, she vowed that she would come back to this heavenly place. There was a situation that needed to be resolved at home, before she could truly settle into her retirement. Her very *active* retirement, she thought proudly, placing her bike outside the bakery, not the slightest bit out of breath.

'*Bonjour*, Brigid,' Madame Gironde, the owner, greeted her warmly when she entered the shop, the smell of freshly baked bread making her feel hungry. 'What a beautiful morning.'

'Indeed it is, Louise. The wind has died. It will be a good afternoon for our boules match.'

'It was strong, yesterday, the Tramontane,' Louise observed, placing two baguettes, a *fougasse* and a brioche in white paper bags, and taking a box filled with pastries from a shelf. 'Keelin asked me to put these aside. Is she doing a holistic day today?'

'She is. I'll do the morning meditation, but I'll be in the square for the boules this afternoon,' Brigid assured her.

'Ah, *bonjour*, Brigid! Would you like to join us on a painting trip to Casteil next Thursday? Monsieur Delacroix has offered to take us in his minibus.' Madame Janvier huffed and puffed into the shop, wheezing loudly, swathed in a fog of Gitanes smoke. She was a chain smoker, which Brigid hated, but she was a talented artist and an excellent teacher.

'I'd love to. *Merci*,' agreed Brigid enthusiastically, forgetting that she was planning to return to Ireland.

'Excellent, we will bring a picnic. Louise can bake a few extra baguettes on Thursday morning. And some of your delicious éclairs. Enough for six of us,' Madame Janvier ordered bossily, and Brigid hid a smile at Louise's exasperated expression. Madame Janvier was the mayor's wife and she had introduced herself to Brigid as the First Lady of Bois d'Abbés. As Brigid's late Aunt Nellie would have said of the mayor's wife, she was 'a right consequence'. Nevertheless, the Frenchwoman had made Brigid feel most welcome in the village when Keelin had made the introductions.

It seemed like only yesterday, Brigid reflected, cycling along the narrow, winding main street, past the butcher's and barber's and up the hill where the small chapel dominated the square where the little coffee shop and local bar were the focal points of the village.

Had Keelin not been hosting one of her holistic days,

Brigid would have stopped for a coffee, a vice she had given in to with guilty pleasure for the past few months. She'd miss these little treats when she got home. She'd be back to being Reverend Mother and not Brigid, the Irish woman who was Keelin's aunt and who could speak fluent French. She hadn't told anyone that she used to be a nun. She'd merely said that she was retired from a nursing career.

Would she have been treated differently if she'd said she was a nun, she wondered. It had been so emancipating just being *her*: Brigid Dunne from Ardcloch. Going home to Ireland, she'd have to put back on the old skin she'd sloughed off, and she didn't want to. Whether she stayed in the Four Winds, or the convent in Limerick, there'd be constant reminders of her old life. The life she now had so many regrets about.

'Nothing I can do about it now,' she sighed, freewheeling down the hill with the breeze kissing her cheeks and ruffling her hair.

How she would love to stay longer in France with Keelin and Armand, enjoying the friendships she'd made in the village, reading the thought-provoking books that filled Keelin's bookshelves, and absorbing the energy from the mystical mountain that she had grown to love. But there was unfinished business between her and Imelda and, until they made their peace, if such a thing was possible, there would be constant misery for both of them.

For the sake of her family, Brigid would have to make the first move. But before she left this heavenly place she would climb the peaceful slopes of Canigou once more, she promised herself, glancing over to the dawn-caressed mountain that dominated the landscape, as she pedalled across the cobbles to her niece's kitchen door where she could smell the aroma of coffee brewing for *petit déjeuner*.

'We've loved having you stay, Mère,' Keelin said as she and Brigid sat looking out at the moonlight painting the slopes of Canigou, etched sharp against an indigo sky.

'And I have *loved* being here, *alannah*,' her great-aunt smiled. 'Keelin, would you mind if I borrowed that book, the one you recommended about Mary Magdalene and Iona? It sounds intriguing.'

'*Pilgrimage to Iona* – oh, it's lovely, Mère. It made me long to visit Iona when I read it and when I did visit, very briefly, I was blown away.'

'I'd like to go there myself,' Brigid confided. 'It seems so deeply mystical and esoteric, much like Canigou.'

'How about we go for a few days in May?' Keelin suggested out of the blue. 'Maybe Marie-Claire could join us.'

'That's a *great* idea!' approved Brigid excitedly. 'I'd love to visit Rosslyn Chapel too—'

'Oh, it's amazing, Mère. And we could go and see the stained-glass window of the pregnant Magdalene in Dervaig on Mull. I've always longed to see it.'

'Ooohhh *yeeessss*!' Brigid clapped her hands her eyes alight with excitement. 'Oh my! Did I ever think I'd be having such adventures? It's so wonderful to have you to share this awakening with. But you need to make your peace with your mother. And I need to make peace with Imelda too. *You* should be sharing adventures like this with *her*.' Brigid sat up straight in her chair. 'Keelin – that's it! Will we invite Imelda to come to Iona with us? It could be a pilgrimage of reconciliation. For once and for all, let us sort out all our issues so we can live the rest of our lives in peace, whatever the outcome. What do you think?' She turned her bright, blue-eyed gaze on her niece.

Keelin made a face, not enamoured with the idea. 'It sounds good, in theory,' she sighed. 'But I don't think she'll come. And even if she agreed, she'd probably ruin the trip with her shenanigans.'

'But on the other hand, having had all this time to think about her bad behaviour, she might welcome the chance to heal the rift with us,' Brigid pointed out calmly.

'You're far more forgiving than I am.' Keelin made a face. 'And more honest. But you're right, Mère: it's time I practised what I preach. Do you think she'll come, though?' she asked doubtfully.

'Oh she will. Don't you worry. You leave that to me, Keelin. Imelda will come with us. You wait and see,' Brigid said with a gleam of anticipation in her eyes at the challenge ahead.

CHAPTER FORTY-FOUR

It was a bitterly cold day. There'd been snow the previous week. Marie-Claire felt glum and unsettled. According to Lizzie, Marc and Amelia were still seeing each other and Amelia had been promoted to assistant office manager and was, in her breathless, sycophantic way, passive-aggressively throwing her weight around. Marc was totally involved in setting up the New York office and Amelia often accompanied him on trips. It didn't seem to Marie-Claire that he was missing her as much as he proclaimed in their infrequent online interactions, when she played the part of carefree girl about town. Why should she care anyway? She wouldn't go back to him for all at the tea in China. But it was all his friggin' fault that she was unsettled, unsure of her future, and working at a different career to pay the bills.

Oh for God's sake, will you get over yourself and cop on, she thought irritably, photocopying a travel itinerary.

The job she'd taken as a tour rep in a company that

specialized in organizing guided tours for French tourists was interesting enough, and the salary was good, but her manager, Chloe, a snooty blond from Foxrock who sported a Trump-like coiffeur, whiter than white veneers, and red shellac nails that could be seen from space, was hard going. 'Networking and contacts are what it's all about,' she was fond of saying whenever she tottered into the office in her vertiginous Louboutins, a little the worse for wear after too many flutes of champagne over lunch.

'Quite the pantomime,' Ines drawled. 'The r-rolling goes into overdrive when she's pissed.'

Marie-Claire laughed. Ines was on a year's exchange from the French head office, and was not greatly impressed by her manager's *manigances*, as she so derisively termed Chloe's carry on.

Ines wasn't overly friendly. She had the Parisienne's hauteur and her narcissistic navel-gazing was wearing. 'I'm so fat,' she'd wail, studying her thin frame critically in the bevelled mirror in the foyer. 'I am mired in depression because of this *fatness*.' All because she might have indulged in a Malteser.

'I've never known anyone quite so fascinated by herself as Ines. Her life is a *permanen*t existential crisis,' Marie-Claire moaned to Ella, one Saturday afternoon, about six weeks into the job, having had enough of Ines's traumas to last a lifetime. 'And what with Chloe thinking she's some sort of high-powered executive *à la* Meryl Streep in *The Devil Wears Prada*, it's no wonder I end up doing most of the work. I can't stay there, Ella,' Marie-Claire declared.

She and Ella were marching in a Pro-Choice demonstration in Dublin, ahead of the upcoming referendum to repeal an amendment to the constitution, which currently forced women to travel abroad for abortion – sometimes with tragic consequences.

'Let me have a look and see what's on the books,' Ella soothed, attributing her friend's moroseness to her lack of satisfaction at work.

'I dunno. Maybe I should go back to Canada,' Marie-Claire mused as the good-humoured marchers around them chanted slogans.

'You haven't really given it a chance,' Ella responded, tucking her arm in Marie-Claire's.

'It's weird, Ella. It's hard to settle back. Everything and everyone's changed. They've all moved on with their lives. I feel a bit of an outsider, to be honest.'

'It's going to take a bit of time, ducky. We're not fresh out of college and rarin' to go anymore. Most of us are tied down by kids and mortgages.'

'I know. It's all about the kids now, and maybe that's why I'm feeling like an outsider. 'Maybe I feel left behind.'

'Did you feel like this in Canada?'

'Nope. I felt totally in control, vibrant, anticipatory. The complete opposite to what I feel here.'

'And if you go back to Canada, do you think you'll feel like that again, without Marc in your life?' Ella asked delicately.

'I don't know. I would hope so. I didn't hand *all* my power over to him!' Marie-Claire retorted indignantly.

'Good. I never thought you did. That's not you.'

'I'm still gutted though.'

'Why wouldn't you be? It's still early days. Break-ups are like bereavements, it takes time to get over them. Don't be so hard on yourself. Come on. Cheer up. Take your selfie to post on your "I'm not missing you, dickhead" Facebook page,' Ella grinned.

'Ha ha!' Marie-Claire retorted. 'When you say it like that, you make me feel like a silly teenager.'

'Sorry, I didn't mean it like that. I'd do the same if I was in your shoes.'

'No you wouldn't. You'd have kicked him in the goolies and given him a bloody nose to boot.' Marie-Claire gave her friend a hug. Ella was a far more forceful character than she was and met things head on.

'No, actually. I think your strategy of not letting him know why you left him is absolutely *brilliant*. So come on, take a photo of the two of us with big happy grins on our faces.'

'I'm hopeless at selfies; I never do the right angle. I end up with a plethora of chins or a nose like Pinocchio's.' Nevertheless, Marie-Claire positioned her mobile phone to snap the pair of them.

'Look, the march is nearly over, we don't need to listen to the speeches, we know why we're protesting. I *was* one of those women who had to travel for a termination.'

'I know, Ella. That was *so* hard for you and Shay.' Marie-Claire squeezed her friend's hand, remembering the horrendous trauma her friend and her husband had gone through when they were told Ella was carrying a baby with a fatal foetal abnormality.

'This brings it all back.' Ella had tears in her eyes. 'And it's why it's so important for me to be here to help protect other women from going through what thousands like me went through. And of course, poor Savita Halappanavar. She *died* because of the eighth amendment. We must *never* forget her.'

'Savita won't be forgotten, Ella, *ever*. She's part of the reason we're here,' Marie-Claire said solemnly, and they walked along in silence thinking about the young Indian woman who had died of a septic miscarriage because she was refused an emergency termination, even though her pregnancy loss was inevitable and pending.

'So you don't want to stay for the speeches.' Marie-Claire cocked an eye at her friend when clusters of chanting marchers began to fill up the square.

'I do not,' grimaced Ella. 'To be honest there's a couple of limelight hoggers and bandwagon jumpers here that are doing my head in with their patronizing shite,' she, said crossly, catching sight of two of the more prominent social influencers hugging dramatically for the TV cameras. 'Let's hit McGrattan's for a bit of grub and a bottle of red. My treat.'

'"Limelight hoggers, bandwagon jumpers!" God, you're cranky.' Marie-Claire laughed.

'I *am* cranky, aren't I?' Ella grinned, leading her friend through the throngs.

'OK, so tell me: why are you cranky?' Marie-Claire asked

Ella half an hour later as they tucked into the finger-food platter for two, the heat and conviviality of the bar a welcome respite from the bitter cold outside.

'Teenagers!' her friend said succinctly, devouring a portion of black pudding and apple wrapped in bacon. 'They had a big row with Dad yesterday. A mega one, actually, about the referendum.'

'What on earth made you get into a discussion with your da about *that*? You know his views. You know how hide-bound he is where the Church is concerned. He's livid that you'd vote Yes, to repeal, presumably?' Marie-Claire had never liked Ella's domineering father.

'You know *I* wouldn't deliberately get into an argument with him about anything like *that*,' Ella groaned. 'Jada was saying how she hoped we picked a villa with a swimming pool in France for our summer hols. Julie said she preferred Italy. They're gas, aren't they? It's far from villas with swimming pools you and I were reared. Dad asked when we were going and I said late June, and Jada – wouldn't you know it would be her – piped up and said we'd better wait until after the referendum.

'"You won't be able to vote, if they hold one," Dad told her, and she eye-rolled him! Imagine you or I doing that to him when we were her age. And then she said, "I know that, Granddad, but Mum and Dad will be entitled to vote, and we'll need every Yes vote we can get!" *We'll!* Even though I was mad with her for mentioning it, I loved her sense of ownership of the issue,' Ella said proudly.

'Ooohhhh! I'd say that went down well,' Marie-Claire exclaimed.

'He nearly had a heart attack. "I sincerely hope your parents won't be voting to kill babies," he said. "I didn't raise your mother to be a murderer!"'

'Oh God! How *horrible*. Was there uproar?'

'That doesn't even *begin* to describe it. Jada leapt to her feet and shrieked at him, "Don't you dare say things like that about Mum! She'll be voting to give women choice so no woman has to travel to another country for something that might save her life if she's in difficulties, because our own country won't look after her, or me and Julie, if anything happens to us. How would you feel if I was *raped!* Would you want me to keep the baby?"

'"Yes, I most certainly would," he roared back at her. "We'd all look after you. And don't you be so cheeky to me, madam!"'

'Wow! *I* wouldn't be that brave, arguing with your da. Well done, Jada!' Marie-Claire approved, highly impressed at her godchild's nerve.

'I know. In fairness, I was very proud of them, but I didn't want them involved in a shouting match with their grandfather, not with poor Mum in tears over it all, so I said, "Enough! This subject is not to be discussed here again. Let's go."'

'Probably the wisest course of action.' Marie-Claire nodded.

'"And don't come back here if you're voting Yes," he shouted as we were leaving. "A fine way to be rearing your children to ignore the teaching of the Catholic Church!" So then *I* lost it and said: "Yes the Church that allowed priests to rape children and get away with it, and moved the paedophile priests from parish to parish. The Church that silenced those victims of abuse and tried to buy them off. The Church that sent young women to Magdalene laundries and tore their children out of their arms to sell them off, and kept those women as slaves. The Church that lies through its teeth and calls it 'mental reservation'. The Church that excommunicated a nine-year-old child who was raped – and her mother who took her for a termination because she would have died otherwise – but did not excommunicate the rapist! Is *that* the Church you're talking about, Dad?" And when I'd finished shouting at him, we left. I'm telling you, Marie-Claire, the patriarchy is still alive and well in Ireland,' Ella raged.

'How are the girls?' Marie-Claire asked sympathetically.

'Ah they were shocked and upset initially, but now they're being self-righteous with all the superiority of youth,' Ella chuckled. 'I had to point out that *everyone* was entitled to vote as they saw fit, and No voters had their point of view and it was important to respect their democratic right to exercise their vote, *even* if it was a No and harmful to the lives of women. I explained to them that centuries of the Church's teachings had cowed whole generations into not opposing them, regardless of how much they might want to, and I said there were some people who felt their No vote was morally right and that was their decision. Just as our decision to vote Yes, was ours.'

'Fair dues to you. I suppose balance is everything, but I might not have been so gracious.'

'I know, it's called motherhood,' Ella said wryly. 'But today I needed a break from them, march or no march.'

'*Whaaaatt?*' Marie-Claire wasn't sure if she'd heard her great-aunt correctly. 'You want to go on a pilgrimage to Iona with Maman and bring *Granny*? Controversial!' she grinned.

'I do,' Brigid replied calmly settling herself into the front of Marie-Claire's borrowed car. They were in a car park in Dublin airport. Marie-Claire had come to collect her from her flight and in the morning they would be heading west to the Four Winds for the weekend.

'Well good luck with that, Mère. When I texted her after I came back from France in January, telling her I'd like to come and visit, to talk about what had happened, she told me not to bother. She's done with all of us, according to herself,' Marie-Claire grimaced, reversing out of the parking space.

'That is why I propose that you and I show up on her doorstep, any day that suits you. Perhaps over the Easter holidays, if you're willing – and free, of course?' Brigid proposed.

'And if she closes the door in our faces?' Marie-Claire glanced across at her aunt, who looked twenty years younger than when she'd last seen her. Brigid was tanned and healthy from her mountain walks, her bright periwinkle blue eyes shining clear.

'So be it! She won't be able to say that we didn't try

to mend fences. I'm hoping though that her wrath will have abated.'

'And what about ours?' Marie-Claire asked drily.

'As that inspiring woman, Michelle Obama, memorably said. "When they go low, we go high!"' Brigid shrugged. 'I won't have my latter years spoiled because Imelda has issues with me. I'll give her an opportunity to discuss them. That's all I can do.'

'And Maman is happy to make this trip to Iona with Granny?' Marie-Claire queried. Privately she thought it would be another disaster.

'Yes, we spoke about it before I left. She's very troubled by it all. She wants to have some sort of closure on all their issues. Perhaps my party was a catalyst for the air to be cleared. If it was, well so be it.'

'You're so forgiving, Mère. I certainly wouldn't be asking her to go on holidays,' Marie-Claire said firmly.

'One thing's for sure: if Imelda comes with us, it won't be boring,' Brigid chuckled.

'And I suppose you'll also be going on the Magdalene Trail to Iona,' Marie-Claire asked as they scorched down the M1 towards the Port Tunnel.

'We *are*. Isn't it mind-blowing to even *consider* that Jesus and Mary Magdalene were married, after all we've been taught? I would have been kicked out of the Order for apostasy if I'd ventured such an opinion. Yet now, it's openly talked of in France, especially in the Languedoc. I've read *so* many of your mother's enormous stack of books, Marie-Claire. It was fascinating, discussing such concepts with your parents. Wait until I put it to Maura – she'll think I've gone doolally,' Brigid laughed mischievously.

'And *do* you think it's true?' Marie-Claire swung left at Whitehall church onto Collins Avenue.

'It's a possibility, certainly. I think. And some of the books I've read propose that Jesus – who had mastered matter during initiations as an Essene, in the Mystery Schools – may not have died at the crucifixion. Honestly, Marie-Claire, there's so much to learn and read about. I wish I'd known these things. How different my path might have been.'

'What do they say? "When the pupil is ready, the teacher will come." I'm sure it's all happening the way it's meant to.' Marie-Claire smiled at her great-aunt. 'And right now, my path is leading me to *this*.' She indicated right and parked in front of a pretty bistro called 53 Avenue. 'I booked us a table. The food is fab. I hope you're hungry.'

'I'm hungry all right,' Brigid agreed. 'That rubbish they serve on planes these days is woeful. I didn't eat anything.'

'We'll feast in here, so,' Marie-Claire said cheerfully. 'Their seafood risotto is out of this world, and their chicken wings ... yum, yum.'

'I'll be putting on weight! I'm eating like a horse since I retired,' Brigid confessed. 'My discipline is going to pot.'

'You've had enough discipline for this lifetime,' Marie-Claire told Brigid as they made their way into the restaurant. Having agreed to drive her great-aunt to Glencarraig tomorrow, they were both going to need sustenance. What happened when they got there was in the lap of the gods.

CHAPTER FORTY-FIVE

Imelda wheeled her grocery trolley along the frozen food aisle and threw a packet of Aunt Bessie's roast parsnips on top of the packets of Jus-Rol puff pastry, to which she was particularly partial. Noticing Carmel Hennessy up ahead of her, she hastily rearranged the shopping so that the pastry was well covered. She wouldn't give Carmel the satisfaction of knowing that she no longer made her own puff pastry. Shortcrust yes, but the palaver of rolling the butter in, folding the pastry, adding more butter and doing more rolling was so time consuming that the readymade was a godsend.

Carmel was, as usual, looking like she'd just stepped out of *Vogue*. Dyed jet-black hair coiffed and sprayed to within an inch of its life (Carmel always did her weekly shopping after getting her hair done), red tailored trousers with a crease so sharp it would cut butter, and a very smart paisley-print devoré-velvet jacket that looked as though it had cost a fortune.

Carmel was a great woman for the designer gear, and the body maintenance. It was rumoured that she'd had a facelift. She certainly had a very surprised look about her. Her skin was stretched taut and shiny across her cheekbones and the McDonald's arches of her eyebrows nearly reached her hairline. 'Definitely done,' was the word in the book club.

She wasn't the only one to have had 'work' done, Imelda thought smugly, squaring her shoulders and holding in her tummy. She was wearing her Karen Millen black belted trench coat, bought in the Brown Thomas sale last January, and a pair of smart L.K. Bennett ankle boots, bought during the same spending spree. After the 'party episode', as Imelda privately called it, she'd felt the need to spoil herself.

She'd been reading an article about cosmetic surgery and enhancement in a magazine at the hairdresser's and had been most impressed by some before-and-after photos of an older lady who'd had fillers and Botox. Shrouded in a black gown, with her damp hair stuck to her head while she waited for her cut and blow dry, Imelda had stared at her image reflected in the square unforgiving mirror and wondered who was that pinched, lined, vexed woman. She looked far older than Brigid, she'd thought crossly.

As soon as she got home, she'd gone on her computer and spent hours on the Internet to find someone whom she felt would be suitable for her particular needs. Imelda was wary of cosmetic clinics and their boasts. Even the young one, who'd washed her hair earlier in the salon, had had her lips done; they looked like they were ready to explode. Her eyebrows were like two black caterpillars on her forehead. No, best to steer well clear of the money-grabbers and go to a 'proper' doctor, Imelda decided, making an appointment with a consultant.

She'd told Cormac and Felicity she was treating herself to an overnight stay in Dublin because she wanted to shop in Arnott's basement to replenish her bedding and kitchen ware. They didn't pay any heed to it, because Imelda had always gone to Dublin for the sales and stayed overnight.

She'd driven to Dublin very early, shopped in Arnott's basement, and then driven to the Blackrock Clinic for an appointment with a 'proper' cosmetic surgeon. He had been so kind and encouraging during her initial appointment that when she lay on the couch to have her treatments, Imelda felt exhilarated.

The needles had been very painful, but she didn't care. This was something she was doing for herself and worth every penny for the comfort it gave her after that upsetting family gathering.

She'd booked into the Royal Marine Hotel, down the coast road in Dun Laoghaire, treated herself to a room service dinner, unwilling to show her bruised face in the dining room, and rested against the pillows in the large luxurious bed, plotting how she would lavish more money on herself. A new car was next on the agenda. An automatic at that. Larry would want her to make her life easier, and feck the lot of them, that was exactly what she was going to do. There were no pockets in a shroud, and now that the rest of them were out of her will, she might as well spend, spend, spend.

It had taken a couple of weeks for the discreet Botox and fillers to settle, but Imelda was *delighted* with the results. Everyone was telling her how well she looked. If only they knew, she laughed to herself. They wouldn't believe what she'd done. Felicity and Cormac kept looking at her, wondering . . . Well, let them wonder, Imelda thought defiantly.

She opened the side pocket in her Desigual Madeira bag, slid out a small bronzer compact and opened the mirror to have a quick look. Not 'done' but very subtly 'refreshed', she thought, admiring the new plumpness of her cheeks and lip area, where the dermal fillers had taken years off her appearance. The Botox around her crow's feet and frown lines *had* hurt but it was all worth it, Imelda thought proudly, snapping the compact shut.

Never had a moment of madness worked out so well.

'Good morning, Carmel,' she said perkily, coming abreast of the other woman.

'Morning, Imelda. Isn't it a lovely day after the terrible weather we've had?'

'It certainly is,' Imelda agreed. 'I needed to stock up again.'

'But sure, wouldn't Cormac do your shopping for you and have it delivered?' Carmel remarked.

'Indeed he would. He's always telling me he'll get the van to drop by with anything I need, and it *was* handy to have that facility in the bad weather. But I like to do my own shopping – after all, it was *my* shop once,' Imelda said, reminding Carmel that she too was a woman of substance.

'Well, Cormac's made a great job of it. Who would ever have thought we'd have such a fine supermarket in Glencarraig? It's as good as any you'd find in the city.'

'Indeed it is. Cheerio, Carmel, I must get on. I want to make a start on *The Immortalists* today, to have it read by Tuesday.'

'A strange book. A Greek tragedy and all that, but superbly written nevertheless,' Carmel observed knowledgeably, and Imelda thought irritably that she shouldn't have let on she was behind in her book club read.

'See you on Tuesday,' she said, waving at Mags Reid, who was coming down the aisle in the opposite direction. 'Mags, I heard Dickey Casey is laid up with cellulitis and won't make bridge tomorrow night. So you could partner Susie Murphy Hemsworth, seeing as you don't have a partner either for this Sunday?' she said to the other woman.

'That would be great, Imelda. Glad I bumped into you. Poor Dickey. He's having a hard time of it.'

'Indeed he is, the craythur. I'll see you on Sunday so.' Imelda carried on to the next aisle, very pleased with her Saturday morning.

'Morning, Imelda.' Sergeant Kenny saluted her when she passed him with her trolley. He was carrying a basket with cartons from the deli counter and a tub of ice cream and a rhubarb crumble.

'Morning,' she returned coolly. She didn't like Sergeant Kenny. He was a nosy ould yoke who thought he was a cut above everyone and loved the deference showed to him. He was in her bridge club and always pontificating about something or other. He'd won the last two games they'd played against each other.

'Doing your shopping?' The Sergeant cast an eye over the contents of her trolley.

Imelda bristled. 'Well you wouldn't need to have gone to Trinity to get the answer to *that*,' she said tartly. 'And you'd want to cut out that ice cream and crumble stuff or your uniform won't fit you, and the taxpayers will have to pay for another one.'

'You're quare cranky, Imelda,' he scowled at her. 'I was only trying to be polite.'

'Hmmm,' she sniffed. 'I'll see you at bridge.' That gave him his answer, she thought smugly, rounding the corner to the next aisle. She would treat herself to a cup of coffee and a cream cake in the café adjoining the supermarket, she decided, looking forward to her treat.

The new café that Cormac had added on was doing a roaring trade. She was lucky to get a seat. It was astonishing that having breakfast out had become such a thing, she thought, watching a couple at the table next to her tucking into an enormous fry.

She was proud of her son, immensely proud, though she couldn't help feeling a pang of guilt when she remembered how much he had wanted to study architecture until she'd browbeaten and emotionally blackmailed him to take on the family business. Peter had gone out to Australia when he'd left school, determined to make a life for himself abroad. He had no interest either, in taking over the supermarket.

She'd done to Cormac what had been done to her, Imelda realized with a shock. How come she'd never thought of it like that before? He had been the one left to shoulder the family burden. Keelin, like Brigid, Sean, and Peter had taken off, getting as far away as they possibly could to escape the binding ties of home.

Had she ever thanked her son properly for the sacrifice he'd made? Not really, she thought ruefully, biting into her cream cake. She'd never actually put into words that she was grateful and proud. Her thanks would be the leaving of the business to him and the index-linked stash in her savings account at the bank.

She heard a woman laugh. A hearty, smile-inducing laugh, behind her, and it reminded her of someone. But who? Her brow went to furrow but could not because of the Botox. Marie-Claire, that was who it sounded like. Her grand-daughter had a great sense of humour. Imelda smiled, before remembering that she wasn't speaking to Marie-Claire.

When Marie-Claire had texted her saying she wanted to come and discuss the family row, Imelda had been in the height of her annoyance with them all, and had fired off a cold, unforgiving text. She'd heard nothing since. Felicity had mentioned last week that Brigid was still in France. She could stay there, for all Imelda cared. Her mouth drew down into a thin line. What was she doing, thinking of them and ruining her enjoyable morning? She would buy a box of crème cakes at the bakery and drop them in to Felicity and tell her to keep the éclair for Cormac because they were his favourites, and then she would run the mower over her lawn, a chore she quite enjoyed. Afterwards, she would settle down to read her book for the afternoon and put her feet up. Pleased with her plan for the day ahead, Imelda finished her cappuccino, retouched her lipstick and made her way out to the bakery. She was glad she'd packed her shopping into the boot of the car earlier. Nothing worse than lugging shopping bags around. There was a queue, of course. The bakery was always busy. She stood behind an elegant grey-haired lady, admiring the cut of her hair. Stylish and modern. Should she stop colouring her own hair and finally go grey? Imelda wondered idly.

'The loos were packed,' she heard a voice say as a young woman stepped in front of her. Imelda's heart almost jumped out of her chest. 'Marie-Claire!' she exclaimed involuntarily.

Both women turned in her direction.

'*Granny!*'

'*Imelda!*'

Imelda stared at the grey-haired woman in shock. '*Brigid!* Where's your veil? Your habit?' she said idiotically.

'I don't wear it anymore. Hello, Imelda, how are you?' her older sister said calmly.

'What are you doing here?' Imelda snapped, flustered.

'We had our breakfast in the café after the drive from Dublin, and then we decided to buy some cakes to bring to you, hoping that you wouldn't close the door in our faces,' Brigid said matter-of-factly.

'Oh!' Imelda was gobsmacked. 'I wouldn't close the

Patricia Scanlan

door in your face,' she muttered, unable to meet her sister's steady gaze.

'We weren't sure what sort of a reception we'd get, seeing as you didn't want to meet me when I texted you and asked if I could visit,' Marie-Claire said quietly.

'*Oh!* Yes. Well, I was *very* upset then,' Imelda said defensively. 'Did Cormac and Felicity know you were coming?' She eyed her granddaughter suspiciously, anxious to get off the subject and pleased that she'd made sure they knew that *she* was as wounded by them as much as they had been offended by *her*.

'Nope! It was all very spur of the moment!' Marie-Claire shrugged.

There was a strained silence as two pairs of eyes studied her expectantly. Imelda was in a complete tizzy. She hated being caught on the hop.

'Can I help you?' a young white-coated assistant asked Brigid.

'So, will I buy a few cakes for us, Imelda?' Brigid cocked her head quizzically, her blue-eyed gaze never wavering from Imelda's.

'Oh go on then. A cherry-and-walnut slice for me,' Imelda said grudgingly. She would have preferred to make her peace with the family at a time and place of *her* choosing – she'd imagined many deathbed scenarios – but she couldn't deny the way her heart had lifted when she'd seen Marie-Claire. And Brigid, who by rights should have been very snooty, after having her party ruined, was showing admirable forbearance. Maybe it was time to let bygones be bygones,

Imelda acknowledged in the welcome solitude of her car, as she drove towards home, followed by her relatives.

She felt butterflies flutter around her innards and her hands tightened on the steering wheel. Would Brigid go for the jugular and attack her for her behaviour on the night of the party? She'd every right to, Imelda had gone *way* too far, especially announcing to all and sundry, including Brigid's Mother General, that she'd seen her sister having sex with Johnny Larkin.

It was time to face the music. She would just have to sit there and zip it and take what was coming to her. If the Botox had permitted her to frown, she would have.

'That was a stroke of luck, wasn't it?' Marie-Claire followed Imelda's silver Volvo out of the car park.

'It certainly was,' Brigid agreed. 'It couldn't have worked out better. We weren't left standing on the doorstep with the door closed in our faces. Or left standing because she wasn't in. The Lord works in mysterious ways,' she smiled.

'She looks great, in spite of everything. So fresh and rested. The quarrel certainly hasn't taken it out of her, the way it's taken it out of Maman,' Marie-Claire observed crossly, indicating left, to follow her grandmother off the main street.

'Imelda doesn't have the responsibility for the shop anymore. That must be a great weight off her shoulders. She's got a good life now, I suppose, after all the running around she'd had to do, and she deserves to take it easy, in fairness,' Brigid pointed out.

'I love the coat and the bag. Granny always looks smart. She never buys this side of the Shannon, she told me once. She doesn't want to be seen in anything anyone else would have. She always goes to Dublin for her clothes.'

'She's *always* gone to Dublin to buy her clothes. Larry was very generous in that regard, and of course Imelda is an almighty snob and excels in one-upmanship,' Brigid said ruefully. 'I'm thinking now – and excuse me for changing the subject, dear – but perhaps we'd best not get into the whole "you said", "she said", "I said" carry on. Yes, eventually we'll have to address the things she threw at us at the party, but I think initially we should take a restrained approach. Have our tea with her and ask her will she come to Scotland with us. It would be good to talk things over in a neutral setting. You know what Imelda's like: if she gets *defensive* she'll get *offensive* and there could be another row, then we'll be out the door before we know it.'

'Right. Good thinking. You're very wise, Mère, and she doesn't deserve the leeway you're giving her.' Marie-Claire swung into the drive behind Imelda.

'Trust me, running a convent with women in various stages of hormonal disarray was a *great* training in how to manage disagreements, large and small,' Brigid laughed.

'Well, I think you're awesome. *You're* the one she should be apologizing to instead of letting us think she's doing *us* a great favour by seeing us,' Marie-Claire said indignantly.

'It's all a front. Remember, there was a lot of hurt and resentment behind that explosion of anger. Imelda had a point about being left to look after the farm and our parents, as well as looking after her mother-in-law and her own family. I can see that, looking back at it now, from her point of view. So let's play it softly-softly. What do you say?' Brigid studied her great-niece quizzically.

'I say I'm in awe of you. Come on, Saint Brigid. I'll follow your lead,' Marie-Claire said fondly, switching off the ignition, glad she hadn't come to see her grandmother on her own in January. She would have ended up making matters worse.

'Go into the sitting room and I'll make the tea,' Imelda instructed when they followed her into the house.

'The cakes, Imelda.' Brigid handed her the square white box.

'Thanks.' Her sister managed a small smile.

'I'll make the tea if you like, Granny,' Marie-Claire offered, as she always would when she was staying with her.

'No, I'll do it myself. Go in and sit down,' Imelda gestured into the sun-drenched front room, before marching down to the kitchen.

'We're being treated like guests.' Marie-Claire made a face, sinking into the plump-cushioned burgundy sofa.

'We're in, that's all that matters.' Brigid took off her coat and scarf and sat in one of the armchairs. 'This isn't where she sits, is it?' she asked.

'No, she sits in the one by the fire.'

'Grand.'

'It's a bit like going to confession or something, isn't it?' Marie-Claire whispered.

'What will our penance be, I wonder?' Brigid chuckled and Marie-Claire giggled.

'I feel like a naughty child, it's weird.'

'She has to keep control. That's how she can save face,' Brigid observed sagely. 'I had to do it myself many times when I was a young Reverend Mother in charge of older nuns.'

'Not easy I suppose.'

'What's not easy?' Imelda appeared at the door carrying a tea tray. Marie-Claire jumped up to take it from her.

'Being a young Reverend Mother in charge of older nuns,' Brigid said mildly.

'Oh! Well that was no bother to you, I'm sure. You're bossy enough.' Imelda handed her a mug of tea.

'Hmmm, when faced with rudeness and bad manners you needed to be bossy sometimes,' Brigid reciprocated tartly.

A frigid silence descended on the trio.

Realizing that she'd overstepped the mark, Imelda sought a safe topic. 'Er ... I believe you were in France for a while.'

'I was.'

'And how did that go?' Imelda handed her sister a plate with a selection of pastries.

'It was absolutely wonderful.' Brigid took a custard slice. 'I'd only had a very brief stay at Keelin and Armand's, years ago. It was *so* delightful to get to know the people in the village, and take walks on Canigou,' she enthused.

'I like walking Canigou too,' Imelda admitted, relaxing a little.

'Perhaps we might walk it together someday?' Brigid seized her opening.

'Er ... well ... ah ... I don't think I'm flavour of the month with my daughter and her husband right now.' Imelda was stunned at her sister's invitation. Was Brigid in her right mind?

'Well, that's one of the reasons we came to see you, Imelda. Keelin, Marie-Claire and I are going to Scotland for a long weekend, Thursday to Sunday, and we wondered would you like to come with us so we could spend time together and heal old wounds,' Brigid asked.

'Keelin wants *me* to go?' Imelda could hardly believe her ears.

'Granny, Maman is very unhappy about being estranged from you, and she's very hurt by what you said about Papa – as am *I*, by the way. But she feels we all have to make an effort to resolve our issues so we can put the past behind us and move on,' Marie-Claire said bluntly, feeling that her grandmother was getting a very soft ride from Brigid. 'If she's prepared to do it so should you.'

'And why Scotland?' Imelda ignored her granddaughter's last comment.

'We're going on the trail of Mary Magdalene. A pilgrimage, if you like,' Brigid interjected swiftly, seeing Marie-Claire's truculent expression. 'We're going to visit Rosslyn chapel in Edinburgh, take the ferry from Oban to Mull, stay at a B&B in Fionnphort and take a ferry to Iona and spend a day there. I've read some fascinating books about it. We're also planning to visit a little church that has a famous stained-glass window of a pregnant Magdalene and Jesus.'

'You *believe* this – and you a *nun*?' Imelda was incredulous.

'Let me tell you, Imelda, my eyes have been opened, and there are *many* things that have been kept from us. I'll send you a couple of books to read before we leave so you can see for yourself.' Brigid couldn't hide her enthusiasm for their forthcoming trip.

'I must say it all sounds very interesting.' Imelda wondered was she in a dream. This day was turning into a very surreal experience.

'So are you coming?' Brigid demanded.

'When do I have to let you know?' she said warily. Brigid was like a different woman, she thought. Not wearing the habit and veil made her look years younger, and her clothes and hair were most stylish, in a restrained sort of way.

'Sooner rather than later, Granny,' Marie-Claire said firmly. 'We'll get cheaper fares if we book soon and we want to make sure we can get accommodation.'

'It's all a bit sudden, and unexpected,' she said, rattled.

'How about you have a think about it, Imelda? Marie-Claire and I will head down to the Four Winds, and I'll ring you early next week,' Brigid suggested.

'You're getting very adventurous in your old age,' Imelda sniffed.

'*Carpe diem*, Imelda, *carpe diem*. Being eighty concentrates the mind wonderfully, and I intend to seize the day for as long as I can. I'd advise you to do the same,' Brigid said crisply, standing up. 'Thanks very much for the tea. I'm glad to see you looking so well,' she added with a smile. 'Come along, dear,' she said to Marie-Claire, 'Miss Daisy needs to be driven.'

'Do you not drive anymore?' Imelda asked, dismayed.

'Oh, indeed I do, but it's a luxury being driven and I love spending time with this one,' she said affectionately, smiling over at Marie-Claire.

'I know you do. I do too,' Imelda surprised herself by saying. 'If you'd like to stay for dinner, you're welcome to.'

'Thank you, Granny, but we won't put you to the trouble, and Una's expecting us anyway so she'll have a meal prepared.' Marie-Claire looked at her grandmother, noting the brief expression of disappointment that crossed her face. Her heart softened and impulsively she stood up, put her arms around her and hugged her.

'Thanks for the tea. I hope you'll come with us to Scotland. I'll ring you next week.'

Imelda stayed in her granddaughter's embrace. She'd missed the hugs so much.

'We'll see,' she murmured. 'I'm glad you called and I'm sorry I was curt with you when you texted me. And I'm sorry about what I said about your father, and for ... er ... well bringing up his past.'

'I won't deny it was a shock, and we were all hurt by your behaviour, Granny. Come to Scotland with us and let's put the past behind us there.' Marie-Claire couldn't hold on to the grudge. It wasn't her way.

Imelda followed them to the hall, and impulsively reached out and took Brigid's hand and gave it a brief squeeze before letting go. 'Safe journey,' she said awkwardly.

'Thank you, Imelda,' her sister responded. 'I'll be in touch.'

She watched the car disappear from view, emotions churning inside her. 'Let's put the past behind us,' Marie-Claire had urged. But it was Keelin she really needed to hear these words from.

If only it was that easy, Imelda thought sadly as the tears that she'd struggled to contain when she watched them drive away flooded her eyes and slid down her cheeks.

She felt a movement against her ankle and looked down to see the cat rubbing his furry black head against her.

'Come in and I'll feed you, mister,' she gulped, wiping her eyes, grateful for the little cat's affection. 'I wish you could talk, Sooty, I wish you could tell me what to do,' she said, pouring his kitty treats into his bowl. 'Because right this minute I don't know if I'm on my head or my heels with the surprise of it all. If Keelin knew what I've lived with all these years, she might not be so bitter towards me. But do I tell her, little kitty cat? Do I tell her?'

CHAPTER FORTY-SIX

'I can drive, if you'd like,' Brigid offered. She was sitting in Imelda's kitchen drinking tea and eating a delicious slice of homemade apple tart. She'd driven up from Limerick to meet with her sister before they drove to Dublin.

'Not at all, you had the drive from Limerick. Sure, it's a doddle driving to Dublin now, once you get on the motorway,' Imelda said briskly, wiping pastry crumbs off the kitchen counter. 'And besides, I know exactly where the hotel is and how to get there.'

'Do you go up much?' Brigid asked, wondering how she would cope with being Imelda's passenger. Brigid liked driving and liked being in control. Just like Imelda did, she realized with a start. In some ways they were quite similar.

'I do. I think it's important not to let your world shrink. Some women down here say they wouldn't drive on the M50 for love nor money, but for goodness' sake if you can drive into Galway in the rush hour you can manage a five-lane highway in America, let alone the M50,' Imelda scoffed at the notion. 'Living on my own after Larry died taught me to be very independent.'

'I can see how it would and I admire that about you, Imelda,' Brigid remarked before taking a sip of tea.

'Really?' Her sister looked momentarily astonished at the notion that Brigid would admire *anything* about her.

'Oh yes indeed. You're very get-up-and-go. I've allowed myself to become quite institutionalized in the last decade or so. I scurry back to the safety of the convent, or the Four Winds. I haven't had to look after myself, as in cooking, shopping for food, and the like, for a long time. I don't know if I would have the nerve to live on my own now,' Brigid admitted. 'I like having company and not being on my own at night.'

'I've no choice,' Imelda shrugged. 'And it's not as great as you might think. It's lonely rattling around a house on your own. And it's hard feeling I'm beholden to Cormac and Felicity, although I don't think they look at it like that. But when the weather was so bad I was depending on them to shop, and clear the drive when I got snowed in. You on the other hand have company, conversation and people to mind you. You wouldn't, I'd imagine, feel like you're a nuisance.'

'No. In fairness to the Order they have always looked after their elderly nuns very well. I'm sorry you're lonely, Imelda.'

'Ah, I get on with it. I'm in the ICA and the book club and I play bridge. It's only when the door closes behind me at night that I feel it. Drink up now and we'll make a move.

There's no point in paying for a hotel room in Dublin if we don't make the most of it. If we leave now, we'll beat the rush hour. We can have a late lunch at the hotel. We could have a rest before Marie-Claire collects us for dinner, after picking up Keelin at the airport.' Imelda topped up both their cups and emptied and rinsed the teapot and put it away.

'We should bring a pack of cards with us,' Brigid suggested. 'The four of us could play Twenty-Five or Sevens. Remember when we lived at home the mighty games of cards that used to go on?'

'I more remember the mighty rows that used to go on – Daddy was a divil for cheating,' Imelda retorted, and the two of them laughed, united by the memory of a happier time in their lives.

Please let there be no rows. Please let this be a time of healing, Brigid prayed silently as Imelda washed their cups and she dried them. So far the hour she'd spent with her sister had been unexpectedly pleasant, but there were five more days to get through, and with Imelda, anything was possible.

The trip up to the capital had sped by, Imelda reflected, taking the Ballymun exit of the M50. She indicated to get into her lane to turn left at Northwood. Now that they were getting close to the hotel she was beginning to feel nervous. In a couple of hours she would be face to face with her daughter. She knew it was an encounter that neither of them were looking forward to.

They hadn't spoken yet. Imelda had sent a text saying

that she was looking forward to the trip to Scotland, and rather pointedly, she supposed, adding that it was nice to be included.

Keelin had responded with an equally insipid text saying that she was looking forward to it also and that she was glad Marie-Claire could join them, and that three generations of the family would be on Iona to give honour to Mary Magdalene.

Nothing about the row at Brigid's party. And not a word about Armand. She would have to apologize, Imelda supposed, but the old indignation began to rise and she felt herself becoming grumpy.

Stop it! She silently rebuked herself. She'd given herself a talking-to that morning before Brigid arrived, telling herself to be on her best behaviour and not to make snippy remarks. It actually hadn't been as hard as she'd anticipated. Brigid had been most affable and interested in all that was going on around her as they zipped along to Dublin.

'That's a very nice building, very modern,' Brigid observed, noticing a curved glass structure to the left of them.

'That's the Santry Sports Clinic. That's where I had my hip done, under Denis Collins. He does complicated ones,' Imelda informed her. 'And if you ever have trouble with your shoulder, go to Hannan Mullett. He's an expert. The *best* in the country,' she added knowledgeably. 'I get cortisone injections from him for the pain. I hurt my shoulder after hauling Larry's mother into a sitting position in the bed, back when I was minding her.'

'Oh dear,' murmured Brigid. 'Lifting people is difficult. When I was doing my nursing training all those years ago, I knew dozens of nurses and nuns with crocked backs and shoulders from lifting. Lifting children was so much easier.'

'Do you know, I almost forgot you did nursing,' Imelda remarked, driving into the car park of their hotel.

'It was the thing I was happiest at. A time when I felt my life and work was worthwhile. And I *loved* minding the children,' Brigid confided.

'Of course your work was worthwhile. Why would you think otherwise?' Imelda was surprised at Brigid's comment.

'Ah I suppose when you hear all the terrible things done in the name of the Church, like the revelations about the Tuam babies' mass grave . . . It's very upsetting. And then there's the stuff that's come to light about cases of sexual abuse by the clergy – enabled by the Pope, cardinals, and bishops. I can't help thinking to myself: this was the organization I worked my whole life for, and encouraged countless African parents and children to follow.' Brigid gave another sigh that came from the depths of her.

'That Tuam's a terrible scandal all right. Those poor children.' Imelda saw the glimmer of tears in her sister's eyes and felt an uncharacteristic and surprising pang of sympathy for Brigid. 'We hear all about the bad ones, the cruel nuns in the Magdalene laundries and the orphanages, we don't hear about the good ones like you and all the other nursing and teaching nuns, and Missionaries who gave up their lives in the service of others,' Imelda said supportively.

'That's very true. Good deeds don't make the headlines. We did our caring in different ways, you and I. But we made a difference to people's lives. We brought ease to hardship, Imelda. You didn't have it easy.'

The olive branch was held out, and Brigid waited for the usual rant to follow. But Imelda looked into the distance and said slowly, 'I didn't. I certainly didn't. But I suppose in our own way we *did* bring ease. I never thought of it like that. I was full of resentment at the time, to tell you the truth.'

'That's understandable,' Brigid conceded.

'I've a full bladder too.' Imelda grinned. 'And it's feeling a mite resentful – I'd better get in and pee.' She wriggled in her seat.

'Old age is a terrible thing. The leaky bladder is the worst,' Brigid grimaced. Now that Imelda had mentioned it, she could do with going to the loo herself. 'This looks very nice, Imelda. I feel guilty spending money on a fancy hotel room.' Brigid gazed out at the hotel entrance where well-turned-out people entered and exited, some pulling cases, others looking very businesslike in smart suits.

'Don't be ridiculous, you deserve it – besides, it's not *that* fancy.'

'I'm not used to staying in hotels and taking holidays abroad,' Brigid pointed out, unclipping her seat belt.

'Get used to it,' Imelda retorted. 'There's no pockets in a shroud. And don't you dare leave any of that money John gave you to the Church.'

Brigid laughed. 'OK. And just so you know, the Church has got all it's getting from me.'

Imelda smiled, in good form again, and exceedingly pleased that Brigid had admitted that she'd had a hard time looking after their parents. At last! Even if it was years late in coming. How she wished the others had been around to hear it, so they too could acknowledge her great sacrifice. The urge to wee overtook Imelda's desire to bask in her self-righteous gratification.

'Come on,' she urged, 'let's check in and give comfort and ease to our ancient bladders.'

'I think that's it.' Keelin fastened the straps at the top of her case and zipped it closed.

'Have you got your tickets, passport, glasses, and sterling?' Armand asked, hauling it off their bed.

'I do.' Keelin glanced into her handbag to check her travel wallet *was* safely packed, even though she'd only put it into her bag twenty minutes previously. Armand always double- and treble-checked everything when they were travelling.

'Now, have a fantastic time. Let the past go—'

'I'll do my best, Armand,' Keelin said hotly, 'but you know what Mam's like!'

'I do,' her husband said, enfolding her in a hug. 'But remember, she's old—'

'Yeah, old and mean-spirited.' Keelin snuggled in against him.

'If you were holding a session and someone spoke about

difficulties with a parent, one of the first things you'd say is, "What are they teaching you?" So, what's your mother teaching you?'

'Ha ha! Hoist by my own petard ... *again*! She's holding up a mirror and showing me that I'm a mean-spirited, unforgiving woman.' Keelin grimaced.

'Try and be gentle with each other, *chérie*. The middle way is the best.'

'Yes, Armand,' Keelin said affectionately, drawing his head down to hers to kiss him long and tenderly. 'I'll miss you!'

'We'll FaceTime. I'll be looking forward to hearing about your travels. Take plenty of photos. This is going to be such a special trip, Keelin, in every way.' Armand gave her one last hug before they went downstairs to lock up and leave for the airport.

Later that afternoon, as the plane soared into the cotton wool clouds, Keelin wished she could sit back and enjoy the flight. If it had only been Marie-Claire, Brigid and herself going to Scotland, she'd have been bursting with anticipation. But her mother, long a thorn in her side, had the ability to turn the whole jaunt into a fiasco.

Stop giving it negative energy! she told herself fiercely. This was such a test for her. Every spiritual belief she espoused was now knocking at her door. Forgiveness. Releasing anger and resentment and letting go so she could finally put the past behind her and move on. And hopefully heal her relationship with her mother. Was it too big an ask? Could she and Imelda *ever* get on?

Help me, Dad. Help us both, Keelin prayed as the plane levelled out, heading over the Bay of Biscay.

'Oh not now,' Marie-Claire heard her phone ringing from the depths of her overflowing tote bag as she rampaged around her bedroom looking for her house keys. She'd put them down somewhere when she'd got in from work, and couldn't find them.

She scrabbled to the bottom of the bag, wondering if it was Keelin ringing to say her flight had been delayed, although when she'd last checked flight radar it was scheduled to leave France on time.

Frankie Walsh's name flashed on the screen and she wondered why her old college mate was ringing her. She'd kept meaning to meet up with him and Dee, his wife, but between moving back into her house and being extra busy at work, she hadn't got around to it.

'Frankie, how's it going? Look, can I ring you back? I've to go to the airport to collect Maman and I can't find my bloody house keys. I'll call you from the car,' she said hastily.

'No bother. Stay calm and say a prayer to St Anthony,' Frankie laughed and hung up.

'Oh St Anthony, *please* help me to find my house keys,' she entreated Ireland's favourite saint.

The doorbell rang and she groaned in exasperation, running downstairs to answer it. 'Howya! It's your local friendly policeman just saying the front door isn't the safest place to leave your keys.' A tall, well-built man in jeans and a maroon jersey stood on the doorstep dangling her keys. She recognized him as the next-door neighbour on her left-hand side.

'Oh! Oh, hi! Is that where they were? I've been looking all over the place for them,' Marie-Claire exclaimed, relieved but exasperated at her stupidity.

'Easily done – I've looked for my phone, and I've been talking on it,' he said matter-of-factly.

'I'd ask you in, but I'm legging it to the airport and I'm late. I keep meaning to knock and introduce myself. I'm Marie-Claire Durand.' She held out her hand. It was taken in a firm clasp. He had long fingers and neatly cut nails, she noted. And he had nice eyes.

'Senan O'Connell. Don't let me keep ya. Knock on my door if you're ever stuck.' He handed her the keys and raised his hand in a wave before loping off to go up his own path.

'Thanks,' she called after him before running back upstairs to get her handbag, where she was hoping mightily that she'd put her car keys. She'd been carting bags of groceries into the hall and had clearly forgotten to take her keys out of the front door. She found her bag, and her car keys and sprinted downstairs into the kitchen to turn down the oven where a beef casserole was simmering. The aroma was tantalizing and her stomach rumbled. She'd hardly had time for lunch earlier, making do with a sandwich scoffed on the run. She grabbed a banana and hurried out to the car.

She was halfway down Eccles Street when she remembered she'd to ring Frankie Walsh back. 'Hey, Frankie, how are things?' she said cheerfully, relieved to see that the traffic on Dorset Street was flowing smoothly.

'Let's say they've been better, MC, and it's one of the reasons I'm ringing you. I heard you were back in town.' Frankie's Cavan accent was as pronounced as ever, even after years in the capital.

'How can I help, what's up?' she asked, remembering what fun they'd had in college.

'It's Dee, she's pregnant—'

Ah, Frankie, that's great news, congratulations,' she said warmly.

'Yeah well, we're delighted of course, but the problem is she has that all-day morning sickness, hyperemesis grav- idarum – you know, the one that Kate Middleton had?'

'Oh no! How horrible.'

'It is truly, MC. She's throwing up morning noon and night. She was recording an ad last week and right in the middle, while the voice-over actress was trilling "lazy days of sun and sangria", Dee threw up into a paper bin and added some stupendous sound effects.'

'Oh God!' Marie-Claire laughed in spite of herself. 'How awful for her.'

'Fancy coming back to the business? I heard you're hob- nobbing with the D4 set, so we might be a bit downmarket,' he teased.

'Are you serious?' Marie-Claire's eyes lit up. Frankie had opened up his own post-production company a couple of years back.

'Look, if you want to, I'd love to have you on board. I'm up to my eyes with a project in LA with a good buddy of mine. We're working on the Solfeggio Frequencies—'

'Oh cool! My mum's really into the frequencies in her holistic work. She uses them a lot, especially the 417 Hz.'

'Yeah, that's a good one all right, great for clearing the past,' Frankie agreed enthusiastically. 'We've got funding to develop headphones, with the various frequencies tuned in—'

'Wowza! What a *brilliant* idea.'

'I know, and I wouldn't say this to Dee in a million years, but right when I need her most in the business, she gets preggers—'

'And I suppose you had nothing to do with it,' Marie-Claire joked.

'Ah, you know what I mean,' Frankie laughed. 'Don't get me wrong, I'm delighted, but she can't stay at work. She's as sick as a dog. She keeps having to go into hospital so they can put her on IV fluids.'

'Gosh, that's terrible, Frankie. Poor Dee.'

'Fancy taking charge of the post-production end?' he asked hopefully.

'Really?' Marie-Claire felt a frisson of excitement.

'You bet. When I heard you were back, there was no one else I wanted. We were a good team together, you and me.'

'We were,' Marie-Claire grinned, remembering some of their college escapades. 'Look I'm going to Scotland for a few days. How about we hook up when I get back and have a chat?'

'Great stuff,' Frankie agreed.

'Give my love to Dee.'

I will. Great talking to ya, MC. Looking forward to catching up.'

'Me too. See you soon,' Marie-Claire smiled.

Things are looking up at last, she thought, cruising through the Whitehall, Griffith Avenue junction, which usually took an age. An opportunity to get back into post-production was exactly what she needed, she realized. She was back in her own house, not quite sorted out yet, but getting used to it again. And now this. Maybe Dublin *was* where she would settle, after all.

Marc had called several times, urging her to come to New York to take charge of his new business there: 'Marie-Claire I know you'd make a fantastic success of it. I trust you implicitly,' he'd implored. '*Please* come back. I *miss* you, babe.'

But I don't trust you! she'd thought, enjoying his grovelling. He wanted her in New York because she was excellent at her job, but he wouldn't pay her the salary he was going to have to pay to get someone as qualified and experienced as she was. She knew Marc of old.

She'd thought about it. Working and living in New York would be a whole new experience, even if she weren't romantically involved with Marc anymore. New York moved at a much faster pace than Toronto. There'd be a lot of schmoozing and networking required to attract new clients. Did she really want to put in all that effort for someone else's business? Did she also want the upheaval of uprooting again, when she'd got her house back and was beginning to settle?

The unexpected offer of a job from Frankie, right when she felt she couldn't stick Chloe and Inez for another minute, was a sign from the universe. Frankie was highly thought of in the business. They'd worked well together in college and she had a lot to bring to his company. They would be working as equals, with genuine mutual respect. That very much appealed to her.

Marie-Claire felt a flicker of happiness and optimism. Something she hadn't felt since she'd overheard that phone call the previous Christmas. She saw a United Airlines jet descending over the M1 on its flight path to land. Maybe last week she might have been tempted to book a ticket Stateside, but today she was happy to be in Dublin. It was the first time she'd been able to say that since her return from Toronto. Now all she'd to do was get her mother and grandmother reconciled and life would be well and truly on the up again.

CHAPTER FORTY-SEVEN

Keelin's eyes lit up when she saw Marie-Claire waving at the Arrivals barrier.

'*Chérie*, what a treat!' she exclaimed, throwing her arms around her daughter. 'I love that you're back living in Ireland. It's so much easier to get to see you.'

'Maman, you look great. I love the hair.' Marie-Claire drew back and studied her mother. Keelin's new ash-blonde highlights and flick-out cut, tucked behind her ears, emphasized the green of her eyes and her high cheekbones.

'Hmmm, I needed to do something with it. I'm too old for long hair now and there's more grey than there used to be, so I'm embracing it,' Keelin laughed, tucking her arm into her daughter's. Together they set off towards the exit.

'Granny and Mère are at the hotel, so they survived the trip to Dublin together,' Marie-Claire grinned, sliding her parking ticket into the machine.

'Well that's something, I suppose,' Keelin said. 'To tell you the truth, I'm dreading the next few days. I don't know if it was such a good idea to invite Mam.'

'I know. We don't want to be watching our P's and Q's every time we open our mouths. But I think, from the short time I spent with her when Mère and I called in unexpectedly, she's relieved to have an opportunity to sort things out and move forward with the rest of us. Maybe it might be a blessing in disguise,' Marie-Claire soothed, rooting for coins.

'Yes, hopefully,' Keelin said, but doubt lingered in her voice. 'All I know is that a mirror is being held up to me and I don't like myself very much. I never realized how angry I was at her and how resentful. I'd buried it for years. So I suppose it's time for me to walk the walk, put my spiritual beliefs into practice and clear all this toxic energy between us. No matter what the outcome.'

'You're very hard on yourself, Maman,' Marie-Claire said. 'None of us have found Granny easy to deal with.'

'I'm the one teaching holistic classes and holding spiritual retreats and pontificating about how to live our best lives.' Keelin followed Marie-Claire into a lift, glad they were alone. 'What if I can't do it, though? What if I can't hack it with Mam. Then where are we?'

'What would you say to someone in that position if they were asking your advice?'

'I suppose I'd say, provided you've done your best, let them go. We can't love, or even like *everybody* who's in our lives, and that's OK. Bless them and let them go, basically.'

'Well, that's what you'll do then, Maman,' Marie-Claire

said pragmatically. 'Stop beating yourself up. Who knows, a miracle might happen and we'll have a fun time,' she added. 'Speaking of miracles, you'll never guess what happened to me today,' she exclaimed, hoisting Keelin's case into the boot of the car. 'An old college friend phoned me, out of the blue. His wife is pregnant and very sick and he needs someone to run the post-production side of his business, and that some-one might be *moi*!'

'Terrific,' enthused her mother, settling into the pas-senger seat.

'That's a real sign that I've to stay in Dublin, isn't it? I was so unsettled, I didn't know what to do with myself and thought of going to the States—'

'And going back to *Marc*?' Keelin couldn't hide her shock.

'No!' scoffed Marie-Claire, reversing out of the parking bay. 'I'd never go back to him – though I did think about taking the job in his NY office. But now this has come up and I really like the idea of it.'

'And you've moved back into your lovely house. It's per-fect,' Keelin encouraged, relieved that Marie-Claire was staying put. 'Mary Magdalene is working her magic already – let's hope she gifts us with a serene few days in Scotland.'

'Somehow I don't equate the word "serene" with Granny,' Marie-Claire replied, and they laughed heartily as they headed for the hotel.

Brigid knocked on Imelda's door. She'd got a text from Marie-Claire to say that she and Keelin were leaving the airport, and to be in the foyer in ten minutes. She was thoroughly enjoying this great new adventure. Staying in a hotel was a real treat. Whenever she'd travelled for work, she'd always stayed in convents.

She'd had a lovely post-lunch siesta, lying on her bed flicking TV channels before losing herself in her latest Patrice Chaplin book, which was all about life in a small French village. They were going to dinner in Marie-Claire's house, and make plans for their Scottish itinerary. She hadn't been this excited since she was a small girl waiting for Santa to come.

For so many years, there'd been nothing in her life to make her feel really enthusiastic. Now every day had a new joy and a new sense of freedom for her. It was thoroughly invigorating, Brigid thought happily.

Imelda's perfume wafted out the door when it opened. Brigid could see that her sister had taken extra care with her make-up. She really was looking very well for her age.

'I must get you to give me make-up lessons sometime. You look very glamorous,' she complimented her sister.

'I try.' Imelda admired her reflection in the mirror. She'd got a new foundation the last time she was in Brown Tomas and it was very smooth compared to the old one, which had always looked patchy.

'They're on their way to collect us. Marie-Claire said to be in the foyer waiting,' Brigid explained.

'Did they ring you?' Imelda asked sharply.

'Text.' Brigid wondered why the tone.

'Huh, they could have sent me one. Just as well I was ready in time,' Imelda said snippily, gathering her bag, scarf and jacket.

Don't start your nonsense. Brigid felt irritability prick her bubble of anticipation. Imelda's humour had changed. She wore that dour expression that Brigid was more familiar with. She realized that Imelda was nervous. It was her first time to meet Keelin after the row. It would be awkward for both of them.

'Do you want to take the stairs or the lift?' she asked.

'I suppose we should take the stairs. It's good exercise.' Imelda arranged her scarf just so over her shoulders as they walked along the corridor.

'The Dunne ladies shall make their impressive descent, then,' Brigid said light-heartedly. 'Remember after we went to the cinema to see *Gone with the Wind*, we wrapped Granny Dunne's shawls around us and pretended to be Scarlett and Melly, walking down the stairs.'

'We did, didn't we? I'd forgotten that.' Imelda brightened at the memory. 'You forget so much, don't you! Oh look, there's Keelin waiting for us,' she murmured. 'I wonder will she be snooty with me.'

'She wanted you to come with us,' Brigid reminded her gently. 'She's probably wondering will you be snooty with her.'

'Well she *was* quite nasty to me,' Imelda said self-righteously as they reached the last step and walked past reception to where her daughter was waiting for them.

'Hello, Mam,' Keelin said calmly.

'Hello, Keelin.' Imelda felt her mouth go dry and her heart start to beat faster. She didn't know what to say next.

Brigid saved her. 'Hello dear, where's Marie-Claire?' she asked, reaching up to kiss Keelin's cheek.

'She's in the car outside, she's anxious to get home because she has the dinner simmering in the oven, so I said I'd run in for you.'

'Grand, we're all ready to go,' Brigid said, ushering Imelda and Keelin ahead of her.

'Did you have a good flight?' Imelda made an effort.

'I did. It was very smooth and it was such a treat to have Marie-Claire waiting for me in Arrivals. I'm so glad she's back in Ireland for good.'

'Is she going to stay, do you think?' interjected Brigid as they crossed the foyer. 'She was a bit betwixt and between when I saw her last. Couldn't decide what to do.'

'I think so. She's moved back into the house and earlier today she got a job offer in post-production, which is where her heart lies. As I said to her, Mary Magdalene is working her magic!' Keelin smiled at her aunt, who was waving at Marie-Claire.

She jumped out of the car when she saw them and kissed Imelda and Brigid.

'You sit in the front, Keelin, Imelda and I will get in the back.' Brigid took charge, thinking it might be awkward if Imelda and Keelin were sitting in the back, not knowing what to say to each other.

Keelin leapt into the front of the car with alacrity. The last place she wanted to be was sitting beside her mother, trying to make polite chitchat.

'I've a beef casserole in the oven. You'll be my first guests, for dinner. I hope you're hungry, because I'm *starving*,' Marie-Claire said over her shoulder as they set off.

'We had a delicious lunch earlier, in the hotel, but I'm beginning to feel peckish all right.' Imelda settled herself comfortably, beginning to relax.

'That sounds tasty,' Brigid approved, wondering would it be better to clear the air with everyone over dinner, so that they wouldn't all be walking on eggshells for the duration of their trip to Scotland. How many times had she sat at dinners with her community after a row had taken place and antagonism had crackled around the table, despite the silence, while they ate?

Perhaps they should wait, at least until the meal was over. No point in ruining Marie-Claire's first dinner party. 'Tell us about the new job offer Keelin mentioned, Marie-Claire.' Brigid moved the conversation to another safe topic.

Her grand-niece turned onto the Ballymun Road and regaled them with tales of her time in college with Frankie, and his job offer to her.

'And what will the fella in Toronto have to say about that?' Imelda queried.

'He can say what he likes, Granny. It's got nothing to do with him. I'm my own woman and I make my own decisions,' Marie-Claire retorted.

'It really is a time for women to come into their own in Ireland now, isn't it?' Brigid remarked. 'So different from our day, Imelda. It's wonderful to see women standing together and standing up for one another to repeal the Eighth.'

Imelda did a double-take at her sister's words. 'But you're a nun, Brigid – surely you wouldn't be voting yes to abortion?'

'I'm a nun who has been sleepwalking through life, believing what I was told by my Church. Now I'm awake, thinking for myself, making my own decisions. And while I don't condone abortion, neither do I judge anyone who has had one. I've never had to make that decision. There but for the grace of God went any of us. And my Yes vote will give women the chance to make their own decision, so that they'll no longer have to put their lives in danger, or have to travel to a foreign country for a termination, if it comes to that. There's a great liberation in being free to work all these things out for myself after all these years of toeing the party line, so to speak,' she smiled at Imelda.

'Could you be excommunicated for voting Yes?' Imelda asked.

'They can excommunicate away. They got the best of me. Now I'm giving my best, or what's left of it, to myself!' Brigid countered and they all laughed.

'There's a squad car outside your house, I hope there's nothing wrong,' Imelda said, when Marie-Claire turned onto the road where she lived.

'That's my neighbour getting out. He's a copper—'

'He's not wearing a uniform,' Imelda observed as Marie-

Claire indicated and waited patiently to get into her parking space.

'Maybe he's a detective Garda,' Brigid said. 'What's he like?'

'He seems nice enough. I see two young girls staying over part of every week. I think he's probably sharing custody of his kids or something.' Marie-Claire pulled into her spot when the squad car moved off.

'Good to have a guard beside you. Excellent for security. I like the colour of your door,' Imelda approved.

'Nice, isn't it?' Marie-Claire admired the lilac gloss paint that reminded her of window shutters in Languedoc. They all trooped into the hall behind her, oohing and aahing at the light airy pastel décor, and the mouth-watering smells emanating from the kitchen.

'I am *stuffed*.' Imelda sat back an hour later, patting her tummy. 'That was delicious.'

'Very tasty, dear. Thank you.' Brigid wiped her mouth with her napkin.

'Let me clear the table.' Keelin stood up.

'Stay where you are, Maman, I'll fling these into the dishwasher and then I'll serve up dessert. I got a strawberry roulade over in Thunder's,' Marie-Claire instructed, delighted that her meal had gone so well.

'I know what I'll do, while we're waiting,' Keelin said with a gleam in her eye. 'I want to get something out of my case.' She came back in from the hall holding a box in her hands. 'My Mary Magdalene cards,' she explained. 'Let's all choose a card and see what message she gives us. They're cards with guidance and words of wisdom on them, Mam. You always get the message you need. I use them in my work all the time,' Keelin explained to her mother. Marie-Claire and Brigid were familiar with them.

'Ohhh yes,' Marie-Claire exclaimed. Imelda looked dubious, and Brigid's eyes lit up.

'This is what we'll do,' Keelin shuffled the deck, 'We'll pick one each, and whatever the message is, we'll keep it to ourselves. Then we can talk about it on our last night in Scotland, if we want to. Or if you want to keep it private, that's OK too, Mam.' She spread out the pack and held it out to her mother.

Imelda pursed her lips and eyed the cards warily. 'I'm not sure about this woo-woo stuff,' she said.

'If you don't want one, it's OK.' Keelin shrugged.

'Oh, I'll take one to please you.' She selected a card, looked at it, and her lips tightened. 'Hmmm,' she muttered.

Brigid took one eagerly, read it and her eyes widened. '*Oh!*' she exclaimed.

Keelin chose her card, and smiled at the message.

'My turn.' Marie-Claire laid the creamy roulade on the table and leaned over and plucked a card out of the deck.

'I wonder what this means,' she said, studying it.

'Here, you can have this back,' Imelda said, thrusting her card into the deck. 'Messages indeed! They're only cards.'

'No problem,' Keelin said coolly, agog to know what card her mother had selected that had prompted her testy response.

'I'll keep mine, if you don't mind,' Brigid said quietly.

'Me too.' Marie-Claire tucked hers into her handbag.

Imelda sat sour-faced.

Later, after Marie-Claire had driven Brigid and Imelda back to their hotel, she and Keelin sat in Marie-Claire's cosy lounge area sipping a G&T before going to bed.

'I'd love to know what message Granny got. She wasn't impressed at *all*!' Marie-Claire threw a log on the wood burner and watched it blaze up in a shower of sparks.

'You can be assured it was *exactly* the message she was meant to get,' Keelin said ruefully. 'And I think this trip will be make or break for her and me. Finally, after all these years, there will be a resolution to our problems one way or another.'

'She's lucky to be getting this chance, Maman. Not many would be as decent to her as you and Brigid are after her outrageous behaviour.' Marie-Claire raised her glass to her mother. 'Thank God for alcohol! What will be will be. Let the high jinks begin!'

CHAPTER FORTY-EIGHT

'Terminal two, because it's Aer Lingus,' Imelda announced knowledgeably, looking at her boarding pass as they drove along the M1 to Dublin Airport. She was keen to let her family know that she too was an *international* traveller.

'Allegedly,' Keelin threw her eyes up to heaven. We check in at T2, go through security and then have to traipse over to T1 to get to our boarding gate, and then we have to get on a bus to go out to our plane,' she grumbled.

'Well you know, when you go on a pilgrimage, in search of truth, obstacles can be put in the way. You have to prove you really want to seek and find,' Brigid joked.

'"Pilgrimage" is surely a bit overly dramatic. You go on a pilgrimage to Lourdes or the Holy Land. I never heard a trip to Scotland referred to as a "pilgrimage"!' Imelda scoffed.

Brigid's lips thinned as the familiar irritation surged. She wondered yet again why she'd suggested inviting Imelda along. She was going to ruin their trip with her nit-picking and sniping.

'A sacred journey of devotion, no matter where in the world you go, is a pilgrimage,' she riposted tartly.

'Hmmm! If you say so. And we have to fly on one of those propeller yokes? Sure, we might as well have taken a boat. We'd be there quicker,' Imelda fired back.

'You knew that before you booked – you didn't have to come,' Brigid reminded her.

'Stop it, Mam,' Keelin ordered crossly. 'I am *not* travelling to Scotland, on a quest I've longed to go on for years, to have it ruined by petty bickering. Mère is right. This is a pilgrimage and we have to go with whatever is thrown at us and get on with it, propeller planes and all.'

'Doesn't sound like much fun,' her mother said sulkily.

'It will be, if you allow it to be. And remember, you didn't *have* to come. No one twisted your arm.' Keelin couldn't hide her exasperation with her mother. The airport came into view, and Marie-Claire drove to the long-term car park. Ten minutes later they were sitting on the link bus waiting to drive to the terminal. 'When we get airside and are having our coffee, we'll do a kitty purse. We'll divide the car parking between the four of us,' Keelin said when they disembarked at T2.

'Ah no worries,' Marie-Claire said, lifting the cases onto the kerb. 'Let me get a trolley. *Four Go Wild in Scotland.* Enid Blyton, eat your heart out,' she said cheerfully, trying to lift the tense atmosphere.

The others laughed at her banter and Keelin was grateful that her daughter was accompanying them. Marie-Claire had an exuberance and lightness of spirit that might get them through their first – and perhaps, last – holiday together, without ending up constantly at each other's throats. The energy changed from surly petulance to anticipation, and when Marie-Claire returned with a trolley, they cheered and made their way to the bag-drop before heading to security.

Imelda tried not to feel flustered while divesting herself of her coat and scarf. The others were regular travellers. Keelin and Marie-Claire hopped on planes the way others hopped on buses, and she didn't want to let on how very apprehensive she was about flying on a plane with propellers. She'd butterflies in her tummy and felt queasy with nerves.

Brigid swiftly and efficiently passed through the scan and was already putting her coat back on at the other end of the desk.

'Let me help you, Gran,' Marie-Claire offered, neatly arranging her belongings in the tray for her.

'You're a kind girl,' Imelda said gratefully. She should stop fretting. She didn't have to shoulder the burden of being in charge anymore. It was rather comforting to be minded, she acknowledged, walking through the metal detector. To her dismay she started to beep, and felt a tide of embarrassment flood her. Everybody in the airport was probably looking at her.

'Do you have any replacement hips or knees?' the security guard asked matter-of-factly.

'Oh ... oh ... yes ... yes ... I do. I got a hip replacement a year ago, it was a complicated one, I nearly—'

'That's all right, madam, we'll just get you patted down,' the security guard wasn't interested in hearing about her trials and tribulations with her hip, Imelda thought huffily, and gave him one of her 'unimpressed' looks as a female security guard began to frisk her.

'Now hold on to this and lift your leg,' the young woman instructed, pointing to a step beside the conveyor belt.

'What am I? A *gymnast*?' Imelda demanded, glaring at the woman as she carried out the instructions.

Marie-Claire caught Keelin's eye and was afraid she was going to burst out laughing. 'Thank God we're in this together,' Keelin whispered. 'I do so want to enjoy this trip.'

'You will,' Marie-Claire assured her. 'We'll buy a bottle of Hendrick's in the Duty Free and drown our sorrows tonight.'

Keelin laughed. 'You're a divil, do you know that?'

'I do,' smirked her daughter as she walked, beep-free, through the security arch to join her waiting fellow pilgrims.

'Oh, Marie-Claire aren't those bridges a wonderful sight?' Imelda was bubbling with excitement as the commuter plane made its descent over the Firth of Forth towards Edinburgh airport. At her granddaughter's suggestion – once Imelda had seen how smoothly the much-dreaded propeller plane flew and her fears had subsided – they had changed seats so that Imelda could see the stunning scenery as they flew east over Scotland. On the other side of the aisle, Brigid was equally absorbed in the views below them. Keelin and Marie-Claire smiled at each other like two co-conspirators.

Less than half an hour later, they were sitting in an extremely comfortable hired Peugeot SUV, cases stowed in the boot, and Marie-Claire was setting the route they were taking into the satnav. 'Right, Rosslyn Chapel here we come,' she exclaimed gaily, and a ripple of excitement spread through the car.

'I've longed to go to back to Rosslyn for so long,' Keelin exclaimed from the back seat, where she was sitting with her mother.

'But it's not a Catholic church anymore, is it?' Imelda said doubtfully. To tell the truth, she was a little fearful of stepping into the strange church that Keelin and Marie-Claire spoke about so reverently. The stuff they believed in was difficult to credit – it was the one thing she and Brigid agreed upon – but a small part of her, the adventurous and to-hell-with-it part that she'd only lately discovered in herself, was eager for new adventures. Would she feel vortexes and ley lines and see beyond to another dimension, like she'd read about in one of Keelin's books? Apparently, Rosslyn was no ordinary chapel.

'It's not Catholic now, Mam. It originated as a Catholic church in the mid-fifteenth century, but after the Scottish Reformation, Roman Catholic worship was ended and the chapel was closed to the public until it was reopened as a Scottish Episcopal church. Anglicans,' she explained. 'It remains privately owned still.'

'Well as far as I'm concerned, if it started out Catholic, it still is,' Imelda declared.

'And what's your esoteric view of it, Keelin?' Brigid, who had hopped into the front without being asked, turned back to look at her niece.

'Some things are only visible to those that have eyes to see. You know the way I work with the tuning forks with the Solfeggio Frequencies that I use in my healing sessions? Rosslyn Chapel is located on top of a vortex *and* a specific crossing of ley lines, which in my opinion makes it a gigantic frequency generator. I think this place was created to preserve an ancient library of information. When the Masons – as in the Freemasons, guardians of esoteric knowledge – found themselves called in to this magical location, they took advantage of the opportunity and created a virtual library, hidden in plain view. The Solfeggio Frequencies, the semi-tones, are embedded in the cube sequence on the ceiling—'

'They're the frequencies Frankie and his business partner are working on in LA,' Marie-Claire interjected. 'So we're going to find out more about them in Rosslyn? Wooo-hooo!'

'Indeed we are,' Keelin said happily. 'When Pope Gregory forbade the use of these healing frequencies, sometime between AD 590 and 604, it became known as the "Devil's Chord". Because of the Pope's ban, the knowledge went underground, and the Mystery Schools, or Schools of Initiation, kept the information flowing.'

'The church keeping knowledge from us, yet again?' Brigid said crossly.

'Exactly,' Keelin nodded, as they emerged onto the motor-way. 'The translated meanings of the frequencies were found in the original Greek Apocrypha, which made up the earliest books in the Christian Bible, but they were left out of most subsequent translations following the First Council of Nicaea in 325 AD—'

'To think that a council of around three hundred *men* determined the nature of Christ. Man or deity? And *they* *decided* what was to go into the Bible. It's simply *outrageous*!' Brigid exclaimed. 'I believed all I was taught and wasted a lifetime obeying rules and regulations that were man-made, hiding the true nature of who we are. It *grieves* me. It was brainwashing, that's what it was. Mark Twain was right: "*The truth is not hard to kill, and a lie well told is immortal.*"'

'Oh that's a good one, Mère,' Keelin approved. 'I never heard that one before.'

'I'm very partial to Mark Twain. He was a wise man and he had a great sense of humour. According to him, "Cauliflower is nothing but cabbage with a college educa-tion",' Brigid quoted, laughing.

Even Imelda chuckled at that.

'Well, here you are, on a journey of discovery. It's never too late, Mère,' Keelin laughed.

'I'm going in with an open mind, Keelin. I'm ready for revelations,' the elderly nun said briskly.

'So are those frequency things the same as those fork things you twang on me?' Imelda queried. She was somewhat aghast at her sister's pronouncement. After all, Brigid had been a Reverend Mother for *many* years. It was shocking to hear *her* denounce the Church so vehemently.

'Yes, Mam, they're my tuning forks. You always tell me you feel good after a session with me.' Keelin smiled at her mother's description.

'Well they do make me feel relaxed,' admitted Imelda.

'That's the vibration. Everything has a vibration . . . you've heard of good and bad vibes. Remember Brian Wilson's song?' She hummed the tune of 'Good Vibrations'.

'It's very strange to me that you were raised a Catholic, became a nun, and you ended up believing all this—' She nearly said *gobbledygook* but stopped herself in time. 'This, er . . . weird stuff,' Imelda couldn't get her head around all she'd heard.

'"Ask and the door will be opened unto you. Seek and you shall find",' Keelin deftly quoted the Bible at her mother. 'I searched and I found different answers, precisely because I questioned and asked and I followed the leads I was given, just as you are now, even if you are a doubting Thomas,' Keelin teased, and they laughed, enjoying the unexpected camaraderie their trip was engendering.

At Gowkley Moss Roundabout, take the first exit onto Penicuik Rd/B7003, the calm, cultured voice from the satnav instructed.

'Isn't technology incredible, all the same?' Brigid said in awe as Marie-Claire followed the instructions and turned right, before announcing triumphantly and with a sense of relief, 'Here we are!'

They were glad to stretch and unwind and feel the gentle

breeze drifting down from the Pentland Hills. The sun was warm on their faces as they walked towards the impressive glass and stone visitor's centre, glimpsing the massive gothic, honey-coloured stone pinnacles and flying buttresses of the ancient chapel through the leafy trees to their right.

'Isn't that beautiful stonework?' Imelda admired the wall that enclosed the chapel and led towards the entrance.

'I'm so delighted to be back again,' Keelin exclaimed, her head swivelling from right to left, taking it all in. 'Could we please go into the chapel first and then we can meander around the visitor's centre and maybe have a cup of coffee and a sandwich afterwards?'

'It's your trip, you're in charge, Maman,' Marie-Claire declared, following Keelin, who had entered the centre and turned right to make her way to the grounds of the sacred place she'd longed to return to for so long.

'Oh my!' Brigid stared at the imposing edifice in front of them. 'It's quite impressive, and most unusual. I love the colour of the stonework; it makes it warm, not like some of those big gothic cathedrals that are cold and sterile.'

'I don't much fancy the look of that fella. Is he the devil?' Imelda pointed dubiously to a massive, grinning gargoyle. 'And I don't like them pair either ...' She pointed to two smaller ones on either side of the big wooden door that led into the north entrance. 'Are you sure this is a holy place, and not one of those places that have strange goings on?'

'Gargoyles are very common in medieval buildings – they were sometimes used as a form of protection, frightening away evil spirits. Actually, they're water spouts designed to let water flow away from buildings, a bit like gutters. And don't forget this was once a consecrated Catholic church, although it's now Anglican, so you'll be quite safe, Mam,' Keelin explained patiently, reminding herself how new esoteric thinking was to her mother.

'Oh well, if you say so.' Imelda gave a wary side eye to the grotesque figure beside the door.

'Wow!' Marie-Claire enthused, walking into the chapel. 'Where do you begin to start exploring?'

The sun's rays slanted in through the magnificent stained-glass windows, throwing beams of light along the nave, where the visitors exclaimed at each new discovery.

'Look, Auntie Brigid, the Apprentice Pillar with the strands of DNA I was telling you about! You know the double helix? This was carved in the fifteenth century, and guess what? Dolly the cloned sheep was cloned at the Rosslyn Institute down the road. Now don't tell me *that's* a coincidence!' Keelin's eyes gleamed with anticipation, enthralled.

'Good heavens, it's amazing!' Brigid felt a strange sense of excitement stir in her.

'There's the Devil's Chord, the seven semitones the Church banned from being played, that I was telling you about. Remember the frequencies, hidden in plain sight.' Keelin pointed to a set of decorated cubes in the magnificent arched ceiling. They all gazed upwards and Marie-Claire felt a jolt. *This is why I'm here!* she thought in amazement, remembering the message on her Magdalene card.

'You could spend a lifetime here, and never get to the bottom of it. There's so much to discover. Let's join the group over there and hear what the guide has to say,' Keelin suggested, delighted that the others were becoming as keen to explore the mysteries of the magnificent medieval church that she loved.

CHAPTER FORTY-NINE

'I'll drive to Fionnphort, seeing as you drove all the way from Edinburgh,' Keelin offered, as Marie-Claire stood yawning on the deck of the ferry that was to take them across to Craignure on Mull.

'I don't mind driving; it's a terrific car to drive. So comfortable.'

'It's *extremely* comfortable to sit in as a passenger,' Imelda interjected, leaning on the rail, enjoying the sound of the ship's horn wailing above her head as the ropes were cast off and the ferry began to glide across the molten waters of the Sound. The breeze had dropped and the sea was flat calm, much to her great relief. 'The next time I'm changing my car, I might go for the Peugeot,' she added. 'Could I have a little spin in her, somewhere quiet, to see what she drives like. I've never driven an automatic?' she asked Marie-Claire.

'Of course you can – and you too, Mère, if you like. It's so easy once you get used to it,' Marie-Claire said agreeably.

'Thank you, dear. I might do that.' Brigid smiled, gazing at the panorama before her. The throb of the ship's engines reminded her of the many times she'd travelled on boats upriver in Senegal, en route to outlying villages to minister to children. It seemed a lifetime ago. A dream almost, she thought sadly, remembering how young and vigorous she'd been then, and happy to be with her beloved African children, giving them the love she'd never been able to give her own, lost baby. *Don't think about it.* She buried the memories with difficulty, and said 'Isn't that's a stunning sunset?' admiring the streamers of red, gold, and pink that tinted the western horizon. The faint lights in the houses on Mull began to get brighter as dusk deepened and the mountains darkened, etched against the twilight sky.

'Absolutely *beautiful!*' agreed Marie-Claire, snapping away on her iPad and turning the camera towards her companions to take their photo.

'It's a long time since we shared a room,' Imelda remarked, studying their surroundings with pursed lips. The landlady of the B&B they were staying in had shown them to the spacious bedroom with en suite that would be theirs for the night. There was a single and double bed and she didn't fancy sleeping in the narrow confines of the smaller bed. She was exhausted after the early start and all the travelling. And she was hungry.

'Indeed it has, Imelda. A long time too, since I shared a dormitory with my fellow Sisters. I suppose we're lucky we're not sharing a bed like we did in the old days.' Brigid took off her coat and scarf and hung them neatly in the wardrobe.

'You're skinnier than I am, will the single bed do you?' Imelda ventured.

'I'd sleep on a rock, I'm so tired,' Brigid said tartly, annoyed at her sister's selfishness. Typical Imelda. Always thinking of herself first. *Little fat selfish lump*, she thought viciously. Their short *entente cordiale* was wearing thin. It had begun to erode when Imelda had taken the front seat of the car for the long trip from Craignure to Fionnphort with a pointed, 'My turn to sit in the front, but I won't hog the front seat for the *entire* trip.' It was directed at her and Brigid had felt a blaze of indignation, and had had to bite her tongue to smother the retort that came instantly to her lips: *You wouldn't have been on this trip if it weren't for me, you crabby old biddy.*

One would surely think that after her sister's dreadful behaviour at the party, Imelda would be bending over backwards to make amends. But no. Me, me, me to the fore as usual. The way she was carrying on, you'd think Imelda was the one hard done by.

'It was considerate and thoughtful of the girls to put us first, and give us the bigger room. They're *most* unselfish,' Brigid remarked.

'I should hope so, they were always traits I encouraged in my daughter and granddaughter when they were growing up,' Imelda declared, taking ownership of the locker beside the double bed, placing her clock, tablet container and book beside the lamp.

Pity you didn't practise them yourself, Brigid thought crossly, as she unpacked her nightgown and slippers. It would have been an unaccustomed luxury to spread herself out in the comfort of a double bed. Her beds in the convent and the Four Winds were single divans. Sleeping in the double bed in the hotel the previous night had been a real treat.

She felt grumpy and resentful, the high of Rosslyn wearing off at the prospect of spending a night in such close proximity with her sister. It had been Imelda's choice to share a room on the trip to Mull. She should have drawn her boundary and said she wanted a room of her own. It was her own fault, Brigid acknowledged, and that made her even more vexed. She glanced out the window, trying to ignore her irritation. A scatter of twinkling house and street lights dotted the darkness outside, and the hint of dim shadow in the distance, where Iona lay, made Brigid wish for morning's reveal as she drew the curtains on the window that was at the front of the house, while Imelda did the same to the window facing the ferry jetty.

Keelin's knock on the door brought her back to earth.

'Are you ready for dinner?' her niece called.

Brigid, being nearest the door, opened it to allow Keelin to enter.

'Just unpacking, dear.' She smiled at her beloved niece and her heart lifted. How Imelda and Keelin could be mother and daughter was a mystery to her. They were chalk and cheese. Keelin had inherited her father's gentle traits, for sure.

'Oh my goodness, the aromas that are floating up the stairs

426

are to die for. I'm *ravenous*,' Keelin groaned. 'Isn't it a stroke of luck that our host is a real chef?'

'I'm famished myself,' Imelda declared, running a hair-brush through her hair, and touching up her lipstick.

How Imelda could be famished was a mystery to Brigid. Her sister had scoffed her way through sweets and chocolate bars for the entire car and ferry journey.

Are you hungry, Mère?' Keelin smiled at her.

'I'll certainly enjoy my dinner, Keelin, I haven't eaten since lunch, apart from the Danish on the ferry.' She refrained from saying, *unlike some people*. 'Eating between meals is not our way in the convent, so I'm used to it.'

Imelda's flaring nostrils let her know that her barb had hit home and that gave her a good dollop of satisfaction before guilt got the better of her and Brigid mentally chastised herself for her childish, unchristian, mean-spiritedness.

She and Imelda had been united in their interest and curiosity about Rosslyn, and that had made the experience all the better. She should try to rise above her lower self and see the good in her sibling. That was part of the journey of life: seeing the good rather than the bad, Brigid reminded herself, switching off the bedroom light and following her family down to the large conservatory where dinner was about to be served.

'Well, we survived our first day,' Keelin grinned, clinking her glass of gin with Marie-Claire's.

They were sitting on the side of their beds, in their

pyjamas, having a private drinks party with the Hendrick's Marie-Claire had bought for that very purpose in Duty Free.

'They were grand during the flight and when we got to Rosslyn, but I sensed an edge sliding in soon as we got off the ferry. And over dinner there was a lot of shade in some of the tit-for-tat comments.' Marie-Claire took a slug of her gin.

'I know. One was as bad as the other. Brigid's restraint didn't last very long. She's giving as good as she gets. This is the first time they've been in such close quarters since they were teens. And a *lot* of water has flowed under that bridge.'

'I still think we were right to invite Granny. I think it was meant to be.' Marie-Claire yawned widely. The sea air was so rich and pure she knew she'd sleep like a log.

'Me too. It'll be a rocky road, but healing *will* come on this journey.' Keelin tried to stay positive. Privately she was wishing she'd come on her own; this was a journey she'd wanted to undertake for such a long time. Her mother was being her usual spiky self, and Brigid's responses were a master class in passive-aggressive behaviour, unlike her earlier restrained impassiveness. Clearly, being in close confines with her sibling was peeling off the façade of polite non-engagement.

That was what this trip was all about though, she conceded. Stripping away the layers and getting to the kernel of disaffection and resentment between them. Identical too, to what was going on with herself and Imelda. The day of reckoning had come and issues had to be faced, no matter what the outcome. Family dynamics weren't easy at the best of times.

'It's too late to turn back now, Marie-Claire, we're stuck

on an island, at the mercy of the weather. Do you hear the wind getting up? And heavy rain is forecast, unfortunately. God works in strange ways, for sure. It will all be OK though, I truly feel it.' She spoke with more confidence than she felt.

Marie-Claire laughed. 'Maman, all I can say is, as I've said before, thank God for gin ... and your optimism. *Sláinte*,' she added, raising her glass.

'To family,' Keelin responded comically, and they laughed heartily.

'Oh excuse me,' Imelda burped. She put her hand to her mouth as another unladylike belch threatened. She was sitting against the pillows in her double bed, a few rollers tucked under her hairnet, ready to settle down for the night. Brigid was reading her missal in the adjacent single bed.

'Indigestion?' She arched an eyebrow at her sister. 'Well, you did eat rather a lot at dinner. At our age, second helpings aren't good for us.'

Imelda's mouth tightened into a thin line and her eyes narrowed to slits of annoyance. 'I'm not used to eating late at night, and neither am I used to people watching and commenting on what I eat. The height of bad manners, if you don't mind my saying so.'

'I was merely making an observation, Imelda. I was a nurse once. I have medical experience, and I know that overfilling the stomach late at night causes flatulence and discomfort. I'm merely thinking of your comfort, dear. Sleep well,' Brigid returned sweetly.

'You don't have to worry about *my* comfort, *dear*. And I sleep *very* well thank you. *There's no pillow so soft as a clear conscience*, as the old saying goes. Goodnight,' Imelda retorted bitchily, switching off her light.

Cow, thought Brigid, in a most un-nun-like manner. What a spiteful response. A real dig at her. She racked her brains for a pithy comeback: 'I rather like what James has to say in the Bible: "*God resists the proud but gives grace to the humble.*"'

She heard her sister's sharp intake of breath and smiled. *Put that in your pipe and smoke it, madam*, she thought, snapping off her light, hoping against hope that she would fall asleep quickly and wondering had she lost her senses entirely to take this journey with her *extremely* annoying and acerbic sibling.

CHAPTER FIFTY

The sound of a shower running woke Imelda and she lay in her warm bed, wondering where she was. This wasn't her bed, or her room. She blinked rapidly to clear her eyes from sleep. A faint ray of light splashed through a chink in the curtains on the window opposite her bed, and she remembered she was sharing a room with Brigid and they were on the Isle of Mull, in Scotland.

Thanks to the half sleeping tablet she'd taken, she'd conked out. Had her sister fared as well, she wondered. There was nothing worse than lying in the dark, listening to someone else snoring and being unable to sleep.

Brigid's bed was already neatly made and her case packed for their departure. She'd obviously taken care to be very quiet, because Imelda had not stirred from her sleep. Brigid had become extremely disciplined and immaculately tidy, Imelda acknowledged, remembering how untidy she'd been when they shared a room at home. And her sister had made an effort not to wake her. She would try hard to be nice today, Imelda decided. She'd been a bit spiteful in her comments last night.

Out of the blue, Imelda remembered what the message on her Magdalene card had been and her jaw dropped. Was it really a message from beyond the veil or just some random choice of card that she'd selected? It certainly was most pertinent to her behaviour towards her sister, she thought uncomfortably.

'No! It's all nonsense,' she muttered, shaking her head. But was it? Keelin had such faith in these things, and when Imelda had been in Rosslyn Chapel, she had to admit she'd felt *different*. From the moment she'd walked in through the big church doors she'd felt a ... a ... great welcome, and a sense of tranquillity. A feeling that someone had said, 'Well done. You're here'. Was it her imagination, or was there more to it all? *Was* Mary Magdalene guiding this trip, as Keelin so firmly believed?

Imelda threw back the duvet and went across to the window, pulling open the curtains to reveal a rain-spattered window and a gloomy vista ahead. The roiling sea was as grey as the sky. In the distance she could see a shadowed Iona melting into the gloom. Shrouded in mist, she could hardly make out the small village behind the ferry port across the water, where lights had glimmered so brightly the previous night. She hoped she wouldn't feel sick on the journey across. She'd done well on the ferry from Oban the previous evening, but the sea had only rippled gently across the Sound of Kerrera, on the short trip from the mainland to Craignure.

Imelda turned her back on the dismal view and went and rooted in her case for a clean pair of knickers and vest. Keelin had advised her to pack layers of clothes to wear on their jaunt to the windswept isle.

'Good morning, Imelda.' Brigid emerged from the bathroom, already dressed, with her winceyette nightdress folded over her arm. She was wearing a pair of black tailored woollen trousers, a mauve roll-neck jumper and a pair of sturdy brogues. Imelda couldn't hide her shock. She'd never seen her sibling wearing trousers.

Brigid noted her surprise. 'Keelin said I should wear trousers. I do feel rather strange wearing them,' she explained, a tad defensively.

'It's so unusual to see you out of your habit.' Imelda stood with her own clothes over her arm, studying her. 'It takes a bit of getting used to.'

'You can say that again,' Brigid said drily, packing her nightdress neatly in her case. 'It's taken a while for *me* to get used to. My head is fierce cold without the veil sometimes, and ... well ... it's strange seeing my ... er ... figure. The habit hides a lot.'

'You have a neat figure,' Imelda conceded, and, noting the seeming thaw in relations, added magnanimously, 'I *could* do with less second helpings, I suppose.' She made a face and patted her portly tummy.

'I'm a skinnymalinks and always was,' Brigid said ruefully,

noting her sharp angular hips in the mirror. 'I have Mother's genes and you have Daddy's.'

'You could be right,' Imelda agreed. 'Was the water hot?'

'It was grand. I opened the window in there to let out the steam; you might want to close it. There's a howling gale blowing. You hear it at the back of the house, not this side. We'll be bouncing around on the ferry.'

'Hmm, it's a pretty miserable day out there, unfortunately. What a shame. It was so nice and summery yesterday. You can hardly see Iona.' Imelda pointed to the view from her window.

Brigid walked over, glanced out and sighed. '"Blessed are those whose strength is in you; who have set their hearts on a pilgrimage." I can't remember who said that. We can't let the rain stop our trip, now that we're here. We'd better eat a good breakfast to keep our strength up.'

Imelda tittered. 'That's my kind of talk. I hope they offer us a fry.'

'We only have a fry every second Sunday. It will be brown bread and marmalade as usual, for me,' Brigid said briskly.

'Ah for goodness' sake, you're retired now, Brigid, You're on holidays. *Have* a fry if you want it. You *deserve* it,' Imelda exclaimed, thinking how awful it was that the meals one ate were dictated in the convent. *She* would never have lasted in a nunnery. She'd never be able to hold her tongue if she was getting chastised, *and* she loved her grub too much. She had a fry at least once a week and a bacon butty for lunch whenever she felt like it.

'I bet all those overweight cardinals in Rome tuck into fine food and drink. Mrs Reilly in the Post Office told me, back in the eighties, that her sister's young lad was doing electrical work in the Bishop's Palace in Dublin, and he said the black sacks were filled with empty wine bottles – *unbelievable*! And they made that laddo a cardinal, despite him paying off abusers and hiding the fact. It's all "do as I say and not as I do", with them ould yokes! You eat your fry and *enjoy* it!' Imelda decreed imperiously, disappearing into the bathroom.

Her sister seemed in good spirits, so Brigid would start afresh this morning, repent her unkind thoughts of the previous evening, and perhaps the trip to Iona – albeit a wet one, judging by the rain-drenched vista outside – would be as happy and exciting as the visit to Rosslyn had been.

'Och, ye'll nay be travellin' to Iona this morning. The ferry's been cancelled,' their convivial landlady announced matter-of-factly, handing menus to the four women as they sat at the dining table in the bright, airy conservatory listening to the rain hammering on the glass roof. They were the only guests and had the big oval table to themselves.

'Oh, no.' Keelin couldn't hide her disappointment. 'Will we get there today at all?'

'Ye may. If the wind dies down. We can have four seasons in one day here on Mull. Dinna give up hope,' the landlady replied with a laugh, being well used to the vagaries of island weather.

'Well that puts a damper on things. Excuse the pun,' Brigid sighed, unable to contain her disappointment. Imelda lifted her head from the menu and laughed.

'Daddy used to say that, didn't he? Or he'd say, "Well, what do you want me to do about it? Burst into tears and wear a black tie?"'

'Yeah, that always made me laugh.' Brigid smiled at the memory of her father's teasing. 'There's not much point in us driving around in that weather. What will we do?' She looked at her companions.

'Och we won't throw ye out – relax, read, play cards, hopefully by lunchtime the ferry will be sailing again,' the landlady said reassuringly.

'I'll have the fry with a hard egg,' Imelda got down to the business of eating. They could work out a plan after breakfast.

'The scrambled eggs and salmon for me,' Keelin said.

'Me too.' Marie-Claire handed back the menu.

Imelda looked enquiringly at Brigid.

'A slice of bacon and a sausage, and some toast, please,' Brigid said. Imelda was right. She was retired, she might as well enjoy it, and besides, she hadn't gone the whole hog and had the large fry – she was doing well with the puns today, she thought ruefully.

'I've googled the distance to Dervaig where the stained-glass window of the pregnant Magdalene and Jesus is. It's fifty-eight miles, so if we went there this morning and came back again that's a round trip of over a hundred miles. And, *if* the ferry is sailing, and we get to Iona, then we'd have to drive back another fifty miles to Tobermory where we're booked in for tonight. We'd be doubling back on ourselves and spending more time in the car than seeing what we came to see,' Marie-Claire lifted her head up from her iPhone where she'd been checking out their options.

'Stay calm,' Keelin lifted the big teapot and began pouring the tea, 'I have every faith in Mary Magdalene. She will get us to where we are meant to be today. How hard do we want to do this, seems to be the way she's taking us. We have to surrender to the pilgrimage and whatever perceived blockages and trials beset us.'

'That's all very well,' replied her mother, who – at times like this, when the brakes were put on something she wanted to do, found Keelin's 'mumbo jumbo' as she sometimes privately termed it, hard to take – 'but we only have a day here. And we fly home the day after tomorrow.'

'I feel that we have to do nothing,' Keelin reiterated. 'So let's have our breakfast and enjoy it and see where the day takes us. It must be the sea air, but I'm hungry again,' she grinned, putting down the teapot and slathering a slice of crusty homemade bread with butter.

'Were you ever any other way? You were a gannet when you were a child,' Imelda said with surprising fondness.

'And, tragically, I've taken after her,' Marie-Claire joked, tucking into orange juice and a dish of muesli and yogurt before her scrambled eggs and salmon came.

*

'Oh for goodness' sake,' Imelda exclaimed irately, throwing her cards on the table when Brigid knocked, for the third time in as many games, to announce she'd won the round.

'I can't help it if I'm good,' Brigid said smugly. She was enjoying herself immensely. Imagine playing cards in the middle of a morning with no convent bells ringing to call her to prayers, or whatever duties she'd to turn her attention to. It was almost decadent.

'Ah you were always the same, winning at everything,' Imelda said grumpily. She was not a good loser.

'It's only a game. Mère is having a run of luck, calm down, Mam,' Keelin said, gathering the cards together to shuffle them.

'Oh typical of you – take her side as always,' Imelda snapped.

'Mother, that's not fair. Don't start,' Keelin retorted.

'I'll start whatever I want, miss,' Imelda shot back, irritated at being told off. 'You take her side, same as Mother and Daddy always did, and let me tell you, it hurts sometimes.'

'Imelda, you're exaggerating,' Brigid said crossly. 'Mother and Daddy didn't treat me any different than you. That's being childish.'

'Are you *serious*?' Imelda scoffed. '*Everybody* treated you differently. You were Granny's little pet, always going over to her and sucking up to her to get money for sweets—'

'I liked going over to Granny's to listen to her stories,' Brigid said hotly.

'Ah yeah,' jeered Imelda. 'Tell that to the marines.'

'Our granny had a very interesting life, if you'd bothered

438

to spend time with her and listen to her talk about the times she grew up in, Imelda. But no! Not you! *You* were too busy going around feeling sorry for yourself to take notice of *anyone* else,' Brigid retorted.

'You're right, I *did* feel sorry for myself, because I had to do everything while you swanned over to Granny's, to hear all about her . . .' – she paused and glared at her sister – ' "interesting life".'

'Excuse *me*,' Brigid interrupted. 'I did housework in Granny's. I cleaned and polished, and helped her make her bed, and churn butter, and bake bread and scones. Otherwise, Mother would have had to do it. So stop your nonsense.'

'Ah, really, let's not row. We were doing so well. We're meant to be getting over the *last* one, and enjoying a mini-break,' Keelin said wearily.

'Oh, am I not entitled to say anything—'

'Stop it, Mam. You're always the same. Every time I come home I get the "poor me" litany.'

'Is that so? Well, you did nothing to make my life easier, Keelin. Just remember that,' Imelda shot back.

'And you'll never let me forget it, will you? Until the day I die, you'll hold it against me that I got pregnant, left the convent and married Armand.'

'You should never have joined it in the first place. That was all because of *her*. She took you from me.'

'You made that accusation at my party, Imelda, the night you made a holy show of yourself, and I didn't challenge you as vigorously as I should have. Because *I wanted to*. Unlike *you*, I wouldn't embarrass either you or my guests. But I will rebut it now. I did *no* such thing,' Brigid, said furiously, wrath staining her cheeks red.

'Yes you *did*, Brigid! You took her to become a nun, and then, when she had Marie-Claire, you inveigled your way into *her* affections and made her prefer you to me. You took my own granddaughter from me. She always wanted to stay down there with you instead of in Glencarraig with me,' Imelda shouted.

'That was your *own* fault, Mother,' Keelin stood up in fury. 'You wouldn't let me come home when I was pregnant and when she was a baby. You were too ashamed of me. Where else was I to go? The Order more or less disowned me. They would have put me in a home and taken my baby from me for adoption – that was their plan. Mère *fought* for me to stay in the Four Winds. She took me in and saw me through my pregnancy, and then she made sure my baby was looked after. Don't you dare berate her for that or tell lies of omission. I won't stand for it.'

'Maman, Granny, Mère, please! Stop fighting,' Marie-Claire begged.

'But you *have* abandoned me for her.' Imelda turned on her. 'You do your duty visit and then you go and spend all your time at the Four Winds. You don't bring *me* shopping for clothes, do you?' she snapped waspishly.

'Listen to yourself, Granny. Did you ever think that it's your own behaviour that drives people away from you? You can't see anything beyond your jealousy. Maman—'

'*Maman* and *Mère*,' Imelda mimicked. 'You're Irish, for God's sake, not French. And you're all such saints, aren't ye? And I'm the black sheep. The sinner. Not for me the "Calling". I'm the poor old servant like Martha in the Bible, doing all the work while Mary swanned around with her jar of expensive oil, taking the easy way out. Some of us have to do the dirty work. Why I came on this daft journey with all of you, knowing you dislike me so much, I'll never know.' Tears welled up in her eyes and she stood to leave, mortified that they would see her crying.

'I had no "Calling", as you put it, Imelda,' Brigid said quietly. 'You were right about that from the beginning. I went into the convent to atone for my sins – especially the sin against chastity – and not because I was called by God. I went in to get to Africa. To escape Ardcloch. It was the greatest mistake of my life.'

Silence fell like the unexpected snowflakes that drifted down from the leaden skies outside.

Keelin stood up and put her arms around her mother. 'Sit down, Mam. This is all happening for a reason. Now I know why we weren't meant to go to Iona this morning. All this had to *finally* be cleared between us, before we can carry on.'

'I'm sure Mary Magdalene won't want me in Iona after what I just said about her,' Imelda muttered shakily, but she didn't resist her daughter's embrace, feeling the need for comfort.

'Why don't I make us a pot of tea and I'll get the chocolate Goldgrain I have stashed in my bag.' Marie-Claire jumped up and put on the kettle that the landlady had left filled for them, before going across the hall to her ground-floor bedroom.

'Can you talk to us about why you entered, Mère?' Keelin reached out and touched her aunt's shoulder.

'I'd like to,' Brigid nodded. 'I'd like Imelda to know why I've lived a lie all these years.'

'It's all right, Brigid, you don't have to if you don't want to. And I'm sorry for the things I've said,' Imelda said gruffly.

'I'm sorry too, Imelda, and I have to thank you . . .'

'For what?' Her sister sniffed and wiped her eyes.

'Because you've made me face up to and acknowledge the fact that entering was the wrong thing to do – and that's not easy to deal with sixty-four years or so later.'

The kettle whistled and Keelin busied herself making the tea. This day was not turning out the way she'd imagined, but at last the boil of bitter resentments was being lanced. No wonder they had not been allowed to visit Iona. Keelin knew without a doubt that setting foot on the island would be the most healing thing to ever happen to their family. After all these years, it seemed the peace of Mary Magdalene's dove was coming upon them. Imelda had been the catalyst. She'd played her part in all their healing.

Marie-Claire came back and shucked the chocolate biscuits onto a plate while her mother poured the tea. She kissed her grandmother and great-aunt. 'We're family, that's all that matters, and we're together.'

Brigid took a sip of her tea and tried to stop her hands from trembling.

'Have a biscuit,' Imelda offered, handing her the plate. 'You had *half* a fry for breakfast, you might as well go mad and have a chocolate goody while you're at it – break *all* the rules.' She gave her sister a tremulous smile.

'Ah sure, maybe I will for the day that's in it,' Brigid smiled back and in that moment felt a peace unlike any other settle around her. Whatever their differences, she and Imelda would go back to Ireland with a strengthened bond. Her sister, in a strange way, had freed her from the ties of the sixty-four years of religious life. That was a gift that could not be ignored.

'You know, Imelda, I envied you so much,' Brigid confessed, wiping a crumb from her lips.

'*Me!* You envied me?' Imelda squawked in astonishment.

'You had everything I ever wanted. A husband. Children. A home of your own. For years all I had was a lonely cell and a bed with a hard mattress and a burden of guilt that I wasn't a real nun like I should have been, that I was in the convent under false pretences—'

'Because you had sex with Johnny Larkin—' Imelda interrupted.

'Yes . . . although, in my own defence, I did tell him no. Nowadays they would say consent wasn't given. Perhaps I didn't fight hard enough. I did try and push him away but he was very strong, and then it was all very rushed. Over almost before I knew it. So the loss of my virginity was not the way I expected it would be. Not like the movies, for sure,' she said wryly. 'I know it's all very different for you, Marie-Claire. You young women embrace your sexuality. There's no shame involved like there was when we were young.'

'Thankfully no, I was lucky never to feel shame about having sex, and my first time was enjoyable because I was with a boy who was gentle and anxious for it to be good for me, and I wasn't afraid of getting pregnant because my parents were sensible and gave me a good sex education.' She flashed a grateful smile at Keelin. 'I could talk to them about anything. But, having said that, for me the best sex was when I felt loved.'

'*Was*?' Imelda noticed the use of the past tense and pounced. 'What about that fella you're going with? I thought that was going places.'

'So did I,' Marie-Claire said lightly. 'But it's over. I didn't say anything to you because of what was going on.'

'And did you end it or did he end it?' Imelda probed.

'I did. I . . . er . . . I discovered he was cheating on me.' To Marie-Claire's dismay a lump rose to her throat and tears blurred her eyes. Marc had sent her a text the previous night *pleading* with her to contact him. She'd texted back saying that she was mostly out of coverage in the wilds of Scotland and she'd phone him when she got home. She'd spent the night listening to her mother's gentle breathing, in the other bed, while trying to suppress her sobs of grief and loneliness.

'Ah the . . . the . . . *bastard*,' Imelda cursed, something she rarely did unless greatly provoked. 'He's not worthy of you, Marie-Claire. Don't waste your tears on him, the sly weasel,' she counselled, standing up to go and put her arms around her granddaughter in an uncharacteristic display of grand-motherly solidarity – much to Keelin's surprise. Imelda was not given to overly affectionate behaviour.

'Thanks, Granny, I ... It was a shock; I thought we were going to make it as a couple. I saw me having a future with him, children ... a home, working the business together.' Marie-Claire broke into fresh sobs and Imelda's mouth tightened into a grim line and she wished she could have five minutes with the cheater who had made her grandchild weep such bitter tears.

'What's for you won't pass you by,' she murmured, strok-ing Marie-Claire's thick auburn hair as Keelin handed her daughter a tissue.

'I'm sorry I was so unforgivably rude, earlier, Granny I shouldn't have said those things,' Marie-Claire said, shame-faced, breaking away from her grandmother's embrace to look up at her.

'Maybe I needed it saying, child. I've become a bitter old woman and I was a bitter young woman too, because I thought everyone else had a better life than me. And how wrong I was,' Imelda said sheepishly.' I wasted my life feel-ing sorry for myself. Don't go down that path because of that Canadian fella. Don't hold on to the bitterness, and end up like me, a foolish old woman with a lot of regrets,' Her two plump cheeks were pink with emotion. She'd never expressed herself like this before, and it was ... what was that word Keelin often used about women? *Empowering*, yes, that was it, she felt empowered by speaking her heartfelt feelings in a very honest way. Not trying to make others feel bad, or not making herself out to be greater than anyone else. Just saying what felt real and true to her. What an emancipation! What a revelation this morning was proving to be. If only it had happened years ago, Imelda thought regretfully.

'Perhaps his cheating broke a bigger cross for you,' Brigid said reflectively, unaware that her sister was having a life-changing epiphany. 'If it had happened when you were married and had children, and he cheated *then*, it would be much more difficult to deal with. Now you can make a complete break with no ties.' Brigid's blue eyes, undimmed by the passing of the years, focused laser-like on her great-niece. And as always, Marie-Claire admired their beauty and especially the tiny flecks of gold in the iris that sometimes caught the sun's light.

'I know you're right, and I know, as Maman always says, "things happen for a reason",' she sighed. 'But it's bloody hard starting over again in my thirties, I'm at a crossroads and I don't know what road to take and it all happened so unexpectedly, I'm still trying to adjust.' She took a deep breath and wiped her eyes, trying hard to compose herself. She was shocked at how upset she'd become. She'd thought she was over the worst of it.

'At least you're young enough to have plenty of enjoyable sex – not like us ould wans,' Brigid teased, trying to ease Marie-Claire's pain. The others laughed. 'If Mother General could hear me! If my Sisters could hear me, they'd think I've lost my mind. Me, the one who was so starchy and prim and proper in the convent. Me, living a lie all my life and suppressing every emotion, every surge of longing that flooded my body. I was very happy in Africa. I should have left the convent and gone back there as a lay person,' Brigid sighed. 'But I didn't have the courage to stand on my own two feet. At least you're *living*, Marie-Claire, even if right now your heart is in flitters – and I know the pain of that. But you're not running away from life like I did,' she added forcefully.

Imelda looked at her sister quizzically, 'I never thought of you like that. A young woman with needs and desires, and emotions. Once you put the veil on I thought of you as . . . don't laugh.' She eyed her sister with a glint of affection. 'I thought of you as holy.'

'Holy! *Me*? I was far from holy,' Brigid snorted, amused at the notion. 'I battled myself night and day to conquer my *real* self. When I wasn't envying you, that was.'

'I don't know what you were envying me for. My life was a life of . . . of . . . disappointment,' Imelda confided ruefully. 'My first time wasn't great either. I was petrified. I was afraid it would hurt, and it did. I didn't know anything about foreplay and lubricants. I cared greatly for Larry. He was a good man, but I wasn't *in* love with him – I'm sorry to say that to you, Keelin,' she turned to her daughter. 'He was my opportunity to get away from home and working the farm and looking after Granny, seeing as you were gone, Brigid. I wanted a home of my own and that was the reason I married your father. There was no great *coup de foudre* for me.'

'I'm sorry to hear that, Mam,' Keelin said quietly. 'It's a shame those were the reasons you married. I'm sorry none of you have known real love like I did, and do, with Armand.'

'Well he *is* a Frenchman,' Brigid joked, breaking the tension, and they all laughed again.

'And was *your* first time good, Keelin?' Imelda asked, astonished, yet feeling decidedly liberated that she was having such a conversation with her daughter. *This* exchange was what being a mother and daughter was about. This was the way Keelin and Marie-Claire interacted, and now she was part of it, no longer the one on the outside. Imelda felt a surge of joy like she'd never felt before.

'It was. He was a nice chap and I fancied him like mad. It was when I went on holiday to Rhodes. On a moonlit night by the sea,' Keelin admitted. 'Everything I wished for. So I wasn't a virgin when I entered the Order. And then of course I met Armand in the Ivory Coast and fell for him hook, line and sinker, and there was no going back. But I'd decided to leave before we became intimate. I couldn't take the inequality, the way the Church treated women. And then I remember so clearly, when I discovered that I was pregnant, any guilt I felt disappeared. I *knew* I was meant to have my child. The power and privilege of carrying another life within me overcame everything.'

Brigid took a deep breath. 'I felt that too.' She smiled at her niece.

'You were *pregnant*?' Imelda nearly fell off her chair in shock.

'Yes. For three months. And I too felt that glory that Keelin talks about, despite the shame and guilt; I revelled in the knowledge I had a child inside me. It was a primal joy, unlike anything I've ever felt before or since. I lost my baby out on the hills, on my way home from Granny's the Christmas Eve before I entered. I lost my baby the night a Virgin gave birth to hers. The irony was never lost on me.'

'But that was a *terrible* thing to happen, Brigid. Did you tell Mother?' Imelda couldn't hide her dismay.

'What do you think? I was *terrified*. I was afraid I was going to end up in a home and have my baby taken from me. That was why I was determined Keelin would not be sent away, even though it was what the Order wanted. I understood what she was going through because I'd been there myself. In our day, getting pregnant outside of marriage was the worst catastrophe that could befall a girl. The family name would have been ruined. How could I tell Mother and Daddy?'

'And you never told me either. You went through it all by yourself. Oh, Brigid, I *am* sorry. I wasn't much of a sister to you.' There was a lifetime's regret in her apology.

'We didn't have that kind of relationship, Imelda. But it's never too late.' She reached out and took her sister's plump little hand in her own bony, thin one.

'What a waste of our lives – you envying me, me envying you, and each of us knowing nothing about the other's turmoil.' Imelda stroked her hand gently.

'At least we didn't go to the grave estranged, my dear. Let's make up for lost time and enjoy the years we have left.

Now that I'm a free woman, I'm game for anything,' Brigid declared briskly.

'There's something else I need to say. Seeing as we're being so honest with each other,' Imelda said slowly. 'Keelin, I treated you so badly when you got pregnant, and then I let you think for all those months afterwards that it was your fault that your father died, when it had nothing to do with you, and was a result of that awful haemochromatosis. Something happened with me and Larry, years earlier, that had a terrible effect on me—'

'Ach, ladies, would yae like some sandwiches? The wind is dying down, yae could be lucky yet?' The landlady breezed into the conservatory; oblivious to the moment of revelation she'd interrupted.

'Um, perhaps later, thank you, we've not long had tea,' Brigid said calmly, noting Keelin's tense expression and Imelda's pale strained face.

'Right, I'll be away tae our wee house at the back. Call if yae need anythin'.'

'Thank you *so* much.' Brigid smiled graciously, thinking privately, *Go, woman, and let us get on with things.*

'We certainly will,' Marie-Claire said pleasantly, but her fingers were curled into her palms under the table and she felt sick. Were Imelda and her mother finally going to come to grips about their dysfunctional relationship and try and sort it out? *Please let it go OK, please, please let Maman and Granny make their peace*, she prayed silently as the door closed behind their friendly landlady and they were alone again.

CHAPTER FIFTY-ONE

She could feel it bubbling up inside her, wanting to be expelled out of her with volcanic force. That awful thing which she'd swallowed down and kept secret all her adult life. That cruel situation, which had poisoned her with grief, resentment and envy, and ruined her marriage, and all that went with it.

Imelda looked at her family, gazing at her, concerned, expectantly and knew it really was now or never. She cleared her throat.

'Keelin, well, the thing is ... I have a revelation too,' she blurted, 'but I think it's going to hurt you and I don't know whether to tell you or not.' Imelda bent her head, uncharacteristically stuck for words.

'What is it, Mam?' Keelin's voice had an edge of anxiety which Imelda misunderstood. Was there a hint of exasperation in her voice? Did her daughter think she was trying to steal Brigid's thunder? Perhaps she *should* have stayed quiet.

'Tell us what's troubling you, Granny?' Marie-Claire said kindly, noting her grandmother's heightened colour and unusually bright eyes.

Imelda swallowed. She felt her throat close. 'Give me a hot sup of that tea, will you?'

'Don't say Johnny Larkin got you pregnant too, Imelda,' Brigid exclaimed in consternation.

Keelin blanched. Was her mother trying to tell her that Larry wasn't her father?'

'No! . . . Oh no, Brigid! I was a virgin on the night of my wedding, for all the good it did me.' Imelda took a gulp of tea and gave a little splutter.

'Take it easy, Mam, sip it,' cautioned Keelin, feeling very uneasy about whatever disclosure was coming. Why would her mother say a thing like that?

Imelda took another drink of tea, putting off the moment of telling the others the secret she'd kept to herself for decades. It was a strange feeling to know that it was going to be released from her now, like a genie from a bottle.

'Mam what is it you have to . . . er . . . *want* to tell us?' Keelin tried to hide her impatience. She'd a feeling that what was coming might explain her mother's behaviour, but then again, knowing Imelda, it could very well be some molehill she'd built into a mountain.

'Larry was gay!'

Stunned silence descended on the other three women.

'*What?*' whispered Keelin, bewildered. Had she heard right? Could this actually be happening?

'Your father was a gay man, Keelin,' Imelda said quietly, all the adrenaline gone out of her. Her shoulders slumped and she felt quite exhausted.

'He *couldn't* be. He fathered three children,' Keelin stammered, not thinking her response through.

'That was when he was hiding it from me,' her mother explained wearily.

'*Imelda*!' Brigid stood up and hurried over to her sister and put her arms around her. 'Why didn't you tell me? Why did you keep this to yourself all these years? Have you told *no one*?'

'Why didn't you tell me *your* secret, Brigid?' Imelda shrugged. 'We didn't have that kind of relationship, you and I. And sure, what good would it have done? It wouldn't have changed anything. I still had to live with it. I never told a soul,' she added sadly.

'At least you wouldn't have lived with it alone. I would have supported you, Imelda,' Brigid said, devastated that her sister had lived most of her life with a burden that big to shoulder.

'And I would have supported you, Brigid,' Imelda reached out and took her sister's hand. 'We're a right pair,' she managed a weak smile.

'Mam, you should have told me this *years* ago! It explains so much,' Keelin said slowly.

'How *could* I tell you, Keelin? You loved him so much. Far more than you loved me.' Imelda couldn't resist the dig.

'I always thought you were mean to him. And he was so

kind to you. I could never understand why, and now I do.'
She started to cry, heart-wrenching sobs, her shoulders shaking. Marie-Claire jumped up and put her arms around her.

'It makes no difference to how he felt about you,' she assured her distraught mother.

'I know that. And it makes no difference to how I feel about him, but it made a difference to *our* relationship,' Keelin wept, pointing at Imelda.

'How so? Believe it or not, I love you very much. That's why I kept your father's secret from you until now.' Imelda wiped tears from her eyes.

'If you loved me that much, why wouldn't you let me come home with Marie-Claire when she was a baby? Why did you treat me like a pariah?' sobbed Keelin.

'Oh, Keelin, when you got pregnant I felt I was being punished by a very harsh God. And your pregnancy was the last straw. I couldn't cope. I was looking after the parents. I was starting an early menopause. I was always afraid Larry's secret might get out one way or another. I know it's not an excuse for turning my back on you. And I *genuinely* didn't want everyone pointing the finger at you ... for your own sake. There was no excuse for how I behaved in the early years when you needed me most,' she said earnestly. 'But it's my reason. From the moment I saw your father and the man that he loved, together, something twisted inside me. I felt unlovable. I felt unworthy of love. I felt I was a bad person and that this had been sent to me as a punishment.

'When I saw them kissing and heard Larry saying "I

love you" with such passion – words that I had longed with all my heart to say to a man and have him say the same in return, and then knew it would never happen – my life was blighted forever.'

'You saw them kissing?' Brigid exclaimed. 'Oh, Imelda, how traumatic for you.'

'It was. I can still remember the shock and fright of it to this day. He and Fran Cassidy, who was the art teacher in the school, were in the storeroom behind the shop when I came upon them—'

'But Daddy wasn't in any way effeminate,' Keelin interrupted, unable to get her head around her mother's disclosure.

'Ah now, Keelin, you know better than that. Look at Rock Hudson. Look at Leo Varadkar—' Imelda raised an eyebrow at her.

'Yeah, that was daft of me. Sorry. I'm dumbfounded. I never had any inkling.'

'Nor had I. The young man he was in love with was less of a masculine type than Larry. He was on the slender side, very quiet. He loved art and poetry and stuff like that. He left for England soon after I saw them together, and committed suicide a year later. Your father was devastated when he heard the news. He had a sort of nervous breakdown. I tried to keep it from you and the boys, and to keep him going as best I could—'

'Oh, Mam, that's *awful*!' Keelin burst into fresh tears. 'Poor Dad! And that unfortunate young man. And poor *you*!'

'It was very hard for them. Ireland then was a far more

harsh and intolerant place than it is now. When I saw them kissing ... well, to tell the truth, I felt sick. I was horrified. Disgusted. In turmoil. I didn't understand it.' Imelda's eyes darkened at the memory of that unspeakable time. 'Gay men and boys in those days got badly beaten up and chased out of villages and towns for "dropping the hand", as they called it. Homosexuality was a jailing offence then. And of course the Church's preachings about it were vile and so condemnatory. There was none of God's love for you if you were a gay man or woman, which was another reason I turned my back on that lot of Pharisees and why I didn't want you becoming a nun for them.' She shook her head as memories flooded back. Imelda reached out and took her daughter's hand. 'I didn't handle it well a lot of the time and that was why I often lashed out. I was worried that the boys would be gay – not because I was against it anymore, I came to understand it, believe it or not – but I didn't want them to go through the hardships their father and other gay young men went through in this country.'

'No wonder you were so anti-religion, so anti-Church. I never understood why,' Keelin said slowly. She was in total shock at what her mother had disclosed. It explained so much of Imelda's behaviour.

'Thank God that has changed,' Imelda sighed. 'How I wished Larry had been alive for the same-sex marriage referendum. When I made my mark against the "Yes" box, I whispered, "This is for you, Larry." Because I felt very guilty too, about marrying him. He knew I didn't love him when we stood at the altar.'

456

Imelda gave another sigh that came from the depths of her. 'Even if your father wasn't gay, Keelin, I should never have married him. I married for all the wrong reasons. I thought I was in love with Johnny Larkin, but Brigid was right' – she flashed a glance at her sister – 'it was first love and a teenage crush. I thought I'd never fall in love with anyone else, so I took the first escape route that was offered, and that was with your father. And he was looking for someone to marry, too. To conform to what was "normal" in those days and pretend he was someone other than who he was. He denied who he was to himself, until the day I walked in on him with Fran. After that, there was no denying it. No going back. And believe it or not, it was a liberation of sorts for him.

'We never had sex again, and he felt terrible guilty because he felt I should have a proper married life, and because of who he was, I was denied it. So we struggled, I can tell you, especially in those early years after I found out. But, believe it or not, Keelin, your father was my best friend and I was his and we eventually accepted each other for what we were and found a middle way. He knew what was behind my unhappiness and bitterness and he made allowances for me, just as I made allowances for him. It wasn't all bad. I did miss sex, though, because I was a healthy woman with rampant hormones and desires, so I might as well have been a nun,' she gave a shaky grin.

Brigid gave her a sympathetic pat on the hand. 'It's the pits, isn't it? Being horny and wanting a man. I'll never forget my menopause. Those surges that would sweep over you—'

'Oh *yes*! Did you have them too? They nearly did my head in. Girls, you pair are so lucky, have as much sex as you can,' Imelda joked to Marie-Claire and Keelin and they stared at her, astonished.

'Don't look so surprised,' Imelda said. 'Brigid and I were normal young women, once, too. You know the biggest irony?'

'What?' asked Keelin warily.

'The day I found your dad and Fran together, I had come back from Dublin with condoms Teresa had bought for me, up in Belfast, when the women went up North on the Contraception Train, as it's called now. Who says God doesn't have a sense of humour.'

'My God, Mam, you've kept this to yourself all these years. Could you not have shared it with me, even when I was older?' Keelin squeezed her mother's hand.

'Why would I? You *adored* your father and he adored you. You were the light of his life. I didn't want to make you miserable and burden you with my problems. I had made you unhappy enough in life as it was. I wasn't a good mother and I'm sorry. I hope you can find it in your heart to forgive me.'

'Mam, if only I'd known, I would have understood more. I *wish* you'd told me sooner. It explains so much. Let's try and put the past behind us and make the most of what we have now, will we?' Keelin came around the table and put her arms around Imelda.

Imelda exhaled a deep, weary sigh. Now that she'd finally said her piece she was shattered. 'Keelin, that would be all I could wish for,' she said quietly, nestling into her daughter's embrace. 'I think Larry helped us plan this trip. You were right, Brigid, it *is* our time of healing.'

'I think so too, Imelda. It's a fresh start for us after all these years. And a new beginning for you and Keelin,' Brigid agreed wiping tears from her eyes.

'I think the four of us are going to have a lot of fun for the rest of this trip, despite everything,' Marie-Claire put in her tuppence-worth, hardly able to believe what she was hearing. Never in a million years had she expected a revelation like this from her grandmother. 'When we get to the hotel tonight we're having a champagne celebration,' she announced.

'Maybe, sherry, not champagne,' demurred Brigid. 'That might be a step too far.'

'I will if you will,' Imelda declared. 'I've never had champagne.'

'Oh well we can't have *that,* then,' Brigid said with a twinkle in her eye.

'*Four Wild Women Go on a Bender,*' Keelin interjected, shakily wiping her tear-stained face.

'Oh, look!' exclaimed Marie-Claire, pointing to the window. 'There's a rainbow over Iona. The sky is clearing.'

'Well, isn't that gas? Snowflakes one minute, rainbows the next. I feel right at home. Just like the weather in Ireland – four seasons in one day,' Brigid observed. She'd thought Imelda had had the ideal life. How wrong was she? The old Native American proverb came to mind: *Don't judge someone*

459

until you've walked a mile in their moccasins. She'd judged her sister harshly, being too smug and superior to find out what lay behind Imelda's behaviour. Some sister she was.

'Imelda, I'm so sorry I didn't know of your burdens. I failed you badly.' Her lip trembled.

'Ah look, we can't change the past, but we can change our future, Brigid.' Imelda stood up and held out her arms to her sister and they hugged tightly.

Keelin and Marie-Claire looked at each other, hardly able to believe what they were seeing. This truly was a life-changing moment for all of them. A day they would never forget.

'Look, the wind's dying down. We'll be getting to Iona today, I'm sure of it.' Keelin raised her cup to her companions. 'And no better women to go exploring than us. I bet we were *all* nuns over in that nunnery in a past life.'

'The more I'm reading and learning, Keelin, the more I'm beginning to think you might be right. Perhaps that's why you and I entered. Because of a past life.' Brigid mused.

'Maybe that's why we've all come back together in this life. All I know is that everything is happening as it's meant to be.' Keelin had no doubts about that.

'I wonder which of us was the Reverend Mother then, if that's the case?' Imelda teased. She'd never been on a holiday like this in her life. She felt so delighted that she was free of her burdens she wanted to hug *everyone*.

'If it was my turn this time, it could have been you then, and I'd say you were a right ould rip,' Brigid joked and the pair of them burst out laughing. They were still laughing when the landlady popped her head around the door. 'The ferry's heading up to the pier. I was keeping an eye on it for yae. Yae'll be away tae Iona after all, ladies. Yae need to pack up.'

A chorus of delight greeted the news and they left the conservatory in a flurry of light-hearted excitement to gather their bits and pieces for the next step on their Magdalene Trail, free at last from all that had divided them.

CHAPTER FIFTY-TWO

The sea was emerald green, topped by foamy whitecaps. The sky had cleared. The gloomy rainclouds were now a distant bank of grey out on the horizon. It was what Marie-Claire called a Simpson sky. Patches of blue dotted with white scudding puffballs. Fionnphort grew smaller behind them as the jetty in Baile Mòr came into view, and the abbey to their right, dominating the landscape of the small island of Iona.

'Baile Mòr – big town – it's the same as the Irish version. Scottish Gaelic and Irish Gaelic are practically the same,' Imelda observed, relieved that she would soon be off the rocking ferry that was ploughing through choppy sea. Still it was a very short journey and she didn't feel queasy. In fact, she felt quite exhilarated. *Free!* she thought in awe. Released from the prison she'd created for herself, she felt an unexpected wave of happiness. She wasn't an outsider with Keelin, Brigid and Marie-Claire the way she'd always felt she was. Now she truly was part of the quartet. Sharing the truth of their lives with no more secrets and façades. She wished she'd shared her burden years ago. Imelda inhaled the salty sea air, watching the spray dance ahead of the bow as the ferry dipped and rose in harmony with the sea. She felt alive and excited.

'Are you OK there, Mam?' Keelin came and stood beside her at the rail.

'I am now, Keelin. I feel like an awful heavy load has been lifted from me. This is a day I'll never forget.'

'I'll never forget it either. A turning point for us all,' Keelin dropped an arm around her mother's shoulder. 'Mary Magdalene certainly cleared us all today.'

'Keelin, will you tell Armand I'm sorry for those terrible things I said. I'll phone and say it myself to him on the land-line when I get home. I can always hear better when I'm on it,' she said hesitantly. She knew how wounded her daughter had been by her harsh, unkind words to her son-in-law.

'I will, Mam. I'll be talking to him later when I can get a signal. It's not great at the moment,' Keelin assured her.

'I ... em ... I do love you very much, Keelin. I know I wasn't a good mother. I'll try my best from now on to make it up to you,' Imelda said awkwardly. 'And I'm very proud of you, the way you help so many people in your retreat place in France. That's a good thing to do.'

'Thanks, Mam.' Keelin swallowed hard, knowing how difficult it was for her mother to apologize, and taken aback but quietly delighted at her praise. 'Things will only get better for all our relationships from now on. I'm so glad you're with us.'

'I'm very glad too,' Imelda said with heartfelt emotion. She suddenly felt that Larry was very close to them on this trip.

The ferry gave a bumpy shudder as the iron drawbridge lowered onto the ramp and they hastened on deck to disembark.

'So this is Iona!' Brigid stared around her at the picturesque village with its cluster of houses and small hotel. Knots of tourists wandered around, and people sat at outside tables in front of a café, eating and drinking. 'Isn't it pretty? So many Irish nuns came to the nunnery here when it was founded in AD 1200. I read up on it when I knew we were visiting. Seemingly it's one of the best-preserved nunneries in Britain. I'm dying to see it,' she enthused.

'And I'm dying to see the medieval abbey.' Keelin felt a burst of anticipation. 'We have a two-hour window, the captain said, because the wind is to get up again and the ferry could be cancelled. I think we should prioritize those two sites. We can visit the craft shop on the way back and get a take-away tea and sandwich. What do you think?'

'Let the pilgrimage commence,' Brigid smiled, pointing to a sign on the end of a row of stone cottages. 'The abbey and nunnery this away!'

They walked up a narrow hilly road, passing a Spar and craft shop before turning right at a T-junction to turn right again into the nunnery. 'Well, that took all of a minute. Big place, Iona,' Marie-Claire grinned as they walked along a stony path to explore the ruins. Part of the church was still upstanding.

'It's very Irish too, isn't it? Those triangular-headed windows and the rib vaulted ceiling can be seen in every church in every small village in Ireland,' Brigid noted, running her hand along the pink-hued stonework. 'My goodness, life would have been hard here in the winter. It's very exposed. Oh look! There's the cloister. Let's have a look.' She took off at a clip.

'Good Lord, there's a Sheela-na-gig on the wall of the refectory!' Keelin pointed to the carving of the naked woman with an exaggerated vulva. 'That would have been placed to ward off evil and also used to celebrate the Mother goddess and fertility,' she explained, loving the female energy that emanated from the very stones of the cloister.

'*Saoghal Nam Ban*, World of Women,' Imelda read the plaque, illustrating the nunnery as it was. 'Look at the dormitory—'

'Oh, and look at this,' exclaimed Brigid, '*Seòmar Blátchaidh*. The Warming Room. This was where the poor craythurs came to thaw out on cold days. It was the only place where a fire burned. Can you imagine how cold it was here in the depths of winter?'

'Eeeewwww, I like my comforts, I doubt I was ever a nun in any past life, no matter what you say,' Imelda declared, glad the sun was warm on her face, even though it was so breezy. 'Now why do you suppose some of those gravestones are bigger than others?' She pointed to a line of flat, grey slate slabs in an enclosure at an outer wall. 'Did it signify rank? Did the Mother Superior get a bigger slab stone than the ordinary nuns, do you think?' she asked her sister.

Brigid shook her head. 'I don't know the answer to that, Imelda. Maybe some of the nuns were fatter than others. It could be that simple,' she shrugged.

Imelda's jaw dropped and she broke into chortles of laughter. '"Fatter than others!" You always were funny, Brigid,' she said fondly, and Keelin looked at Marie-Claire and gave a tiny wink, loving that her mother was starting to enjoy herself.

They wandered around, immersing themselves in the history, wishing they could stay longer but knowing their time on the island was limited. The abbey held another treasure trove of discoveries that would have needed a day at least to study everything but it was the cloister walkway in the medieval part that most resonated with Keelin. 'The Cathars were here – look at that sculpture. It's like the one in Minervois. Remember I took you there, Mère?'

'I do. I remember that beautiful dove sculpture that the sun shone through,' Brigid said.

'Look how they use the dove, here. The symbol of the Magdalene. I *know* she was on Iona. There are even rumours she's buried here.' Keelin traced her fingers along a carved pillar. 'I'd like to come back and explore that mound we saw. There's something about it that draws me to it. Pity we can't stay longer,' she said regretfully, glancing at her watch.

'I thought she was buried in Saint-Maximin-la-Sainte-Baume in Southern France.' Brigid looked surprised.

'Not buried, but she is supposed to have lived in a cave there and healed the sick, for part of her life,' Keelin said.

'And what about Rennes-le-Château?' 'Marie-Claire arched a quizzical eyebrow.

'We'll just have to go to visit all these places,' Imelda's eyes lit up. 'You've got me hooked, Keelin.'

'Have I, Mam?' Keelin laughed. 'After all these years! Who would have thought it? But if you don't want to spend the night and tomorrow here, we'd better get a move on. The wind's getting up again,' she cautioned, noticing that the sea, though still sparkling in the early afternoon sun, was looking decidedly choppy.

'We'll *definitely* come back.' She cast a last glance around the arched cloister, filled with the sound of birdsong and the breeze whispering through the grass.

'Isn't there an old saying, if you visit Iona once, you'll come back three times?' Brigid reminded her.

'What a peaceful place,' Imelda said a couple of minutes later, leading the way into a tiny, whitewashed stone chapel with flagged floor, a minuscule stone altar, and triangular candle stand, tucked in the left-hand corner. They each lit a votive candle, the flames flickering into light and illuminating the ancient wall behind them, casting dancing shadows that became one golden glow. Four very different women, and yet ... not so different ... joined in a silent prayer of thanks, that love had won out over that which had once divided them.

'Oh wow! Look at that tower. Is this the church? Is that Dervaig across the valley?' Marie-Claire steered the car round a high narrow bend on the one-track road and saw a pencil-slim white tower in the distance. 'How very French it looks.'

'I think so.' Keelin studied the vista ahead intently, thinking how beautiful the small Scottish village looked nestled against a hillside, the round Magdalene tower almost incongruous in its setting.

'It's quite strange, isn't it, that the tower features so strongly on Iona and Mull? Brigid said.

'The name Magdalene means 'Tower' in Hebrew. Some say that the prioress's tombstone on Iona depicts Mary Magdalene with the child of Christ, John Martinus, allegedly born on Iona. If this is true, it would suggest that Anna MacLean knew about this legend,' Keelin told her rapt listeners.

'How do you *know* all this?' Imelda asked, astounded.

'I've been reading about, and studying Mary Magdalene for years. I think that's why I was drawn to a Frenchman who lives in Magdalene country. This is my life's work. To bring her to the fore and help restore her to her rightful place in the world, as the equal of Jesus. In the Gnostic texts she is referred to as "the apostle to the apostles", until she was airbrushed out and branded a fallen woman and a penitent sinner. So now it's time to restore the balance of the Divine Feminine with the Divine Masculine. We've had the patriarchy, and now the pendulum has swung to the other side and men are seen as the enemy. It's all about bringing back balance.'

'And you really believe that she and Jesus came to Iona and had a child?' Imelda still found it a hard concept to swallow.

'So the Mystery Schools have taught their initiates for the last two thousand years, passing the teachings on from generation to generation. Her story represents the entire regeneration of women. Now it's all being revealed, Mam. I mean, don't you think it's *extraordinary* to see a white tower on a church on an island off the Scottish coast, and inside a stained-glass window depicting a heavily pregnant Magdalene holding the hand of Jesus? It's *fascinating*! Don't forget we have a Magdalene tower ourselves in Drogheda.'

'I never knew that,' Brigid said, intrigued.

'There are towers all over Europe actually, but this one here is very special.' Keelin was bubbling with excitement as Marie-Claire parked the car outside Kilmore church and they got out, eagerly anticipating the next stop on their itinerary.

They pushed open the iron gate, walked up the winding path and entered the tiny porch that led into a small, homely church, filled with light and serenity. The evening sun streamed multicolour rays through the striking stained-glass windows.

They gazed in awe at the window Keelin had so longed to see. Again, in 'plain sight' the clues that this was indeed Jesus and a beautifully pregnant Mary Magdalene, depicted in stained glass. A halo with a cross, seen above the window uniquely symbolizing Jesus, the Christ and below a banner that read *Mary hath chosen that good part, which shall not be taken away from her*.

Keelin googled her notes on her iPad. 'That gospel text,' she pointed out, 'it's from Luke, chapter ten, verses thirty-eight to forty-two, where Martha complains of doing all the work while Mary sits listening to Jesus teach—'

'I always felt sorry for poor old Martha. Someone had to do the housework,' Imelda said firmly, having for so long felt that she was very much cast in a Martha role.

'I know,' Keelin laughed. 'But there is a theory that Jesus was actually explaining to Martha that women can achieve a higher path with their lives, rather than the traditional role – the path of study and higher spiritual learning.'

'Hmm,' Imelda studied the window.

'Look at their positions: doesn't it remind you of the ancient Celtic marriage ceremony of the hand fastening? That would have been very familiar to the people of the isles, and recognized by "those with eyes to see" – the truth hidden in plain sight. Look at all the Cathar symbols: the sheaf of corn, the bee, the grapes, the towers, the dove. And look at the beautiful mural of the dove. *Her* symbol, painted over the pulpit. It's all much more than coincidence. Esoteric truths are here for all.' Keelin positioned her camera to take a photo.

'It's so peaceful here, isn't it?' Brigid sat on one of the wooden pews and let the tranquillity of the place wash over her.

'Why don't we have our flask of tea here? There isn't a soul around. I don't think Jesus and the Magdalene would mind,' Marie-Claire suggested, gasping for a cuppa. They had bought a flask and a carton of milk in Fionnphort, and the landlady had filled it with boiling water for them and given them a handful of teabags to take with them for their trip.

'Great idea,' agreed Imelda, who was wandering around looking at the intricately carved pulpit upon which rested a Bible. It wasn't a Catholic church, and didn't have the solemnity of one, so she felt she could drink tea and not feel she was being too disrespectful.

Marie-Claire went out to the car and carried in the plastic bag with the flask and biscuits, then busied herself pouring out the tea. Keelin opened the chocolate biscuits and they sat companionably enjoying the welcome brew, feeling quite at home in the mystical, magical energy, under the benevolent gaze of the Divine Couple in the beautiful stained-glass window, in a little chapel perched on a hill in the middle of nowhere.

'I've something else to tell ye,' Imelda confessed, her cheeks rosy from the champagne she'd imbibed earlier. The four of them were sitting around the fire in a cosy nook of a hotel in Tobermory, a coastal town not far from Dervaig. They'd eaten dinner and repaired to the lounge for coffee and a glass of Baileys.

Keelin felt a pang of anxiety, waiting to hear what her mother was going to spring on them next. 'What's that?' she murmured apprehensively.

'Ah don't worry, it's nothing serious like earlier,' Imelda chuckled. 'Do you know what I did?'

'What?' Marie-Claire grinned. Imelda didn't realize it, but she was slightly tipsy.

'I treated myself to a bit of Botox and a few fillers!'

'You're *kidding*!' Keelin exclaimed, hardly able to believe her ears.

'I *knew* there was something different about you. Didn't I say that to you, Mère, that day we surprised Granny in the supermarket,' Marie-Claire exclaimed triumphantly.

'It's very discreet,' Imelda said proudly. 'I went to a surgeon in the Blackrock Clinic. No fly-by-nights for me,' she smirked.

'It's so natural,' Marie-Claire peered at her.

'It makes you look very fresh. Did it hurt?' Brigid was curious.

'It did; I'm not sure I'd get it done again. I was done in little over an hour.' Imelda let out a hiccup.

'What made you decide to do it?' Keelin asked, marvelling at her mother's ability to constantly surprise her.

'Ah ... I was feeling down in the dumps after ... eh ... well you know, the upset at the party,' Imelda said delicately. 'I needed a bit of a lift. Not a facelift now,' she added hastily.

'Well you look great on it – years younger,' Brigid approved. 'I might try it myself.'

'If you decide to do it, I'll give you the surgeon's contact details,' Imelda yawned. 'I'll sleep well tonight.'

'Me too,' agreed Brigid, delighted that tonight she would have a room with a double bed in it, and a TV, all to herself. 'I've really enjoyed these few days. It's hard to believe we've done so much.'

'I certainly got what I came for, and more,' Keelin said, eyes aglow. 'My card was so apt.'

'So was mine,' Marie-Claire smiled at her mother.

'Do you want to say, or will we keep it private?' Keelin ventured.

'Mine said *Revelation*. And the minute I saw the musical notes in Rosslyn, I knew I've got to bring Frankie and his business partner over here. It was a real affirmation that their work on the Solfeggio Frequencies is spot on,' Marie-Claire declared. 'What was yours?'

'*Sacred Sexuality*. What could be more apt after what we saw today? The balance of male and female. The marriage of the Divine Masculine to the Divine Feminine. And the guide in Rosslyn confirmed that the Double Helix there symbolized the same. Win-win for me.' Keelin gave the thumbs up. 'Mère?' Do you care to tell us or would you like to keep it private. No pressure, honestly,' Keelin invited.

'Believe it or not, mine was *Little Children*,' Brigid said softly. 'How appropriate for me that today, I told you about my own child. And how lovely for me also that Mary Magdalene acknowledged my work with the African children I was so privileged to serve.' Brigid's eyes glistened in the firelight.

'Ah, that's *lovely*, Mère.' Marie-Claire felt a wave of love for her great-aunt.

'I suppose you want to know what mine was?' Imelda made a face.

'Only if you want to tell us, Mam. We don't want to

473

invade your privacy,' Keelin said firmly. The visit to Iona and Dervaig had gone so well, she didn't want anything to spoil their evening.

'I might as well be honest, it was *very* blunt,' Imelda confessed. 'I got a bit of a start, to tell you the truth.'

'Don't tell us if you don't want to, Imelda,' Brigid patted her sister on the arm.

'No. I'll tell you. Today has been all about the truth,' Imelda said stoutly. 'It said *The Judgement*, and what I took from it was not to be making judgements about others anymore, and hope that they wouldn't make them about me.' She jiggled her Baileys over the ice cubes and took a sip. 'I like the taste of this though – judge that if you want,' she jested in a most uncharacteristic fashion, lightening the mood.

'That could apply to us all, dear,' Brigid said kindly. 'All in all, a very successful trip so far. Here's to new adventures together.' She raised her glass and they all did the same, clinking their glasses together.

CHAPTER FIFTY-THREE

'I'm definitely buying one,' Imelda declared, loving the camera screen on the dash, as she reversed neatly into a parking bay. 'I feel like the queen on her throne.'

'The Queen of Glencarraig,' grinned Marie-Claire, who had spent the past twenty minutes instructing her grandmother to keep her left foot on the floor and not to keep trying to change gear. In fairness, both her grandmother and great-aunt had mastered the rudiments very well and been equally impressed with the smooth drive of the car that had taken them over six hundred miles in the past three days. If she could ever afford it, she'd buy a Peugeot 3008 herself, she thought in amusement as the trio walked into the airy foyer of the Premier Inn in Dalkeith where they were spending their last night in Scotland.

Keelin was in her room Skyping Armand, and they had all decided to meet up for dinner at six-thirty, giving them time to freshen up and get sorted for the journey home.

Imelda eased her feet out of her shoes, glad to wriggle her toes. They'd walked a lot these past few days, much more than she was used to, and she was impressed at how sprightly Brigid was. She might walk to the shops in future, instead of driving, as she was wont to do, she decided, feeling her waistband tight around her waist. They had eaten very well on their trip. Some pounds would need to be shed.

Had she ever thought that she would be happy to go on holidays with her sister and daughter, and not feel like a misunderstood outsider, with the weight of the world on her shoulders? It was still hard to believe that she'd told her deepest secret to her family.

Keelin had been very upset about Larry, as Imelda knew she would be, and she'd endured a moment of guilt, wondering should she have kept her troubles to herself. But, by telling Keelin, a blockage had been cleared between her and her daughter, and she could only hope that Larry would be pleased for them.

Keelin had *such* immense knowledge. She'd been far too dismissive of it, Imelda thought guiltily, remembering the Judgement card. She would try to be more open to the woo-woo stuff in future, because it had turned out to be very thought provoking indeed, Imelda conceded, enjoying the way the evening sun stippled the branches of the trees in light and shade.

Her thoughts turned to Brigid's revelation that she'd got pregnant by Johnny Larkin. Imelda had been utterly dismayed, not because her sister had got pregnant, but because she'd not felt able to confide in Imelda. Now they knew everything about each other. It was true, blood *was* thicker than water, and she was glad of it.

Marie-Claire lay on her bed studying a selfie she'd taken of the four of them as they sat on a stone wall at the edge of Loch Lomond, cups of tea in hands. Imelda was looking at Brigid, laughing at one of her witty asides; Keelin, hair swept up in a loose knot, sunglasses perched on top of her head, was looking effortlessly chic, the worry lines of the past month softened now that her estrangement from her mother was over.

Marie-Claire was joining in with the laughter, looking carefree as she gazed up into the camera lens, held up high to get them all in, her auburn hair tumbling around her shoulders, her green eyes squinting in the sun, surrounded by the three women she loved most in the world.

A happy photo. One to cherish, Marie-Claire thought with pleasure, logging out of her Facebook page. A thought struck her: she hadn't given Marc a thought these last few days. There'd been no posting photos to impress him with her allegedly wonderful life. It was time she stopped acting like a teenager, she thought, with a dart of shame at her previous behaviour. A woman in her thirties uploading fake happy posts was *so* not cool. She'd never do *that* again.

'Maybe I'm *finally* over him. I was happy these past few days. Now *there's* a welcome revelation, Mary Magdalene!' Marie-Claire murmured, picking up her phone to call

Frankie to tell him that it was absolutely *imperative* that he get his skinny ass over to Rosslyn because she knew in her bones that his frequency work was going to be big! She wasn't her mother's daughter for nothing, Marie-Claire thought to herself as her friend, and potential new boss answered the phone.

Keelin stood under the hot jets of the shower, visualizing a glorious white light washing all over her, cleansing every cell and atom of her body. What a day of reconciliation and liberation it had been, but a day of immense sadness too, when she thought how difficult life had been for both her parents. Her poor Dad must have been in turmoil for most of his life. How sad that he'd never known what it was to be his authentic self. And then the tragic end to his affair, learning that the man he truly loved had committed suicide, far away in another country.

Tears slid down her cheeks. How lucky was she that she'd taken her great leap of faith with love. If only Larry had been able to do the same. They had borne their burdens stoically, Larry and Imelda, and Keelin felt a deep sense of gratitude to her mother that she'd stayed with Larry and, in her own awkward way, supported him. It must have been so hard for her to set aside the physical side of their life. If a situation occurred where she could never make love to Armand again, she would be devastated. She wished Armand were right there in the shower with her, making love to her, at this moment.

Their reunion would be delightful. And all the more

so because, thanks to the graces of her beloved Mary Magdalene, a healing that she never thought possible had been brought to their family.

'Thank you, thank you, thank you,' she murmured, more at peace with herself than she'd been in a long, long time.

Brigid sat in the chair beside her bed watching *The Chase*. She enjoyed the general knowledge programme. It was even more delightful being in a hotel room all by herself, surfing the TV channels and looking forward to sleeping in her wide double bed.

She was tired, but pleasantly so. The trip to Scotland was almost at an end. They had packed so much into the three days. She'd bought a stack of books in Rosslyn and Iona and was looking forward immensely to reading them. The gift of retirement was a wonderful thing. She'd never dreamed she would have so much to do. She'd feared her days would drag interminably but now, after all her years of service, she was finally honouring her own needs and wants and requirements, and not feeling one bit selfish about doing so. It was liberating also to be freed from the narrow confines and the tyranny of Church doctrine.

I'm so glad I too have lived long enough to find my own truth, Brigid thought gratefully, remembering the words of Sister Martha who had been in the Suez crisis and lost her faith in the Church. Most of all, she was relieved that she and Imelda had finally made peace with each other. How sad, after all the wasted years, to think they could have been friends if they had trusted and liked each other enough to confide in each other. There was still time left. They could be the friends in old age that they could not be in their youth, and enrich the years they had left. Imelda had mentioned that she would like to go to Lourdes. Perhaps they could take a trip together and then stay with Keelin for a few days. That would be lovely, Brigid thought. Her eyelids drooped and she fell asleep and dreamed she was on the summit of Canigou looking right across to the sparkling blue Mediterranean.

'Now I'm not getting into the habit – excuse the pun – of this drinking lark,' Brigid avowed, as Marie-Claire urged another glass of red wine upon her.

'Brigid, that was good ... "habit" ...' giggled Imelda, who had made no protest to the offer of a top-up.

'It's the last night of our mini hols, we deserve it,' Keelin assured them. 'We'll all be back to normal next week.' They were sitting in the comfortable dining room of the Premier Inn, having decided to stay put for dinner instead of going back into Edinburgh. The hum of convivial chat and laughter from the other diners added to their own.

'I see the Pope's coming to visit Ireland,' Keelin remarked. 'How well I remember John Paul II's visit in '79. I'll never forget walking to the Phoenix Park. Hundreds of thousands of people streaming in from everywhere on that gorgeous morning, and the *wave* of excitement that swept over us when the Aer Lingus jumbo he was on swooped low over the park. It was the last time the Church was in control and people behaved as good, obedient little Catholics should,' she added acerbically.

'It was a great day, all the same. And in Galway, when he said, "Young People of Ireland, I love you," I actually believed him. And he probably did mean it – but oh, he was such a disappointment in the end,' Brigid said sadly.

'He was,' agreed Imelda. 'And he's a saint now for his trouble. This new fella is dishing out sainthoods to beat the band.'

'Are you going to go and see him, when he comes, Mère?' Marie-Claire asked.

'No, dear. Are you?'

'I think that would be a no too.' Her great-niece shook her head, smiling.

'Are you going, Mam?' Keelin looked across the table at her mother, who was larruping into the wine.

'As the Dubs say with such expressive vulgarity: I am, in me hoop. And all them bishops and cardinals, who turned their backs on my kind, gentle Larry can put that in their gold pipes and smoke them.' Imelda tittered at the dumbfounded expression on their faces. The others fell about laughing and Imelda raised her glass, delighted with herself.

CHAPTER FIFTY-FOUR

'Good morning, dear, I hope I didn't wake you up,' Marie-Claire heard her grandmother say as she groggily held the phone to her ear.

'It's time I was up, Granny. I was having a lie-in. It's been a mad week.' Marie-Claire yawned and glanced at her alarm clock. It was only nine a.m. on a Saturday.

'I've been thinking,' her grandmother said, and Marie-Claire waited, intrigued to see what was coming next. Imelda sounded perky enough, so she didn't think there could be anything wrong.

'And what were you thinking?' She hauled her pillows into a comfortable position and settled back against them.

'I know your strategy is never to tell that yoke in Canada why you dropped him, but if you don't mind my saying so, that's what they call passive-aggressive type of behaviour, and you're better than that,' Imelda declared.

Marie-Claire's jaw dropped.

'Oh!' she managed. She'd *not* been expecting this.

'In my opinion – and you may not agree with me – I think you should say it straight to his face,' Imelda carried on, oblivious to her granddaughter's stupefaction. 'End it properly. Or if you really love him, give him another chance and forgive him. An affair can be got over, if the bond is strong enough,' Imelda advised briskly.

'You think I'm being *passive-aggressive*?' Marie-Claire made a face, trying not to feel insulted.

'I do! And do you know why?'

'Why?'

'Because I'm an expert at it. And look where it got me – nowhere. It's wasted energy, as Keelin would say. And you'll always have that bitterness in you. You don't want that. That's my advice to you now. Take it or leave it. Now, I have to go – Brigid and I are meeting up to go to a cousin's funeral, in Ennis. I'll talk to you again soon.'

'Oh, OK. Give my love to Auntie Brigid. And thanks for thinking of me, Granny,' Marie-Claire said, not knowing whether to laugh or cry when she hung up.

Passive-aggressive! That was telling her straight, she thought glumly. And the annoying thing was that Imelda was right. Even though she wasn't in contact with Marc as much as she'd been, there was unfinished business between them. She'd had her revenge, and that was what her behaviour had been about: revenge. Not very adult of her, Marie-Claire admitted, though it had been satisfying for a while. Her grandmother was right. It was time to draw a line under her relationship with Marc. She needed to bring closure to that chapter in her life, one way or another. Make a decision on whether she was going to work with Frankie on a long-term basis, or cover Dee's maternity leave. She also needed to make up her mind as to whether she was going to stay in Dublin or go back to Toronto. And if she was staying in Dublin, she needed to take her belongings out of storage and ship them home from Canada. It was time to stop acting like an ostrich.

Marie-Claire stretched over to her bedside locker, picked up her iPad and googled flights. She was working her notice, much to Inez and Chloe's dismay, and she was owed five days' leave. She could use that time to take a trip to Canada. Perhaps when she got back to Toronto she might find that she wanted to stay there.

It was hard to believe so much had changed in her life in less than six months. And just when she'd felt she was beginning to settle back home in Ireland, Granny had put her spoke in and made her face up to the fact that decisions had to be made.

Marie-Claire tapped in a message to Lizzie on her phone:

> I'm planning on coming to Toronto for a week.
> FaceTime me when you get up. MCx

Then she threw back the duvet and went into the shower, wishing Imelda had kept her thoughts and very blunt suggestions to herself.

*

'I'm so excited,' Lizzie beamed from her kitchen counter where she was drinking coffee and eating a bagel. 'I've missed you so much.'

'I've missed you too,' Marie-Claire laughed. 'I can't wait to see you.'

'You'll be staying here, of course,' her friend said.

'Where else would I be going?'

'I'd better stock up on the liquor then. Will you bring me some Taytos and some of that gorgeous Green Angel eye gel?'

'I will. And some handmade chocolates and O'Neill's rashers.'

'Get on the next flight, girl.' Lizzie gave her the thumbs up. 'So, listen, are you going to see Marc while you're here?'

'Yeah! I guess it's time to put an end to the charade,' Marie-Claire sighed. 'How is he?'

'He's fine, spending a lot of time in NY. Things are taking off there.'

'Yep, he told me that the last time we spoke. How's Amelia?'

'As breathy and wide-eyed as ever. She got hair extensions. She's worse than freakin' Rapunzel, twirling it around her fingers.'

'Bioch,' laughed Marie-Claire, entertained as always by her friend's acerbic wit. They chatted for a while, until Lizzie had to head off to the gym. Then Marie-Claire dusted some light bronzing powder onto her face, added a slick of lipstick and mascara before picking up the iPad to call Marc.

It rang for a while and she was on the verge of hanging up when he answered. He was wearing a towelling robe and his hair was wet, and he looked tanned and fit and, she had to admit, as sexy as ever.

'Babes, how are you? This *is* a surprise,' he said delightedly.

'Hi, Marc,' she replied, keeping her tone light. 'Listen, I'm booking a flight for a trip back to—'

'You're coming back?' His face lit up. 'When?'

'I'm not sure of the exact date. I want to see the prices. Next week sometime. Will you be around or will you be in New York?'

'Honey, I'll be sure to be around if you're coming to Toronto. Let me know and I'll collect you from the airport,' he said eagerly.

'No, it's fine,' Lizzie can collect me,' she said firmly.

'Don't be like that, Marie-Claire,' he protested.

'Look let me book my flights, and I'll let you know the details and we'll arrange to meet up if you're free. I need to talk to you, Marc.'

'And I need to talk to *you*! I can't wait to see you again. It's been lonely without you. I've so much to tell you about NY.'

'I'll be looking forward to hearing it,' Marie-Claire assured him. 'See you soon, Marc.'

She waved and hung up and felt a great emptiness. If she hadn't overheard that phone call of Amelia's, they would still be together and she'd have been happy. Imelda's words came to mind. 'An affair can be got over.'

Could she get over Marc's fling with Amelia? Had she punished him enough? Had she punished herself enough, distancing herself from him? Could she take him back?

Brigid had told her forgiveness would make a relationship stronger. Imelda was saying that an affair could be got over. Was the universe sending her a message? Did she actually believe in that stuff her mother was so caught up in?

Her trip to Toronto would find the answers to all these questions, Marie-Claire knew. One way or another it was make-or-break time.

CHAPTER FIFTY-FIVE

Toronto

'I knew you'd come back to me when your six months' self-imposed exile were up. We're meant to be,' Marc said smugly, swinging Marie-Claire into his arms and kissing her passionately.

'Marc, stop!' she protested.

'Why? I'm kissing my girl, who I haven't seen in nearly six months,' he said, holding her tight, smiling down into her eyes.

'It's very public here,' she murmured, relaxing against him. It was good to feel his arms around her.

'You wouldn't meet me at my place,' he chided.

She'd arranged to meet him in the Amsterdam BrewHouse on Queens Quay, where they'd often gone for brunch. She'd made sure to be there first, and had ordered a coffee while she waited for him.

'I fancied a smoked brisket sandwich and a craft beer,' she said easily. 'It was one of my favourites.'

'You look great,' he complimented her, pulling out the chair opposite hers and waving at a waiter to catch his attention.

'You look pretty good yourself, Marc,' Marie-Claire returned, leaning her elbows on the table, smiling at him. For a few moments at least, it was easier to pretend that there was no hidden secret between them.

It was a warm, sunny day. The boats were bobbing gently on the lake, which glistened and rippled in the sun. She remembered how lovely Toronto was in summer and what happy times they'd had and suddenly felt unutterably sad.

'So ... how are things at work? Is New York doing well?' she asked as he reached across the table and took her hand in his.

'Flying – it's really starting to take off, like I knew it would. You'd love it, MC.'

'Would I?' she said slowly. 'How would Amelia feel if I came back? I don't imagine she'd be too happy.'

Marc's eyes narrowed and he looked uncomfortable.

'*Amelia?* What about her?' He frowned.

'You take her to New York—'

'Ha! I knew that got back to you,' he grinned. 'When you tweeted about being there with me, at Christmas. I knew you were pissed. See, I *can* make you jealous. You *do* love me, MC,' he exclaimed triumphantly.

'I was just wondering where is she in the picture. I presume you *did* sleep with her.' Marie-Claire took a sip of her coffee with pretended nonchalance. If he admitted *everything*, there might be the faintest chance, she argued silently with herself. Or maybe not. At least if he was honest and owned up, she'd have some respect for him.

'She's not my type. Don't be silly,' he shrugged dismissively. 'She's only a junior.'

'Really? But you promoted her. Lizzie told me. We *do* keep in touch, you know.' There was an edge to her voice.

'What are we talking about Amelia for?' Marc said irritably. 'She's of no consequence.'

Marie-Claire took a deep breath. It was now or never. 'She's the reason I left, Marc. I know you're having a relationship with her, and you were sleeping with her when you were with me before Christmas,' she said steadily, not taking her eyes from his.

He reddened and dropped his eyes, unable to meet her unwavering gaze.

'Look, the thing is, it's only a fling. And it was only a fling when I was with you. My last one before I settled down with you, if you want to know the truth,' he said gruffly. 'How did you find out?'

'That's neither here nor there. I just did. And you know, to hear a man say about a woman that he's sleeping with that she's of "no consequence" is pretty disgusting. I'm sure Amelia thinks she has a future with you – and why wouldn't she?'

'I never gave her reason to think that,' he said heatedly. 'It's a casual thing. She knows it.'

'Does she know that I'm back and we're meeting today?' she challenged him.

'It's none of her business—'

'Marc, are you for real?' Marie-Claire retorted angrily.

'Ah you know what I mean,' he blustered. '*You're* the woman for me, Marie-Claire, no matter how many women I sleep with, or slept with. I love *you*! That's what I meant when I said "of no consequence". There won't be anyone else if you come back to me, I *swear* it,' he said earnestly, gripping her hand.

'Marc, when it happened, and when we had dinner on Christmas Eve in Edulis – which was the day I found out about you and Amelia, by the way – I swore I'd never let you know why I left you. I wanted to keep you wondering. I know you love me, in as much as you're capable of loving someone – and, strangely enough, I love you. But I *can't* be with you. Not because you had an affair – although that was pretty shitty – but because you haven't been honest with me. Even today, now, you had an opportunity to come clean and clear the slate, and you didn't.' She looked him in the eye. 'I came back because I wanted to give you that chance. And, if you had taken it, perhaps to see if we could try again—'

'We *can* try again. I'll never do that to you again, Marie-Claire, I *promise* you. Stay with me. Give me another chance,' Marc pleaded, and she knew that at that moment he truly meant what he said.

A clip from an old western *High Noon*, which she'd seen on TV a while back, came into her head. Talking of Kane, the marshal, Katy Jurado had said to a cowboy, 'You're a good-looking boy. You have big broad shoulders. But it takes more than big broad shoulders to make a man, and he is a *man*!' It had resonated deeply with Marie-Claire because she knew that Marc – handsome, personable, successful though he was – did not, and never would have, that indefinable quality, that strength of character, that made someone a *real* man.

'I'm sorry,' she said, and a lump came to her throat. 'I can't do it. But I hope when you do meet someone, again – and you will, Marc – that you will remember this, and stay on the straight and narrow with her. And that's what I wanted to say to you today.' She stood up and picked up her bag. 'I wish you every good thing in life, Marc. I had very happy times with you, and that's how I will remember us,' she said quietly, before turning and walking away from him with tears streaming down her cheeks, leaving him bereft.

'You did what was best for you. And if it's any comfort, I think you did the right thing, Marie-Claire,' Lizzie said forcefully as they necked a couple of beers on her patio that evening. 'He's one leopard that will never change his spots.'

'Yeah,' Marie-Claire sighed. 'I gave him his chance. He didn't take it. I know when he was telling me he'd never betray me again that he believed it. But in years to come, whenever temptation reared its head, when our marriage had settled into domesticity and all the rest of it, and he became bored, as he inevitably would, I'd always be checking up on him because I wouldn't trust him. Some women can cope with men like Marc, and fair dues to them. But for me, infidelity is a deal breaker. I couldn't live like that.'

'Me neither.'

'And I guess being honest was, in the end, a lot more satisfying that being "passive-aggressive",' Marie-Claire said wryly, remembering her grandmother's accusation.

'There was nothing passive-aggressive about what you did today, MC. You told him straight. Guess who's going to come into work tomorrow in a fouler?' Lizzie grinned, chomping on her Tayto crisps with relish. 'How about I meet you at the Amsterdam for lunch and I can tell you all the news from the office and you can have the smoked brisket sandwich you never got to have today?'

'Sounds good to me, Lizzie.' Marie-Claire clinked bottles with her friend and lay back in her lounger and felt the stress and tension that had built up in her since she'd made her arrangement to meet Marc begin to drift away on the balmy Canadian breeze.

CHAPTER FIFTY-SIX

Dublin

'Have I got news for you!' Marie-Claire stood up and hugged Ella, who had emerged through a throng of people on Dame Street, into Eddie Rocket's, where Marie-Claire had managed to secure a booth. Town was heaving as the people who had voted Yes and worked on the campaign for the Repeal referendum, came to mark another step on the long hard road of choice and equality for Irish women, with a landslide victory announced earlier in the day.

Ella and the girls had arranged to meet her to be with the thousands of women who were finally going to have a say in the right to make decisions about their own bodies. It was a momentous day in the lives of Irish women and Marie-Claire, remembering what her grandmother had told her about the Contraception Train all those years ago, wondered whether Ella's daughters realized that the freedom they took

494

so much for granted was hard won, and what a debt they all owed to that small group of women who had ploughed the furrow of liberation.

'Where are the girls?' Marie-Claire sat down and took some of Ella's shopping from her.

'They're getting a cross-town Luas. They'll be here in the next twenty minutes or so. I don't care; I'm not waiting for them. I'm ordering a Coke. I'm parched. Do you want another coffee?'

'Might as well add to my high. Yes, I'll have another,' Marie-Claire agreed.

'Why are you high? Because we got a great Yes vote?' Ella slid in behind the table and grinned at her friend. 'Isn't it heartening, women in Ireland finally got the support we need after all these years of being second-class citizens.'

'I'm very glad I'm here for it and so proud of everyone who flew home to vote Yes, especially the younger generation. It gives me great hope for the future.'

'So,' her friend raised an eyebrow. How did it go with Marc? You gave him his walking papers, I presume?'

'I did!'

'Aaahhhh, Marie-Claire, I'm so proud of *you*! Well done, missus!' She half stood up and leaned across the table and hugged her. 'Tell me *everything*!'

' . . . then I said I hoped he'd never do it to another woman, and that was that,' Marie-Claire concluded five minutes later.

'Perfect, Marie-Claire. I *love* it.' Ella applauded. 'What a way to take back your power.'

'Yep, I was rather chuffed with myself, because I *did* love him, and I was gutted when I found out about him and Amelia.'

'I know you were, sweetie. I was worried about you for a while.' Ella took a swig of her Coke.

'No need to worry about me, Ella, life's just peachy,' Marie-Claire assured her.

'And not even the merest *flicker* of wanton desire when he kissed you?'

'Not enough to make me ride him, and you know how I envy you your shags with Shay,' Marie-Claire laughed.

'Hmmm. How is your bogger detective from next door?' Ella teased.

'He's not a bogger; he only has a *hint* of a Connemara accent. Anyway, I'm not interested. He's got two pre-teen daughters, and a divorce coming down the tracks. I don't need a man with baggage,' Marie-Claire said firmly.

'He's good at unblocking pipes in washing machines though, and I thought he had a very sexy ass and *deliciously* muscular thighs, lying on your utility room floor trying to get at your ... ah, stop ... cock ...' Ella said innocently. She'd called over to Marie-Claire with a birthday present before she went to Toronto, to find her standing beside her next-door neighbour, whose head was stuck in a press under a sink, effecting an emergency shutdown of Marie-Claire's water flow.

'Give over,' grinned Marie-Claire. 'Not going to happen.'

'Indeed!' Ella grinned back. 'Here's the girls.' She smiled

at the sight of her teenage daughters barrelling through the door. 'They're in a good mood today,' she whispered. 'We must be thankful for small mercies. And thankful too that they'll never have to worry about being denied necessary medical treatment in a maternity hospital in Ireland. They'll never have to go through what I went through.'

Marie-Claire squeezed her best friend's hand in silent support, before she was enveloped in hugs and kisses from her 'posh besties', as she called them, warming the cockles of her heart.

'Isn't it a great day for Irish women, Marie-Claire?' Julie, her younger godchild, said fervently, scooting in beside her.

'Empowering, sweetie. A day when we came into our own, at last,' Marie-Claire agreed.

'History in the making and we were part of it. Like the civil marriage referendum,' Jada remarked proudly.

'It's a far different country to what your mother and I grew up in, for sure—'

'You sound like our parents,' grinned Ella.

'And God knows they had to put up with so much we didn't have to. When my mum was training to be a teacher in a college run by nuns, she'd to kneel down and have her dress measured to see if it was long enough to go out. If it didn't touch the floor, she had to change.'

'OMG!' squealed the teenagers.

'That's like from the ark!'

'Wow! Like, unbelievable.'

'You certainly wouldn't have been getting piercings,

tattoos and the like, if you were growing up in our day!' Ella pointed out, and laughed when Julie did a dramatic eye-roll.

They ate their meal, and for once the girls put their phones away and lively chat and banter went to and fro across the table. Later they mingled with the throngs of people gathered together to affirm the result of the referendum, which had been divisive and bitterly fought.

There was no air of triumphalism, no wild celebration. What struck Marie-Claire most was the undercurrent of relief that permeated the crowds of women, and men who had fought the battle for sisters, wives and daughters, and the sense of a coming of age in dealing with a problem that had been hived off to other countries for generations.

If she ever had a daughter, she would have one less worry for her, Marie-Claire thought gratefully, smiling into Julie's camera for a selfie of their little group.

EPILOGUE

Sunday, 26 August 2018

'Here's a packed lunch for you now, and you have the flasks.' Maura handed Marie-Claire a basket filled with freshly baked scones and brown bread and Tupperware containers of cold cuts, salads, and pasta.

'That's a feast, Maura. Thanks,' Keelin said warmly. 'What a treat it is to be here,' she added gleefully.

'I suppose that's one good thing about the Pope's visit, we got to see ya! I think Una's mad to go traipsing up to Phoenix Park to see him, but to each his own.' Maura was less than impressed that Una had gadded off to Dublin. 'I thought you might have been up there too, Imelda,' she remarked casually.

'Huh! *Me*? There was a time I might have, but those days are long gone. I've no time for him and his ilk.' Imelda drained the last drop of tea from her cup. 'That fifteen million of our money we've to spend on this visit could have gone towards housing the homeless. It's *disgraceful*! The Church has billions! And there were well-known people fundraising for this carry-on, expecting the hard-put tax-payer to dip deep into our pockets yet again.' She shook her head in bewilderment. 'We're a strange little country some-times,' she said crossly.

'We're getting better,' Brigid smiled. Her hair was damp against her head. She and Marie-Claire had been for a swim in the sea and were having a quick cuppa before getting ready to leave the Four Winds on another 'small pilgrimage', as she'd put it when she suggested today's trip to the others.

Keelin had flown in from France the previous afternoon and she and Marie-Claire had driven directly to Glencarraig to collect Imelda, and then driven to the Four Winds.

So different from the last time they had all been here in January, Brigid thought, loving that they were all sitting in the kitchen chatting and laughing, the hot August sun splashing daubs of light all over the table, through the old-fashioned sash windows.

Una and Maura had welcomed the trio warmly the pre-vious day, and had been exceedingly gracious when Imelda had apologized for ruining Brigid's party. 'I wasn't myself,' she explained by way of mitigation.

You were very much yourself, Maura thought acidly, but she refrained – heroically, in her opinion – from making any smart remarks and let her sister take the lead.

'These things happen in families. The important thing is that you all rose above it, so that can only be a good thing,' Una replied, a little embarrassed to see the usually cocky Imelda displaying unexpected humility.

Once the awkwardness was over, and they'd unpacked, Keelin suggested a walk on the strand before dinner.

It had been invigorating. The sand was warm under their bare feet. The heat, which had been a feature of the long, hot summer, was tempered by the southerly breeze that caressed their faces as they strolled along the golden beach below the Four Winds. After an afternoon spent bringing each other up to date on what had occurred in their lives since the trip to Scotland, they gathered to eat dinner on the small patio overlooking the pale blue sea. Una had cooked bacon, cabbage, parsley sauce and new, flowery queens that melted in the mouth.

'These are such an occasion of sin,' Brigid sighed, scattering salt and a dob of butter on her spuds and eating them with relish.

'That was a real saying of the old days . . . "an occasion of sin"!' Keelin laughed.

'Everything was a blinkin' occasion of sin, then.' Imelda threw her eyes up to heaven.

'Don't remind me. I hated going to confession when I was training to be a nurse. The priest was always asking me had my work in the men's ward ever been "an occasion of sin" for me,' Brigid grimaced.

'Are you serious?' Marie-Claire was astounded.

'I wish I weren't,' her great-aunt retorted.

'It must have been strange for you, though, a young woman and a novice at that, having to nurse men and see their wobbly bits an' all.' Imelda dipped her forkful of bacon into the mustard smeared on the side of her plate.

'Eeewww, we're eating, Gran!' Marie-Claire reproved.

'Ah get over it, as the young lot say. You've seen plenty of those in your time, I'd imagine,' Imelda gave her the eye.

'Well, I'll never forget the first time I saw the male appendage – because I never saw Johnny Larkin's, it all happened so quick.' Brigid put her fork down and her eyes creased in amusement at the memory. 'Needless to say, I *was* curious, but apprehensive at the same time. We really were so innocent in those days, weren't we, Imelda?'

'We were. There was many a virgin on her wedding night got a lot more than she bargained for, I can tell you,' she chuckled. 'Come on then, let's hear about your first "vision".'

'I was so disappointed when I saw that little soft wobbly thing that I'd tried to imagine for so long when I used to dream about being rescued from danger by William Holden – he was a famous film star, dear,' she said in an aside to Marie-Claire. 'So anyway, I'm looking at this most disappointing sight and I had my tutor, Sister Ignatius, standing beside me with a silver spoon in her hand. "If it rises up, slap it down, Sister Dunne. *Slaaap* it down," she ordered. The poor patient didn't know where to look and neither did I. I was *mortified*.'

The others exploded with laughter, guffaws echoing across the garden.

'Oh God, Mère, that's *hilarious*,' gasped Keelin, wiping the tears of laughter from her eyes. 'I'm going to bring a spoon to bed when I get home, and when Armand gets frisky I'll give him a tap with it, just for the laugh.'

'Oh, Maman! Could you imagine his face?' Marie-Claire hooted, almost choking.

Imelda was chuckling heartily, unable to believe how much fun she was having. She'd told Felicity she was going on a 'girls' weekend'. Had she ever envisaged sitting in the Four Winds, laughing with her sister, daughter and grand-child? There was a time, in the not too distant past, when she would never have believed such a thing could happen. She was as happy as she'd ever been in her entire life.

Now, as she placed her cup in the dishwasher the following morning, Imelda relished how much a part of their little group she'd become. And most importantly today, she was here to support Brigid who had suggested that, as a protest against the Church's handling of widespread abuse, instead of joining those watching the Pope celebrate Mass in Phoenix Park, they would travel to the town of Tuam, where the bodies of almost eight hundred children were buried in a mass grave. All of them had agreed to the suggestion instantly when Brigid had broached it.

'Not only were those poor little children and their vulnerable, unfortunate mothers betrayed, the Catholic Church and their corrupt hierarchy has betrayed *every* good nun and priest who has ever lived and worked for God. I *abhor* the Church I gave my life to,' she'd raged one day to Keelin, provoked by news coverage of the Pope's impending visit.

'Don't think of it like that, Mère. Think instead of all the lives that have been touched with such goodness, integrity and pure intention by you and your fellow nuns and priests. You have all done so much to raise the vibration of the world. The darkness *has* to have a spotlight shone on it to be healed. That's why all these atrocities are coming to light now, all over the world,' Keelin counselled.

'I suppose you're right, dear.' Brigid found some small comfort in her niece's words. Keelin had a way of looking at things that would never have occurred to her. 'But it's terrible to think such a thing happened in Ireland and nothing was done about it. That far from stopping it, the Church enabled those responsible to continue.'

The more she thought about it, the more determined she was to make a mini-pilgrimage to Tuam.

They left the Four Winds half an hour later and took the N68 to link up with the motorway to Tuam. It was warm but cloudy, and the fields on either side of the road were scorched brown. Dry as a bone for the want of rain, after forty days of drought.

They were lost in their own thoughts when Marie-Claire slid a CD into the player. 'Listen to this. I was at a gig this fabulous singer/songwriter was playing at a while back and

I've absolutely fallen in love with her. What a voice. What a talent. What a committed activist,' she enthused. 'Midwives for Choice, Repeal the Eighth, she's always quietly working in the background, seeking no fame or glory. But wait until you hear her voice and listen to the song she wrote for the Magdalene women. It blew me away. Her name is Ciara Sidine. It's called "Finest Flower".'

She turned the CD on and a voice, pure and resonant with depth and emotion floated from the speakers.

There's a valley of stone
Deep down in my soul
A restless place where stories roam
Nights when I lie awake
In a traceless haze
Of steam and smoke
There's a sisterhood of fallen dreams
Landed in a godless place
And oh though I lost you there a long time ago
Oh, my joy to care in a barren zone
Not for one minute of an hour
My finest flower
Did I ever let you go

Mary said she'd get free
Though she made good her plan
Did she know she'd be running still
When out into the night she ran?

Patricia Scanlan

For Jenny Dwyer
The same night came
By a fever taken so they told us
They who took her name

And oh though she lost you there a long time ago
To live and die unmarked, unknown
Not for one minute of an hour
My finest flower
Did she ever let you go

Me, I guess that I was blessed
For I knew love
Could know no shame
When I held you to my breast
And called your name
Till the day I found
An empty space
The day I never let you go
Oh the weight of the love you have
But cannot hold

Cos I lost you there a long time ago
My joy to care in a valley of stone
Not for one minute of an hour
My finest flower
Did I ever let you go
My heart my joy my very own

Not for one minute of an hour
My finest flower
No I never let you go

The last poignant notes faded away. Brigid sat stock-still in the back seat beside Imelda, tears pouring down her face. 'That could have been written about me, if I'd had my baby,' she wept. 'But even though I lost her, those words – "Not for one minute of an hour, My finest flower, Did I ever let you go" – that's my life every day. I think of my child and know that she is always with me. *Always*,' Brigid sobbed. Broken.

'I'm so sorry, Mère, perhaps I shouldn't have played it,' Marie-Claire exclaimed, upset to see her beloved Brigid in tears, and nearly in tears herself.

'No, no! It's a sacred song. A very empowering song to all of us who've lost a child, no matter how the loss occurred,' Brigid assured her, trying to compose herself. 'I know now why I was so driven to come to Tuam. I needed to release this grief that I've carried most of my life.'

'Are you sure you're up to standing with the families, when we get there?' Keelin asked gently. 'We can just light a candle ourselves and leave, if you prefer?'

'I'll stand with the families, in solidarity,' Brigid said resolutely. 'And my tears will mingle with theirs.'

'We'll be with you, Brigid. This is *one* ordeal you won't have to endure on your own,' Imelda said firmly, taking her sister's hand in hers, in the gentlest of clasps.

*

Leaden clouds threatening rain overhung the crowds of people gathering for their silent vigil at the town hall in Tuam, as Brigid and her stalwart companions took their place in line, waiting to begin their walk. The vigil was organized by a Manchester woman whose sister had vanished from a mother-and-baby home, and the crowd resonated with sombre sorrow when the many hundreds of people began their walk at the same time as the Pope was celebrating his Mass in Dublin.

There were no accusatory speeches, no songs of protest, just a dignified recitation of each precious child's name and age, that seemed to go on for an eternity, there were so many of them. Hundreds of candles, lit in their memory, illuminated the grey, grim afternoon. At the site of the former Bon Secours Home, a special sculpture in the shape of a baptismal font, made by a Flemish woman, was placed under the glowering skies.

Brigid's lips trembled and she broke down in tears again. The sight of all the small teddy bears and toys posted along the route had seared her heart and she'd struggled not to cry. But now, in this desolate place, her tears overflowed and she wept along with many others.

Marie-Claire moved to comfort her, but Keelin held her back when she saw Imelda wrap her arms around Brigid and draw her sister into a close embrace. Brigid rested her head on Imelda's shoulder and released her years of pent-up grief and loss.

'Healing,' Keelin whispered to her daughter. 'Difficult as

it is, the healing that will come for the both of them, and for me too, today, cannot be described, *chérie.*'

Much later that night, the four of them sat watching the Nine O'Clock News, with segments about the Papal Mass. The concert at the Garden of Remembrance was covered, and then their own silent vigil in Tuam.

'There we are,' Imelda pointed excitedly to the lower left of the screen, where the camera panned along the lines of men, women and children who had come to pay respect and honour to the mothers and their babies who had suffered such appalling neglect and abuse at the hands of those to whose care they had been entrusted.

'I'm glad I stood with them. I'm glad I made my protest,' Brigid said tiredly.

'I'm glad I was there with you,' Imelda said purposefully.

'Me too,'

'And me,' echoed Keelin and Marie-Claire.

'And do you know, something?' Brigid said slowly. 'I understand now why I got *The Little Children* Magdalene card. It's about never forgetting them and always holding them in our hearts, including the unborn ones lost to miscarriage and abortion. Today's silent vigil and that beautiful song we listened to affirmed that for me, more than anything else could have. This was a very powerful and a very liberating day for *me.*'

'For all of us, Mère. It was such a comfort to be here with you, and share the experience.' Marie-Claire smiled at her.

509

'That will give them something to think about in Rome,' Imelda declared with satisfaction, listening to the discussion on the news about the low turnout for the Papal Mass, in comparison to the previous Papal visit. 'Sure you'd get more at the Galway Races than were in the park today.'

'And a wishy-washy apology had to be dragged out of them, and that is *so* much to their shame. Their day is over,' Keelin remarked with disgust.

'And not before time,' Imelda said tartly. 'They have a lot to answer for.'

'So let's try to plan a Magdalene Trail week in Gerona and Rennes-le-Château, and see if we can manage to climb to the summit of Canigou too, sometime around mid-October, then?' Brigid suggested, looking at them expectantly.

They were sitting outside in the morning sun, enjoying the lullaby of the sea and having a last cup of tea together before Marie-Claire, Keelin and Imelda began their trip back to Dublin via Glencarraig.

'I can go any time,' Imelda chirruped.

'I'll make sure not to have any retreats planned for whatever week you come. Let me know as soon as you can.' Keelin clapped her hands in delight.

'I'll check out the work diary and see what's scheduled and clear my decks – that would be an in-joke at work,' Marie-Claire grinned.

'Something wonderful to look forward to.' Brigid

smiled broadly, the grief that had been etched upon her face softening at this unexpected treat in store. It had been Imelda's idea.

'I'm going to read as many of those books of yours as I can, Keelin, to see if I can make some sort of sense of the stuff you talk about,' Imelda assured her daughter.

'You know something, Mam, if a thing resonates with you, go with it, that's all you have to do,' Keelin said easily.

'And I'd just like to say, I very much appreciate all your understanding and forgiveness. I'll try not to be as cranky as I used to be, but if the odd sharp word or two comes out, you know I don't mean it. I doubt I'll be able to change my ways overnight,' Imelda said awkwardly.

'We'll all try and practice tolerance, Imelda. We're all on this path together,' Brigid said reassuringly. 'But neither of us will be canonized yet,' she added good-humouredly, and Imelda laughed.

'I suppose we'd better hit the road,' Marie-Claire said reluctantly, standing up to shake away the crumbs of Una's light-as-a-feather sponge cake.

'I wish you could all stay longer,' Brigid said regretfully.

'We'll be in touch with Skype,' Marie-Claire assured her.

'And you're coming to me in September for a few days, Brigid,' Imelda reminded her.

'I am. And I'm looking forward to it,' Brigid assured her.

'So am I, believe it or not. Now did you ever think you'd hear me say that?' Imelda joked with a mischievous glint in her eye.

They laughed, and followed Marie-Claire to the car, which was already packed up and ready to go.

'Happy days are coming!' Brigid hugged Marie-Claire and the others, and stood waving at them as they drove slowly along the narrow drive to get onto the coast road.

'I'm looking forward to the week in October. That will be great fun,' Marie-Claire said, glancing into her rear-view mirror for one last look at Brigid, who was waving vigorously after them, against the background of their beloved Four Winds.

'I am too. Immensely. And thank you for offering to put us all up, Keelin,' Imelda declared, turning to her daughter in the back seat.

'It will be my pleasure – and I mean that,' Keelin said, smiling at her mother.

Imelda turned back to face the road ahead. She was loved. There was no mistake about it. After all these years, she knew without doubt that she was very much loved. It made her giddy with happiness. *I must change my will back*, she thought suddenly. She would ring Fitzpatrick's Solicitors first thing in the morning to make an appointment.

They turned a bend in the road and the coastline rose up to greet them. The sea a palette of blues and greens, tipped by white. On the horizon, the most splendid rainbow that Imelda had ever seen. A gift from Larry, she thought, feeling his presence very near. 'Look, Keelin. Look what your dad has sent us – like on Iona. I feel him so near these days,' she exclaimed.

'I know, Mam, would you believe I was thinking the same myself.' Keelin leaned over between the seats and held out her hand. Imelda took it, squeezed tightly, and all the years of turmoil and strife between them slipped quietly away. Brigid, in the shelter of the Four Winds, caught one last glimpse of them as they crested the hill, and blew them all a kiss before they disappeared from view.

ACKNOWLEDGEMENTS

As always my first acknowledgement is to my Spiritual Team led by Jesus, Mary, St Joseph, the Divine Feminine Energy of Mary Magdalene, Saints Michael and Anthony (the stalwarts) and all my Angels, Saints and Guides. My books would never be written without your Divine Inspiration.

To my sister, Mary, who is always there to share the highs and lows and keep me going. Thanks for all the fun times too.

To all my family. And a special thanks to nieces Rachel and Maria, who uncomplainingly carried bags, helped me dress, cut my food, did my make-up and did all manner of chores, when I crocked my shoulder, and to Fiona for all the lifts and kindness.

Two very special women helped me greatly in my research about the life of a nun on the Missions. Dear Sister Una Lennox and Carmel Bracken RSM, you gave so much and touched so many lives in the tremendous work you did, and do. Thank you for setting me on the right path with my own nuns, Brigid and Keelin. We are in your debt. I wish I could have included everything you told me. Perhaps in another book. Thanks, Mairead Conlon and Aidan Storey for the introductions.

To my dear manuscript readers and precious friends Caitriona, Yvonne, Pam, Mary Helen and Mama Helen Hensley, Aidan, and Breda, who encouraged me so much with their laughter, tears, comments and gentle pointing out of my errors. (Rachel found a three-year-old nun whilst doing my chronological order!) I am blessed to have such loyal and loving friends. And thanks to Aidan and Murtagh for my 'Writer's Retreat' on the Curragh.

To Helen McKean my amazing Publicity Manager and dear friend. I could not do this without you.

To Geraldine and Antoinette, and Marian Lawlor, dear friends.

To Ray and Dee O'Callaghan, who have given me my haven in Wicklow, where so much of my work is done in such a wonderful setting. Thank you both SO much.

To Michelle Connor, AIB Finglas, who keeps me on track and remembers things I forget! You're the BEST!

To Sarah Lutyens and all my wonderful team at Lutyens & Rubinstein. Thanks, my dears, for all the hard work you do my behalf and for your continued support and friendship.

A huge thanks to Jo Dickinson, my editor for the past six years. It was a joy to work with you, especially on this book. I'll miss you enormously. Your new authors are *very* lucky.

And to Alice Rodgers, Anne O'Brien, Sally Partington and all in the editorial department, a very grateful acknowledgement for your expertise in bringing the manuscript to completion. To SJ, Rich, and ALL my Schusters in the various departments, a massive 'Thank you'.

To my team at Atria Books, and to my editors, Haley Weaver and Loan Le, thank you. And to all my US Schusters for your enthusiasm and continued support.

To my Schusters in Australia, India and South Africa, a big thanks for the great work you do on my behalf.

To all my translators, foreign publishers and sub agents, it is such a thrill to see my books in other languages.

To Simon at Gill Hess & Co, who always has my back and who works so hard with all his team, on my behalf. There aren't enough thanks.

To Mr Hannan Mullet, Grainne Roche, Finn and Orla, who got me through this book in my great hour of need. Thanks for the injections, surgery, and very kind care, as always. This book would not have been written without you.

A big thanks too, to Garrett Fitzpatrick, solicitor. His immense patience and good humour in all his dealings with me are hugely appreciated.

I'd like to also acknowledge Ciara Sidine, a dear friend and wonderful songwriter and musician. It's an honour to have your beautiful, poignant song, 'Finest Flower' in my novel. (You can listen to it on the link below.)

https://www.youtube.com/watch?v=e3ubrOZGPSA

A loving thanks also to Patrice Chaplin, a wonderful writer, and precious friend. Her books are mentioned in the novel and *The Portal and The Stone Cradle* are gripping reads if you want to treat yourselves to something different. Fiona McLaren's *Da Vinci's Last Commission* is also a fascinating tale, which we will be hearing a lot more about!

A huge thanks to all in the book trade, worldwide, who have supported each and every one of my books. And most importantly to my dear and ever loyal readers, and social media followers: you are the ones that make the writing of my novels such a rewarding and gratifying endeavour. Your enjoyment of my writing means so much. You keep me going. Thank you, m'dears. XXX

PATRICIA SCANLAN

City Girl

Whatever life holds, friends come first . . .

Dublin, late-1980s. A beautiful blonde, a quiet
brown-eyed girl and a redhead looking for
adventure: meet Devlin, Caroline and Maggie.

Their staunch three-way friendship is born while
sharing a house in Dublin and, as they each battle
through changing times and turbulent love lives,
soon becomes the only certainty they have.

Through good times and bad, the bond they share has always
been a refuge. And with big life changes on the horizon,
the three friends will need each other more than ever . . .

**Full of warmth, wit and wisdom, *City*
Girl is a brilliant family drama from a
trailblazing author in women's fiction.**

AVAILABLE NOW IN PAPERBACK AND EBOOK

**SIMON &
SCHUSTER**

booksandthecity.co.uk
the home of female fiction

Follow us online to be the first to hear from
your favourite authors

booksandthecity.co.uk   **@TeamBATC**

Join our mailing list for the latest news, events and
exclusive competitions

Sign up at
booksandthecity.co.uk